SEARCHING FOR SANCTUARY

AN ENCHANTMENT AVENUE NOVEL

CHRISSY WISSLER

BLUE CEDAR PUBLISHING

ACKNOWLEDGMENTS

A story that couldn't have been written without the love and support of my family. For Sean, who continued to believe in me, my dreams, and my goals despite the many sleepless nights and long days with our young daughter (and soon-to-be-arriving son). For my mom, who came over to help and to play so I could get in those few moments of writing. For Kate, who gave me enough of those quiet moments when it was just the two of us, enough so that the story in my head somehow ended up on the page.

And also to the Wildlife Waystation in Southern California, a place I visited many times as a child and then later volunteered as an adult. Clearly, the memories and the love put into this place made a lasting impression.

For Kate

CHAPTER 1

$\mathcal{A}$isha leaned against the cage's rusted chain-link fence. The hot surface heated her dark skin, but she ignored it.

The tiger Lanhi lay sprawled and uncaring on her wooden hovel of a house's flat roof. Massive paw hanging off. Not even swinging in the nonexistent breeze. Not the way she used to, like she was batting at some stray hopping-kangaroo mouse that'd wandered in from the southern pen enclosures.

It'd only happened once, not long after Lanhi had arrived, when she'd barely had the will to even eat her food. Aisha hadn't respelled the mouse enclosure lock against hair-thin whisker-picking abilities (the hopping-kangaroo mouse's master having not informed Aisha of their peculiar talents—the same talents that'd gotten them banned from hearth and home and a much nicer, much more expensive Familiar Sanctuary).

But the little adventure of hopping-kangaroo mice had given Lanhi (and the mice) some of their own spark back. Both sides had survived (thank goodness), and while the doors were now safely locked and secure, the spark had held.

Especially for Lanhi.

Until today.

Until whatever had made her change, made her revert back to the tiger with barely the will to live.

And yet, even now Lanhi lay on her roof with her paw hanging down as if the memory of the mice was still with her. Still hanging on. Perhaps even a small spark remained for her to be on guard for the next silly hopping-kangaroo mouse foolish enough to come into her domain of faded and tearing circus posters, elephant stands, and flung-about clown noses on the dust-dirt floor of her enclosure.

Even though her paw just hung there. Unmoving. Uncaring.

"Come on, sweetheart. Please." Aisha felt the magic within her gut stir. Slowly, as if reaching out to the tiger…testing and unsure.

Aisha held her breath.

She hoped Marcelle had reported wrong. Hoped her magic would prove otherwise, that their dancing Lanhi was fine.

Lanhi ruffed and grumped. A hot puff of air spewed from her massive mouth of teeth and tongue, blowing at the tattered, pale-pink tutu hanging from a skirt hook.

The sparkly sequins, no longer sparkly.

The ruffles wrinkled and limp.

The tutu had been a recent addition. As had the clown noses. Insisted by Lanhi's master, the witch Ghazille.

Fat lot of good that had done Lanhi.

The unrelenting Simi Valley sun beat down on Aisha, the outside cage, the lines and lines of other Familiar cages in her Waystation, barely a narrow, dirt footpath between them. Even the tiniest movement caused a small twister of dust to billow upwards. The dust didn't even spare poor Lanhi, her no longer shimmering, no longer carefully groomed orange-, white-, and black-striped coat and instead, now dull and faded. The Waystation's famous dust coated every surface, made Aisha's skin look a pale tan instead of the dark, sun-kissed skin of her grandfather's people, the Hadzabe tribe.

A tribe she couldn't *actually* remember.

Aisha snapped her eyes closed. Squeezed them shut.

She needed to focus on Lanhi. Focus on someone she *could* help.

Who *wanted* help.

Sweat trickled down Aisha's forehead. Dripped off her nose. She didn't move. Not even when the salty sweat slid into the corner of her eye.

Any movement, sudden or even slow, could send the tiger Familiar into another set of fits.

It was one of the main reasons Lanhi had been banned from her previous sanctuary. An uncontrollable Familiar was a handful; an unpredictable one, a danger to everyone. The kind of Familiar those high-end Sanctuaries didn't want to help.

But Aisha did.

Her magic continued to circle. To rise up from her chest, reaching her throat. Still tentative. Unsure. Trying desperately to reach out, to find some connection between Aisha and Lanhi, something that would help her understand—would help the tiger keep wanting to live.

She almost wished Lanhi would have those fits again. Anything to bring the tiger back to her usual spirits. Anything at all to show that she wasn't withering away.

Just like so many of the other retired, abused, and often forgotten Familiars.

Lanhi ruffed again. Blew another a sigh of hot air. Made the tutu's ruffles dance just the slightest, but nothing like the way those ruffles had danced before Lanhi had been sent to the finest Familiar sanctuary in the Northern Hemisphere, Paradise Grove Familiar sanctuary —before, of course, coming to Aisha's barely-holding-together Waystation.

There wasn't even the tiniest bit of excitement behind those hooded orange-gold eyes.

The magic in Aisha's stomach settled into a cold, hard stone.

Not even a stirring remained.

"Damn," Aisha whispered. "Not another one."

Aisha swept off her felt-brimmed cowboy hat. Slapped it against her khaki pants. Dust billowed up and into her nose, tickled it. Right alongside the tang of animals and sweat, rotting meat, and just plain hot-dry Waystation.

She sneezed. Then sneezed again.

Felt a familiar ache for home, a longing to go back to another time. Funny how a sneeze could remind her of the hot summers at her parents' thriving sanctuary in the Serengeti Magical Proper. Back when her life was going just fine and climbing upwards, upwards to where no sky, no magic was the limit.

She slapped the hat back on her head.

She'd never change that clock, though.

Never.

This was exactly where she needed to be.

Who she needed to be.

Aisha gave one last look at Lanhi. She'd have to call the witch, Ghazille. Not that the woman would care. Not that any of them did, not after their Familiars wound up in the Waystation, the last stop on their abandoned, unhappy, and too often short lives.

At least for these Familiars.

Not all Familiars led the perfect lives the Enchantment Avenue Council (hell, even that great and powerful High Council) liked to preach from their safe havens of magic and strength. They pretended ignorance when it came to abuse and misuse of Familiars, turning a blind eye especially when it came to the highest among them.

But Aisha knew better, and so did the Enchantment Avenue Council.

Her Waystation was living proof, and they knew it, too. Did their best to keep it all under wraps. An open, unacknowledged secret.

Even if they needed her.

Needed someone to take in the Familiars who couldn't handle the strain of performing like a monkey for unrelenting magical masters. The kinds of masters who didn't even deserve a pet, let alone the special, magical bond shared with a Familiar.

An old argument, though.

She sighed, knowing there was nothing she could do. Not about the Council and not for Lanhi. And all the Familiars like her.

But she wouldn't let them go out alone.

Whatever it took, she'd be there for them.

CHAPTER 2

*A*isha's feet dragged as she left Lanhi's circus-outfitted enclosure and passed the rows and rows of Familiar cages. Each, hemmed in by even more cages. The spells sparkled above the fences, bright and strong and holding up against the heat and often brutal winds in her crick of a valley, fortifying the metal and links, but she noticed some were already fading.

The locksmith had done his usual piss-poor job just because the bastard could.

She slapped at her pants. Dug her hiking boots into the thick, dust-dirt path. If she'd had even a smidgeon of money like those big fancy Sanctuaries had…

A usual complaint.

One that usually ended up with her having a glass of wine and sneaking in some Normal television of the world beyond their magical one. The one where lions got to be lions, monkeys scratched their butts and wore nothing but monkey fur, and they all roamed good and free across the Serengeti like they were meant to.

Like Aisha remembered, growing up.

A raven cawed down at her from above. Flapped to the nearest tree, dark wings rustling and blowing off the other half of the empty, near-leafless, spindly tree. He settled there, a message scroll glowing in his claws.

"Message from Marcelle, Einstein?"

Einstein cawed back and lifted up his foot.

The scroll dropped in the air, arcing towards her. Then slowed and hung there, carefully unfurling with a snap. The image of Marcelle, with her pink, spiky hair now glowing with what looked like her latest conditioner, turned towards Aisha.

She took one look at Aisha and her face fell. "I was right, wasn't I?"

"Afraid so."

"Oh, Aisha. What could possibly be wrong with them?"

"I wish I knew."

Because it wasn't just occurring at her Waystation, but everywhere. Even if the Sanctuaries refused to admit it—to the public, and especially to her. But rumors were leaking out, and she (and Marcelle) were good at ferreting out truth from rumors.

It was happening slowly, it seemed. At least at first. But then once a sanctuary became "infected." the rate of sickness grew.

Fast and steady.

Aisha was just lucky enough to have been the last stop for most of these Familiars, when all the well-to-do of magical standing had grown tired of pouring resources towards their retired and now useless Familiars.

She got to see them pass. Stand by them, hold their paw or wing or claw, and remind them that they weren't alone. That someone out there cared for them. A driving need that had made her leave all those high and mighty establishments and start her own place.

But it was still never enough.

And now, not even Aisha's Waystation was being spared the wasting sickness.

Lanhi had contracted it, along with a few dozen before her.

She couldn't deny it anymore.

"She was such a good girl. So filled with life." Marcelle sniffed. Wiped at a dark-lined eye, but no smudges or runny lines appeared underneath.

One of the many benefits, Marcelle liked to claim, of living a magical life over a Normal one.

Aisha could think of one point in the Normals' favor. Their pets, at least, usually died of natural causes (though neglect and abuse were still part of their culture, as it was in all humans). But at least they were just pets. Nothing more. Normals didn't carry the same special, magical, and psychic bonds that often spanned decades.

Sometimes, generations.

And Normals didn't simply toss aside their pets when they no longer fit in their pre-determined mold. When they no longer performed as was their role.

Instead, Normals (many of them) saw their pets as family.

The only family Lanhi had left were Aisha and Marcelle. Just like all the Familiars here. The ones that didn't fit in magical society anymore. The ones that no one wanted. The ones that had even given up on themselves.

Heart twisting at the thought of sending Lanhi into the great beyond—she'd probably last only a few weeks at best—Aisha knew she needed to prepare. To start making plans for the next Familiar on the list.

"Damn it."

"I know, sweetie." Marcelle gave her a wobbly smile. "I know you care."

Aisha flinched back. Mostly because if Marcelle was standing beside her, she'd do something silly like try to squeeze her hand or something.

Or hug her.

Aisha didn't hug people.

She hugged Familiars.

The ones she could actually understand. Respect.

"Look, I'm making my rounds right now," Aisha said. "Did you sense any vibes from the others?"

Marcelle shook her head. "Just the usual. But the undercurrent here, Aisha, it's really strong. *Something* is going on with them and it's here. Like I can almost feel it, but…"

But couldn't.

They'd been over this before.

"I'll keep searching," Marcelle said.

And find nothing. But didn't matter. If there was something here and harming her Familiars, they'd find it. Destroy it.

The Waystation was a safe place. A true sanctuary, even for the poorest and most unwanted. Aisha wouldn't let anything—magical or human created—affect that.

"Oh! One more thing." Marcelle managed to catch Aisha before she snapped the scroll closed. "You've got another call from that fancy-pants Lord What's-His-Name. Really, Aisha. I think he's pretty serious about sending his Familiar our way. You should call him back."

Aisha reached for the scroll.

"You seriously need to call him back—"

She snapped it closed. The heavy parchment closed with a furling-flap. She tossed it back to Einstein, who took off of the branch in a flap of hot air and dust in her face.

"Maybe."

The last thing she needed was a stuffy lord anywhere near her Waystation. She'd played that game once already.

Only once.

And once was all it took for her to turn her back on her family, the country and land she loved.

Aisha continued her slow, studious search of the compound. She didn't have Marcelle's gift for searching out psychic energies, but Aisha had another gift, and that was reaching out to Familiars. Her "gut" magic. Even if it didn't always work. Even if she didn't under-stand it.

Maybe if she was diligent enough, aware enough, she could find the next Familiar before it was fully touched by the wasting sickness.

And if not...well, what she could do, what *was* in her control, was make some calls. Find out from the other Sanctuaries—demanding an answer this time if they stalled, delayed, or flat-out lied, as they tended to—what the hell was going on.

Before it was too late to save her Familiars.

CHAPTER 3

$\mathcal{N}$ate Darkwood stood as far from the enclosure as possible. If he dared even call this a "snow leopard enclosure."

Or even a leopard.

He didn't.

His appropriately polished and shined shoes sank into the plush, four-inch-thick carpet that lined the enclosure's "lounge and viewing are." The window gazed out into a room that looked like it'd fit right at home in father's family home.

His father's study, even.

At least, from a ten-year-old's memory of it. Before…before it had required the renovation.

Still, the enclosure seemed all too perfect. Just like what a Familiar owner at Paradise Grove Sanctuary would want. An armchair with thick, recently reupholstered cushions. A smoking pipe resting against an ashtray, complete with a spelled, never-ceasing stream of lightest gray smoke, which shared the small mahogany end table with a leather-bound book, its pages cracked and aged yellow.

A sputtering fireplace in one corner, complete with iron-bond safety bars. A grandfather clock tick-tocking away in another.

And there, lying in a sorry, sad lump in the center of all this grand finery, the best that the magical community had to offer—especially with the sanctuary just a tiger's leap to the great Enchantment Avenue itself—was the snow leopard.

Elsa.

A silvery-white crown hung limp on her head. The black and white shades of her ears, no longer longer shining, and seemed to sag against her head. Not alert. Not perking up, twitching back and forth as she catalogued and listened to the sounds Nate made. The slight footfall of his shoes brushing against carpet. The rise and fall of his chest. His heartbeat.

Instead she just lay there, head tucked against her massive, declawed paw. Just…just completely passive. Uncaring.

Even her ice-blue eyes, and a leopard's eyes (or any of the large cats) were always unnerving to Nate. There was something truly feral yet intelligent in their eyes—but Elsa even kept her eyes closed. As if she didn't care to even open them to see who'd come calling.

Sweat dotted his forehead.

Couldn't help the reaction. A reaction he felt any time he came face-to-face with the white-and-black spots.

Even though Elsa wasn't a tiger. Wasn't the tiger he'd seen, off and on, in his dreams, his nightmares.

The tiger that had killed his mother.

Still, Elsa's massive size dwarfed every little trinket in the hideous enclosure. Made every misplaced object seem miniscule. Tiny. And yet…yet her spirit was barely a spark now.

Barely a glowing ember.

Not long left here.

The sharp, whistling voice of Timiculous echoed in Nate's mind.

Nate reached over to his shoulder. Brushed Timiculous's long black beak with his fingers. His blue-and-gold macaw rubbed his whole head into Nate's hand. Needing the comfort.

Which was fine. Nate needed it too.

But he agreed with Timiculous. Elsa had a few days at most.

At best.

Timiculous sat, still and silent, huddled on Nate's shoulders. Bright blue wing feathers shaking. Brilliant golden breast shivering. He dug his narrow black claws into Nate. Managed to pinch the skin even through the thick robes Nate's station required.

This was the first Timiculous had spoken a single word—aloud or in Nate's head—since they'd arrived.

And that made him more nervous than anything.

Right along with this place.

The second he'd set foot in the sanctuary, he'd felt the wrongness. As if it crawled along his skin.

Something dark and oozing and unnatural.

Even now, Nate could practically smell the phantom smoke. Right from his nightmares. His half-memories. The memories his father had stolen from him, and the ones Nate hadn't managed to fully reclaim.

But Nate could still see the fire in his father's study. A fire that burned low until just the glowing embers remained. But there was no ventilation. No wind. Nothing to carry that thick, clogging smoke out and away.

Nate backed up another step from the viewing window.

His back pressed against the wall behind him and Timiculous gave a quick unfurl of his wings. Beat them once to steady himself, then a second time to settle down, before pressing his entire side against Nate's cheek.

Bad place. Bad air.

Nate wanted to be far from this place.

Far from that dull glow that clung to Elsa.

Couldn't, because of his father's order. And also, because, somehow, Nate felt there was something here...some answer to what had happened all those years ago.

An answer that burned in his gut.

A knowing.

Something was happening. Now. Something his father and the Council wanted to remain hidden.

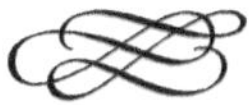

CHAPTER 4

Behind Nate, the "wall" was in truth yet another window, this one showing a perfect, panoramic view of the entire Paradise Grove Familiar Sanctuary. There were many "enclosures." Hundreds of crystal-clear glass cages separating the carefully selected, carefully monitored guests who stayed at the Paradise Grove Familiar Sanctuary.

All paying guests, of course.

A single night's stay being more than Nate could afford in a year. Unless, of course, he ever received his father's inheritance—and since his father refused to ever die, that at least left Nate with a clear understanding of where he fit into the greater picture.

Which was why he was standing here, with Timiculous shivering on his shoulders, staring out into a "paradise" that was the furthest thing from it—all at his father's command.

It was, he admitted to Timiculous through the bond that they shared, a perfect view.

As if snow leopards cared about perfect views.

As if he did, either.

"So, I see you've met our little queen," a voice boomed from the small, mostly hidden door to the viewing lounge.

Nate felt his shoulders tense—just for a moment—before his training took hold. With his training, and Timiculous's presence (though his Familiar was anything *but* calm), he regained control.

Nate turned. The dark robes of his office—of the Council—swayed with him. Flowed about his legs. The special blue-and-silver-etched lining running up its length, the embroidery of an ocean wave on his left breast.

To most people, this would immediately cause a hastily retracted hand, smile, or even a quick turn around in the other direction. If they were smart, anyway.

Not Lord Victor Asher.

If anything, those gold, beady eyes only brightened. The curling gray mustache rising up, practically gripping his face in complete joy.

The last thing Nate wanted was to shake the man's head.

But he stepped forward. Body and face and aura in complete control. He shook the lord's hand.

"Lord Asher. I came as soon as I heard."

Timiculous tugged at Nate's ear with his beak—nearly twice the size of Nate's ear. A beak that had no problem cracking the hardest Brazilian nuts within moments. Timiculous almost nipped Nate's ear, the pinch just a little too hard, hard enough to *almost* draw blood.

But Timiculous didn't.

He was also too well trained for that.

Lord Asher's smile fell. "Are you sure he's safe? He didn't—"

"Merely a sign of affection." He sent Timiculous a very cold, hard warning through their special, gleaming bond.

A bond that appeared bluish-red to Nate, something that no one but he could see, but it was there.

Just like a bond existed between every Familiar and their wizarding companion.

"Ah, yes, well—he's quite charming." Asher held out his hand, motioning that Nate should come closer to Elsa's enclosure.

A hand that, Nate noted, stayed far from Timiculous.

Interesting.

And this man was supposed to be the top curator and expert in Familiars and rehabilitation—or in most cases, retirement.

"We have several macaws in residence," Asher went on, "though thankfully they've seemed resistant so far to…well, to whatever this contagion is. Do you have any thoughts? Elsa was one of my prime Familiars. A real breakthrough with how she reintegrated into society."

Yet if she was doing so well, why hadn't she actually been reintroduced into society?

Of course, Nate kept his silence.

Had to.

Father's orders were quite clear.

Find out what was wrong. Do not engage.

"This enclosure has been mirrored after Elsa's home?" Nate asked. "With her master, I take it?"

"Down to the last detail, I'm pleased to say. My home, actually. And I'd just recently finished the final touches on the renovation. Quite pleased with the results, actually, as if Elsa were curled up at my feet like a good little cat."

Asher's mustache bobbed and twitched at every word. "We take great pride in our work here. In the comforts we provide our guests. See there, in the corner? That's actually the lavatory. Complete with plumbing, of course."

Nate had no choice but to follow the short, foppy man. "Has she used it, yet?"

"Sadly, no, I'm afraid. But we did have hope. At least, at least until this…."

"Which is what the Council sent me to investigate."

"Yes, yes, your father. He's a good man. Quite a good friend, actually. Spoke highly of you"—Asher's gaze flicked to Timiculous—"and your Familiar's talents. Would you like to look around? Perhaps meet Elsa?"

Timiculous immediately nipped again at Nate's ear.

Harder this time.

This time, Nate felt the tiniest trickle slide down his neck. Blood.

"No," he said. "We can sense just fine from here."

"Yes, of course, if you change your mind…"

Asher's voice trailed off.

A young woman, had to be barely out of her magical studies courses, poked her head in through the door. "I'm so sorry, Lord Asher. But I have a call for you. I told her that you were on important sanctuary matters but she was quite…rude. Wouldn't take no for an answer."

Asher's mustache dropped. A scowl creased his face, showing wrinkles he'd carefully hidden through a spelled-perfection disguise. "That's quite all right, Chelsea. Thank you for trying."

Asher excused himself to Nate, but as he walked through the doors, Nate clearly heard Asher ask the name of the caller, and the answer.

"It's that Waystation woman. That Aisha Faye."

The woman's—girl's—voice dropped to a whisper, but Timiculous took off. Flew right towards the slowly closing door, and heard and saw just fine for the both of them.

"Lanhi, the tiger you sent over a few months ago, is sick."

Asher froze. Back straight and taut. "The wasting sickness?"

"She wouldn't say, but my magic clearly picked up on her emotions. She's scared. I think it might be happening throughout that hovel."

Nate immediately turned his back on them. Jammed his hands into his trouser pockets. Stared into the enclosure that was meant more for a man like his father than a leopard, one bred for that super-cold, northern weather.

Damn.

Not there too.

He'd hoped, prayed, there might be one place, one holdout….

Elsa, he noticed, still lay there. Uncaring. Her beautiful, sleek and spotted form completely devoid of life. As if the will to live had simply vanished. Her spark barely even a flicker.

He'd been wrong about her.

She didn't have a few days.

Like many of the others, she'd be dead by nightfall.

And there was nothing he, nor even Timiculous, could do to save her.

CHAPTER 5

*A*isha gave the curling-mustached face of Lord Victor Asher—shimmering in her cracked speaking-mirror—her most serene, calmest smile.

It didn't matter that her hands slightly shook.

Or that she'd purposefully made the call outside, sitting crossed-legged on the still superheated sand with no tree in sight, sweat sticking to her forehead, slipping down her nose and forming a puddle of its own—which then immediately evaporated. But hot or not, uncomfortable or not, the sun behind her cast a silhouetted glow over her features.

Concealed the tension in her face.

Disgust to have the mirror in her hands. Staring into his serene, perfectly spelled face.

She'd made the call here so he couldn't see one ounce of her compound—of her living space or office in that patched-together building beside her. Or that her Waystation was hidden out of sight in that slit of a valley below the bluff.

She *was* making the call.

That was what mattered.

Even if those eyes of his gleamed brighter than she'd ever seen them. Wider, too.

Correction.

She'd seen him this excited once before. When she'd just arrived from Tanzania. Carried only her one bag and the clothes on her back, her entire being missing the home she'd been forced to leave. Lord Victor Asher had been thrilled to shelter and offer her sanctuary—especially while she still felt that loss, the rejection by both her parents and her sister. A loss she'd felt with every breath.

One she felt, still, so keenly.

An ache circling in her stomach.

And with the ache came the shadow, which crossed over her heart. The dark, curling, cold touch of a man she couldn't see clearly but could feel.

Aisha shivered. Closed her eyes for a moment.

She wasn't sleeping now. Wasn't in her deepest nightmares.

Forced herself to remember Asher, who was on the mirror call right this moment. She'd accepted Asher's help, she remembered. The moment she'd gotten off the dragon transport, she'd allowed herself to be cared for and sheltered by him.

Until she understood the man. Until she saw his sanctuary.

"Was there something you needed?" Asher asked, calling her back to the present.

The tips of his mustache curled upward. Reached his ears in the exact same manner she remembered. Behind him, she glimpsed his fancy, frivolous office. Nearly three times the size of her whole home, complete with its little trickling fountain in the back. The high-backed, cushioned, black exotic wood chair he sat in—completely at odds with her hot dirt and rocks digging up her butt.

Then there were those windows overlooking his perfect sanctuary. The little world he ran and controlled like a god.

Bile crept up her throat.

Aisha swallowed.

She wanted to end the call right there.

Her hand nearly swept across the mirror's surface to close the connection.

No, she reminded herself. She needed answers. Even if it meant getting them from Asher. The man who'd proven himself nearly as bad as her parents. Just as fake and social climbing and completely uncaring of the Familiars he supposedly cared for.

"Aisha, dear, I'm so glad you called." Asher's voice preened as if he were right beside her and not in the southern tip of California's famous coastal beach area. No where near her hot, sticky valley where legions of black gnats buzzed around her head, following her like her own personal black cloud.

Persistent little buggers.

"I've told you to call me, time and time again, when you're in need of help," Asher said, "and here you are. Tell me, dear, what can I and my humble sanctuary do for you?"

He was no better than the mosquitos—at least the mosquitos were right up front with what they wanted.

But she *did* need the help. So she ignored the way her stomach and the magic there twisted. Churned. And told him about Lanhi.

"I confirmed it today. She has a wasting sickness," Aisha bit out the words. "I'd appreciate any information you might have."

"Is she the first case?"

Her grip on the mirror's wooden rim tightened. Forced herself to breathe in. Out. "I've heard rumors that several of your Familiars have this as well."

"Well." Asher cleared his throat. "I can neither confirm nor deny that statement, as the privileges of our clients prohibits me from discussing their Familiars' condition...."

Which meant yes, damn him.

Asher drawled on, firing more questions at her. Who was the first case? When did this occur? Have any deaths been documented and at what rate? Was she doing any manner of quarantine or did her facility even have such...capabilities?

The heat in Aisha's face rose. Crept up her cheeks.

With every question, he gave her one more piece of the puzzle. One more fact he wasn't telling her.

They did have deaths.

Multiple.

Spreading fast.

Even with quarantine procedures.

She was grateful for the sun and her dark skin, he wouldn't be able to see, to notice the anger building within her. Because even with the Familiars and their lives at stake, he was still trying to use her.

She had expected his response. All of it.

She'd have been better off contacting one or two of his employees who still worked there, and still chatted with her on occasion. But Asher...he never accepted her calls.

Not that she called often (did her damn best to avoid it), but ever since she'd been disinherited by the famous and internationally popular Familiar sanctuary revolutionaries, Rosaline and Albert Faye, Lord Asher had suddenly lost his interest in her work, finding it inconsequential and small-minded. Of course, the disinheritance hadn't happened until *after* she'd arrived and settled in the States. After Asher had taken considerable time helping her adjust to her new life and fit in. After she'd broken away from his sanctuary to start her own.

She had a feeling he held this against her. As if *she* could control what her parents did.

But still, what truly mattered was that everything Asher asked of her, about Lanhi and the other Familiars, told her more than he'd ever expected: this situation was serious and he didn't know how to control it.

Otherwise, he'd never have accepted the call.

She cut him off.

"Thank you, Lord Asher, but if that's all you have to say on the matter, I believe the rest of this conversation is pointless."

Asher sputtered, tried to smile, though it seemed more like a curling grimace behind that gray mustache of his. "Come, come, dear. You were trained at my sanctuary. You understand our rules and our privacy. I simply cannot divulge that information. But your simple little Waystation with all its forgotten Familiars, well, you don't have that kind of restriction. So tell me, dear Aisha, *is* Lanhi the first?"

"No, she's not," Aisha snapped.

Couldn't help herself.

Nearly said more.

Didn't.

"And that's all *I* will say on the matter." She swept her hand over the mirror.

Asher's face shimmered. As if a rock had been thrown straight into his too-sharp noise. A ripple effect traveled across the mirror and the image finally faded. And she managed, just barely, not to chuck the mirror into the valley.

"Gee, that sounds like it went well," Marcelle said behind her.

Aisha spun. Gripped the mirror's wooden handle as if she'd use it for a club.

Marcelle stood there, pink hair glowing almost neon in the sun's orange-streaked line. Hands on her hips—wrists that once again sported spikes leather bands around them.

How she didn't manage to poke herself with those things...

"What are you still doing here? I thought you went home." Aisha shoved the mirror back into its special pouch—little more than a burlap sack she'd found in her storage closet—and slung the thing over her shoulder.

"You said you were making some calls." Marcelle tipped her head to the mirror. "It didn't take a psychic to know you'd need someone near."

"I don't need anyone."

She didn't. Hadn't in years.

And she'd proven it, damn it, time and time again.

"Uh-huh. Right. Well, that may be, but I figured since we've had a really shitty day and since we've actually finished *before* the sun went down, I thought some quiet and fun girl time was in order."

"Girl time?"

It sounded frightening.

"A shower," Aisha said, "would be just fine."

A hot one, too.

Hopefully.

If Marcelle hadn't already used up all the hot water (which the shorter witch with her short hair probably had).

Marcelle just smiled. "I was thinking a bit of foot pampering. How do you feel about Dusky Sunset glinting off your toes?"

Absolutely frightful.

Instead, Aisha said, "My toes need a shower."

Marcelle hooked her arm in Aisha's. Patted off the dust and whatever that black smudge on Aisha's jacket was. "Trust me, dear, more than your toes could use that. You, shower. Me, get wine and nail polish."

Aisha had no choice but to follow. Captured by the tiny psychic with a will that'd out beat even her stubborn, closed-minded mother.

Except Marcelle's smile was much, much more friendly.

And she cared, too.

About Aisha.

And even more importantly, cared about the Familiars here who depended on them.

ate's eyes shot skyward at the slowly darkening sky. A high-whistling keen of an airplane broke through the barrier surrounding Paradise Grove. Too high up for even the best spell caster to block out, even as the airplane slowly worked its way to LAX airport just a stone's throw from where Nate stood outside that glass compound.

With its manicured lawn. Elaborate fountains.

Extravagant promises to existing and potential clients of the care their Familiars would receive while staying at Paradise Grove. As if it were a luxury hotel and not a place to dump the unwanted has-beens.

But those engines kept on whirling. Turning.

Nate shielded his eyes from the sinking sun un-obscured by the bare scattering of clouds. He couldn't see the plane, but heard it just fine.

Smiled.

The airplane didn't care about magical sensibilities. Didn't care about those living here who needed the utmost privacy from all things considered "Normal."

Just went about its job and damn the magical people it pissed off.

Some of the knots in his chest lessened.

Nate reached over and stroked Timiculous curving beak. "Must be nice."

You try sometime.

"Right."

Starting with Father.

And while pissing off his father would be on his top of his wish list, what he really wanted was to hop into the nearest shower, clothes and all, and wash away that dull, clingy glow.

Felt like it clung to his skin. His aura.

Hell, maybe he'd just burn his clothes. Had more than enough robes for his damn position to last a month.

"You up for a shower, buddy?"

Timiculous unfurled his brilliant gold wings. Flapped them in agreement.

Shower first. Then, maybe a drink.

From the way his head pounded, from the tainted glow his own aura had taken, just from being near the leopard…he might need more than that just to clear the air around him.

But a shower sounded like a damn fine place to start.

Nate tucked his hands into his pockets. Crossed that perfectly cut lawn—probably no more than three inches high or some such nonsense—completely ignoring the cobblestone walkway leading to the parking lot, and headed towards his sleek black Mustang.

Whipped out his wand instead of keys and flipped open the lock, which disengaged immediately as the engine started.

With a rolling, rumbling purr.

He hoped some of the uppity types heading to visit their precious Familiars had their perfect existences disrupted by his loud, blasphemous car for even a moment….

Company, here.

"Good." Nate grinned.

But then that hope was squashed when he spotted the brilliant red-tailed hawk sitting on the hood of his Mustang. Those narrowed eyes, sharp-curving beak, talons meant for ripping and tearing.

His father's Familiar, Artemis.

Nate hadn't expected his father's call.

Not this fast, anyway.

Not two steps outside of Paradise Grove.

Nate shoved his wand back into his robe. Crossed his arms and glared at Artemis, who just glared right on back. Those talons curled, just a tad. Turned towards Nate. Caused the thin, shining black of his hood to screech.

Probably scratched the paint too.

"Well?" Nate snapped.

Artemis lifted her talon; a thin parchment slid out from between those piercing claws.

Unfurled. Opened.

The face of Nate's father appeared. Not a single line or wrinkle. Just the allowance of gray around his temples. But there was a shadow about him. His eyes. No matter how hard and long you looked, you never got a clear, full image of him. Nate, however, got a clear, full image of the distasteful expression he always wore whenever it was necessary to speak with his *son.*

Heir.

Because even the great Lord Sylvester Darkwood, the High Chancellor of the Council itself, the politically rising and powerful wizard that he was, needed one.

Timiculous rubbed against Nate's check—helped him realize he'd held his breath. Again.

Damn it.

"Father," Nate forced out. "As you can see, I was just leaving my inspection of Paradise Grove—"

"Far too soon."

"Yes, well, there's nothing I can do for the snow leopard—"

"I don't care about the tiger. I care about the problem, which you've clearly given a great deal of time and attention to discovering what is actually *causing* this sickness and why it is affecting our most important Familiars. *Especially* since you were in the facility for less than a sun's turn."

Every word, Nate felt the heat rise. A slap right in his face...that only made him want to slap back.

Fight back.

For once.

Timiculous again rubbed his soft feathers against Nate's cheek, but Nate ignored it.

His father had no idea...no idea how long Nate had already searched. Studied. Worried over this. Stayed up at nights, unable to sleep, unable to get that suffocating smell of smoke and death from his mind. The shattered, broken images of his mother. Pale and lifeless on the red-soaked carpet. So many sleepless, nightmare-filled nights.

Timiculous tugged at Nate's ear.

Nate tensed.

Out of control. He was getting out of control.

What mattered, though, was that his father *didn't* know.

"I need you to look into this," his father was saying, "with all that same care you give those Normals and their trinkets, like that infernal, screeching car of yours."

"It doesn't screech—"

"And I need you to do something even more important. Something you must discuss with no one."

His father's glinting gray eyes narrowed on Timiculous. "And I expect you to keep your thoughts on the matter protected even from your Familiar."

Nate felt a stone fall in his stomach. Rolled there.

Above him, still high and still working on its descent, was that airplane. Didn't seem to care at all that Lord Darkwood was speaking and all should be silent.

Should listen.

"You've been reassigned to another project. I'll have Racine Faye follow up with Paradise Grove, investigate the matters further there. You, on the other hand..." His father leaned in. Closer to the message parchment. Pointed, hooked nose nearly touching it. "You will go to The Magical Waystation for Unwanted Familiars."

Nate didn't dare breathe. Didn't dare move.

Just waited.

Knowing what was coming.

"It's been reported the wasting sickness has appeared there as well, just as I expected."

Timiculous was practically on top of Nate. His whole body pressed against the side of his head.

In support.

Or in warning.

Probably both.

"Father?"

He couldn't actually ask. Didn't want to know, though part of him knew he had no choice. Had this been the plan from the beginning? Had this sickness been somehow orchestrated by his father? By the Council? Did they know of Nate's interest there? How he'd been trying for weeks to contact the owner?

Nate found his hand reaching into his rope, curling around the dark wood of his wand. For comfort, and, more. His grip tightened. A warning spark crisped up his knuckles, but he didn't let go.

Couldn't.

Because he knew what his father would ask. Knew what he would want his son to do.

His father's cold eyes never left Nate's. As if daring him to disobey, to even attempt some silly form of independence.

Nate didn't move. Just stood at attention even while his stomach flipped. The contents of lunch slowly swirling up his throat.

"This," his father said, "is the opportunity I and the Council have been waiting for. Identify the truth of the matter. Find conclusive evidence that the wasting sickness has, in fact, contaminated the Waystation. Bring this back to us, conclusive and irrefutable, and we'll finally shut down that wasteful disgrace of a facility down."

The smile Nate's father gave him, that sneer of joy and pleasure, reached all the way to Sylvester's unkind eyes.

Nate simply, and slowly, nodded his acceptance.

Of the assignment. Of his fate.

Couldn't help but wonder, as Timiculous climbed onto Nate's arm and settled on his perch in the car, if this was the moment his Familiar had mentioned earlier.

The moment where he damned the magical community, and his Father, and told them to piss off. And whether or not he could do it.

Instead, he slid the Mustang into reverse and drove home.

To prepare.

CHAPTER 7

Sylvester Darkwood leaned back in his cushioned mahogany chair. His private study, quiet and dark in this deepest of night except for a small burning fire in the great fireplace. Just embers remained, as his servants had carefully prepared and spelled, which now cast the perfect red glow.

Tinted everything to be either that shadowed dark.

Or red.

He held a crystal glass. It hadn't been passed down among the family, not like other great families, because the Darkwoods hadn't been great until Sylvester came along. Until he finally emerged from the shadows, from his quiet, secret life fulfilling those not-quite-legal contracts and...requests the great families had need of handling. When he'd made his name on the larger, more political front, with all his years of contacts and "information," it had been only too easy to solidify his power.

To make his family great.

Sylvester swirled his wine glass. Once. Twice. Allowed the most exquisite red wine within to breathe, to release every hidden fragrance.

He breathed in the wine, forcing himself to relax, regardless of the recent developments. To take this moment to enjoy this time. Always, as late evening approached early morning, was his time.

No one to control. No frilly Council members to manipulate or coerce—and using such a delicate hand that none were the wiser. Were even aware of his influence.

But relaxation didn't come to him. Not tonight. Not with the news so fresh, having been confirmed by his son. He couldn't help but reflect. To think of his mistakes and his lost wife, Trishia, and... others he'd made.

Like the girl.

Perhaps he should have Aisha all those years ago.

Should have used the ruthless, cold calculations that was so necessary, so common in his former life. But he'd been too new to the change. Too new to living out in the open. Under scrutiny. Surveillance.

He'd thought the memory-block spell had been the right maneuver.

Perhaps, he'd been wrong.

Or perhaps the whole operation with the Tanzanian Wizarding Council had been a mistake.

There was no point reliving the past. Dwelling on it. Power was gained only by moving forward.

And right now, he wanted to enjoy the wine.

Which he'd enjoy more if he were actually alone. If the looking mirror didn't chime and ripple, the image of that weasel Lord Asher glinting back at him.

Sylvester slowly lowered his wine. "You do understand, Lord Asher, that I do not accept calls at this time."

"Why, yes, great sir, but I believe this is a matter of utmost importance." The tips of Asher's gaudy mustache curled up and into his nose.

Sylvester placed the wine down in disgust.

Couldn't possible enjoy the exquisite delicacies with this man in front of him, mirror reflection or not.

"I have already done what I can. Sent my son. Redeployed Lady

Racine, whom you will remember, including her connections, even if you'd not been formally introduced."

"Yes, yes, I cannot begin to tell you how overjoyed I am to hear of her visit, but there's more and it simply can't wait—"

"Racine will be arriving tomorrow. My son will be arriving at the Waystation tomorrow. I assure you, he and his Familiar will find anything untoward happening there."

He wanted this man gone. But Asher fought with every polite deflection, completely ignoring the two dismissals Sylvester had just given him.

Politeness wouldn't last long.

Especially when Asher needed Sylvester more than Sylvester needed that foppy, pretending lord—

"But you see, sir. It *is* the Familiar."

Sylvester sat up straighter. "Go on."

"I've been wondering over his visit. With your son. I've heard great things of them both, the great work they've done, together, but the Familiar's reaction to the sanctuary, it was almost as if he couldn't wait to be gone of my place. He spoke not a single word to me. Or to Nathanial the entire time he was there. Our sensors picked up very little in the way of mind speak as well."

"And you believe this is a cause for concern?"

Sylvester couldn't know for sure. Hadn't taken on another true Familiar, hadn't spoken with one—even the ones he still had—since that night. With Trishia.

"A great cause for concern, Lord Darkwood. It was almost as if Timiculous *understood* what was going on. What we were...omitting from your son. About Lanhi, and the others that were...under treatment before her, and then quietly removed from the sanctuary. As soon as I realized the connection—"

"I'm losing my patience."

"The Familiar. Your son. His Timiculous. I believe he knows."

Sylvester's hands gripped the armrest. Fingers dug into those ornate, ancient carvings. "Knows what?"

"Knows the cause. Of the sickness."

Sylvester's grip tightened. "He couldn't possibly know."

The Enchantment Avenue Council, of course, knew the cause. To some degree, anyway. As did all the Councils. And each had been careful. Very careful at keeping all incidents, all the signs, hidden.

Until that night.

Until Trishia.

"But the way Timiculous was acting, what he said…" Asher sucked on a tip of his mustache. "Somehow, he knows. The truth. About what happened to your wife."

Sylvester stood. Hands clasped behind his back. The silk of his dark robe giving slightly, but made not a single sound.

Just the little pop, every so often from the fire, and that foolish Asher still sucking on his mustache as if he were a child. The mirror followed Sylvester, but behind him. Discreetly. Gave him privacy to think. To process.

If this were, indeed, possible…

Sylvester stroked his chin. The always clean-shaven skin. "Timiculous may know some form of the truth, but not the whole of it. My son did not procure him until after the event."

"But who's to say what he's learned from your son?" Asher objected.

"My son doesn't know."

Couldn't, because Sylvester had personally, carefully, blocked those memories.

That was why, after all, Nathaniel had pushed for the unique Familiar to begin with. A Familiar to help him understand, and prevent, such an event from ever happening again.

A Familiar that now sat beside his ear, day and night.

Never leaving him.

"Yet…" Sylvester gave his chin another stroke. "Yet, even if Nathanial doesn't know, we cannot say the same for his subconscious. Memories he's blocked or forgotten. Correlations, scents. He would have not have access to such things, but the Familiar…"

Sylvester let his words trail off.

"The Familiar may have, though," Asher put in. "We understand so little about the bond. Especially with a Sensitive."

Sylvester only nodded. Grateful that while Asher was a fool, the man wasn't completely brainless.

Nathanial and Timiculous's bond was little understood, simply because the Council rarely allowed such Sensitive Familiars to live in the first place.

Sylvester would need to be careful.

They'd need to be separated. Kept at a distance until Sylvester learned the truth of this sickness. Precisely how it was caused. To think, all these years of work and effort by the Fayes and their picture-perfect sanctuary, and he still didn't have concrete evidence. Proof of why their Familiars could so easily, so quickly, turn.

Become feral.

Sylvester would learn the truth, and bury it.

He finally lowered his hands. Slow and careful. In control.

Even as thoughts of Trishia fought against him.

Struggled to be free.

Not tonight.

Not ever.

Sylvester turned to the hovering silver mirror and that pasty man staring back at him. "I will inform my son that Timiculous is to remain within the Waystation. To limit their contact. You will inform Racine of the change in plans. Pray you learn those answers soon or your sanctuary, like all the others, will be shut down permanently."

Asher squeaked. His face gone a sticky white. "S-sir? But we offer a great service to the magical community—"

"And I will not risk this information surfacing. Ever. Get your Familiars under control, and if you can't, destroy them."

After all, what was one more dead Familiar when they could be replaced? While his Trishia could not. And once the truth was revealed, about the Familiars and how the Councils had known, for all these years, the danger lurking within every household, Sylvester's place in their world, his power, could never be replaced.

Not ever.

The High Council would make sure of it.

Sun filtered through the leaves and branches of the half-sized trees scattered through Aisha's carved-out valley. The tint of dawn and dew still holding on. Even the breeze carried a crisp kick to it that worked its way past her light jacket to her tank top below.

But underneath all that she tasted the promise of heat. The sweltering, unrelenting sun that'd fill her Waystation in just a few short hours.

Aisha lifted her arms up, yawned, and groaned. Yawned because she'd had another sleepless night. Wisps of shattered images through a thick, hazy smoke. The shadow man again, ripping into her. Into her heart. Her magic.

Aisha stretched her arms up further, used the ache and the stretch to shove aside the last remnants of sleep and memory. She groaned because her muscles ached something fierce—she'd already been at work for two hours.

Working with Familiars meant the day started before the sun, before the Familiars even knew it was time to start their day. At least for some. Some just started their day when she finally, finally collapsed on her beat-up couch.

Aisha smiled.

It was good work, though. And always worth it.

Always.

Even if those like the great Lord Asher, like her parents, with their fancy Sanctuaries and fancy clients, didn't understand.

Could never understand.

But the sting she'd felt last night, the burning in her gut when she'd dissolved the call to Asher, didn't hurt so bad anymore.

Thanks to Marcelle.

As much as Aisha hated to admit it, she'd had a good time last night. Even the toe-polishing part—but they'd stayed up late.

Much later than Aisha expected.

And more importantly, even after the fun and the wine, Marcelle had gone to her little garden of rocks and knickknacks (which she claimed helped center her chi or whatever). Marcelle did her best work at night, which was fine by Aisha 'cause seriously, she did *her* best sleeping at night.

Sometimes.

But not only did Aisha's dreams not cooperate with the idea of sleep, neither did Marcelle, who'd gone and overdone it with her psychic searching. She'd stumbled into Aisha's home, bleary-eyed and pale, taking any chances of Aisha actually getting some quality sleep.

The poor witch had pushed herself a bit too close to exhaustion and had barely made it back inside. Aisha hadn't gotten much out of Marcelle and what had happened, but she did manage to shove the witch into the spare bedroom...err, pull-out bed thing...and she'd been out like a phoenix's tail-fire light.

Aisha could, and would, handle the chores.

She'd gone by herself before. She'd do it again.

She only wished that Marcelle had found some clue, something that would really help her link together whatever pieces she was missing. She'd have to wait until Marcelle was conscious again.

But Aisha *knew* she was missing something.

Her magic, her gut, insisted that the answer was right there.

Her magic kept trying to pull up memories, to recall feelings and smells from her life back home...well, back in Tanzania. On her parents' sanctuary. Of that short but amazing time she'd spent with the Hadzabe tribe, her grandfather's tribe. Before her mother had figured out where Aisha had gone off to.

But try as Aisha might, even as she strained her senses, her memory, she simply couldn't recall whatever it was she was missing.

As if she was blocked.

As if her mind simply shut off. Blacked out. Skipped right on over it.

Which didn't make any sense at all.

Aisha tossed her dark hair, wrapped in a braid to keep it out of her way, over her shoulder. Tipped the brim of her hat up. It was probably pointless. The answer couldn't be there. In Tanzania. She'd come such a long way, such a long way from that time...there was no way the answer was there.

Couldn't be.

"You need to focus, girl. Stop dreaming in the past."

Words were usually spoken to bring comfort and conversation between one human and another.

Aisha found that words to Familiars, and even to herself, did just fine without adding another annoying, difficult-to-understand human into the mix.

So, she did as she'd instructed herself, and focused on the work.

She carted a dinged-up slop bucket of day-old veggies and half-turned apples, mangos, and some other green fruit Aisha wasn't even sure was a fruit...but she wasn't about to turn her nose up on the free, discarded food from the Normals' grocery store.

What wasn't fit for Normal consumption, animals had no problem eating.

Yet another point in the Normals' favor.

The magical, well, they'd expect payment for any kind of favor, gift, heck, even donation.

And money, well, she'd purposefully glanced over *that* stack of bills when she'd set on this morning.

Chimpanzees hooped and hollered as she made her way to the aviary center. They catcalled, too, even though she wasn't within sight of their enclosure. They were some of her more difficult residents—flinging poop being their least offensive action. No, it was those unregulated, unbalanced spells they'd either managed to sequester away without their magical masters being aware or, even worse, they had learned the rudimentary basics of those spells that didn't actually require a wand.

Aisha and Marcelle made a habit of never going to *that* enclosure without a backup, a subdue spell (or six) at the ready, and a big, big bottle of Mountain Dew.

There was another *he-he-yep*! Followed by the usual screaming chorus.

They probably smelled her from here.

She'd get to them soon enough. Probably bring two cans of that Mountain Dew concoction today. They'd be taken care of soon enough, including the two younger ones, the ones she'd already noticed had the wasting-glaze in their eyes, their aura.

Aisha came to the giant, ringed net enclosure. It reached up, high into the sky, the highest point of her whole Waystation, though if Normals were on her back-end-of-nowhere dirt road to begin with—a rarity, for sure—they'd see nothing more than the stunted trees and steep inclines cutting through the valley.

Nothing, at all, of interest to see.

One of the only spells she actually paid good money for.

The aviary net, she noticed, was fraying again in a few spots.

Damn.

More mending on her part. But it wasn't the kind done with spells or wands. Instead, she just used a pair of hands, hooks, and some cobra-thick rope. Nothing like the silvery-spelled stuff her parents had at their sanctuary, hard as dragon-hide scales but light and quiet as an owl's feather. Still, her Normal rope did the job.

Another sign of good, hard work, and it made her smile.

Unlike the locks she needed to rely on that locksmith for, already fading and flickering—the bastard—her netting held good and strong.

And she could trust it.

Aisha lumped the bucket up to the locked enclosure doors, her muscles still protesting. She managed to slip her wand from her back pocket.

Perfectly balanced, made of a rowan tree as wind passed through its leafy bough, with the core of a phoenix feather centered within. It was considered a true treasure among the Magical folk.

Aisha scrunched up her nose. Gave a half-flick of her wrist—not at all elegant or graceful as her mother's instructors had spent years teaching her—but it did the job.

She didn't use wands often. Didn't like them and didn't trust them.

The rusty lock, one of the first she'd purchased what felt like a hundred years ago, gave a *click, click, whirl* as the dial turned to the correct combination and slipped open.

Tucking the wand back into her pants, out of sight and out of the way, she somehow kept her hold of the bucket. She also resisted the urge to wipe off her hand where she felt the glowing spell's residue clinging to her fingers, soaking into her skin. Mostly because she didn't want to dump the birds' breakfast.

She always got that sensation after using her wand and the magic that spilled from it.

As far as she was concerned, wands were used only when needed. And, if she could help it, only for emergencies. Course, regulations required that the locks be spelled and keyed to individual wands and not strictly for emergency-only. Still, that was one rule her parents had taught—why, exactly, she didn't know, but it was one rule Aisha still followed.

"One of the few good ones they gave me."

Even if they *had* also taught her the proper form and all that other upper society nonsense crap.

Wands couldn't be trusted.

Neither could the wizards and witches flinging about those wands.

Familiars, however, were a different matter.

At least, until recent years, it seemed.

Until she'd noticed her Waystation was growing more and more filled, not just with the retired and abused, but the Familiars who actually, truly could no longer be trusted.

"Which just doesn't make any sense."

She shook her head.

Animals, and therefore Familiars, were about the only thing that she *could* trust. Trust that they'd behave and act in a certain a way, a way that was always—always—based on instinct.

"Just add that to the growing list of answers I don't have."

The chimps, still a-hollering and a-screaming, even way off beyond the hill rise and down into the next dip over, answered her with their usual insults.

She snorted.

They probably did know the answers. Probably got plenty of enjoyment watching her spin and hiss and kick in frustration. She wouldn't put *anything* past that bunch of chimps.

Just like Asher and those other uppity sanctuary owners.

Using her Waystation as their testing ground. Not caring if any of *her* Familiars up and died.

Her Waystation, after all, like Aisha, simply wasn't important to the magical community. The great-ass Enchantment Avenue Council made sure of that. Would *always* make sure of that.

Even thought they needed her.

Needed her Waystation to take in their unwanted. Their garbage. Because, after all, someone had to.

CHAPTER 9

A mix of dust, dirt and broken bits of asphalt swirled up and around Nate's legs as he climbed out of his Mustang. Stepped onto that too-hot ground in a parking lot that was nothing more than a thin patch of dirt. Not a single building in sight for miles.

Just tumbleweeds.

Stunted bushes locals liked to call trees.

A road held together by paint and luck—one earthquake out here and the whole thing would fall right into those rolling hills.

"Answers here!"

Timiculous flapped his swings from Nate's shoulder. Stirred up some dust of his own, which only made Nate cough. His eyes, water.

The sun hadn't even really climbed over the tall foothills behind him and already the sweat clung to his armpits.

He slammed the door to his Mustang—then winced. Because, really, it wasn't his car's fault.

It was no one's fault.

Except his own.

Nate leaned forward. Peered over the edge where a dirt road—he presumed the one that led into the Waystation—dove right into a ravine. Simply fell off the planet without a blink.

A perfect place for an unwanted Familiars.

A perfect place for his father and the Council to dump their own unwanted garbage. This Waystation for the Unwanted. This dark blemish on their otherwise pristine little world.

Nate snorted. Wanted to roll his thick, dark robes up to his elbows, but didn't. Not when he felt that familiar touch on his mind. That brush. That warning.

"Company coming."

"Real company or just a message?" Nate growled.

The last thing he wanted was his father, Asher, or anyone else from the Council checking up on him—especially when he hadn't set one damn foot into the Waystation yet.

This time, at least, it wasn't the soaring, graceful flight of a red-tailed hawk he saw—but a pelican.

Giant beak sagging open. Like the guy was gasping for breath. His wings beating as much as they could, but only made him limp along.

"Really? Poor guy. Asher could at least have sent a pigeon."

Timiculous nodded his bright blue head.

Some bird, any bird, accustomed to the heat and dryness further inland.

But then again, Asher, being the kind of lord he was, probably didn't have something as mundane as pigeons or crows—hell, probably not even a raven.

Well, it wasn't Artemis with his father's cheerful face. That was something. At least.

"Why don't you go give the poor guy a hand? I'll wait right here."

And with that, Timiculous launched himself from Nate's shoulders. Just the hard flapping and beating of wings in that still-ass air. The extra-strength cloud of dust that sent Nate into another round of coughs.

And eyes tearing.

By the time Nate could see again, Timiculous had helped the poor ocean bird settle down on the hood of Nate's car.

Relief flowed from Timiculous—and from the pelican, exhaustion.

Nate swore. Leave it to a man like Asher to not even *think* about the consequences. Of what would happen to his bird, sending him so far inland. In southern California, even seven miles from the beach could mean ten degrees hotter. Not a single breeze and a serious need for air conditioning.

"All right, fella." Nate held out his hand. "Hand over the message so you can get home before it really heats up."

The pelican's dark eyes bulged at that. Opened its mouth and spat out a rolled up parchment message.

Which immediately unfurled.

The pelican immediately took off again.

Nate kept on coughing and wiping up his eyes—even as Asher's gaunt face rolled out before him. Anger, the pretty pissed-off kind, rolled off that man so hard and fast, Nate didn't need a sensitive (or even Timiculous) to tell him what was up.

"You were sent to help us!"

Asher's concealment spells, Nate noticed, had nearly faded. Wrinkles lined every inch of his face. Dark, hollow eyes glared at Nate as if from a skull. The spells had left open the truth of that man in his bright red and blue robes. That fancy office behind him with the fountains and birds of paradise huddled in the corner.

And Asher was too upset to care.

Wonderful.

Nate got another swallow of spit down. Managed to hold down another round of growling, throat-scratching coughs. What the hell was in the dirt, here?

"Lord Asher, I'm sorry to say I've only just arrived at the Waystation—"

"My Elsa is dead!"

Nate closed his eyes. Both for the relief from that dirt, and for that brief flare of pain—pain he didn't want Asher to see.

"I'm sorry to hear," Nate whispered.

He felt Timiculous then, that light touch against his mind. A feather touch. Comforting.

Reminding Nate that he wasn't alone.

"You were supposed to save her," Asher wailed. "She was my prize. Do you know how long it took to hunt her down? To train her?"

Manipulate her? Morph her into something other than what she was?

Instead, Nate shook his head. Focused on Timiculous and that welcoming touch that didn't abandon him.

"I want you to find out everything—*everything*—about that Waystation. Do you hear me? Whatever Aisha is hiding. What she had for breakfast. I must know it all. Every detail. I will find out what's causing this and *you* will be the one to bring it to me. Is that understood?"

Nate crossed his arms. Leaned back against his Mustang.

"I'm a little confused. I thought I was being sent to investigate the cause of the wasting sickness."

"You are!"

"Except...we've only just received reports that it's appeared here. To my knowledge, Paradise Grove and other sanctuaries have had this sickness much longer—"

"Because she lied." Asher's face distorted into a roadmap of wrinkles and lines. "She lied. There is no way, no possibility that this, this *sickness* would strike my Paradise before her wasteful little facility. I'm sure of it."

There was nothing for Nate to do but nod.

He was, after all, more a politician than a therapist for Familiars. At least, so far as the Council was ever concerned.

Timiculous flew from the Mustang's hood to Nate's shoulders. Settled there. Rubbed his soft feathered head against Nate's cheek.

Which only made Asher glower further.

"I will continue on as instructed," Nate said. "The new instructions. Yes, my father contacted me last night." With strict orders that Timiculous was to *stay* at the Waystation.

Without Nate.

His fists clenched at the thought.

He wanted Timiculous beside him. Helping him finally understand what this sickness was, who had it and, just maybe, how to stop it.

Nate forced himself to breathe. To relax. "I'm sure I have you to thank for those changes."

"It's necessary. If we are to understand what Aisha has unleashed in her vile, backwater place—"

"I am truly sorry to hear about Elsa"—even though he'd warned Asher before he left that she wouldn't make it.

Asher straightened. Tugged at his curling mustache until he got himself under control. The great lord and powerful Sanctuary Director, the one accustomed to his perfect life by the ocean and beach, returned.

"One more thing," Asher said. "It would be best if you didn't mention your involvement with the Council."

"Obviously."

"Or with me, for that matter. Aisha and I have a…history. We didn't part on the best of terms. She won't be…open…to your visit if she knew about me. Or my Paradise."

"Of course, Lord Asher."

Just like Nate wasn't going to mention a word about Lady Racine being in residence at the sanctuary. Nate had done his homework, even more so since his father's latest orders.

Nate knew everything, or as much as one could know, about Aisha Faye, her disgrace from her family—even if the "why" of it wasn't listed or explained.

Anywhere.

Still, he at least knew which spell mines to avoid and right now, he'd take whatever help—big or small—he could get. Especially since he hadn't a clue what he was going to do.

About the Waystation.

The Council.

The sickness.

He shivered. Felt the distant, hidden memory of that night pull at him. Those memories might be blocked, mostly, but there some things that *couldn't* be blocked, even with the greatest of spells. Bits and pieces of a memory that refused to stay buried. Like the smells of smoke, clogging his throat, stinging his eyes as he tried to get to her.…

All that was still there.

Timiculous flapped his wings. Squawked.

Nate blinked. Focused on the lordling before him. "Now, if you'll excuse me. I have a job to accomplish."

He didn't wait for a reply. Just furled up the message parchment with a wave. Then turned that whole thing into a smoldering, burning crisp with another wave.

Whatever job that was; he still hadn't decided, still didn't know which side of the coin he and his loyalty would fall on.

And this time, he'd be alone.

No Timiculous to guard his back. To watch him.

Completely alone.

Just like he'd been that night. When he'd found his mother and his father's precious Familiar, Apollo, found them in the one place his father had always called his sanctuary.

Both of them, dead.

CHAPTER 10

*A*isha shoved her way past the aviary's double doors. One door swung in, the other swung out. It was a simple Normal technique to keep birds from flying out, better than some complex mismatch of spells most sanctuaries used to keep the birds in line (even if those spell might accidently zap off a feather—or permanently ground the bird).

Course, the Normal way sure was a pain when she had a bucketload of sharp, tangy, and well-past-ripened fruit bucket bulging in her arms.

Still, she managed.

Just like she managed every morning and night. And the birds heard her racket as she shoved and banged and even thunked her own hand against the door—and swore too in the language of her grandfather's brethren, a guttural *click, click*.

The kind of word even her Familiars gave her funny looks at.

Even if cursing was one of the few things she seemed to remember from her short stay with the Hadzabe.

The birds called right back to her. Joy and whistling and the constant singing of feathers in flight.

Unlike her other enclosures, which had barely enough metal and spells to keep a cage together, in addition to the necessary roof and place to sleep—just the bare necessities of living—the aviary was the one place she'd put every extra penny and spell in.

The ones she could spare, anyway.

And sometimes, even when she couldn't.

Water fell off the small-sized waterfall, the kind where streams decided to jump off a higher elevated area. The water which then tumbled down and over rocks, swirled around a trickling bend, pooling into the small pond by the entrance where a pair of newly mated wood ducks, with their bright feathers, dipped and dove and played in the morning-cool water. Moisture and humidity hung thick in the air, seemed to bounce off the palm leaves and moss, but the birds merely flew and jumped from branch to branch.

Bright colors of red and blue and gold.

Calling and cooing at her coming.

And just plain ol' hungry.

"Yeah, yeah. I'm happy to see you too."

But despite her grumping, she smiled.

Already felt the kinks and knots in her neck loosening. Oh, not fully working themselves out, an impossible task in her line of work where happiness rarely fell in line after all the sad and stressful times, the bills and demands that seemed to pile up in both her mailbox and spelled-letter box...but it was something.

She breathed in.

Let the sounds and calls, wings, rustling leaves, water rushing over and even, simply, trickling over rocks—Aisha let all of that roll over her.

Carried her away to another time.

Another place.

Even as she didn't want to, she also didn't fight it.

Couldn't help but feel the shadowy, remembered movements of a horse underneath her. The heavy, sure clomps over the dried-out Serengeti plains from yet another of adventures, sneaking out of her parents' secure and carefully controlled compound. As she followed the herds during the spring crossing, watched and studied and simply joyed in the play of nature and survival and the mere beauty of the animals around her.

Animals who were simply, and only, just animals.

There was a soft turn of dirt. A little scrape of metal on wood.

It pulled her back from that hot, dry heat she remembered of Tanzania, her home, and she blinked at the aviary. Wondered, briefly, why the memories were coming closer, and then forgot because her newest aviary addition, an African Grey parrot named Charlie, stood on a branch just a few inches from her face.

He was one of the smaller parrots—not the smallest—but a good size to fit comfortably on the shoulder.

Of course, his witch master insisted this never be allowed, as the bird would sudden taken a liking to biting ears. Or, more specifically, pecking at the bright emerald earrings the size of plums she'd insisted on wearing.

"Are you hungry?" Aisha asked.

Aisha didn't pull way, even though her ears were in striking distance. Instead, simply gazed right back.

"Or do you have something to say?"

It was her magic again.

Sparkling in her gut.

Telling her something.

Hinting at it.

Charlie tilted his light gray head to the side. Flipped out and spread his small red tail—the only color African Greys had—except, of course, for gray.

His small tiny eyes stared right back her.

The magic in her gut swirled faster. Turned from dancing butterflies in her stomach to rolling tumbleweeds.

"Well?" she asked.

"No future in the past. But future in the past. *Wrrack!*"

Then, without another thought or comment, he took off, flew somewhere deeper into the forest of planted trees and hanging moss.

"That," she said, "wasn't very helpful."

The magic in her gut stilled.

Aisha sighed. Already, her shoulders grew heavy again. Weighted.

Remembered, again, her call with Lord Asher.

Amongst all the natural greens and flowing water, there were the telltale signs of wizardry littered throughout the place. Little knick-knacks and reminders the Familiars had brought with them or that Aisha had added over the years.

Rubber duckies floating in the pond—some with pirate hats and patches, others with the glitzy, sparkling pink sunglasses worn only in places like…like Hollywood and Anaheim. There were knitted scarves with the bright red-and-teal knitting half-pulled apart tied to trees, branches, made into nests. There were a handful of crystal balls on pedestals (not the working variety—she'd been insistent on *that*—the last thing anyone needed was a Familiar making a prediction without authorization). There was even an open book or two—covered, of course, in bird crap.

Some of these items were still in use. They had a bit of a glow about them. As if the Familiars' magic still touched those objects, those pieces of remembrance. But mostly, she noticed, they were fading. Dulling. Just like Lanhi's pink tutu. They'd grown…deadened, almost. Even those objects that still seemed to resonate with the Familiars. It was certainly true for the other objects, the ones the Familiars had simply…forgotten along with that part of their life.

"Interesting."

Aisha dropped the bucket onto the dirt walkway with a hard thump.

The birds kicked up a squeal and a squawk—one thing that never seemed to fade was their ability to pick up emotions. Especially anger.

"Sorry," she mumbled, and got back to work, though her mind was still focused…still watchful of whatever thought, whatever idea was nagging at her.

At Charlie's very unhelpful words.

The magic dug at her to notice.

So, she listened to her gut.

This was yet another of her magics.

Awareness was what she liked to call it, but it might as well be magic considering how few people actually used it.

Aisha made her way through the aviary, shoveling out fruit and veggies, and heck, even some good-sized, and fairly aromatic, chicken legs into dishes and feeding stands. But still, watchful.

She studied the Amazons with their bright green bodies and yellowed heads—but they didn't follow her around and chat like they normally did. The small, darting bodies of caciques' with their yellow and white and green feathers—whom she secretly called her little "attack assassins" because of the way they quickly judged and assessed guests to their aviary (most of the time, taking any sign of flinching as a sign for "prey"). But today, they also ignored her. Just dove right into the dropped piles of fruit. Even the macaws, who usually liked to play and get some amount of attention, even head rubbing and ruffling, paid her no mind.

Like she didn't exist.

"Strange."

The intelligence she was used to seeing, sharp and uncanny, had dimmed to something more…primal.

Their masters, of course, would call that "basic."

Primitive.

Feral, even?

She was so focused on the birds, so in tune with *them*, that she almost missed the shuffle behind her. Soft shoes on the fine dust. Shoes not made for the Waystation but for fancy pubs and council rooms, the way they didn't grip the ground but simply *slid* over it. No traction. Completely unbalanced.

There was a sharp whistling, followed by a loud, "Good morning!"

A macaw.

Right behind her.

And not one of hers.

"I'd say," came a deep, very male voice, "that they're trying to tell you something."

CHAPTER 11

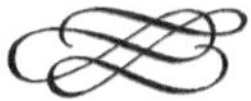

*A*isha spun. Her hiking boots kicked up dust from the small, narrow walkway. Felt her heels smack into the pond's outer rim. Her balance, tipping her back.

Back.

And over.

A hand darted out.

Grabbed her wrist. Shoved her balance forward.

A sharp, keening squawk echoed right into her ears. Right from the man's shoulders.

At least, so she thought. Hard to tell when she was falling.

Although she didn't fall into the pond. Fell, instead, into a very hard, very male body. A muscular body that didn't match the soft shoes her mind had heard earlier.

Had heard, registered, and completely glazed over.

So much for awareness.

Aisha gazed up into the large, dark pupils of a macaw—definitely not one of hers and definitely perched on a man's shoulder.

She realized all of this in a split second.

Right after, of course, she realized this male body should absolutely not be in *her* aviary.

Especially without her knowledge.

Aisha used her weight. Shoved into the man and made *him* stumble back.

The macaw's wings flapped. The bright, deep blue and yellow-gold of a blue and gold macaw. Stretched out those wings to maintain balance, just as the man now did with his arms.

She yanked out her wand.

Didn't care about the sudden spark of magic slicking over her hand. Clinging to her.

Only for emergencies.

This, she thought, staring at man who stood nearly as tall as her… no, taller. A good handful of inches taller. Even with his polished shoes, long, tied-back dark hair, a too-heavy cloak for the valley, personally tailor-made robes she recognized from when she'd lived that high society life….

His eyes as gray as Charlie's feathers. Deep and intelligent and very, very aware of her.

He finally caught his balance. Somehow. Even with those shoes.

Something about him, something familiar she couldn't quite put her finger on…

The macaw kept flapping, though. Drew her attention to him. A macaw who kept staring at her, just as aware and calculating as the man.

Who in the heavens were these two?

Her hand didn't shake and she sure didn't lower the wand.

"I apologize," he said, "for startling you. That was rude."

"Yes. I'd say it was."

She raised her wand an inch. Held it to his throat. Oh, yes, this definitely counted as an emergency.

"Now," she said, "who are you and what are you doing in my Waystation?"

A smile pulled at his lips. He didn't answer, just gave that small half-smile (the kind she'd learned long ago, back in her other life, to never trust). He reached into his robe pocket. Ignored the dig of her wand into his throat.

If he tried it.

If he went for his wand.

She didn't care if a Familiar perched on his shoulder or not. She'd defend herself. Defend her Waystation.

But then he pulled out a small piece of walnut, held it to his flapping macaw….

Who immediately calmed. He gazed at the man, then nodded and accepted the walnut.

"No danger here," the bird squawked.

For most normal folks, understanding parrot speech could be… difficult at best. Parrots couldn't quite mimic human sounds and words, and sure, some species and some individual birds were more adept than others, but Aisha was an expert. She'd heard as clear as day what the macaw had said. And as far as she was concerned, her standing there with a loaded wand counted very much as "danger."

"You're so sure about that?" she asked.

The macaw swung his head to her, peered at her from the side so he could look at her full on. Unlike humans with their nifty peripheral vision, parrots had only one eye on either side so if they wanted to "see" you, well, they had to actually look at you.

This one did.

Intelligence, true, deep, and very, very magical, gazed back at her.

"A Familiar," she whispered.

And one she'd never felt and seen so clearly before. This bird was beyond special. Probably cost just as much, too.

She swallowed a curse before it left from her lips—neither this man nor his super-magical bird belonged here, especially not at this particular Waystation, even if there *was* something wrong with the Familiar—but she still didn't lower her wand.

"Just because you have a Familiar doesn't mean you're allowed to be here. Especially since I have no idea who you are."

"It would help," he said, "if you actually returned my calls. Lord Nathanial Emmanuel Darkwood. At your service. But please, call me Nate."

He bowed, all nice and neat and trim, practically glowed with the upper-level education he'd had, and his bird, well, wonders to all, the bird bowed with him. Even swept out his wings in a grand gesture.

"I only call people I'm *familiar* with by their given name."

Still, Aisha lowered her wand, and after only a slight hesitation, tucked it away again.

This time she did wipe her hand. Couldn't help it. Not when the magic practically glowed off her skin. Sticky and unwelcoming.

She wasn't used to holding the thing for so long.

Darkwood's eyes focused on the movement. She immediately stilled.

Apparently she wasn't the only one with a gift for awareness. As if she'd done so well this morning.

"Fine. Lord Darkwood. You're here."

She crossed her arms. The humidity and moisture from the aviary was already doing its thing. Sweat clung to her underarms. Dripped from her forehead.

Even Darkwood wasn't immune. A small rolling dot of sweat slipped from the bridge of his perfectly sculptured nose.

Well, the man might look perfect, but he at least wasn't wearing any enhancement or deterrent spells. Even when she'd lived that other life, she'd despised those people who refused to live in a world without perfection.

A point in his favor then.

Even if he'd trespassed.

She tugged off her jacket. Tossed it over her shoulder. "Unless you feel like starting your own sweat-river right there, I'd suggest you ditch the robe. Heat's picking up and it'll only get worse."

He hesitated half a second, as if he didn't trust her. As if *he* wasn't the one trespassing on *her* property.

He glanced at his parrot again. Got a nod—a head bob that looked more like a laugh—but as she'd done, Darkwood removed his robe. Carefully, of course, so as not to dislodge his parrot.

"I wasn't expecting the conditions." Darkwood wiped his brow.

"Clearly."

She purposefully did *not* look at the dust coating up his legs, practically reaching his knees. And that was pretty far.

"We're not like your usual variety of sanctuary," she said. "We rely on donations and whatever support local or national is willing to give us. No monthly fees for Familiars in residence. No initial down payment for their stay. But I'm sure you already know this. Just like you know we don't have a rotating staff or even a single staff member assigned to one section, or even one Familiar. Which leads me back to the call I should have returned."

She gave him and the bird and pointed look. Turned, and headed back to the entrance. Managed to pick up the bucket—now much lighter without the smelling, quite-ripe fruit—without pausing in her step. Or looking at him.

He reminded her too much of someone she'd long forgotten.

Or tried to.

There was a reason she didn't serve clients of the lord's stature here. A damn good one, too.

"You're right," Aisha said. "I should have returned your messages. I'd have saved you a trip here."

She tossed a look over her shoulder. He followed, just a pace behind her. Just barely the appropriate distance society instructed as acceptable.

She narrowed her eyes. "It'd have saved your shoes and pants as well."

There was that half smile again, while the macaw bobbed his head up and down.

"Apology accepted."

This came from the man, not the macaw.

Aisha flushed. Heat warming her cheeks to a softer pink than they already were from the sticking heat. She shook her head. Something was wrong with her. Something about him just rubbed her wrong. Got to her in all the wrong places she just didn't want to go to.

Made her uncomfortable.

Made her want to toss him out on his fancy behind while at the same time made her...unsure. Hesitant. Put her off balance.

And if there was a time when she needed focus, needed every ounce of balance, of awareness, it was now.

Now when all these Familiars depended on her. Were trying to tell *her* something and for whatever reason, she just couldn't understand....

Around her, the aviary birds still took little notice of her. They flapped and lunged off branches. Dove into the trickling pond or simply ate up the mess of fruits and veggies, half of which ended up on the ground.

Quite the growing collection of half-eaten food.

She'd need to schedule an extra stop here just to clean up. Fun, especially with Marcelle out today.

Aisha's head pounded at the thought. Too much to do. Not enough time.

Not enough energy.

Another reason she needed the good lord out, so she could get back to work. So she could focus on what mattered....

Not steal glances at him. At those unnerving gray eyes as he assessed, *studied,* her aviary.

In fact, it was as if he wasn't even aware of Aisha. All his attention was on the aviary.

What was he looking for? Why was he even here?

She opened her mouth, prepared to drill him—as she *should* have done instead of being sidetracked by the past—but then her mouth clicked closed.

Her eyes widened. Realized what was odd. Different. Her awareness once again kicking in.

The aviary was silent.

No chattering or tweeting or tittering.

Nothing.

Her birds were *never* silent.

CHAPTER 12

While the birds didn't care about Aisha, or even Darkwood's presence, they did, however, take notice of Darkwood's macaw.

Aisha studied the birds, each one, as they passed. How they'd stop what they were doing. Necks upright, eyes wide.

Straining to see them.

Watching.

Following as Darkwood's bird passed by them, before returning to whatever had interested them. Then whatever spell or psychic presence faded, and they dug their beaks back into split mangos or bathtime water fun.

Curious indeed.

Not curious enough to ask Darkwood to stay.

He followed almost at her heels. A warmth—no—an inferno seared the back of her neck.

As if he was closer than he should have been. As if she could *feel* him.

Again, she felt her traitorous cheeks flame. Thanked the stars he couldn't see her face.

No.

Even if there was some interesting quirk about his bird and hers, she needed him gone.

Fast.

"I'm sorry," Aisha spoke over her shoulder. Quickly. Didn't dare look at him or risk losing her train of thought. "But I just don't think the Waystation is the right place for your Familiar. As you can see, he won't receive the attention or accommodations you're used to. We only have two on staff. No on-call service. Not even a good storage facility for any of his personal items. No—"

"Sounds perfect."

Aisha's boots slid into the dirt. Stopped just short of the aviary's double-door entrance.

She spun.

Her braid, dark hair and all, slapped at her cheek. She moved so fast the empty food bucket nearly slipped out from her fingers.

"Didn't you just hear anything I said?"

"I did."

Darkwood stepped closer.

Narrowed the already small distance between them.

He didn't seem to care that the aviary's heat, humidity, was rolling off him. His dark clothes absorbing every ounce of it. Misty streams of moisture evaporating off him.

And he gave no sign, none at all, that it bothered him.

Again, she wondered, couldn't help it…who was this man?

"In the end, though," he said, "your opinion doesn't matter. Nor does mine, for that matter."

He was closer now.

Wasn't he?

It was hard to tell. Especially the way her head spun. Seemed to blend between the here and now, and with before.

The heat wasn't helping either. Like a perfect bridge back to that day. Heat from Africa's dry season. Scorching the parched, and what looked like dead, land.

The day she'd been found by *him*.

The day he'd forced her to leave the Hadzabe, all the learning she'd done (and she had learned something, must have, even if she couldn't remember). She wanted to remember, desperately, with everything she had, wanted to remember...but then he was there.

It was enough for her to shy away from those blocked memories. That blocked, joyful, and peaceful time.

Because of him. Lord Daniel Blakeley.

That was a moment she wanted to forget.

Blakeley hadn't given her a choice. Not when he'd been sent by her parents. Not when he held that shining, diamond-glinting offer in hand. An offer attached to all those wonderful, dreaming promises. That all she had to do was simply stop running wild, stop playing the child, and return with him.

Return back to their world.

Aisha shook her head. The memories slid away, one by one.

Realized that the man before her *was* Darkwood. And he had a parrot on his shoulder, not a bare-headed vulture.

Heavens above, talk about character signs she'd flat-out missed.

Aisha made herself forget the aviary's heat, how it fogged her mind. Made the past go right back to where it belonged.

Instead, focused on the man before her, in *her* aviary.

But seriously, Darkwood *felt* closer.

Or maybe that was just her nerves or awareness plugging at her to back up, to knee his groin or do, do something. Like she hadn't done that day.

Darkwood froze suddenly. Gray eyes narrowed. As if sensing... then, he backed up a step.

Actually, it was the macaw who nipped at his ear and Darkwood, Darkwood *froze* at the reminder.

The warning.

"I apologize. I did not mean to bring up bad memories." He retreated a step. Then another. "As I was saying, neither my opinion or yours matter. Timiculous has chosen your Waystation and there's nothing to say on the matter but to accept payment."

"What? Excuse me?"

Aisha's mind still reeled.

First from the past and those lurking memories. From the bond Darkwood shared with his bird—with Timiculous—something she'd never seen in all her years working with Familiars.

Familiars listened to their masters.

Not the other way around.

Not like this.

Her hesitation, the few seconds that it was, was just enough for Darkwood to lift his arm, for Timiculous to step on, and then....

"Good place. Safe place. Right place," Timiculous said.

And then Timiculous took right off into her aviary. Flew off with those blue and gold feathers shimmering in the heat and sun, and finally disappeared amongst the thick foliage.

That was 'bout the time her temper finally kicked in. Finally let loose the holds and bonds of the past.

CHAPTER 13

"What the hell?" Aisha snapped around. Smacked Darkwood in the chest with the heel of her palm.

Didn't care that he was a mighty lord.

Just. Didn't. Care.

And it felt good.

Really good.

"Look," he said, "I'm truly sorry about that. I wanted to talk with you before, but Timiculous was most insistent that we arrive today. As I told you, it was his decision."

Darkwood raised his hands in surrender.

Apology. Whatever.

She didn't care.

"And it's *my* decision." She smacked him again. Both palms. Hard into his chest. "Over who and what stays in *my* Waystation."

"Not in this case."

That did it.

Snapped her back to that day. That moment. When her life, her future, her freedom had been snapped from her. Stolen away.

Just because she'd told *him* yes didn't mean *he* could control her.

That she wasn't her own person anymore.

It would never happen again.

Ever.

Aisha didn't hold back this time. "How's this for a decision? Get your bird out of my aviary."

She used all her muscles, arms, the core of her center, her legs pushing off the ground. All her years, even the ones in Africa when she lived and worked the Serengeti Magical Proper—even as unlady-like as it was—used all of that and shoved him again. Hard. Shoved with all her frustration, her helplessness of who she'd been, her refusal to ever be helpless again.

Again, Darkwood didn't resist. Even when her push had him backing up.

One step, then another.

Backed right to the ledge of the same trickling pond he'd saved her from earlier.

He tripped over her discarded fruit bucket. Nice shoes smushing into a mush-slick melon rind, he fell right on in.

The splash that woke the whole aviary—if everyone wasn't already awake and eating breakfast.

Darkwood didn't flail, didn't sputter or splash to get out of there.

No.

He just sat there in the green-tinged water. Strands of dark hair had slipped free from its tie and now dripped down his face. His dark clothes, soaked and clinging to him, revealed that he was just more than a stuffy lord. Clearly, he was a lord who cared about physical exercise and health.

Nothing at like the kinds she was familiar with.

And through all that, he just sat there in the mucky water and watched her. Didn't curse or scream. Didn't threaten her with the magic she knew he had at his disposal.

After all, the Council didn't declare just anyone (or their families) lords.

Aisha's head spun. She didn't know what to make of this.

Or this man.

He brought out all those memories, and yet, yet...he'd done nothing of the things she was expecting. That she familiar with.

Darkwood wiped a hand over his face. Shoved bangs out from his eyes. Those gray eyes that just watched her, no anger, just an apology.

It was enough to make her breathe in. To let go of the anger and realize exactly what she'd done....

Oh, no.

"I suppose," he finally said, "I deserved that."

Damn. Damn again.

Aisha shook her head. Knelt at the pond's edge, her khakis soaking in the puddle his splash had created. She held out her hand.

"No, you didn't."

His hand clasped hers. His touch just as hot and searing as she'd expected, but she said nothing about it. Even did her best not to flinch or look at their entwined fingers.

He said nothing either, if he felt it at all.

Nor did she comment on the calluses there. Nothing like the smooth hands she was familiar with. Was expecting.

And she wasn't about to ask. It was none of her business, nor did she *want* it to be her business. She wanted him gone.

Which, of course, wasn't at all what came out of her mouth.

"You do, however, owe me an explanation," she said.

"Fair enough. I suppose I deserve that as well."

Aisha helped haul him out, surprised again by the strength in his grip. The smooth way he pulled himself out with barely any effort from her. As if he'd taken her hand out of kindness and not out of need.

Again, so very different than she was used to from men like him.

But then again, maybe she was finally figuring out that Darkwood was nothing like what she knew.

A smile tugged at her lips. She managed to keep it from showing.

Hoped, anyway.

"I have some dry clothes back at the compound," she said. "Nothing fancy, just work clothes some of the guys used over the years, and I don't know if they'll fit—"

"If they're dry, I'd appreciate it."

She nodded, and as they made their way out of her aviary, closing the double doors behind them, leaving the strange and independent Timiculous inside, Aisha completely forgot to ask why he didn't use a spell to dry himself off.

And then when she did remember, when they were halfway up the steep hike towards the compound, his fancy shoes having a harder time gripping the soft dirt and making sloshing sounds as they went, she noticed how he didn't once complain or moan or bitch about being waterlogged or forced to walk uphill; instead of doing any of those things, he stayed silent and simply studied her. She decided she didn't want to know.

There was something about him…something that made her hesitate on her past mistakes. Past lessons.

Something that made him not fit with the world she knew.

She wouldn't ask.

For now, anyway.

CHAPTER 14

"*I*n here."

Aisha opened the unlatched screen door into her compound. Not a big thing, really, just a couple of rooms and doors, and pretty unkempt with its leaky roof and barely functioning windows (half refused to open at this point), but it did the job. Gave her a place to sleep, to live, and more importantly, to handle all that paperwork that came with owning and operating a Waystation.

Darkwood paused. She noticed he'd turned his attention to the slight tear running down the screen's side, held together by the most ingenious of all Normal technology—duck tape.

"Not magic?" he asked.

"Fascinating, those Normals. Simply amazing what they figure out without using magic." She opened the door wider, the hinges groaning and screeching. But, hey, it worked, and that was what counted in her book.

And in her checkbook.

"Mostly, though," she said, "buying a pack of industrial-strength duct tape is cheaper than buying specialized spells that can only be used once."

Which then deteriorate in a matter of months because the wizards and witches she worked with knew she wasn't a high-class joint.

But despite the duct tape and screeching, rusty door hinges, Darkwood followed her in. This clearly wasn't the right place for him, for someone of his status, but he followed and now stood there.

Right behind her.

So close Aisha felt the dissolving water, now heated from the day's already sweltering temperature, and it wasn't even ten o'clock.

She tried to distract herself. Focused, instead, on the room.

Tried to see it from another's eyes. Not hers, which would be filled with pride over the care and hard work displayed here, the well-used equipment, the threadbare jackets, but instead viewed the room with a more critical air.

The kind of attitude she might have had back in her parents' Proper.

Boots, hiking and rubber, and even a pair of flip-flops lined one wall, each in various stages of dirt and muddiness. Many also sprouting their own duct tape in certain spots. Coats and jackets and rain slickers hung from hooks. Each, also, not having an ounce of cleanliness to them.

This was a working Waystation, after all. Not a fancy vacation resort or retirement home.

Aisha refused to apologize, even as the words trickled up her throat.

No. She wouldn't apologize. This was who they were.

This was who *she* was.

She'd never apologize for that again.

Aisha slung her jacket from her shoulder, tossed it onto a nearby hook. "I warned you. We're not a fancy place."

Those gray eyes met hers. "I'm glad. It's a nice change of pace."

"I doubt that."

But she entered the mudroom, worked the laces of her hiking boots, then kicked them off into their customary, muddy spot by the corner. Darkwood followed, his no-longer nice and shiny shoes a spattered, muddy, and dripping mess, got tossed beside hers as well.

Left them both standing there in dark socks, also slightly mud-stained, which simply wouldn't do to go tramping around her office, her work place, her home.

The socks followed the shoes and Aisha did her absolute best not to check her feet—or the deep purple nail polish, which stood out in a subtle hue from her darker toned skin.

It didn't look bad, exactly. Just different.

Girl time, Marcelle had called it.

Aisha had thought it was more like ridiculous time, but hey, she'd just been happy to be off her feet (as if she could tell the little pint-sized witch no).

Besides, Aisha had been fine with the girl time.

At least until Darkwood glanced down.

Noticed her toes.

There was that smile of his again. Small and barely there, but it *was* a smile. As if he'd told himself some secret joke and thought the result amusing.

She fought the urge to hide her feet. Then, fought the urge to look at *his* feet. Staring at his bare feet, in her mudroom, felt too private.

Intimate.

The last thing she needed was intimate.

What she did need, however, were answers.

"You promised me an explanation."

"I did. You promised dry clothes…?" He lifted up his arms, shirt clinging just a tad to close to his chest.

"Oh, yes. Right."

Aisha immediately turned away. Opened a cubby, ignored the moth that fluttered out—how it even got in there, she hadn't a clue—and tossed him a T-shirt a couple sizes too big and black sweatpants she hoped were long enough.

All, of course, without looking at him.

Or his chest.

Of course, she still saw that little smile from the corner of her eye. Pulling at his lips as if the joke was quite fascinating.

Aisha pointed out the bathroom, just off the right (which, thankfully, she'd cleaned only last week) and waited while he changed.

And he did change.

Completely changed. Sort of. Because when he finally emerged, a handful of minutes later, the T-shirt and bulky sweatpants that barely reached his ankles actually did little to change his presence.

His *magical* presence.

It was as if those gray eyes and sculpted body simply were one and the same with his magical side. Didn't matter if she asked him to wear a potato sack, he would still look, and feel, powerful.

Appearance, on the other hand—he looked more...comfortable. Normal. Not quite the stuffy lord who'd intruded on her aviary, unannounced and uninvited.

If it weren't for that aura, he might just be another regular employee.

Which was ridiculous.

Darkwood caught her staring. Raised an eyebrow in question. "Something wrong?"

"Nothing. You just look different. And, exactly the same."

He simply nodded. "I promised answers. Is there somewhere we can...?"

Darkwood trailed off, glanced over her shoulder to the narrow hallway beyond—and most likely seeing a few streamers of clothes thrown about the place because really, it wasn't like she ever had guests over.

Marcelle didn't count. She got paid, after all.

"Uh, yes. This way. I, umm, wasn't expecting company." And hoped she hadn't left anything too embarrassing, or too well-past the expiration date, lying about.

Again he followed, somehow managing not to trip over tagging equipment, a broken tranquilizer gun (Darkwood did raise his eyebrows at that—which, she quickly explained, went back to cost of Normal vs. magic), and somehow managed to make it to her too-cramped, paper-strewn dining room.

Well, dining table.

Sort of.

It was big enough for four. Although, there was actually only enough room for two because of all the papers, open and dog-eared Normal animal biology books, and Marcelle's discarded change of clothes from yesterday's outing into the monkey enclosure to sort out the issue between the pink elephant and the clown nose.

Out of all the items on her table, *anything* from the monkey enclosure should be no where near her dining table.

She shoved *that* one off before Darkwood noticed it (or Marcelle's dark, smudged stains), and kicked it under the table. Where would be perfectly hidden along with all the other piles of clothes and fallen papers.

But there *were* two chairs. Mostly in paper-covered, scattered conditions.

"Uh, I, told you we weren't a fancy place." Then realized she'd apologized yet again, which stirred the fire she missed so much, to return. "Which, I told you in the first place. You can clearly see, we're not at all equipped to handle someone of your, or your Familiar's, stature. This just isn't the right facility for Timiculous."

Aisha's mouth closed shut. Realization dawning.

She'd been so focused on Darkwood, on all these emotions and waking up her past, that she hadn't actually asked anything about his Familiar.

"I'm sorry, but what exactly *is* wrong with your Familiar? He didn't seem to display any of the early signs for fading or disheartenment."

Not even disobedience, which, sadly, was quite a common reason for Familiars to be tossed out of hearth and home.

Darkwood pulled out the least covered chair, carefully placing the paper stack on an open avian book, then sat. Crossed his legs and stared at her.

It really wasn't fair that he sat at her messy dining table, wearing sweats and a baggy T-shirt, and still felt like a great lord while she was just some Familiar worker who'd never cleaned the dirt from under her nails or in the cracks in her sun-kissed skin.

Aisha snapped her arms to her hips. "You promised answers."

"Well, then. To your last question, there's nothing wrong with him. Not exactly."

"Then he has no business here." Which was when the rest of the realization hit. "You're telling me I've just messed up my entire routine and will now be working until midnight simply to catch up on the work that *you* interrupted, and there's nothing wrong with him?"

"With him? No. And I am sorry about the disruption. Perhaps hiring more workers..." He shook his head. A damp strand of hair clung to his forehead. "Sorry, that was insensitive. Money again. As I said, there's nothing wrong with Timiculous, but he does have business here."

She crossed her arms. Tapped a bare foot with purple toenails on the floor.

Darkwood's gaze flipped down to her foot. Which she immediately stilled.

"And what business," she asked, "is that?"

"To help you with your problem. The Familiars. Their wasting sickness."

CHAPTER 15

*A*isha paled. Felt her mouth slacken. Felt a bit...dizzy all of a sudden. She yanked out a chair of her own. Papers and bills and way too many pink slips tumbled to the floor.

She didn't care.

Just sat down with a thunk. Didn't bother removing the book on entomology.

"How do you know...?"

The *only* person she'd told was Asher. And not even twenty-four hours ago. Was Darkwood working for Asher? For the Council?

Oh, did her heart twist at that. Her stomach. Felt the bile rolling up. Searing the back of her throat.

But Darkwood just sat there. Patient. Understanding, almost. His legs crossed, hands resting on his knees. As if just...just waiting for the shock to pass. As if he wanted it to pass.

Aisha swallowed. Tried again. Tried to find her voice. "How do you know about the sickness?"

"It's not happening just here, you know. In fact, from all my research, it appears that your Waystation has been the least—and last—afflicted by this sickness."

"Oh, heavens."

Aisha dropped her head in her hands.

She'd been right. About Asher. About all those rumors.

And not a single one of those arrogant, brainless—they didn't tell her! Didn't warn her!

She'd had a feeling it was bad. Her magic had *told* her it was bad (even if everyone refused to talk about it). But to think *her* Waystation was the least afflicted. Her rundown, barely-holding-together Waystation with chain fences and duct tape...

The thought frightened her.

Excited her, too, because maybe she was doing something right. Maybe her magic, the same magic that hadn't felt right since leaving Tanzania, was right. The same magic, her gut, that had pushed her to take a chance and leave that high-class sanctuary life behind—to make her *own* life, to make her *own* sanctuary—had been right.

But no, she decided.

She was more frightened than anything else.

Because of Lanhi. Because of all the other three dozens Familiars sickening each and every day, it felt like.

And hers was the least afflicted?

"How could so much have gone so bad?" she asked. "So quickly?"

She heard the scrape of Darkwood's chair as he stood. Made his way to her side. Felt his hands lightly touch her shoulders, and then immediately pull away as if burned.

"I'm not sure it did."

"What does that mean?" She didn't bother looking up. Didn't want to.

"This news is upsetting you."

"No."

Yes.

Aisha shook her head. Hoped to clear it, but that only made the fear worse.

The sink faucet turned on, and a moment later, she felt a cool glass being pressed into her hand. Cool and slick and moist from water drops that'd fallen down the side.

She glanced up, finally, and stared at the glass held towards her.

Still, she didn't move. Didn't know if she could.

"I'd give you whiskey," Darkwood said, "but I imagine staying hydrated is more important here than where I'm used to."

She nodded. Gratefully took the water.

Chugged the whole thing.

He was right, too. The water helped. If nothing else, gave her something else to focus on—like not choking. She put the glass down, even managed to balance it on the stack of papers without toppling the whole thing off the table—even with her hands shaking.

"I asked how things had gotten bad so quickly," she said. "But you didn't think it did. What do you mean?"

Darkwood gave her a quirk of the lips. Not a smile.

She couldn't think of anything, anything that involved the sickness of Familiars could be associated with smiles.

He sat again, across from her, but didn't once take those deep eyes off her. "Your magic is unique, I hear."

"So is everyone's."

"Yes, but by your background alone and the choices you made…"

Aisha's back straightened. "What do my choices have to with—"

"Everything, maybe. Peace, truly." His hands shot up. Palms towards her. Defensive. Apologetic. "I don't mean to upset you. Only to explain. You wanted to know why a lord of my stature, with a Familiar clearly as gifted—and as in control—as Timiculous is—don't narrow your eyes at me like that, all I did was observe you observing me. The truth is all those other Sanctuaries, the fancy ones, the expensive the ones, the ones that…pander to my kind. They know a lot about Familiars. But you…."

At this, he leaned across her overstuffed, messy table. His chest with that bulky T-shirt, with the hem unraveling from his collar and from his left sleeve. He gazed at her with such intensity, such willingness for *her* to understand him, to hear the words he was speaking— and the ones he wasn't.

Made her wonder if this, this right here was part of his magic.

She still couldn't help the breath she sucked in.

How she held it, full and brimming in her lungs.

Couldn't even help the way her eyes met his and simply couldn't look away.

Didn't want to, either.

A memory tingled at her. A familiar-ness with Darkwood.

And the shadow too.

But both memory and shadow only tingled, then faded away... faded as he spoke.

"You," he said, "you came from a different world. A world that was still mostly wild. You *lived* it, enjoyed it, and from what I can see, you brought that with you."

Anger. Fear. Both rocked through her.

Aisha shook her head. Deep black hair fell across her brow. She slowly pushed it aside. Ignored how her fingers shook.

She never spoke about her past.

Ever.

With anyone.

Aisha licked her suddenly dry, parched lips. She should have kicked him out. Shown him the door. But he was here for the Familiars. And there *was* something wrong with them.

She'd sworn to help them. To figure this out.

Even if it meant going to the one place that caused her stomach to roll. That made her want to curl up in a tiny ball and shut her eyes tight from the world.

"What did I bring with me?" she asked.

Now he did smile. Full and blazing.

Made Aisha's mouth click closed when she suddenly realized she was staring at him, mouth gaping open like a catcalling chimpanzee.

Darkwood's hand swung towards the table. "Look at all these books you have. Avian biology? Lions in the wild?"

He rattled off a few names from what was on the table. Even flipped through a few pages and paused, pointed out the heavy amounts of highlights and tags she'd put on almost every page, it seemed.

Aisha shrugged. "Most Sanctuaries have books. There's nothing special about that."

"Except those books are about *Familiars*. These"—he lifted up the avian one—"are books written by Normals. Books written *about* animals."

"Which makes most folks think I'm odd." She took the book from him. Dropped it on the table. "That still doesn't explain anything. Or why you're interested in me."

Her mouth shut. She swallowed.

That last had definitely come out wrong.

"I think it does," he said. "You brought the wild with you. The wild that is Africa."

"That's silly. Completely, completely…"

"Are you so sure?"

Aisha opened her mouth. Denial, thick and heavy on her lips.

"Why are you here? Exactly. Tell me, right now, why I shouldn't shove you and your bird out of my Waystation?"

"Because Timiculous believes that the wild is the key. And that you can show him, and me, how to save them."

CHAPTER 16

The last place Nate wanted to go, was home. An empty home with nothing but his thoughts. His loathing.

Nothing but the truth to keep him company, the truth and his meeting, and the bad ending of it, with Aisha.

So, he didn't go home.

Instead, he pulled his Mustang right up to The Cackling Cauldron, that rundown, mishmash of a building with the best deep-fried mushrooms in town—magical or Normal.

He revved right into one of the few vacant spots—between a flaming chariot and a legion of neon flashing brooms, each one sporting the wood-pressed signet of a pointed, wart-pinched nose.

Gave the brooms a hard look.

Looked like the Hags were in. Meant he'd be a fool to go in, himself.

Especially if Hilda was there.

They were the only witches' gang any sane upper lordling would take care to avoid. Especially if he wanted to avoid five marriage proposals and ten death threats, each followed swiftly by a wizard duel.

Or two.

Sounded exactly like what he needed.

Nate turned off the engine with a hard, fast swipe of his hand. Didn't once look at the empty perch attached to his passenger window. Didn't look at the clean cloth protecting his seat. Just shoved open the heavy door—and got out.

And barely managed to avoid stomping on a yellow-and-purple flying carpet that had curled up on the line separating his space from the brooms.

"Careful, buddy." Nate side-stepped the carpet and its fraying tassels.

Faded colors too.

His stomach rolled. Bile and hatred crept up his throat.

Towards himself.

He'd seen too many like this one, from flying horses losing their feathers, mermaids who'd lost their tails' sparkle, carpets that unraveled even as their owners flew high over the Los Angeles skyline.

The kinds of things magic gave life to.

The kinds of things magic couldn't replace once it was gone.

"Got to be watchful, you know? Even here."

The carpet gave a weak nod before crawling closer to the curb.

Nate hoped he didn't meet the witch or wizard who owned it inside. He had enough weight on his shoulders. Didn't need a reminder of everything else that was just plain wrong with their world.

Everything else that was on his father.

On him.

For not daring to do anything about it.

Not everyone on—or near—Enchantment Avenue was adjusting well. Not with magic so out of balance.

Failing.

Leaving witches, wizards, even the magical creatures a choice to become more traditional, more magical focused, to or walk more into the Normal world and forever be shunned. Great choices his father and those Council members dished out.

Choices he knew too damn well.

It was no wonder the Familiars were finally developing a sickness of their own. Dying. Just like the rest of them, in one form or another.

Nate almost reached up, almost touched the spot were Timiculous's beak would be.

His hand froze in mid-air.

"Damn it," he whispered.

Reminded him of his own choice ahead of him. Of family loyalties. Of his own beliefs.

Aisha and her Waystation.

Nate shoved his hands into the pockets of the borrowed sweatpants. He *should* have gone home to change. Scrub away every reminder from today. Even the sweat and pond water that had dried on his skin, his hair.

But nothing could, or would, scrub away what he felt inside.

Nothing except some piss-poor beer and a fight or two with a witch who had every right to be pissed at him.

"The hell with it."

He'd do what he came here to do. And maybe, for five minutes, forget the ass he was becoming.

A lord, like his father.

Nate strode right into the bar, ducked his head under the sagging, flashing neon sign of The Cackling Cauldron (even though the two Cs had fizzled out before he was born), and shoved aside the swinging doors.

And came face to face with Hilda.

Hilda, and the pink feather boa wrapped around her neck. Her ass-long wavy blond hair shimmering with pixie dust, and a scowl that'd send any grown man running.

Especially when Nate, of all people, practically trampled the shorter witch.

She lifted that head of hers, hair cascading around her in perfect symmetry, and that scowl turned ten degrees hotter than even hell allowed. Still gorgeous. Intelligence gleaming in those eyes of hers. Everything he'd been attracted to and everything his father had hated.

She was also still damn pissed at him.

"What the hell are you doing here?" Hilda snapped.

"Hoping to get good and drunk," he said. "Shall I buy you a round?"

Her eyes narrowed, first at him, then at his empty shoulder where Timiculous usually perched. They somehow narrowed even further, turning to tiny pink slits—but really, that was from all the glitter she insisted on wearing. Her, and the other two dozen Hags behind her, some just as beautiful and overdone as Hilda, others just as hideous and in need of some over-doing themselves. Including the pointed, wart-pinched noses.

'Course, they all—to a one—crossed their arms and glared.

"You..." Hilda growled.

But then she tilted her head to the side.

Studied him.

Did it in the way she looked at all the Familiars that came to her for care and aid, as if just by looking at him she saw all the mess he was underneath the surface. He wouldn't put it past her that she did. Still, she might be a blond, elf-side of hottie in the witch's gang, but she was the best Familiar veterinarian on the coast. Glitter, long-ass nails, and all.

Nate nearly backed right out those swinging doors under that gaze. Didn't like what she might be—and probably was—seeing.

"You," she said, "can buy us all a round and I won't incinerate you. Right now."

Should have gone home, damn it.

"Done." Nate signaled to the bartender.

Chaz, the half-minotaur with his half-sized loin cloth and his head brushing that sagging, slime-coated ceiling—was doing the honors today. The man, err, horse didn't wait even a hoof's beat to get the Hags their order.

The rest of the bar, Nate noticed, had finally stopped staring—which, he only noticed because of the sudden pick up in noise and conversation. From pint-sized, glitzy and glowing pixies with their skin shriveled like a banshee's, to the black, nightmare water horse with moss and kelp dangling from its mane…they all did their damn best to not look at Nate.

As if every one wanted to quickly forget they'd seen, or heard, anything.

A good place, The Cackling Cauldron.

And a damn good thing he didn't ever come walking in, flaunting his clothes as the Council's official lapdog.

Otherwise, he probably wouldn't make it back outside.

Nate pulled up to the bar, yanked out a stool that scraped against the wood-shaving-littered cement floor, plopped down.

His too-big T-shirt billowing out at all sides. Made him look even more out of place than usual.

Didn't care one whit. Especially when Chaz quickly poured him a pint of the house's specialty.

"You're a lifesaver."

Chaz snorted. "You say that now. Got company coming."

It'd been the second time in two days someone had said that to him. Both warnings had been as bad as he feared. Especially when this time it was Hilda who sidled up beside him. Plopped her perfectly sculpted butt down on the stool next to his and straight up stole his beer.

"You gonna tell me what this visit's all about? You only come here when bearing bad news, bad tidings, or the will of your father."

Nate resisted—barely—the urge to grab his beer back. Settled instead for the replacement Chaz shoved in front of him. The minotaur might be one of the strongest and tallest members there, even over Timmy the Troll, but he also wasn't stupid.

Neither was Nate.

Most of the time.

"This time I'm not breaking off our engagement."

"Of course not. You've already done *that*." She gave him a curling smile, lips redder than blood, before tipping back the beer and downing half in one gulp. "Which begs the question, then, if not bad tidings...I'm guessing the will of your father?"

She leaned closer.

A trail of lavender and spiked whiskey rolled off her.

It was nothing like the heat and sweat and plain hard work scent that'd followed Aisha around all day.

He shook his head. Leaned away. "Can't I just come to enjoy the company? And the beer?"

"You never enjoy the company. Or the beer."

Then, Hilda's eyes widened. Considered him.

He nearly squirmed in his chair. Settled instead for sipping the burning monstrosity they called beer here.

Hilda wasn't wrong about *that,* anyway.

"So. Not just your father then, is it? All right. I'll play. Who is she?"

CHAPTER 17

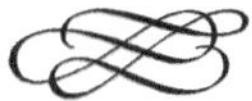

ate did not spew his beer out all over the sticky, stained-wood bar counter. Or over the recently deceased banshee with her talon-like teeth nearly half the size of Nate's arm.

For that, he was proud of himself.

For not covering up his blush, or the fumble as he tried too quickly —and carefully—set the frothing beer down, not so much.

Hilda's bloodred lips—and he was sure those lips *had* had some fresh blood at some point, even during their short but heated engagement—quirked up.

Triumph lit her face.

Definitely should have gone to his empty, dark home after all. His demons were a hell of a lot easier to deal with than a witch on a mission.

Especially one that'd seen him naked.

"Well, isn't this interesting. The great son of the great Council wizard has a new girl."

"She's not my girl. In fact, I'm fairly certain she hates me. Maybe even as much as you."

"I'm not so sure about that," Hilda purred. Ran a finger along her bottom lip—a finger that came away red. "I'm not sure that's even possible. After all, you had your *father* break up with me."

"I warned you. Told you about him the moment I walked into your clinic."

"Yes. I remember. But you were just *tooo* cute to pass up. Especially when you stood before that Council of mean-ass hard-asses and defended my practice. Defended the Familiars I treated who *weren't* licensed." She scooted closer.

Hilda's legs—bare legs, he noticed, practically all the way to the curve of her butt—slid beside his.

"You stood before all of them. Even your father. You argued my case. When you didn't have to. When everyone was sure you would lose."

A bloodred finger nail curled up and around his T-shirt sleeve. Tapped his bare skin. Sent too many chills up his arm.

Nate forced himself to sit still. To not squirm.

To not breathe in that intoxicating smell that was Hilda.

"It was the right thing to do," he said.

Somehow. Had managed the words.

"It was," she agreed. "Which was why I didn't bat an eye when you came carrying all that nasty father baggage."

Hilda leaned in closer. "*And* which was why I was so pissed when you couldn't stand up to him. About us."

"The situation was different."

"Was it? Was it really? Or did you just not know the type of person you really are?"

"I know who I am."

"Yet you let *him* dictate our relationship. Let him end it. All because you didn't care enough to risk his anger."

"You don't know what I was risking."

She didn't. No one did.

Even though she'd been with him the moment he'd finally broken through his father's memory spell. The spell that had taken, and blocked, most of his memories of that night. Of his mother's death.

But Hilda hadn't trusted him.

Hadn't let him be as the memories came back…such a delicate, important process. She hadn't given him the space to heal and reconnect with the missing pieces of himself, which was why he still had, and could smell, mostly the smoke and not always see *through* it.

Hilda snorted. "You risked it once. For those Familiars."

Her whiskey and spice and lavender messed with his head. Made his eyes tear. Made him remember too much.

"Familiars," she whispered, breath circling round and round his ear, "that you hadn't even met. And I guess that's the real problem, wasn't it? You didn't love me enough to even try."

"That's not true—"

"But you loved them, sight unseen."

That, he didn't argue. Couldn't.

Because she didn't know the full truth. The truth he was relentlessly searching for, and why.

"I wonder, did that come only from you?" Hilda's fingers crept up along his arm. Tickled the spot on his shoulder. "Or did that come from your other, true half? Timiculous, who, surprisingly, is not here."

"My relationship with Familiars is complicated."

Had been. Ever since that night.

But unlike his father, Nate didn't start seeing them only as tools. Slaves. He saw them as something more. Something, *someone*, to be helped. Prevented so nothing like what happened to his mother—and the cover-up—ever happened again.

"So, where is he?" Hilda asked.

"Timiculous is helping me with work."

"Right. Your *father's* work. The *Council's* work. And they have got their finger right on top of the both of you."

At least, she'd said that last quietly. Nate did his best not look around to see who might've overheard. Thankfully, Chaz was at the other end of the bar, drying a glass with a towel that had a bit too many dark, rust-burnt stains, while trying to make New Miss Banshee feel less sorry for herself with his usual charming grin.

Most banshees, Nate had noticed, liked guys with lots of teeth.

All the while, Hilda just watched him with those pink, glowing eyes of hers. Eyes that were way too intelligent for the leader of the Hags. Eyes that told anyone sane enough to look who she really was—the best damn Familiar vet on the coast. Maybe both coasts.

Which was why she even knew—why she'd even been able to guess who and what Timiculous even was.

"Which I guess goes right back to my first question—what is it, then? What is it he's after you to do now? Whose life is he trying to ruin?"

Her hand still dangled on his shoulder. But her fingernails had bit into his skin at that last bit.

He didn't blame her.

But that place, his shoulder, was meant for Timiculous. No one else.

He cupped her hand. Removed it.

"I'm here for myself."

"Because he wants you to do something. Because you need to forget for five minutes what a weak and terrible person you are."

Nate let go of her hand. Tried not to think about how right she was.

Even in that short time, she'd learned so much about him.

He also tried not to think how her touch could still burn. Could still feel like a fire lit through him. But that was just Hilda. It was her light. Her magic.

Why she was so good at saving Familiars' lives.

And all of it made him wish like hell he had Timiculous back on his shoulder.

But he didn't, though.

Timiculous was in the Waystation.

At his father's orders.

But there because they might save all those Familiars. To keep them from changing. From turning on those they loved most.

If he disobeyed his father.

But it was enough of a reminder—of where Timiculous was, and who he was with—to shove aside that magically spelled scent.

"Been to the Sirens lately?" Nate asked instead. "Pretty powerful tonight. I'd say you're out trying to catch a particular fish."

She ignored the question. Just kept on playing with his shirt sleeve—the shirt that Aisha, of all people, had given him.

Aisha.

It was as if she'd gone and dumped him in another pond all over again. All it took was thinking her name.

Hilda's fiery touch dissolved to nothingness, and Nate removed her hand from his arm, from his sleeve, again. Lowered it.

Then completely let her go.

"Aisha," Nate said. "That's the woman's name. And she pushed me into a pond five minutes after meeting me. You, on the other hand, kissed me."

"What did you expect? You'd just proclaimed you would be my knight in shining armor against the evil Council! Of course I kissed you." She smiled. Hot. Seductive. "I'd kiss you again, too. For the right reason."

"And I'd have to pass, with great dismay."

She hmphed. "Well, you're saying this Aisha pushed the great and powerful lordling into a pond?"

"Filled with bird crap. I'd say she definitely out beat you on that score."

"Really!" Hilda smiled. Clapped her hands, with those red taloned tips she called fingernails, together. "Oh, I like her already. You will bring her by, won't you?"

Nate snorted. "Not going to happen. She's more of the outdoorsy type."

Which was a far, far cry from Hilda and her love affair with glue-on eyelashes and electric hair dryers.

"Pity." Hilda pouted. "Well, I still want to meet her."

Then, she snagged Nate's god-awful beer and finished that one too.

He shook his head when Chaz headed his way with another. After a conversation with Hilda, the last thing he'd need was alcohol in his system. Driving home would be challenging enough as it was.

With a half-sized square napkin, Hilda dabbed the froth from her mouth. "You do realize, though, the real reason you came?"

"I thought I was here for the bad beer?"

"Which you had *so* much of. No, Nate dearest. You came looking for me."

"I didn't—"

She pressed that red-tipped, sharp finger to his lips.

"You came, because you don't want to make the same mistake twice. With her. With this Aisha and whatever it is your father is frothing at the mouth for you to do. I told you once before—we need you on our side. Not theirs. And *that's* what your dear dad is truly frightened of."

Hilda slid off her stool. Trailed both hands down the sides of her slim, trim body. Pressing any wrinkles away in that skimpy, wrinkle-less dress.

But he didn't look away.

Couldn't.

Not when her words were like a punch to his gut. One, right after the other.

"He's terrified," she said, "of you, and that bird. And, I'm guessing, it's because what you might do. Together."

CHAPTER 18

It had been one hell of a day.

A really, really long day.

Aisha slumped into her office chair—aka a dining chair—not even bothering to remove the stacks of bills, Familiar registry notices, and concerned letters from the magical community about the living conditions her Familiars resided in.

She gave her butt another good rub into *those* papers before finally resting her cleaned, scrubbed, and bare toes onto the table.

The sun had long set and she hadn't bothered to turn on any lights.

No point, really. Not when she just wanted to curl up and fall asleep.

And stay asleep. Maybe. If the dreams let her.

Not like she'd even be able to fall asleep, no thanks to Darkwood. His interruption. Then his…his audacity to even claim that Aisha and her past—of all things!—could save her Familiars.

Her stomach growled. Weak, but insistent.

Probably weak because she'd gone and ignored it for an extra…oh, five hours or so, if the amount of starlight blazing in through her uncurtained window was any indicator.

She dropped her head back. Rested it on the chair's headrest.

"Shit."

It felt like it was nearly time for bed and she hadn't even eaten yet. Hadn't even gotten to the bills and bookkeeping part of her job.

There was a stirring and a rustle from one of the papers. And she remembered Marcelle.

Aisha sat up straighter. Knocked away all those stupid bills and complaints, freed Marcelle's message scroll from underneath all that crap. The Waystation was big enough that scrolls and other forms of messaging worked best instead of trudging up and down the hills and valleys of the place. Unless, of course, you wanted to sweat your ass off for the heck of it.

Sure enough, a rolled parchment unfurled and straightened, revealing Marcelle's no longer…glowing face. In fact, her eyes looked dim and shadowy.

"That's because you need to hire more help," Marcelle said through the message scroll—reading Aisha's mind again.

"How you do that without even being in the same room—"

"Psychic, remember?"

But the joke fell dead in the air. Didn't have Marcelle's usual spark or jazz.

"Something happened," Aisha said, "didn't it?"

"Gee, you think?"

Sure, Aisha had known. Had even helped Marcelle that night as the psychic witch stumbled into the compound. But that was a lifetime ago. Wasn't it? And she'd actually gone and forgotten about Marcelle and whatever she'd learned during her psychic hunt.

Because of Darkwood.

Aisha's stomach tightened. The magic there, warning her, warning something terrible was coming.

She huffed, mostly to keep the pretense that life was normal, and didn't remove her feet or her head from their comfortable spots.

"You look like shit," Aisha said.

"So do you."

They both nodded in agreement.

"Didn't have any luck, did you?" Aisha asked.

"I thought I was the psychic one." Marcelle managed a small smile at that, but it was as weak as her pink glow and it faded. Quickly. "No, I…Aisha, I don't know what's going on, but it's strong. Really strong. I should have told you earlier…but I needed to go home. I needed my place to, to recharge."

A slight tremor trailed off in Marcelle's voice.

Aisha sat up. Energy and fear licked up and down and through her body. She pulled her feet down, nail-polished toes and all, and leaned closer to the message.

"Were you attacked?"

"Yes." Marcelle shook her head. "I mean no. Not exactly, at least I don't think so."

"Tell me what happened. Everything."

Marcelle's mouth twisted—after all, psychics naturally wanted to keep their abilities in the mysterious sector as much as possible—too many possibilities for abuse—but apparently their ten years of friendship, of working together, meant something….

More than Aisha ever realized as Marcelle slowly, but carefully, explained what had happened.

Marcelle had set up, as she usually did, in the small garden of rocks and stubby plants that didn't need a whole lot of water or care (the kind of plants that actually liked the semi-arid desert that was the southern California valley and not the fancy green grass Normals were so enamored with).

Everything had gone fine, Marcelle explained. She was able to reach into the Waystation, for her consciousness to examine each section, each Familiar.

"There were more, Aisha. More Familiars are already showing the fading colors. It's moving faster now. I had no idea…. There were, there were so many of them. So many more."

Marcelle's voice broke.

It was anger, Aisha realized, at herself.

But no more than Aisha.

"I should have seen the signs too," Aisha said. "Don't blame yourself."

Marcelle nodded. Then went on with her story. Explained that she couldn't see anything when she went and looked so closely. There was nothing tying the Familiars together, no clues other than the similar colors once the wasting sickness took hold.

"So, then I went higher. Thought I might get a better picture higher up above the compound, to see it as a whole, and that's…that's when I noticed it." Tears rimmed the corners of Marcelle's eyes. "A dark cloud, Aisha. Like a net."

Aisha's hands gripped the chair's armrests. The stuffing slipping out the seams. "Someone is doing this on purpose."

"I don't know. I couldn't tell. I only saw it for a moment and then I swear, I swear that *thing* turned its horrible gaze on me. Like I was some other bright light for it to consume. I ran. It touched me. Slightly. I fled as fast as I could back to my body. I didn't think I'd make it."

Marcelle's whole body was shaking.

"My magic, I could barely touch it," Marcelle whispered. "Could barely feel it."

Which was Marcelle had then gone home to her place…where she could center her magic and her soul. The one place that she felt truly safe, that was truly *hers*, where could heal from whatever…whatever that darkness had done to her.

Aisha could understand that.

Did, in fact, understand that.

She wanted to reach across the parchment and hold the smaller woman. Comfort her, like no one had done for Aisha since she was a small child.

"I should have been there for you," Aisha said.

"You didn't know. Heck, *I* didn't know and I'm the psychic. Whatever that thing is, it's almost like it's alive and it's drawn to our Waystation. To this place."

"The Familiars?"

"I don't know. I'm going to make some calls. I know a few other psychics who are helping out at the sanctuaries, maybe they know something."

Aisha finally relaxed her grip on the armrests. The imprint of the chair's seams in her palms. She'd gripped it so hard. So long. Had not even noticed.

She should have.

Just like she should have noticed this, this dark net or whatever it was that was killing her Familiars.

What had happened to her magic? And why was it failing her?

They needed answers.

Desperately.

She closed her eyes. Thought of Darkwood and Timiculous. As much as she hated to admit it—hated that they'd arrived, that they had some hidden plan of their own—she might need their help.

That bastard Asher wouldn't tell her, but Darkwood knew. That was why he'd come here. Looking for answers, thinking that Aisha just might have them.

But still, he knew more about what was going on than Aisha did, and she needed every bit of knowledge she could get.

Aisha thought of mentioning the unexpected guests to Marcelle, but with one look at the shadowy eyes, the dark rims circling the other witch's eyes, she changed her mind.

There would be time enough for that tomorrow.

Right now, Marcelle needed rest. Not more questions.

"Whatever this is, this spell or net or whatever, it's not going away, is it?" Aisha asked.

"I think it's staying. Staying until it's consumed whatever it came for."

"Familiars."

Familiars who were suddenly and without explanation being struck by a wasting sickness. A sickness that slowly sapped their spark, their magic, their life. Didn't stop until there wasn't even a breath left in their body.

Which meant it was staying.

Staying until every last of her Familiars were dead.

CHAPTER 19

*A*isha hefted a bucket of mostly thawed chicken pieces and a red, oozing piece of meat into Lanhi's feed bowl. Flies buzzed about her head, ears, the bucket. Already swarmed in thick, black packs.

Promised to be another hot, sweaty day.

Her muscles groaned with every twist. Pull.

She moaned.

Even though it was still early, the sun barely kissing the valley, it felt like she'd been up and moving for hours.

Mostly because she hadn't lied yesterday when she'd told Darkwood that she'd be working to midnight—and damn straight had she refused his offer of help when she'd finally gotten him to leave. But still, maybe she shouldn't have been quite so hasty....

She stretched her back, arching it to relieve the soreness.

Hadn't gotten much sleep either.

And how could she? Knowing that somewhere above her, some thing she couldn't see was killing the Familiars she cared for.

That she loved.

Not to mention, when she finally did pass out, it wasn't the oblivion of sleep waiting for her, but shattered bits of memories of

Tanzania. The arid, dry air. The distant, throaty howls of baboons on a moonless night. Cracked earth beneath her bare feet. And the shadow man slowly appearing as if he were a mirage. Except he wasn't a mirage because even now, she felt his icy-cold magic searing into her. Ripping her into tattered, fraying shreds....

And once she got passed the nightmares, it felt as if she'd only just fallen asleep when her resident rooster, Elvis, gave the usual morning wake-up.

Right outside her window.

Aisha shook her head. Focused on where she was *and* who she was with.

She shoved the slop bucket through the now-unlocked cage door. Did her best to ignore Darkwood, who stood just outside, barely marking the five-foot distance she'd warned him to keep from the chain-link fence.

But he kept it.

"Damn fool," she muttered.

She couldn't believe he'd actually came back. Sure, he'd left his precious Familiar in her aviary—*without* her permission—but after tossing him in the pond, after him trudging through her compound in sweat and dirt, part of her had been *sure* he'd never come back.

But he had.

Bright and freakin' early.

But at least he wasn't smiling.

Wasn't acting like he was the king of her little world, with him knowing all these little secrets he just wasn't telling her. Instead, he had just shown up this morning, with that same dark expression on his face, same matching shadows that Aisha had under her eyes, and told her again he wanted to help.

And she was the fool for letting him follow her around. Fool for even thinking, for half a moment, that she had the answer to all their problems. As if her time in Africa, her *choices* in Africa, were the answer.

Not after what had happened to Marcelle.

Aisha's past, even a past tied to the powerful and ancient Serengeti plains, couldn't stop whatever that thing was.

She glanced up.

Couldn't help herself.

Stared into the blue- and green-tinged sky from all the Normal smog and pollution that just sort of sat above the valley, hung there because of the constant movement and growth from nearby Los Angeles.

It looked like any other day. Didn't look like the killing poison Marcelle had described.

"Something wrong?" Darkwood called.

"No. Nothing at all."

She turned her back on him. It wasn't Darkwood or his Familiar that were the fools, believing she could fix this. Hell, her magic couldn't even do its thing and tell her there was a floating poison cloud or whatever about her Waystation.

But, really, *she* was the fool for even believing him.

Trusting him.

That he might actually help her.

She glared at him from under the brim of her hat.

Darkwood gave her a small nod. He even made sure the toe of his boot—a real hiking boot this time, made for tromping about back-country trails and not the fancy, shiny clunkers he'd first worn—stayed behind that glowing line in the sand.

She'd slapped that line down, used her wand and everything, just to prove she was the one in charge. If he wanted to help, if he wanted in on her Waystation, he would listen to her.

And no more escaping Familiars into her enclosures without authorization.

She almost wished he'd step over it.

He didn't, though.

He just stood there, watching like a good boy—except she didn't trust that "watching" at all. Hell no. That gaze took in every detail. Every crevice and creak of her rust-hinged doors and sagging fences.

Almost like he catalogued the state of Lanhi's ruffled tutu skirt, the no longer sparkling sequins.

Almost as if he were searching for something—something he wasn't telling her.

And Aisha trusted her gut.

Trusted the magic there—even if it usually only worked on Familiars and even though it'd completely misread the whole danger-floating-above-them thing—but still, she *knew* Darkwood was up to something.

Which only pissed her off more.

"I don't need his damn help," she growled to herself.

Except she did.

Damn it.

She carried the now empty food bucket out of the enclosure. Then, went in where the hose's water supply was slowly filling up Lanhi's water bucket and turned it off with a quick turn of the nozzle. Then went and lugged that heavy, extra-thick, snake-like mess out of Lanhi's enclosure.

And all the while, Darkwood just stood there. Studying Lanhi as if she had the answers—answers he wasn't planning on sharing.

"Screw it," Aisha muttered.

Might as well get one thing out in the open.

She threw the whole thing, that heavy-ass hose, nozzle, coil, and all, straight at Darkwood—who blinked.

Saw the approaching hose. Then, moved. Pivoted before the lump fell right on his shoes.

Almost didn't quite make it.

So.

He had been in his own world.

"What the—"

"Do you think I'm an idiot?" she snapped. "Do you think I haven't seen it before? A hundred times? A thousand times?"

Aisha planted herself right in front of him. Smacked him in the chest with her palm.

He didn't move an inch. Made her want to smack him again—but she resisted.

For now.

"I really have no idea what you're implying—"

"That you're not the first person to come here, to come to *my* Waystation, under false pretenses? Saying you're interested in one thing when it's really something else you're looking for?"

She narrowed the distance between them. Got in closer.

Her nose practically touched his.

She didn't care about personal space. She was all fire and really pissed-off anger.

"Who are you?" Aisha stood on her toes. The brim of her hat folding and bending on his forehead. "And what the hell are you looking for?"

Darkwood didn't back up. Didn't back down, either. Just glared right back at her.

"I already told you. I'm here to help. And yes, I am watching this Familiar closely. Why? Because she clearly has the sickness."

Aisha clamped down on her bottom lip. Made herself breathe in.

"She does, doesn't she?"

Aisha kept surprise from her face. Hoped she'd succeeded. "How do you know?"

"Just look at the state of her belongings. They've faded too. Just like her coat. Just like the magic that should be shining off her. The spark in that little pink skirt, the magic that is the *tiger's*, should be all over it. Coated in the ruffles and lace. But it's gone. Vanished. Like it was there a hundred years ago and now it's just...just gone. Forgotten."

Now it was Darkwood's turn to step closer. To force her to either back up, or stand there.

How that was even possible...

Aisha didn't budge. She planted her hiking boots into the soft, mud-spattered dirt from the hose.

Her hat smushed further into Darkwood's forehead.

Their breaths seeming to mingle until it was difficult to tell whose was whose.

Aisha refused to back down. Instead, she tilted her chin up further.

"Anyone," he said, voice dropping, lowering. Heating. "Anyone with a lick of awareness can see what's right in front of them."

Suddenly, and without reason, she wanted to squirm. To slide away from that suddenly intense gaze.

A hard, cold, and calculating gaze of gray eyes—that some intense, studious look he'd given Lanhi and her enclosure, her belongings.

The kind of look that saw a hell a lot more than she wanted him to.

"And what," she asked, "do *you* see?"

That gaze narrowed. Practically dared her to look away. To give in. To admit defeat.

She didn't.

Wouldn't.

"I see someone who's terrified of the past. Someone who, if she doesn't figure herself out, is going to lose a lot more Familiars besides this one."

CHAPTER 20

*A*nd what makes you think I have the answers?" Aisha's breath was a mere whisper.

She didn't think she could speak any louder.

Didn't even know if her words were intelligible.

It was good they stood so close. That she could smell the heat and sweat already dotting his brow. Made him feel—and look—like just another ordinary wizard covered in dirt and a spattering of feces along his boots and pant legs.

The more normal he appeared, the better.

Because he'd hit her—right in the gut.

The gut where her magic rested, which stirred slightly, as if giving its own slow nod...in agreement.

Didn't deny what he'd said.

Which was silly because her magic only worked on Familiars. And even sometimes, at that. At least, ever since she'd left Africa.

Ever since she'd had the awful situation with *him*.

Her magic worked on Familiars and Familiars only.

Until now.

Now, it stirred and reawakened.

Pushed to what it'd once been before, maybe?

Aisha didn't dare hope.

"Why are you here?" she asked again.

Demanded.

"I already told you." His voice, barely above a whisper, remained hard. Unwavering. "Timiculous believes your Waystation, and you, are the key."

Truthful.

That was what her magic was telling her.

He was telling the truth.

About everything. Including…what he'd said about her.

Darkwood backed up a step. Then another. Gave Aisha her space —which was good because her legs had suddenly turned to mush and it was all she could do to keep herself upright. To keep from falling into a heap and pulling her legs to her chest, or flinging herself at him, smacking and hitting and denying everything, *everything* he'd just said.

She wanted him gone, *gone* from her Waystation. Couldn't handle this, not on top of her Familiars.

"I don't believe you," she said. "There's something you're not telling me. Something you're hiding."

At *that*, her magic gave a small leap.

Truth, then.

"That may be." Darkwood shrugged, a great roll of his shoulders in his loose shirt—his robes long discarded from the valley's growing heat. "Then I suppose it's for you to figure out. Or not. Maybe me too."

He glanced away at that last. Refused to meet her gaze. "But I am here to find out what's causing this, what went wrong, and hopefully, how to fix it. That means studying your animals. You, as well. But it's your choice. Like you said, it's your Waystation."

Aisha turned away from him. Her boot sinking into the small mud puddle her hose had dripped out when she'd filled Lanhi's water.

She didn't like her options. Hated them.

Every one.

Hated that her Familiars were dying. Hated that, no matter how much she and Marcelle looked, searched, hoped, they couldn't find a single answer. Not even a clue as to what was happening and why.

She clenched her fists. Then yanked Lanhi's enclosure door closed and sealed the lock with that distrusted wand.

"You said you'd help me," she repeated.

"I did."

Darkwood hadn't moved, hadn't come up behind her, for which she was grateful, but his voice was still clear.

Still deep and still very much not belonging here. Not part of her Waystation.

But he was no longer the stuffy lord with the shiny shoes and overheating robes.

And that, she realized, counted for something.

He might be here, might have his own agenda, but he was trying to work with her. Trying to bend into something she might be able to trust with her precious Familiars.

Damn him.

Finally, she wiped her own brow. Sweat smudged between her fingers. She rubbed her hand on her pant leg. "I don't trust you."

"You don't know me."

"No, I don't." But she needed the help, damn it all. "But I need you."

For now.

Until she figured out this wasting sickness. With help, or on her own.

But she wasn't about to let her Familiars suffer for her pride.

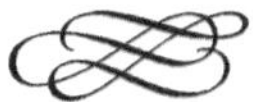

CHAPTER 21

Nate managed to steal a few minutes away from Aisha—back pressed against a sagging, rusting chain-link fence. A pint-sized, claw-like bush grabbing at his ankle. Pulled and scraped at his pant legs every time he moved.

But this was where the shade was.

Not that it did much good.

Sweat covered about every inch of him. Glued his shirt and pants to his skin. The muffled roars from lions came every couple of beats now. Louder. Could practically hear the padding of large paws over the soft-packed dirt.

Excitement.

Anticipation.

Nate's own heart sped up a few beats. Those were really big-ass cats. At least they weren't tigers.

White-striped ones.

And Aisha didn't seem to have a whit bit of concern about the lions. Just ducked into her steel shed, ordered him to not move an inch, and went about rummaging for—well, who the hell knew what.

Just like he didn't know what the hell to make of her.

Nate ran a hand over his head. Pulled at his sweat-tangled hair.

Not like he knew what to make of…this thing between them.

Had he almost kissed her?

Maybe Hilda had been right. About why he'd gone to The Cackling Cauldron in the first place. If she was, it wasn't doing a damn thing for him and not repeating mistakes.

There was a light, gentle touch on his mind. He could almost see the glowing bond, the pulsing light stretching between him and Timiculous.

It was thinner now. Weaker, but only because of the distance.

"You there?" Nate whispered—keeping his voice down so Aisha couldn't overhear.

Which would be difficult, at best. Considering she was banging away at drums or whatever was in that metal monster. And those lions, getting all excited like they were about to get breakfast.

"You upset. Why?"

"It's complicated."

"Feels so. Why?"

Sometimes talking with Timiculous was like talking to a toddler. Not like Nate had much experiences with those—and for a good reason.

Plus, his father didn't tolerate children.

Of any age.

Including adult children. Including his own.

Nate swiped the sweat from his chin. Forehead. "My father. Aisha. What we're even doing here. Pick one."

His mother.

He was upset about them *all*.

And torn—all over again. Just like with Hilda, when he'd defended her methods, her practice, but not the future with her.

This time, though, was worse. This time there *were* Familiars at stake and not just a happily-ever-after with a beautiful, damn intelligent witch. There could very well be the answers he'd been searching for after all these years.

Plus this time, someone else's dreams were at stake too.

Aisha's.

"Still not feel right. You still of two minds."

Two minds because Nate couldn't choose.

To side with his father, his orders, and the Council, to keep his cover and his quiet investigation into the Sanctuaries, the legal means Nate was opening to fully reveal everything his father and the Council had kept him hidden from them. He could do all that, by keeping his silence and following orders...or Nate could side with Aisha and all her unwanted Familiars.

"You choose."

"Right."

Easy enough. Except for the consequences.

And this time it wasn't just his happiness at stake, like it had been with him and Hilda, though he'd rightly come to doubt that after she hadn't trusted him to piece his memories from that spell back together. And this time, it wasn't even just Nate's search for the truth at stake.

Not anymore.

It was Aisha's, too. Her, and her Familiars.

Nate glanced up. Searched the sky and that...whatever it was he could feel. Like oil rubbing against his skin. Not natural. Not what should be there.

Almost...familiar.

Somehow.

Probably yet another of those half-pieced-together memories.

He—or more to the point, Timiculous—had felt it the moment they'd gotten out of his Mustang. Stepped onto that hot dirt ground. Breathed in the sweltering, unforgiving air. The air, which was so completely different than Paradise Grove with its cool, salty ocean breeze. And of course, those huge jetliners touching down for the thousands of landings they did in one day.

A smile pulled at Nate's lips. Couldn't help it.

But out here, in the middle of nowhere except for the dirt, sand, and really freakin' hot sun, there wasn't a hint of civilization. Not really. Just what Aisha had managed to throw together to keep her Familiars in one place and not roaming about the countryside.

Aisha.

Nate squinted at that pale blue sky, not a single cloud—with its glorious relief shade—in sight. Aisha had confirmed it too—he'd noticed her staring at the sky, glared at it, as if was the source of all her problems. It, apparently, just might be.

She hadn't realized he'd seen her. Noticed the change in her demeanor. Even her magic. But he'd noticed.

Nate noticed everything.

That was part of *his* magic.

While Timiculous…while Timiculous was the other half.

"What have you learned?"

Timiculous didn't tell him. Not so much in words.

Instead, Timiculous opened the link further between them. It would make him slightly weaker, at least for a little while, but this must be important enough.

Their bond blossomed further.

Brightened.

And Nate felt everything Timiculous did.

And was grateful for the fence behind his back. The fence that was now the only thing holding him up.

The shimmering image, a picture, really, sprang into Nate's mind. Not an image of sharp angles, but of colors. Glowing. Moving.

Timiculous was gazing upwards, right at the sky, just as Nate was. As if it'd been Timiculous all along who'd directed Nate's gaze upwards….

It probably was.

There was a reason Nate's father restricted the Familiar Sensitives like Timiculous.

The truth, however, couldn't be denied.

Not when Nate saw that black, oozing net.

He sucked in a breath. Couldn't believe what he was seeing. The net stretched high, high over the compound. Long, black tendrils dripping down. Falling onto enclosures. Staining the dirt black where it touched. Seeped the life from the land, before it seemed to fade. As if nothing was there to sustain it.

One such puddle was right beside Nate.

He immediately stepped away from it—left his shade and got a full glare of the sun's light.

And he didn't care one whit.

"Timiculous?" Nate whispered. "What is this? What am I seeing?"

"The truth."

That wasn't the least bit helpful.

True or not.

Nate concentrated on the net, then on the enclosure beside him. A lion with a very faded, hardly glowing pink tutu, and several oozing strands of black reaching into the cage.

Pooling there.

Didn't disappear like that nasty puddle next to Nate. Didn't, because that enclosure contained a Familiar.

And Familiars *were* magic.

At least, they used to be.

Until that wasting sickness touched them.

But the one thing Nate didn't understand, that didn't make any sense...if the sickness had been at Paradise Grove first, and it clearly had, why hadn't Timiculous seen this net? Felt it? This spell, or whatever it was?

Why the Waystation?

"What is it?" Nate asked again.

"What they've hidden. Buried. Buried in the rotting ground. Tossed into the unwanted ocean. Kept away, dark and deep in histories and in the earth. But they can't keep it away any longer. They have no more hold on magic and magic has no more hold on us."

Which didn't help Nate in the slightest.

He opened his mouth to question his Familiar, who rather liked to talk in hints and riddles, but just then Aisha banged open that steel door.

Nate jerked upright. Turned towards her. Couldn't help but see her the way Timiculous saw her.

Felt her.

Hot, untamed wind whipping through her long, dark, free hair. The scent of wild and freedom and joy. A blaze of colors—orange like sunset and deep green like the tangled forests he'd only see in movies.

She was…breathtaking.

"I told you not to move."

Aisha lugged yet another bucket with those toned arms of hers, trudged right through one of the seeping, oozing tendrils—

And the tendril immediately yanked away. Slithered back as if burned.

As if afraid.

Timiculous closed the bond between them. The quick snap shook Nate from his head straight to his toes. Aisha's bright, shimmering light faded and Nate saw her as she truly was—hands still filled with that bucket, this one full of sloppy meat and chicken breasts and bones.

She glared at him. As usual.

"If you can't listen, can't take orders, you're gone," she said. "I don't care how you or your bird can help. Am I clear?"

"Crystal."

Except nothing about her, about this place, was clear at all.

What was going on? And why here, at the Waystation?

His mind still reeling, still torn between orders and what was right, from Timiculous's smart retreat and Aisha's…light or whatever it was, all Nate could do was follow. He kept close at her heels. Did his best not to sneak too many glances up at that sky, to that net he could no longer see.

All of his training, his hours of studies and helping Familiars, everything he knew about their magical companions—and none of this made sense.

But if he didn't figure this out soon, he doubted it'd be much longer before Aisha realized Nate hadn't come of his own will, but the Council's.

The thought made his stomach turn to stone.

Vengeance didn't even cover what Aisha was going to do to him.

Or what Nate would do to himself when he failed her Familiars.

When he failed her.

Because it didn't matter if he still felt torn, still felt those two choices as if they were a living, breathing being. It didn't matter, because, at the end of the day, he would fail her.

And, he suddenly, didn't want to.

CHAPTER 22

$\mathcal{L}$ion's Row was an echo chamber of rolling roars and ruffs when Aisha with her bucket, and accompanying wheel barrow (which hauled most of the meat), with Darkwood trailing behind, came calling. Other than his stint by the food shed and wandering off (wandering only a *slight* distance away), Darkwood was listening.

She almost wished he wouldn't.

The lions, however, had an amazing way of distracting her, though. Of tugging a smile on her lips even when she felt like screaming or crying—or, often, both.

To them, it didn't matter that her Waystation was open to that blue-and-yellow-tinged southern California sky (not counting that black, oozing netting she couldn't see). Didn't matter that Lion's Row was merely cages and fences plopped down, one after another—didn't matter, because her lions *still* managed to make the place shake with their calling roars.

It took Aisha right back to her days on the grasslands.

Enough to make her forget her new shadow, the unease and uncertainty his presence brought. Even enough to forget the sickness that was destroying both her and her Familiars' lives.

Destroying her little sanctuary.

For this one moment, listening to all their roars, she forgot everything.

And remembered what she—and her memories—had locked away.

The setting sun. Evening stroking on as stars lit up the night by the thousands. Millions. The only sound, other than the constant whirling and chirping and buzzing of insects, was the sudden, long and loud call from a lion.

Echoing and traveling across the whole of the land.

It made her smile.

These particular roars, the ones shaking all her makeshift cages, weren't because the four dozen lions and lionesses in residence were just happy to see her—though a handful were as they rushed up to the chain-link fence and rubbed the full length of their short fur and tanned bodies as if it were against her legs.

In truth, the lions were happy because she'd begun the lengthy processes of lugging up the morning's meal from the food shed. And when it came to a lion's heart (or truthfully, any Familiar, it seemed), food was what mattered.

Mattered even over spells, trinkets, little dolls called Susie-Pals designed for Familiars that clapped their hands and said, "Good morning," if you followed the appropriate etiquette and niceties as deemed by the wizarding community.

Those dolls were just creepy.

Aisha shivered at the thought—even though it was a good 90 sweltering degrees (or something equally uncomfortable) in the valley with that sun glaring down right above them—and not a wisp of shade or cool breeze in sight.

For once, the lions and their excitement drowned out the constant chatter of the chimps and their catcalls from the upper enclosure. Which was good, because she really didn't want to explain—or even show—the chimps to Darkwood.

First, because of the danger.

Second, well, the catcalls *were* a bit embarrassing. And a bit... crude, to put it mildly.

"We hear you," she muttered to the lions. "We're coming."

"They seem happy to see you."

"It's not me. I promise."

Though this didn't drop her smile in the slightest.

Roars meant her lions still had spark, still had life in them, and if it was food that gave that to them, well, she wasn't about to cry about that.

She slowly lowered her bucket filled with the usual sloshing red juices meat, chicken bones, and carcasses. Her poor back protesting and giving her its pissed-off and "you're overdoing it" routine.

Lancing pain, right from her lower back and digging down, tingling, all through her legs. Oh, there went her spinal nerves again.

She really needed to make another appointment for that.

But there was nothing for it. Familiars needed to get fed and work needed to get done.

She must have winced, must have made some noise because Darkwood was there, practically yanking the bucket from her.

"All right, really. That's enough."

"Hey!" She straightened—a little too fast—and bent over, clutching just above her hip.

Oh, yeah, she'd definitely overdone it yesterday.

"Look," he said, "I'm here. I might as well help."

"You'll just get in the way and the only reason I'm hurting is because yesterday—"

"I made you work till midnight, even though *you* refused my offer to help. Well, no chance this time. I'm not about to stand around while you lug this thing around and clean out scat with a hose that weighs just as much as me."

Aisha's mouth, and the protest, clicked right off. "You're willing to clean up poop? Because you know, lion scat smells exactly like rotting, uncooked mea—"

"Yes, I know what it smells like."

He gave her a tight smile, though it didn't quite reach those sharp gray eyes. "My father had a tiger Familiar when I was growing up."

She snorted. "He made you, his clearly magically gifted son, clean up scat?"

"My father never had much time for anyone, including his 'magically gifted son.'" Darkwood's smile soured. "But he did believe scat duty would build character. More than he knew. Now. How about we stop arguing and you just tell me what needs to be done?"

It would be easy to say no, but then...Darkwood was there, and just following her. And it would be nice to actually finish her chores before dinnertime.

Or bedtime.

Finally, she nodded. "But you need to listen to me. Every word I say. I'm the one who knows these Familiars."

"I get it. You're the boss."

Somehow, she didn't believe that for a second.

It also didn't help when he threw in a wink.

Or that she gave him an answering smile in return.

"Come on"—she waved—"let's get these lions their meal, and then the real fun begins. I hope you don't mind having your butt commented on."

His eyebrows rose at that. "Now, I'm interested."

"Yeah. You would be."

At least until he found out it'd be a hairy, bisexual chimp gal named Bertha who had a thing for tall, handsome, and dark male wizards with a shit-ton of magic in them, commenting on his butt.

Aisha followed after Darkwood and that bucket—and couldn't help that small, teensy peek she gave to his butt—and those pants that fit him a whole lot better than those thick robes from yesterday.

Fit better, and looked better.

Bertha would be pleased.

CHAPTER 23

*A*isha tossed her beat-up, fraying pack on the aviary's hard-packed dirt ground. Breathed in the hot, moist air. Lifted her arms up above her head and stretched.

Slow. Inch by inch. Giving her muscles the break they so desperately deserved.

The break both she—and Darkwood—deserved.

In truth, Darkwood had handled the workload—and the chimps—better than had Aisha expected.

So, she'd broken one of her own rules and scrounged up the only shade available in the whole compound for lunch.

The aviary.

The large, open palm leaves, the dangling moss. Trees filling every bit of available dirt. The constant sounding and calling of birds—a mix of old world and new world species, happy in their own niches.

It wasn't the kind of place big fancy Sanctuaries would have.

Her parents had insisted on separate ecosystems and enclosures for the different climates, not throwing them all together as Aisha had done.

As if she'd had a choice.

But it worked.

And the birds, well, they made it work.

Didn't seem to mind the mingling of African Greys from Africa with the Costa Rican Amazons or macaws. They seemed to just like all the company and made sure the aviary was never quiet.

The humidity clung to this place. Was already soaking through her armpits. And the moist sent of earthworms and turned dirt was just a part of this place.

She breathed in. Long and deep.

Felt her body, her soul, relax for the first time in what felt like weeks.

At least, since she'd met Darkwood, anyway.

She unpacked her lunch, a sandwich, and then, with a darting glance at Darkwood and a resigned sigh, tossed him one as well.

He caught it too.

Stared at it.

"Thank you. I wasn't expecting—"

"Yeah. I know." As if she'd expected herself to make a second sandwich either.

Hadn't realized it until she'd slapped the paper wrapping on it and was halfway down the hill before stopping cold. As if she'd been actually looking forward to today.

Which was impossible.

"It's nothing fancy," she said. "Just a meat sandwich. Heavy on the meat. You need the energy in this place."

Darkwood stared at the paper-wrapped sandwich again—as if no one had ever made him a sandwich.

Which was silly. He had to have had like fifty cooks or something growing up, being the lord he was and all. This couldn't be a new thing.

"You keep saying that," he said. "About not being fancy."

"Well. It's not. It's roast beef and mustard."

She slapped the backpack's front flap closed.

"Sounds delicious. I'm starving." Darkwood took a long look at the smoothed-out, dirt-stomped floor (which was also one of the few spots not covered in bird crap, fruit, and seed shells, or shiny marbles and hair beads—Aisha having claimed the other spot, which also had a bit more tree shade).

He cleared his throat. "You, uh, sure about this? I mean, eating in the aviary."

At least he hadn't pushed about the sandwich. "Absolutely. I'm exhausted and it's hot out."

Aisha plopped onto the ground, kicked her legs out (wishing she could take off her boots and wiggle her toes, but not daring to find out what they smelled like in front of Darkwood). She lounged back on one of the rocks and twisted until she heard a good, nice crack in her back.

Of course, the rock *was* covered in bird crap, but considering she'd barely side-stepped a lion's shooting stream of pee in time (Darkwood's boots not being so lucky), she figured a little bird crap couldn't hurt.

And she *was* tired.

Even if, surprisingly, Darkwood had been a big help.

Darkwood.

What a mystery.

She lifted her eyes, watching him under the brim of her hat—but he wasn't paying attention to her at all. Not this time.

She tried not to think about that slight flutter in her chest. Instead, she tilted her hat back further to watch *him* for a change.

His whole focus was on the aviary. Taking in every detail. Every swish and sway of branches as one bird took off while another landed. One of her little attack assassins, Ducky, a cacique with his yellow, white, and green coloring, darted about Darkwood.

Flittered around his ears like a hummingbird. Settled on his shoulders.

He didn't flinch.

Aisha lifted her eyes at that.

Most people flinched.

Most people then got a nip or two behind the ear.

Or on the neck.

But then, Ducky burrowed down the front of his shirt.

Darkwood *did* straighten at that. Eyes went wide. But…happy.

It was the first surprise she'd seen from Darkwood, Mr. Quiet and Mysterious, since he'd surprised *her* that day—my God, was it only yesterday?

She shook her head, unable to help the smile at seeing the small, moving shape of Ducky disappearing down his front shirt and coming out his arm sleeve.

"Friendly fellow," Darkwood said, when he finally got Ducky to come out.

"Most of the time. If you're not afraid of him. If you are…"

She lifted her shoulders. Let them fall.

And absolutely didn't hide her smile—even when Darkwood looked back and those gray eyes gleamed back at her—with a smile of his own.

He was enjoying this, she realized.

The thought came sudden and fast.

Felt the heat rising in her cheeks. Her chest seemed to swell. To pound. In excitement. Anticipation.

She couldn't remember the last time she'd enjoyed someone's company—a male's company. A wizard's company. And in a place she loved with all her heart and being.

And Darkwood being there didn't…detract from that love. Didn't sour the moment or the aviary.

She was enjoying his company. Enjoying how every minute he seemed to flip her beliefs around. To prove he wasn't like everyone she knew.

Like Blakeley.

She lowered her sandwich. The same sandwich she'd been starving for and hadn't taken a single bite of.

And now, didn't want to.

Because she didn't know if Darkwood was like Blakeley. Couldn't. Not until she had answers.

About Darkwood. About his bird.

Why either of them needed to be there and why they thought she was so important when Aisha was, in truth, no one.

And that thought...hurt. Twisted in her chest. Knotted there until it felt like she couldn't breathe.

Fear, she realized.

Fear she thought she'd conquered years ago. When she'd left Africa, her family, her life behind and started a new one.

Darkwood wasn't looking at Ducky any longer, but at her.

The smile was gone. Had disappeared.

There was no more laughter in his eyes. No more pure enjoyment of being in a place as unique and lively as her aviary.

"Time for answers, isn't it?" he asked.

She just nodded. "I think you owe me the truth."

CHAPTER 24

*H*e knew it was time.

Dreaded it, but knew it.

Nate sat on that feather- and seed-littered floor. A floor, in many areas, stained white from the constant spattering of bird droppings.

He forced himself to sit up. To cross his legs. Back straight. Shoulders at the correct posture angle.

Exactly as he'd been instructed. To never relax. To never let his guard down.

Except now dirt and dust coated his pants, hands, even his face.

His father—hell, just about everyone in the Council—would be appalled. Would order the whole Waystation scrubbed down with a hard-bleach spell.

Meanwhile, there was Aisha. Her long legs sprawled out. Pants stained dark brown from mud and poop spatterings. And she didn't seem to care. Not one whit. Instead, she leaned against that white-coated rock as if this were the most comfortable, relaxing place in the world.

As if she wouldn't want to be any other place than here.

Nate couldn't help being the exact opposite. All his training, all that etiquette, it had been ingrained into his being.

He'd like nothing more than to shed it.

Shed that skin like she'd done when she'd left her own high society life to scrape out this existence in the middle of some ravine in the hot California desert.

But he couldn't.

Because of Timiculous.

Nate felt the muscles around his neck and shoulders tighten. Constrict.

Aisha still leaned against that rock but, he noticed, she wasn't relaxed. Anything but.

He could see it.

Saw the way her own muscles tensed. The slow, deliberate way she forced a bite of her sandwich—and the even slower effort to chew and swallow that bite.

His magic, he reminded himself, which was why Father had sent him. To see. To notice everything.

To study.

Which was what made him so very, very good at his job. Even when his job involved someone like Aisha. Even if she wasn't a Familiar.

She'd grown comfortable with him. As they'd sweated and worked together, side by side. As they'd received their fair share of lurid chimp catcalls. She'd grown comfortable with him.

And now he was about to break that comfort.

He'd known it was coming.

Didn't mean he'd have to like it. Only wished he could tell her everything, the whole truth, but because of his father...because of Timiculous, Nate couldn't.

"I promised you answers. One moment, please."

Nate opened the connection to Timiculous—made their bond shimmer. A gold pulse that traveled from Nate to Timiculous. A tingling Nate felt through his whole being. And a sigh, too. How he missed Timiculous. Missed his familiar weight on his shoulder. That brief, delicate touch of two minds—close by, even if they weren't communicating.

Nate sent the request. He wanted to speak with his parrot.

And Timiculous flew over.

As if he'd been waiting.

Probably had been.

Timiculous's brilliant blue and gold feathers cut through the maze of palm trees, branches, hanging moss. Dipped down and twisted left, then right. The pulsing beat of his wings.

Easy. Comfortable.

As if he'd been born into this kind of forest and knew instinctively how to navigate.

The sight made Nate's chest tighten. Made his breath catch, slightly, in the cave of his throat.

Timiculous wasn't a wild parrot. Hadn't ever been in a true rainforest. Hadn't ever been to the untouched forests of Costa Rica or the Amazon.

He was, and always had been, Nate's Familiar.

Had been bred for the role.

Timiculous landed on Nate's shoulder, his small four pounds nothing compared to his size—even the length of those brilliant tail feathers. Carried with him the tinted air and humidity of the aviary, of the wild, of freedom.

His parrot *glowed* with it.

"I've missed you," Nate said.

Timiculous rubbed his head against Nate's cheek in response.

Joy vibrated through the bond, but the same missing feeling that Nate felt for Timiculous wasn't there...not exactly. There was joy, yes, but also another kind of joy. Something Nate hadn't felt from Timiculous before...and it was because of where Timiculous *was*.

Happiness, at being here.

In Aisha's aviary.

Timiculous, and all the other birds, hummed with it. With that same feeling.

"I'm glad you like it here." Nate turned to Aisha. Gave her a tight smile, even though he didn't feel it. Not exactly. Didn't know why, either. "You've built an amazing place. Your birds are happy here. I thought you should know."

"Thank you."

She'd kept her tone cool. Neutral. But her face darkened. A blush that spread from her cheeks and down past her long neck. Disappeared underneath her sweat-stained tank top.

His words had meant a lot to her. He'd had a feeling, a sense, that they would. Nate wondered why, why these birds were so important compared to all her other Familiars, but then immediately forgot as Aisha bolted up.

Dread filled his stomach.

Damn it.

He'd made a mistake.

Knew it the second her whole relaxed posture suddenly vanished.

Her back, now just as straight as his. Her hands, splayed on her wide hips as she glared down at him. Her whole body, humming with energy.

With tension.

"What did you say? *My* birds? Happy here?"

Shit.

Leave it to someone like Aisha, someone who hummed with awareness of her own, to notice his little slip.

Nate got to his feet. Slowly. So as not to dislodge Timiculous from his shoulder.

"Yes."

"How the hell can you know that?" She yanked her hat off. Didn't seem to care that it'd made her sweat-matted hair stick up in all directions.

Most witches would care.

Not Aisha.

She slapped the hat against his chest. Caused a whirl of sweat and dust to smack into his face. Couldn't tell if it came from Nate or her hat.

Either way, he didn't dare move. Not even to sneeze.

"What's going on here? Who are you? And how do you know what my birds are feeling? No one, not even psychics know that!"

He'd said it only to make her happy.

He'd *wanted* to make her happy. Especially with what he was about to do.

"I'm getting to that—"

"The hell you are. If you don't tell me, right this second, I'm going to boot your asses so hard and fast out of my Waystation the Council's never going to find your pants!"

Timiculous whistled.

High and bright in that greeting Nate loved.

Hoping, Nate could feel, to relieve the sudden tension.

Not that Nate blamed him.

He was pretty sure Aisha was going make good on her threat.

Aisha rounded on Timiculous. Pointed a finger at him. "Don't you get in the middle of this. I deserve answers and damn it, I'm getting them. You both have kept me in the dark long enough."

She glared at Nate. "Long enough."

He just nodded. Gave Timiculous a nice rubbing on his head for comfort—more for himself than Timiculous. "I've missed you too, buddy. But I'm pretty sure the lady wants her answers. And she's been rather patient, don't you think?"

Timiculous's bobbed his head.

Up. Down.

Giant black beak slightly open.

Like he was laughing.

"I'm losing patience," Aisha growled.

"So I see. Now, if you'll sit back down, maybe we can have a civilized conversation—unless you want to toss me back into the pond."

"I do." But she plopped back down on the ground. Tucked her knees against her chest. Leaned on that rock. "So you better get talking."

Nate settled down on that white-stained dirt floor. Did his best to ignore the droppings rubbing into his pants—and the witch glaring daggers at him.

Reminded him, very much, of Hilda the first time he'd met her.

The last time, too, now that he thought about it. Which he wasn't going to do.

One angry witch was all a man could handle.

"Now," Nate said to Timiculous, "why don't you tell us what you found. I can tell the other birds are happy here, but what else? How are they feeling?"

Again, Aisha sat straighter. "What does that mean? Feel? How can he? Is he a psychic?"

Which hit right home, again, to one of Nate's biggest secrets. His, his father's, and the Council's.

"No," he answered. "Timiculous isn't psychic. He is, however, a Sensitive."

CHAPTER 25

You're lying." Aisha sat up. No longer pressed against her rock with that perfect grove for her back to lean against. No longer pretended relaxation.

There was no point.

"You're actually, seriously, lying to me."

Darkwood gave one, slow shake of his head. "No. We're not, actually. And we are quite serious."

His complete attention, his focus, was on her.

Made her want to squirm. To glance away.

Anything but to have that gaze on her.

Sweat dribbled down the side of her face. Her neck. Wondered if the aviary had just gotten hotter or if it only had to do with this wizard and his bird. Sitting there, calm and regal, face impassive and quite serious—yet all the while trying to tell her a lie that was so far from believable Aisha could barely get the words out.

And yet...her magic sensed no falsehood.

No lies.

That he believed, anyway.

"There's no such thing as a Familiar Sensitive."

"There is, and you've met one." Darkwood dug into his shirt pocket, popped out a handful of unshelled walnut pieces.

Timiculous gave his low-pitched, excited whistle and carefully picked one out, then another, until there were not even bitsy-sized crumbs left. Darkwood got out another two walnut pieces from his pocket, never once taking those too-calm eyes off her. As if he needed her to listen. To believe.

In him.

But Aisha had played that game, that dance with another arrogant, high-classed wizard and she'd learned. She'd done more than learned her lesson. It'd shaped her. Changed her.

"You expect me to just believe. Take your words at face value without proof?"

"We can keep debating the topic, if you like, but I assure you, he is a Sensitive and to Familiars. Only Familiars."

She didn't believe him. "Everyone knows Familiars aren't sensitive. Not to each other. To their masters, yes, but not...not to each other."

Darkwood's eyebrows lifted. "You'd rather believe your birds aren't happy? That they're the same miserable creatures you accepted into your home? Cared for. Nurtured. Loved, when no one else would. Especially their bonded wizards?"

"It's not about belief. It's about the possibility. It's about proof. And there has been *no* documented proof that Familiars can sense the deep feelings of others. The Council has personally financed these trials and I've seen, *studied* the reports myself."

"You're sure, then, it's not about belief?"

"Absolutely."

Except, her gut swirled and danced.

The magic there awake and rolling. Sparking.

In agreement.

With Darkwood.

Aisha shoved her tangled braid over her shoulder. The small, escaped hairs sticking to her face. Clinging there and distracting her. The hard-packed ground digging into her butt, as if she could feel every rock and pebble and broken, discarded shell piece.

And the rest of her defense caught up to her.

Clicked.

"The Council," she whispered. Blinked once. Twice. "Goddamn it. The Council financed all those trials. That's what you're telling me."

Darkwood leaned forward. Leaned so close his leg brushed hers.

A heat seemed to travel up her leg that had nothing to do with the moist and constant, unrelenting humidity of the aviary, and everything to do with Darkwood.

She refused to move her leg. To budge in response.

She didn't.

Damn, did she want to.

"Proof is, of course, the ideal, but what happens when that proof doesn't line up with another's agenda?" Darkwood merely shrugged, then nodded at Timiculous. "You heard him for yourself, and everyone knows Familiars don't—or can't—lie. Of course, that can go back to this proof falsehood. Send out documented evidence, your proof, of one thing, even if it's not true, and it won't take much for an entire community—magical or Normal—to believe what you want them to believe."

With every word, Darkwood had pressed even in closer. Even sitting there across from her. As if needing to close that distance.

Needing her to see.

To understand.

"The Council," he whispered, "has many secrets. Some, mostly innocent. Some that, if they were to get out, would change the shape of our society. Our world."

Aisha let out a breath. Didn't realize she'd even been holding it.

"You're saying they know? They've always known? Do they know about you?"

"What would happen if Familiars were seen as more than just property? As living, breathing individuals with wants and feelings of their own?"

Aisha closed her eyes. Shuddered. Couldn't help but feel that Darkwood was right beside her now.

She opened her eyes. Stared at Darkwood, and for the first time, wasn't afraid of that intensity.

"It'd mean that my Waystation wouldn't be needed. It'd mean that the abuse I see every day would never be *allowed* to happen."

"More than that, actually. Much more. What would happen if Familiars could have another, someone like Timiculous and me, to speak for them? To defend them? Right now there are no laws, no rights, and if there were…"

He let the thought trail off.

For the first time in years, Aisha felt hope, strong and true and bright, brimming in her chest.

Could the answer be so simple?

Break the news about Timiculous, his abilities, and change the world? Change what happened in every sanctuary? What happened in too many magical households to count, the abuse and neglect of creatures that were supposed to be their psychic companions?

Except, there was more to it than that.

Deadly, too.

"But," she said, "there's some magic out there, some spell or whatever, that is causing Familiars—all Familiars—to suddenly, without reason or thought, to die."

Darkwood nodded. "There is that."

"Could it be the Council? Trying to keep this from getting out? The evidence, again, being changed?"

"The Council isn't immune to the wasting sickness. Even their prized Familiars are being attacked."

"So, what does this mean? For the Familiars? For us?"

The word "us" sprang out.

Aisha snapped her mouth closed.

But it was too late.

She couldn't take it back.

"It's not them," Darkwood said. "The Council isn't behind it."

"Then who is?"

Timiculous, then, gave another flap-flap of his wings. "Birds still good. Aviary still good. Not good outside. Don't want to go outside. Good here."

Darkwood snapped his gaze to Timiculous. "Why? Why here and not outside?"

Timiculous flapped his wings again.

"I'm sorry," Aisha said, "I don't understand—"

Darkwood held up a hand, stopping her. Never once, however, taking his attention away from Timiculous. His eyes even narrowed, sparked, as if he *were* speaking with his Familiar.

What kind of bond did these two have?

Aisha had never seen anything like this before. Never felt this swirling, strong connection. Practically buzzed along her skin. Sparked in her gut.

"Timiculous. We need to know. We need to stop whatever's happening."

She felt it. That trust again.

That deep trust between wizard and Familiar.

Made her own heart ache just seeing it—and she immediately squashed *that* feeling. What was in the past, stayed in the past.

You learned from it. Moved on.

End of story.

The story that mattered, right now, was the one in front of her. Not the one that happened over a decade ago. Not the one that had seen her own macaw, her own blue and gold Familiar, gone from her life forever.

She shoved the feeling, the ache, away.

Hard. Fast.

"Come on, Timmy," Darkwood coaxed. "We need to know. We want to help."

"Good home here. Real home," Timiculous said. "Africa lady make good. Right home. Not their home. Darkness can't touch what's ours. Can't find magic when its ours. Not theirs."

Then, Timiculous took off.

Disappeared right back into that dense forest of trees and moss.

Made Aisha wish it wasn't so dense so she could take off after him and get some real answers—not some riddles that didn't make any sense.

"What"—she glared at Darkwood—"is going on here?"

"I wish I knew. Truly."

Aisha got to her feet. Clenched her fists at her side. Forced herself to breathe. To think.

Timiculous said the answers were here. Right in front of her.

It hadn't been the answer she wanted.

But right now, it was all she had.

Maybe it was time she stopped whining, stood up, and did something about it.

"Then I guess..." She gave Darkwood a smile. Couldn't help it. Couldn't help but feel that maybe, just maybe, they had a little hope. "I guess we need to find how I made this place good."

isha shoved her braid over her shoulder. The sun's unrelenting heat beat against the back of her neck. Seeped through that thin line of shade her hat provided. Kept right on going as if it wanted her on her knees by the end of the day.

Figured she'd pick the hottest damn day to follow her gut—to follow her magic.

Sweat dripped down her nose. Trickled past her eyes. She kept her gaze on Lanhi, who lounged on the other side of her enclosure, in a separate area now closed off and locked from Aisha. It was a precaution. Not exactly necessary with Lanhi, especially since she'd exhibited signs of the sickness, and while she'd been a bit erratic with her moods before, she had never been vicious. But still, it was a precaution. And with some of her other Familiars, it was a vital precaution.

Especially if Aisha wanted to live.

Precautions were particularly useful when it came to Familiars like the chimps. Like the hybrids. Familiars who'd either pushed themselves, or been pushed, to the brink where both mind and bond had snapped. Left them a violent, volatile mess.

Those were the Familiars she didn't dare trust.

And she certainly didn't dare trust the locksmith wizards'

spells to hold. Especially when there was no telling just how much magic or how many spells these Familiars had hidden away in them.

Lanhi just lay on that hot, dusty ground. Eyes closed. Unmoving.

Didn't even twitch her ears from the constant dive and buzzing of flies pecking at her face.

No way to trust what Lanhi would do. Not when the sickness had taken such a deep hold on her.

Aisha might be trained with a wand. She might be trained on Africa's plains in survival and unplanned-for wildlife encounters, had walked side-by-side with the Hadzabe tribe for months—even if she couldn't remember it.

But even still, she wasn't a fool.

Except, maybe, when it came to Darkwood.

Here she was, going into an enclosure confirmed with the sickness and a tiger that, while isolated from her, could react in a way neither Aisha nor Darkwood could predict. And when you didn't *know* the situation, didn't *understand* the circumstances surrounding the situation—and with this sickness they sure as heck didn't understand—all of could lead to mistakes.

And mistakes, when it came to Familiars—and seriously, any wild animal—meant death was a real possibility.

Hers.

And even with all that hanging over her, all that weight pressing down as she stepped into that enclosure with its dried dirt, faded tutu, and circus posters, she still couldn't help but sneak one more glance over her shoulder.

At Darkwood.

He stood on the other side of the fence. No longer kept behind that line in the dirt she'd drawn. Instead, was right up at that cage.

Gripping it. As if afraid.

For her.

And she couldn't help but feel that hard beat in her chest.

Once. Twice

She didn't berate him for getting to close. Couldn't help but admit, deep down, that she liked having him there. Liked knowing someone was standing behind her. Had her back.

In case…in case something went wrong.

"You're sure about this?" His voice, a bare whisper.

She wasn't. But she nodded.

Yesterday, Timiculous had told her she'd had the answers.

Well, the only way to find those answers was to focus on the ones who were sick. And while she was at it, well, Lanhi needed fresh water anyway. Might as well do some chores while she was at it.

"I won't let anything happen to you," he said.

A smile pulled at Aisha's lips. Couldn't help herself. Couldn't help but feel that tiny bit of joy at his words.

He really was standing behind her.

It'd been a long time since anyone besides Marcelle had done that.

"I won't let anything happen to you," she whispered back.

And then, her focus turned to Lanhi and only Lanhi. She shoved Darkwood and that swirling feeling she had for him far, far away.

She pulled out her wand. Checked the padlock on Lanhi's smaller holding cage from here. The spell glowed red from a moment, then lit brightly to green.

Secure.

She let out a breath.

First step, done. Aisha grabbed the heavy, coiled hose, got the water turned on, and entered Lanhi's enclosure. She closed the cage door behind her, but didn't lock it.

If something happened, Darkwood could get in.

Or, he could secure it.

Leaving her inside.

Aisha's hands shook. Sweat slipped down her fingers. Made the wand's smooth wood slippery.

She closed her eyes for a moment. The padlock might be secure, but she couldn't trust it. She'd been taught…by someone, to not fully trust in only one defense.

Then, her hand moved. Muscle memory. Or maybe mind memory.

She didn't know.

Didn't think or question, just...just drew a spell in the air. Felt the sparks and the magic dancing off the wand's tip. When she finally opened her eyes, her breath caught.

She made herself swallow. Made herself take in a second, deep breath.

Before her, outside Lanhi's smaller cage, was a snare. It anchored itself to the door—both sides, as if the spell's trigger didn't matter if the door was forced open by the lock or the hinges. The spell rooted itself to the ground.

Deep. Deep down. Held there.

Glowed and sparked.

She tasted wildness on her tongue. A hot, distant breeze snapping at her tangled hair—even though hers was quite secure in a braid.

It was a snare she'd never seen.

But a snare she'd clearly made before.

Still, it was a good snare and a damn good spell. She could tell, even from here.

"Aisha?"

She didn't dare look at Darkwood. "It's fine. I'm fine."

The hot wind picked up. Snapped around her pant legs, made her braid dance and twist. A dust devil swirled at her feet. As if it wanted to trip her. To stall her. It didn't let up, either. Danced and danced until finally, Aisha just plowed right on through it, dragged that hose and spattering water with her.

Still, the dirt clung to her.

Slipped into every crack on her skin, past the bandage she'd slapped on her fingers yesterday after a wire had snapped free from one of the cages and dug into her something fierce.

She coughed, squinted her eyes, and went deeper into Lanhi's enclosure.

Aisha needed to focus. To sense, to *feel* with her magic. To push past that...hole in her magic. Just like she'd created that snare. Reached deeper, deeper to a place she could almost feel. Touch.

If there were answers, she'd need to find them.

Had to find them.

But even as she moved closer to Lanhi's smaller handling cage and that bucket with day-old water she was intent on changing, with those chunks of dirt sloshing around, Aisha's insides tingled.

Every swirl of dust pricked at her neck.

Something wasn't right here.

Lanhi still lay there, unmoving. Silent. As if dead.

Aisha dumped out the old water, carefully, keeping her eyes on Lanhi. She pointed the hose in the bucket. Lanhi still didn't move, but the feeling of wrongness didn't go away.

As if…she'd stepped into something.

Something muddy and clinging. Seemed to pull at her magic.

Aisha glanced up at the midday sky, a brilliant blue with not a single cloud in sight. Couldn't see that massive, oozing black net that Marcelle had seen. To her, it was just a sky in the height of its scorching power.

And yet, yet.

Her magic gave another tug at her gut. Made her want to turn around…and stare.

Instinct tickled her. She followed it.

Turned.

Stared straight into the gold-glowing amber eyes of a tiger.

Of Lanhi.

Lanhi crouched on her hind haunches. Not even two feet from Aisha.

Face just a breath from the suddenly flimsy-feeling chain-link fence. Her ears, flattened against her stripped skull.

Aisha's breath caught.

Flies continued to buzz. Swirled around her ears. Eyes.

Aisha didn't dare move.

Water spattered out from the hose. Filled the bucket.

There was no more dancing tiger. No more cuddling and ruffing, the way Lanhi used to greet Aisha after she'd first come to the Waystation. Not even the tiger dying and wasting away of a sickness they didn't understand.

That tiger, that tiger wasn't there at all.

A true tiger stared back at her. Watched her.

A tiger whose gaze narrowed.

Focused on Aisha.

Curling growl rumbling in her chest. Barely slipped out of her throat.

A hunting tiger.

CHAPTER 27

*L*anhi didn't blink those glowing-gold eyes. Not once.

The rushing and spilling of water continued to pump out of Aisha's hose.

Filled the water bucket.

Overflowed.

Water splashed onto the ground. Created a muddy puddle that grew by the second. Lapped at Aisha's boots. Seeped into them, into her socks, and then trickling past her.

Still, Aisha held that hose.

Gripped it tight with both hands. Didn't dare lower it. Drop it.

Lanhi crouched lower. Preparing.

Aisha felt Darkwood behind her. The sudden spike of worry. Fear. For her.

But she couldn't think of him. Couldn't think about the strength she suddenly felt. Knowing that he was there. Behind her.

She could only focus on the tiger before her.

The tiger whose movement was so slow and precise, if Aisha hadn't been paying attention, she wouldn't have noticed.

Lanhi's head, her massive shoulders, nearly touched the ground. And those claws... Aisha glanced at them.

Then wished she hadn't.

Lanhi's paws were spread out, gripping the concrete flooring. Claws out, as well.

Lethal claws.

Lanhi had been one of the handful of tigers who hadn't been declawed by her witch master.

One of the lucky ones, Aisha had always thought.

From across the cage, but what really felt and sounded like across the whole compound, came the crinkle and pull of Darkwood's pants as they brushed against each other.

The shifting of feet in the dusty dirt.

As if he were moving closer.

Towards her.

Lanhi lowered her head further. Gaze narrowing to tiny gold pinpricks. Eyes that flicked, just for a moment, past Aisha.

"Aisha?"

Fear and warning laced Darkwood's voice.

Aisha, with her hands still full of the hose, carefully, with the slowest of movement, waved her fingers at him. Hoped the hose and the water hid the movement.

Hoped the message was clear.

He needed to stay back. Not come closer.

Aisha might not want him here, in her Waystation or in her life, but she wouldn't allow him to be in danger.

Couldn't. And didn't dare think why.

Besides, this was her Waystation. She worked with these broken and abused Familiars, most of them exotic, deadly animals like Lanhi, for a reason.

She knew the dangers. Signed up for them. Embraced them.

Darkwood hadn't.

There was another shift in the dirt. A small sucking noise as a foot moved into the growing mud-stream from Aisha's water hose.

Darkwood wasn't listening. Wasn't staying back.

He was coming to her.

Somehow, she knew he would. Just like she'd known, every

morning when she started her long day, he'd be there. Waiting. Ready to help.

Aisha ignored the sudden, harsh pounding in her chest. Had to.

She could imagine him pulling out his wand. To defend her. Save her.

But she didn't want that kind of help. Not when her magic was still swirling, still guiding.

Sure, instinct was pushing her to run. To escape.

That was the human side of her. The prey side.

And she was done, *done*, being prey.

Timiculous told her she had the answers, well then, somehow, right here, was an answer staring right back at her.

Wanting to maim and kill her, sure.

But it was still an answer.

Her training, from all those years ago from where exactly, she wasn't sure, couldn't remember…but while the memory, the knowledge eluded her, the training still took over control of her arms.

Legs. Body.

She touched on something…muscle memory. It had been taught to her. Practiced. A hundred times. A thousand times. She didn't know, only that it'd been hounded into her until it became second nature.

Eye contact meant aggression.

Aisha looked down. Just a tad. Just enough, so she could still completely see Lanhi—and what she was doing, but not stare directly into those suddenly feral, suddenly all-tiger eyes.

"I've got your back." Darkwood's words were strong, though quiet.

And she knew he did.

Couldn't help the feeling of gratitude swell within her.

He was there for her.

Wasn't leaving.

Which was silly. Ridiculous. That she was even thinking about him, while her heart pounded so loud it was thrumming out the streaming noise of water smacking into the ground. That she was practically nose to nose with a feral tiger.

A tiger's whose paws glowed and sparked. Pink first—Lanhi's

magical color, and then, that color faded away into muddied brown. Finally, to black.

But the magic there still sparked. Still kept coming.

Growing.

Aisha slid back one step. Then another.

Felt her magic slide right into a black, oozing puddle. Sticky. Foul.

The netting?

Didn't matter. Not right then. Only that it clung to her. Sucked at her.

Felt it licking away her magic like it'd found itself a great buffet.

"The sickness is here," she whispered. "I'm standing in it."

"I know."

She tried to move again. To inch out. She couldn't.

The sickness was holding her fast.

Even as Lanhi lowered herself further. Hind quarters bending. Bunching.

Ready to spring.

"Darkwood." Aisha's voice caught. Held. From fear. "I—I can't move."

It was all she had a chance to say.

All she could do as Lanhi sprang forward. As she attacked.

CHAPTER 28

*N*ate sensed the change. The shift.

The hot, dry air now tinged and sizzled with magic. As if it were alive.

Heard the fear in Aisha's voice when she said those words—*I can't move.*

Felt his own fear.

Numbing. Freezing. Constricting.

She was alone in that cage.

A feral Familiar just a few feet from her. A tiger whose magic was flaring.

Uncontrolled. Vengeful.

Only a flimsy chain-link fence—and one without a speck of reinforcement magic—separated her from that tiger.

Except Aisha wasn't alone.

Not now.

Not while he was there.

He wasn't going to let this happen again.

Nate didn't wait for Lanhi to attack. Didn't care about Aisha's protocols or that she'd told him to stay out. Just didn't give a damn. He wasn't about to let that tiger hurt her.

Nate moved. Whipped out his wand. Fast.

Didn't call for Aisha to duck.

To move aside.

Trusted, only, that she would. That she'd heard him move. Would know what to do, what was coming.

Magic glinted and shimmered from his wand. He smacked the cage door with his shoulder. Aimed with his wand. Flung the binding spell. Aimed it at Aisha's back. Aisha, who stood perfectly still in front of the tiger.

But then, Aisha dove.

Right as Lanhi sprang for the fence—for her.

Lanhi's magic slashed from her claws. Ripped right through that fence like it was dough.

Her giant, sleek body turned in mid-air. Aiming, again, for Aisha.

But Lanhi didn't have a chance.

Not when Nate's spell—the one he'd learned after his mother died, a spell he'd studied and practiced until he couldn't see straight —struck.

Smacked into Lanhi's chest.

A glowing white-gold rope coiled around her. Struck hard and fast like a cobra. Constricted. Its very touch, numbing—both physically and magically.

Lanhi screamed once.

Sharp. Piercing. Furious.

Her roar tore through the suddenly still, suddenly quiet Waystation. Not even the chimps chattered or screamed. No lions answered Lanhi in return.

That alone, felt like a victory. But even more so, when Lanhi fell.

That giant, killing-predator body crashing beside Aisha—who rolled free—and Nate's heart gave another beat. Sucked in another breath of air.

Thank God.

She was safe.

Mud caked onto Lanhi's fur from that still-running hose water, sucked at her sides, her legs, but her face was up. She wasn't face down. Her sides still heaved as she breathed.

Once, and then again.

He hadn't made the spell too strong.

Nate lowered his wand. Didn't tuck it away, even though he should. His father was always right about spell-slinging and nerves, and the way Nate's hand shook...

Aisha she sprang to her feet.

Seeing her standing there, her own sides heaving; her dark face, now pale. Mud and water dripping from her face, hair, coating her clothes in a thick, black paste. But no blood. Wasn't covered in it. Didn't soak into the ground and stick to the bottom of his feet as he moved towards her.

Aisha's eyes were wide as she gazed down at Lanhi in shock, and something more.

She would do it again.

Would venture near a Familiar whose whole being was coated with that dark, oozing magic. A magic they didn't understand. A magic that fluttered against the edge of his memory.

She would risk herself to find the answers.

Because it was who she was.

And just like with Lanhi, Nate didn't wait.

He rushed over. Grabbed Aisha by her arms. Muscular. Defined. As he'd always imagined.

She tried to pull away.

He didn't let her.

Just held her tight.

Tighter.

"What the hell were you thinking?" He shook her. Once.

Couldn't help it.

Couldn't help the sudden tightening in his own chest. Heart.

He'd nearly lost her.

Would have, if he hadn't been there. If he hadn't known, in that deep place he pretended never existed, never happened—like it had, all those years ago.

To his mother.

Aisha's dark hair had fallen loose of its braid. Tangled strands stuck to her face from the water and mud. But didn't cover the truth. The fear he saw glinting up through her eyes.

She'd known damn well she was going to die.

"You…you were there," she said. Whispered. As if she could hardly talk. "You were there. For me."

"Damn straight I was."

Then, he kissed her.

Full and deep and desperate.

Didn't give a damn that he suddenly felt just as afraid as when that tiger had launched itself at her.

Didn't care, and didn't hold back either.

Just kissed her.

CHAPTER 29

For the first time in her life—or so it felt, or so what she could remember—Aisha didn't think.

Just felt.

Felt Nate. His fingers, digging into her now torn shirt sleeve. Gripped her. Hard. Wouldn't let go.

Didn't want him to.

His fingers, like fire. Burning. Scalding.

Just like his kiss. His lips.

Like her whole being felt.

She didn't shove Nate aside.

Didn't rear her right arm back and clock him in the face as she would have. If he were anyone else. Like she would have if he'd kissed her on that first day they'd met. Or yesterday. Or the day before that.

But not today.

Maybe it was Lanhi. Seeing a full grown, feral, hungry, hunting tiger spring at her. Or maybe it was because she felt that black, slimy magic sticking to her. Or maybe, damn it, maybe it was just about damn time she opened herself up and *felt*.

Her arms circled his neck. Clung to him. Pulled him even closer.

It wasn't close enough.

Not nearly enough.

Not when every inch of her had forgotten this. How, suddenly, it *needed* this.

Needed him.

It was that thought, that realization alone, that rocked her back. She stumbled, boots tripping and catching in that growing mud puddle turning Lanhi's enclosure into a pond, except she didn't fall back or trip.

Couldn't.

Not when Nate, still, held her close. Held her arms.

Like he'd never let her go again.

She nearly kissed him this time. Wanted to. Every inch of her demanding it. Except…she knew better. Had been here before, with a man like Darkwood. She'd been hurt. She'd suffered, and she'd learned. She knew what it meant to be with a man from his world, a world she'd been forever shunned from. The shunning, she didn't mind. The thinking that *he* could control her, dictate her life as he saw fit, *that* she did mind.

But what was more, Lanhi needed her right now. All the Familiars did.

They were who mattered most.

Not Darkwood. Not even Aisha.

But she could barely think of her Waystation, of her Familiars. Could barely force herself to think rationally. With a clear head. With clear thoughts.

Nate must have felt her pulling back. He broke the kiss.

Hot and fast, just like he'd started it.

Stared down at her. His grey eyes nearly black, but shadowed.

Definitely shadowed.

Just watched her, and what he thought then, she hadn't a clue.

Not when she kept going back to that day.

The sun. Sweltering. Unforgiving. Her bare feet in that reddened dirt. She didn't remember much of her time with the Hadzabe, but whatever happened, whatever was done to her memories, she remembered *that* moment.

With perfect clarity.

Blakeley's anger.

Her own as she finally stood against him and said a single word: no.

His rising wand.

His determination to force her, shape her into being the kind of woman only someone like he could be with. Not the woman she was. A woman who wanted to understand her heritage, understand her place in the world as she roamed the plains, half-clad in cloth and hide, pretending to be some savage from a forgotten, ancient time.

The black-tinged, angry spell that flew from the wand.

Came at her.

A spell she'd known, in that moment, her parents had not only approved of, but must have provided. Otherwise, there was no way Blakeley could have found her. She'd been hidden, after all, by a deeper magic.

An ancient one.

The thought rocked through. Made her mind contract. Pain, splicing through her. She nearly doubled over. Saw only a sharp white, then hazy black. The shadow man again. Appearing before her, right out of the land, a mirage that she could barely see through the inky, dark haze.

She'd seen this man before, and not just in her dreams. Had met him.

Just, just couldn't remember *when*.

Instead of pulling Nate again to her, to her aching chest, beating heart, to push away that memory, that feeling of wrongness that suddenly wouldn't leave her...she settled for a long deep, head-clearing breath.

When that didn't quite work, she took another.

Then another.

She was her own person now. Was no longer in Tanzania. No longer controlled by Blakely. Or by her parents. Aisha focused instead on what had just happened—with Lanhi, with that dark magic holding her—*not* with Nate.

Darkwood, she reminded herself.

Not with Darkwood saving her.

Kissing her.

Darkwood slowly released her. Slowly unclenched his hands from her arms.

"I'm sorry." Dropped his hands to his sides. "That was inappropriate."

Aisha felt only cold now, cold where just moments before there'd been fire.

She raised her own hand up. Saw that it trembled.

Darkwood saw as well. That shadowed gaze growing even more clouded.

Hooded.

She didn't try to hide her hand, or the shakes she felt rippling through her. Instead, she wiped away hair from her face, hair that stuck to her cheek from the water, from the mud—realized she'd lost her hat some time, some time during the attack....

Aisha's whole body gave another shudder. Nearly brought her back on her knees, but she kept herself upright.

And Darkwood didn't go to her. Didn't try and help her.

As if he knew.

That thought, that he *knew* she didn't want him to touch her, hurt. Tore right through her chest.

Aisha didn't dare think on it. Dwell on it.

So, her gaze turned instead to Lanhi. Seeing the tiger, the once star of a magical circus performance lying in mud-sucking water. Her once brilliant tutu a tattered, torn, muddied mess...it was as if some clown had thrown all the frigid, icy water they had in the big tent at her face.

Aisha woke up. Fully. And the haze that kissing Nate—Darkwood —had made her feel vanished. And the haze from that day, that memory, vanished as well.

Both, completely. Gone.

"I-I'm sorry." Aisha stepped back. Then again when that wasn't enough. When part of her could still feel him.

Holding her. Touching her. Wanting her.

When she wanted to feel *him*.

"I'm sorry," she said again. "But I can't—I can't afford to feel right now."

Didn't dare.

She didn't wait for him to answer. Didn't even wait for her own answer—of what she was even going to do next. With Lanhi. With the magic that seemed to suddenly want her torn in two.

Aisha just took off. Ran.

Ran to the one place that brought her comfort. The one place that felt like the home she'd long since left behind. A home that, really, hadn't been hers to begin with.

Ran away from Lanhi, from Darkwood, from her own self.

Possibly, even her heart.

Ran until the tears came. Fell from her eyes in a long, streaming burst that wouldn't stop. Until she banged open the aviary's double doors and collapsed on the moist, humid ground of earthworms and life and freedom.

Until she finally looked up and saw she wasn't alone at all.

Timiculous perched on the top of her favorite rock and blinked at her. Darkwood's bird. Darkwood's Familiar.

That thought made her chest hurt all over again. Made her heart ache.

Even here, even in her haven, she couldn't escape the reminder of him.

Timiculous tilted his head to the side. Watched her. "Safe now. Home now."

Yes, she realized, even with Timiculous standing over her, guarding her, she still did feel safe.

Now she could, and would, cry.

Finally.

And when she stopped, she'd be strong again. Would figure out what to do about Darkwood, about herself, and more importantly, about Lanhi.

But right now, she'd just cry.

CHAPTER 30

It was a long time before Nate could move.

Before he wanted to move.

He just stared at the winding, dirt-trampled road. Those trees planted along its edges with the barest handful of leaves clinging to them, mostly brown. Their branches reaching down, as if wanted to snag Aisha as she ran.

He could still see her, in his mind. Running, those long strides, not pausing, not looking back.

Running from Lanhi.

From him.

Mud had caked on her pant legs. Her bare arms. Her shirt somehow torn but not bloodied—thank God—as she disappeared up the hill.

Nate shifted. The growing mud and water from Lanhi's enclosure lapped at his ankles. Created its own stream down the hill, in the opposite direction of Aisha.

He knew exactly where she was going.

It was the one place he wanted to go. The one place he wanted to seek comfort.

But didn't dare.

Right now, she needed it. More than him.

He owed her that.

Owed her so much more, in truth.

And he just couldn't give it to her.

Nate glanced at Lanhi. That tiger, nearly twice his length. Orange-striped fur now covered in that brown mud. Claws retracted now. Lay there, unmoving. Hadn't even shifted as she slept.

The spell had been a strong one. Stronger than he thought he was capable of, but she'd live.

At least, from the spell.

But from whatever had changed her? From what had shifted her to a feral Familiar? One who had targeted and attacked Aisha?

Nate's body shook. Shuddered.

Couldn't think. Not of his mother. Not of Aisha, just inches away from those claws. Claws that had swiped at her—had torn into her shirt, or maybe that had just been from her fall and roll to safety.

He didn't know.

Didn't dare *want* to know.

He quickly crossed the distance to the hose and its turn-off value. Stopped the water.

There. That was one task done. Didn't require much thought.

That was something he could handle.

Just like he could take care of Lanhi. Could fix up her cage.

It would be one thing Aisha wouldn't have to worry about. One thing, one small, tiny thing he could give back to her.

Nate set to finishing Aisha's work. Ignored the heaviness in his chest. The way his heart tightened and held every time he saw Lanhi. Every time his mind supplied the image that wasn't there, that wasn't real.

At least, not anymore.

But the image came again. And again. The one he'd blocked. At ten years old, when he heard the crush. The scream—both his mother's and the tiger's.

Sharp and deadly.

Fearful.

How he'd crept into his father's study, even though he wasn't allowed, even though he knew he'd be punished, he'd gone in anyway. His new wand, gotten just days early, held out.

Saw his mother lying beside Apollo. The white-striped tiger in his father's great study.

The darkening, soaking carpet. Carpet that squished and sucked at his bare feet as he crept towards her, and the tiger.

The same way the mud now sucked at his boots. Turned them black—but not red.

A boy who'd left small footprints where he stepped.

Footprints in red.

Apollo had loved his mother. More than his father, even.

Yet, there they were. Both unmoving. Both dead.

From all his research, all his years of studying, working with Familiars, trying to understand, to learn...the incident with his mother had been the first.

And even now, he was still trying to figure out why.

Why there.

Why *that* Familiar.

And why now, with all of them.

He knew there was some piece he was missing. Something...something he had a feeling, was tied to Aisha.

Nate wiped the sweat dotted his forehead. Dripping down his nose. Stinging into his eyes.

The stinging that was absolutely sweat.

Not tears.

He'd finished with those a long time ago. Ever since he was that boy and had learned, at his father's hand, that crying could do nothing to bring back those we lost.

Or to understand what happened to those we lost.

Even if, now, was suddenly the last time he could see. Clearly see through the smoke. Mostly, anyway.

Nate lifted his wand, ground his feelings, his pain away until they were into a small, tight ball that he kept tucked away—deep in his gut, deep where not even Aisha could reach.

Then, he set to work.

Reinforced every inch of that cage with the strongest spells he knew. Knitted together the fencing Lanhi had so easily sliced away—a circus-escape magic, he equally assessed, and then counter-measured this magic on each strip of that metal fence.

Then, finally, he levitated the tiger back onto the top of her small house. That square box of metal that had bowed in the middle from her weight.

Lanhi still didn't stir. Her breath didn't even ruffle the curls of her pink tutu hanging beside that house. A tutu whose magic appeared even more dim.

More faded.

If Nate had Timiculous with him, he'd have a better sense, a better knowing of what had happened to Lanhi. The change in her temperament. The change in her whole being.

He was equally glad Timiculous wasn't here.

Aisha, being on the ground, was enough of a reminder.

He didn't need Timiculous there as well. The Familiar he'd searched for, spent days, months wooing, coaxing, to help him.

To understand what had happened to his mother.

To make sure it never happens again, and prevent it from *ever* happening again. He would stop his father. The Council. He would reveal the truth about Familiars, about the wasting sickness, about the years of cover-up as the most treasured Familiars turned on their witches and wizards.

Nate finished off the spells. Carried the hose that had created the mud pit in Lanhi's cage back outside, then reinforced the lock—first with a double lock, then a triple.

He doubted Lanhi could react the same way. Could draw on her magic again.

She felt weaker to him, but it was a risk he couldn't dare take.

When he was finished, staring up at the cage now glowing with its own light, Nate couldn't help but wonder if the darkness surrounding the enclosure felt a lit bit weaker. And then, he worried if that was the just the darkness he carried within him.

The darkness that would never let him go.

Especially, especially once Aisha realized the true reason Nate had come to her Waystation.

And who had sent him.

A hawk screamed in the distance. Shrill. High-pitched. Carried down, down from the heated air currents.

Nate buried his hands in his pockets. Turned in his muddied boots and pants, and trudged out the valley of this small Waystation.

A Waystation he'd once thought of as a refuge. A safe haven for Familiars and whatever troubled them.

Now, he knew, that wasn't true.

Whatever troubles his world had created, they had finally found their way to the Waystation. And regardless of what he wanted, the Waystation would be the next casualty to fall.

His father, the Council, would see to it.

The minute they learned of Lanhi. Of her turning feral.

The Magical Waystation for Unwanted Familiars would be closed.

And it'd be on him. All on him.

Unless he stopped them.

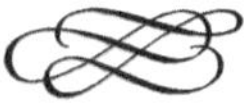

CHAPTER 31

Sylvester stood in his study. Hands clasped behind his back. Tightened.

He'd felt her. Felt the moment the memory spell had strained. As bits and fragments, somehow, had managed to seep through.

To return to her.

The deep red of his robe, the carefully crafted and spelled silk barely made a sound. Silence as he moved. Silence that he had used often to come upon other members of the Council.

A spell he'd used...judiciously in his former life. Former occupation.

But now, it was a spell he used to listen as those fools planned. Listened, without them ever being the wiser.

Sylvester reached for the balcony door.

He curled his fingers. Twisted his wrist, just once.

The spell sparked outwards. Red and gold, with his signature crest burning bright in the center—a white tiger—before it sank into the lock.

The door swung open.

The slowly setting sun on the horizon burst into his darkened study. Made him squint his eyes as he glared at the sinking sun, behind that perfect view of the clear and still, but always moving ocean. Just as there was always that spattering of Normals' rickety boats and ships obstructing his view.

Ruining the pristine beauty.

At least up here, other than those ships, he could pretend. There was no else, but him. A place where only he, mattered. Here, up above, where no other wizard or witch or Normal could see. He could watch.

Plan.

Artemis slowly appeared. Her great red and brown wings beating hard against the wind, then soaring, soaring as she dipped from one air current to the next. Circling, ever closer.

He'd felt her touch. Felt her warning. She was coming.

And with a message.

He thought of calling on Asher, but decided against it. Sylvester had had enough of that fool lord. His demands from earlier that day, the shrieking complaints and warnings that Sylvester should immediately send that Waystation a shut-down notice authorized by the Council. Simply because Racine hadn't yet discovered the solution to the wasting sickness.

And every day the truth eluded Asher, the more real his own threat intensified.

Sylvester was tempted to simply shut down Paradise Grove and be done with the man.

Except, many of the Council's highest clients and members had Familiars...who stayed there.

So he did not send out the notice.

Neither to Paradise Grove or that Waystation.

Instead, he breathed in the cool, breezy evening wind off the waters. Searched for a calm he barely felt, but needed to feel. Too much was at stake. Too much could so easily come undone by one woman.

But there *was* a fail-safe in place. Even if she managed to fully break the spell, she wouldn't live.

Sylvester's hold, and therefore the High Council's hold, over the Familiars, over that Serengeti Magical Proper, would remain.

Would stay strong.

He heard, again, like always, that shrill, high-pitched whirling of planes landing, rising. A noise that never ceased. Day. Night. Even during the witching hours when it was only him and the ticking cloak behind him.

Wished, again, that he could reach out with his magic and send each of those offending beasts constructed by Normals into that pristine ocean. Just as he now wished he'd done with that girl years ago.

But Sylvester just stood there. Waiting.

Artemis touched his mind again, close enough to deliver the message even though she hadn't yet arrived.

He refused.

Finally, she settled on the balcony's curved, black iron rails. Her great wings beating as she landed. Gained her balanced. Stirred both hot and cool air that fluttered his robes, hair.

She gazed at him with those eyes just as sharp and intelligent and unforgiving as his.

"You have a report?"

She lowered her head.

A nod, then. Good.

"And?" he pressed.

"You were right to send me. It has begun. The Familiar tiger has turned."

Sylvester's hands, still together behind his back, clenched. It was the only outward sign he'd allow. And only in front of a Familiar. One he, completely, without question, controlled.

"Was anyone killed?"

"Your son saved the woman."

Damn. Sylvester's jaw tightened. "Timiculous? Was he with Nathanial?"

A turn of the head.

No, then. Good. Very good.

"It seems secrecy is still on our side, then. But not on theirs. Hold, Artemis. I have another task. One that must be completed tonight."

And without delay.

Asher would indeed get his wish. But only because necessity demanded it.

Sylvester reached into the folds of his robes. Only the blowing wind, the distant gulls, and those screeching airplanes made sounds.

He took out the notice. Sealed by with his own seal, a white tiger. Paw extended. Claws out. Slashing. Cutting. Destroying.

"You will deliver this to Aisha Faye. She must sign for it. Do you understand?"

Artemis bent her head to get a clearer look at the seal, at the tiger and the demands of the delivery spell.

If it was possible, her predator's eyes widened, just slightly.

"Is there a problem?"

Artemis shook her head once.

"Very good, then. Keep yourself hidden from my son as you do this. He mustn't know of your presence."

Must not ever know just how close he was to learning the whole truth, to unraveling the secret of the Familiars, of Trishia, and what would happen, again.

And soon.

Everything Sylvester had built, worked for, depended on this.

Artemis accepted the message and took off. Sylvester slammed the balcony door shut and immediately snapped the heavy, dark curtains closed. Snipped off the last bit of the light.

Encased himself in darkness and memories.

No. His son must not ever learn the truth.

Neither could the magical community, nor how their closest companions, their servants, were so close to revolting and breaking free, and Sylvester's role in keeping them chained.

For all time.

CHAPTER 32

"What the hell happened?"

Marcelle's voice boomed out from Aisha's dining/office table. Sharp and piercing and really pissed off. Carried right through the stacks of papers, bills, unwanted memos by concerned magical citizens regarding the health and care of Aisha's Familiars.

Aisha, who'd just barely put up her aching feet on the table and stretched out.

Aisha, who suddenly, barely had enough time to steady herself and her hand.

A hand that held—a very full, very cheap—glass of red wine.

Marcelle's parchment message stirred to free itself from the debris. Shook itself off. Unfurled.

Even managed to toss off the pink notice Aisha had received from the Council.

A notice, which she had received by messenger hawk and had required her signed signature in blood to receive it.

A notice declaring that she reveal any untoward goings-on among her Familiars or immediately desist all activities in her unaccountable and unorthodox Waystation.

It had been wonderful. Really.

Just the thing she wanted after her day of long-ass, hard work. Sizzling kiss with Darkwood. And, oh yes, being attacked and nearly maimed by one of her Familiars.

Aisha tipped back the glass. Felt the sour unripenedness of the wine hit the back of her throat.

Swallowed.

Then, took another long swig.

Marcelle, Aisha's pink-haired psychic and friend, glared at her with all her pint-sized, pink-haired glory. Eyes that narrowed, then sparked, when she saw the full glass of wine.

"What the hell happened to you?"

"Relax. It's not the good stuff. Just Normal boxed wine."

"I don't care *what* kind of wine it is…okay, I do care because the really good stuff means really big trouble—wait a minute. We drank your good stuff last month. You *don't* have any good stuff left and we both know you can't afford more."

Aisha shrugged.

Which sent a glory of agony through her shoulders. Zipped right down to her back from where she'd landed, a bit too hard, during her roll free of Lanhi.

"You're hurt."

Aisha shifted her shoulders. But no matter how she stretched or pulled, the ache didn't lessen. "Not as badly as I could have been."

"Talk. I'm getting every vibe known to man, and even some that man didn't quantify, coming off you. Sexual ones too. I'm serious, Aisha. *What happened?*"

Sexual?

Aisha tipped back her wine glass. Finished it off. Then got herself another good, long pour from the box.

She'd invite Marcelle over, but in person the little witch was even more feisty and right now, all Aisha wanted was a few moments of bliss and quiet where nothing at all mattered except the silence slipping in from her open window and the desert she lived in.

And her own demons that wouldn't leave her alone.

"Aisha!"

"Fine. Fine." There was nothing for it. So, she told Marcelle what had happened since she'd taken her psychic retreat.

Everything.

Or. Mostly everything.

She left out the kiss. And the past.

Which was silly, really. Especially considering, hello, her friend being a psychic.

But Marcelle, thankfully, didn't call Aisha out on those missing tidbits. And, in fact, she didn't interrupt much at all—which was quite unlike her.

Instead, she simply sat there. Hands tucked under her chin. Bent forward. Intent, listening.

Listening to both what Aisha was saying, and what her aura was saying.

You know, that stuff that Aisha was conveniently leaving out.

Like how she'd wanted to kiss Darkwood right back.

"I don't like it," Marcelle finally said.

Aisha managed to keep from laughing. "And why do you think I'm drinking the wine? Not to mention the Council—they sent me a notice, Marcelle. How? How could they know? We haven't told anyone—"

"Except Asher."

"Yeah, but…"

"But what? You know damn well he'd turn on you and on the Waystation in a heartbeat. Especially after your fallout. Especially since you have no value to *him*, being disowned by your parents and all."

Thoughts of Aisha's parents made her stomach turn sour. The red wine not looking so good.

She put it on top of that stupid Council notice. Hoped the stupid thing got spilled on, too.

"But listen." Marcelle unfurled her hands. Placed them on the table in front of her like she needed to hold on. Brace herself. "I said I don't like it, because I haven't been resting exactly."

"You mean like you promised?"

"I just happened to make a few calls. Easy enough to do while you're at home."

"Psychic calls?"

Marcelle fidgeted with her hair. Pulled one of those pink curls out, before it sprang back into place. "Well, how else do you expect not to have your conversation tracked? Or monitored? Look. Stop already and just listen, okay. Something big is going on and those big Sanctuaries are doing their damnedest to keep it a secret."

"From people like me, you mean."

"But not from the Council. They know, Aisha. They'd even sent their shrink-reps to investigate."

Aisha's breath caught. Even though it was still just her, Marcelle's parchment, and the cooling desert air, it suddenly felt like she wasn't alone. That the room was closing in.

Too close.

Not enough room to breathe. To move.

Aisha got to her feet.

Left the wine.

"Tell me," she said. "Tell me everything."

So, Marcelle did. She'd made a few calls—she knew quite a few of the psychics on staff at the Sanctuaries, including Paradise Grove. It took work, even a bit of coercion, but she got them talking.

The same dark netting, that same cloud of magic-sucking energy that fed off the Familiars, and really didn't like psychic, was above their Sanctuaries too. But just recently. And it had grown. Fast.

No amount of attacking or pulling it apart had worked. Had even sent two psychics to the hospital for a magical transplant, they were so bone-dry of magic. And the Council's reps hadn't learned anything either. Hadn't been able to slow the thing down as it slowly constricted. Came closer.

As she talked, Marcelle's face paled.

Aisha expected that Marcelle was reliving that day, what had nearly happened to her, every moment. Waking. Sleeping. Didn't matter because the memory, the feelings, wouldn't let her go.

"You said the guy helping, a Nathanial Darkwood?"

Aisha nodded. "That's right."

"Why does he sound familiar?"

"I don't know." She didn't add he'd sounded familiar to her as well, when she'd first met him. Somewhere along the way, between his following her, his presence, his just being there...she'd forgotten all about it.

"I know I've heard his name." Marcelle pondered. Gave her hair another pull.

"I'm not so worried about him right now." Couldn't afford to be. Attraction. Desire. Or whatever. There was much more at stake. "I don't like that the Council knows about our problems. Enough to send me a certified warning."

Marcelle snapped her fingers. "That's it! I nearly forgot. My source said Paradise Grove had one guy show up, not long enough for anyone to know a whole bunch—I'll do some more digging on that. But listen. They sent another."

Aisha didn't like the sound of that. Didn't like that somehow, without her being a psychic herself, she knew exactly who the Council had sent.

"Racine." The word all but strangled in her throat.

"I'm sorry, Aisha."

Aisha closed her eyes. She shouldn't be surprised. Should have known. Should have expected this. Lord Asher must be thrilled. Must be doing a little Irish jig of his own. He'd finally gotten the Faye contact he'd desired.

Finally had it, and it was right on his doorstep.

Racine was just that good at her job. They wouldn't have sent anyone else. Especially when Racine came so highly recommended. Especially when Racine had been trained by her parents. Trained side-by-side with Aisha.

Even if she had been ten years younger.

She was that good.

"You going to contact her?" Marcelle squeaked.

"No."

Aisha turned her back. Crossed her arms and stared out through her dark, nearly black window. Only the tiniest pinpricks of light—stars—shone out there. A world so far from removed, but apparently, not far enough.

"I have nothing to say to my sister."

CHAPTER 33

*Y*ou look like shit."

Hilda slid onto the wobbling barstool next to Nate. All long, naked limbs with that slip of a fishnet dress covering some of the essentials. She knocked his leg aside with hers so she could shimmy in—then reached right over and downed his half-finished beer.

She wiped her mouth with Nate's napkin. Nodded to Chaz for another. "And you're drinking. Actually drinking. You plan on telling me what's up?"

"No."

Nate reached over, grabbed that foamy, gold-fizzling mug just as Chaz slid it towards Hilda—a mug complete with its usual smudges and dirt residue—and downed a good long chug of it.

Hilda quirked her eyebrows up.

He ignored her. Ignored Chaz, too, when he crossed his double-sized muscle arms across his chest and stared at Nate.

"I plan on drinking," Nate said. "Alone."

"Problems with the job?"

"Do you not understand the alone part?"

Hilda leaned closer. Her usual pulling, enticing scents made him want to reel back. Pull away. Puke.

But that could just be the beer his stomach was clearly not agreeing with. Also that loud noises in the Cauldron. It was, after all, bikini and pool night. All contestants were required to wear bikinis—which meant males, females, karaoke-singing Selkies.

"Nate. You're drinking. In a bar. On bikini night."

"That thought did cross my mind."

He glanced at one quite endowed troll—a male troll in some hot-pink-and-orange fishnet number—and took another long chug of his beer. Hard to believe the troll was ahead—in points and in popularity.

"My point," Hilda said, "is this is my bar. One I frequent. So if this isn't a call for help and company—well, think better about your brooding spot next time. This time, this time you're spilling."

His hand tightened on the mug. The chill from its glass slipping into him, making him shiver, or maybe, it was something else entirely.

The howls and yips as another contestant either made the shot—or bounced it straight off the pool table—seemed...muted.

Probably from the beer. Or Hilda's magic.

She was always good about getting what she wanted.

Nate ran a hand over his forehead. Felt some dirt there that he hadn't bothered to clean from this morning. With Aisha. With Lanhi.

"Definitely problems." He wiped his hand on his pants—which were equally as dirty. "With the job."

"And your dad?"

Nate snorted. "There's always problems with my father."

This time, though, those problems went further, further back. Back to the day his mother was killed. So much so that as soon as he'd left the Waystation, left the slumbering Lanhi in her newer, more protective cage, he'd gone to his father's. Practically tore apart the old archive room and library—the one for storage and useless books, not his father's priceless collection. He'd used every spell and command he could think of. Made up some new ones as well. And when that didn't turn up any answers, went digging by hand for any newspaper articles, letters—

Searched for any hint, any clue from that time.

And found nothing.

Barely even a mention of his mother's death.

Of the *how*.

Nate took another slow drink. The burning, amber-gold liquid glided down his throat. "Maybe I did come here for help."

"I'm listening."

Hilda was always good at listening—just not good at giving him space. But, more than that, he realized, she was always good with *Familiars*. She'd worked with them. Studied them. Had even worked off the Council's radar for *years* until one day, some complaint came in about an unregistered Familiar escaping from her back rooms. Suddenly charging a recently bonded Familiar while they'd waited in the lobby....

He immediately set the beer down.

Why hadn't he thought it before? Why hadn't the incident occurred to him?

He passed the beer to Hilda.

Again, those perfectly plucked eyebrows rose.

"You've worked with all kinds of Familiars," he said. "Treated them."

"You know that for yourself. Both the wanted, and unwanted, kinds. So?"

"Have you treated any...that went bad? Familiars who'd changed all of a sudden?"

Hilda stilled. The mug stilled a bare breath from her lips. Watched him. Studied him with those intelligent, sharp eyes—and not an ounce of flirting in them.

This was the veterinarian now. Not that leader of a witch's gang, but the woman he'd once wanted to marry.

"Why?" she asked.

Nate closed his eyes for a half moment. Remembered Aisha in that cage. Lanhi, springing towards her. Feral eyes. Intent eyes.

On killing.

"Because I think it's happening. Again."

Hilda set the mug down. Rose. Didn't even bother smoothing out her fishnet dress like she usually did. "I'm not allowed to have this conversation."

She turned to leave.

Nate grabbed her wrist. Not hard. Not gentle either.

Determined.

Hilda didn't move.

Neither, he felt, did the rest of the bar. As if they were all, suddenly, watching. But Nate ignored them. Ignored everyone but Hilda.

"You know something."

She licked her lips.

"That was the price, wasn't it? The one the Council wanted for allowing you to stay in practice. You continue to treat any Familiar you wanted, you just need to keep your mouth shut."

Hilda said nothing.

"You were paid off. You. Of all people."

Her wrist felt slick.

Sweat, Nate realized, his.

He let her go. Stood.

Threw some money on that blood-stained and burned bar counter. "I thought you were above all that, and all this while...." Hair dangled across his forehead. He shoved it away.

Fingers, he noticed, shaking.

"All this while, with you hounding me for not standing up to my father, you'd been paid for your silence. Fine, then. I won't ask you to break it. You've got your practice, you've got your little gang."

He saw the other witches, silent and watching the exchange between him and their boss—but kept their distance. After all, Hilda hadn't called for backup.

And he knew she wouldn't, either.

Not when she was the one in the wrong.

Not when he finally learned—saw—the truth.

"You've got everything you wanted, Hilda. So you enjoy it. Enjoy every minute of it—and while you do, just know that I've got Familiars dying by the dozens. Changing and turning feral. Almost watched someone I cared about die today."

Hilda still didn't move. It was as if someone had turned her to stone. But her eyes were wider. The lines and shadows around them, deeper.

Nate sucked in a large, deep breath. Exhaled. "Again. I almost watched someone die again."

Someone he did care about. Deeply.

Even if he, his very presence in her Waystation, was a lie.

But he cared.

And he would find out the truth.

"Did you know this started with my mother?" Nate pushed the barstool in, like a gentleman leaving his coveted place at a restaurant booth—the kind of simple thing, of manners, his mother had insisted he learn. "That's all I know, really, because everything else, they buried. Even tried to bury my memories, but hey, you might have known that too. Is that why you wouldn't let me be? Why you couldn't give me the space to recollect them? Because my father warned you?"

She flinched.

Nate then stepped away from Hilda. From the woman he once loved.

Once thought he'd marry.

She still just stood there, with her siren's scents smacking into his hard, cold barrier. As if she'd turned up the juice to help him forget this conversation—as if his anger could be lulled away from it.

Not this time.

He waved his hand. Pushed the scents away.

"You've done that before. Used that little trick on me. I'd get your money back on that one. And while you do, you can go back to my father and tell him it didn't work. I will find out what's happening and I will let everyone—*everyone*—know the truth."

About the Familiars.

About the darkness.

About his mother.

Nate stuffed his hands into his pockets—pockets still stained with mud and dirt from the Waystation, just like the rest of him—and weaved his way through the crowd of fluttering pixies and trolls and suddenly shy-looking werewolves—half of who were in their most loud and revealing bikinis.

Everyone now knew who he was. An agent of the Council.

Who is his father was.

But that didn't seem to faze them.

It was him standing up to Hilda. Calling her out. And then not running from her.

He was done running.

Done.

"Nate!" Hilda called out.

Once.

He didn't stop. But he did keep listening.

Couldn't help himself.

"I didn't get everything I wanted. I didn't get you."

The Cauldron's swinging door closed behind him. Cutting her off. Cutting off the silence. And even though Nate found himself standing outside, alone, with those sparkling lights and the shimmering Los Angeles skyline in the distance—always lit, never dark—he didn't feel alone.

Even without Timiculous on his shoulder, for the first time in his life since his mother died, Nate didn't feel alone.

Because finally, finally it was all beginning to make sense. Even if he could remember only bits of that night with his mother and Apollo, that didn't matter.

What mattered was right now.

Helping Aisha save her Familiars—before word got back to her of who he was.

And who he worked for.

CHAPTER 34

*A*isha planted her feet on the worn dirt path of her aviary. Slapped her hands to her hips. Breathed in the moist, warming air. Another day. Another day with the sun barely peeking its way through the netting that enclosed her favorite place.

Already the day was heating up—and fast. She'd be sweating within minutes, even this early.

But this early at least meant privacy.

Darkwood hadn't arrived yet and that was what she needed.

Didn't dare allow herself to think why, just that she needed to do this, be here, without him.

She needed a good long talk with his Familiar.

Needed it and needed it now—before the Council sent a full team in to neutralize and destroy her Familiars.

Aisha rubbed her bare arms. Hard.

They'd been waiting for this. Every since she'd opened the Waystation, managed to get the ordinance for her facility passed, those great blue- and pure-blood wizards had been trying to close her down.

A blemish on their pristine little world.

A truth they couldn't deny—that there were Familiars out there who went wrong, who were abused, who just plain weren't wanted anymore.

And they'd finally, finally get their way…and her baby sister was stuck right in the middle of all this. Happily, though, which Aisha was sure of. Her parents' had made damn sure to turn her sister against her.

"All right."

Aisha snapped her head up. Curled her hands into fists where they rested at her hips. Glared out into that forest of living trees and brightly colored feathers and giant-sized beaks—each bird seeming to call out in morning's greeting to her.

Or, really, just looking for food.

"You told me this here's a safe place. All right, Timiculous. Time to own up to your side of the bargain. Time to tell me why."

He didn't wait for her to say more. Just made his way down from the netting itself—right above her head. Large, black beak acting like a hand as he climbed down, using beak and claws, his blue and gold feathers gleaming from the sun's early light.

He hung upside down beside her. Head and body arched towards her.

Shaking. Back and forth.

"Good morning!"

As if…he'd been expecting her.

Then, he purposefully glanced at her hands—expecting food.

Aisha crossed her arms. "No breakfast, mister, not until I get some answers here."

"Already have answers. Have food too."

The little sneak—how in the world did he know her pockets were bulging to the seams with walnuts?

"I said no food." She held up a finger. "Answers first. Deal?"

He just kept swaying back and forth—so Aisha took that as a yes.

"Do you know what's happening to my Waystation? Do you know what is causing the sickness?"

"No."

Aisha swallowed. Hard. "You sure seem to know a lot. How?"

"Nate."

"Nate. He knows?" Her words came out fast. Clipped. Angry.

"No. Not know. Remembers."

Aisha closed her eyes. Counted to five. Familiars were never easy to deal with. She *knew* this. She'd been living with them, helping them for years.

She needed to stop thinking like a human and start thinking like a Familiar.

Or more to the point, an animal with quite a bit of magic.

Timiculous was telling her the truth.

Her gut swirled with its magical nod.

Okay, then. Timiculous didn't know, but he said that Nate knew—no, he didn't. He said Nate *remembered*.

"This has happened to Nate before?" she asked.

Timiculous bobbed his head. Up. Down.

"And you can feel that? From the bond with him?"

Up. Down, again.

She wanted to stomp her feet. Throw her hands up into the air. Scream.

To think the answer could be so simple, so right in front of her—and she couldn't do anything about it.

She had no doubt, if Nate knew anything that could help, so all this made sense, made the wasting sickness disappear...he'd tell her.

She trusted him to tell her.

So it was a memory, then.

Probably not much different than Aisha's—her blocked memories. The ones she couldn't access.

She couldn't blame him for that either, regardless what had happened in his past. Oh, she could get mad—and she was plenty mad, *and* frustrated—but not at him.

Not for something he couldn't control.

Aisha swerved on her boots. Paced up and down that small little path. Vines and plants had grown outwards. Uncontrolled. Untrimmed. They swayed around her ankles as she walked. Some clung to her khaki pants. Others simply parted, easily and without effort. Just slapped her pants with their wide, moist leaves.

She hadn't a chance to get in here and tidy the place up. Trim back the undergrowth. Too much to do. Even on a good day. Even before the sickness had struck Lanhi.

Aisha kicked a rock that had tumbled free from her little strand of forest and wild.

Then, froze.

The magic in her gut, doing a slow, slow turning. That emptiness she'd always felt, ever since that day with Blakeley, ever since the nightmares started…she felt a tug.

A knowing.

It was all just within reach. She just had to trust. To try.

"You said something before, that this was your place. Your home." She turned to Timiculous—who still hung upside down.

And still swayed back and forth.

"Treat?" he whistled.

A deal was a deal.

She kept her breath even. The excitement, she hoped, tamped down.

Aisha fished out a walnut piece, which he gently took from her fingers, and carefully shredded the outside skin of the walnut until he got to the yummy-good insides.

"You said the dark magic couldn't touch you because this was your home…." She shook her head. "Forget that last." She was thinking too much like a witch. "How is this your home? How is this—"

She waved her hands at the aviary. "Your home? *Their* home?"

Aisha held up a treat, but didn't offer it to him.

Just waited.

Timiculous blinked at her. Those large, white eyes as his pupils contracted to black, so black they seemed to fill up his whole eye.

Seemed to measure her. Study her.

What she wouldn't give to have Nate here. Telling her what he was thinking.

And with that single thought of him, even with her earlier anger, frustration, she felt the hot press of his lips against hers.

The warmth and flames she hadn't allowed herself to feel in years.

Aisha shoved it aside. Focused.

On Timiculous. On helping her Familiars.

"Please, Timiculous. I don't understand. I need your help. Please."

He reached out for the walnut piece, paused an inch away from her. So close she could almost feel the brush of his beak against her skin.

"The wild," he said. "Africa lady brought wild back. Gave home back. Home in here."

Timiculous flapped his wings—a little lopsided since he was upside down. The nearest widened palm leaves blew upward at the sudden and different direction of wind.

"But not out there," he said. "No right home out there. Still much theirs. Bring back home, Africa lady. Make darkness go away."

He reached out, grabbed the walnut—again with just a feather-gentle touch—and climbed right back up the netting.

She watched him fly off.

A breath slipped from her chest—one she hadn't realized she'd been holding. Okay, then. That was an answer. More of an answer that she'd gotten before.

And this time, finally, it was making sense.

Aisha took a long, slow turn where she stood. The overarching, blending trees. Branches and leaves crisscrossing. Like a forest. That humidity, that moist hot air that literally breathed *rainforest*.

And the sounds.

Her birds calling and chatting and tweeting.

But not her. Not the witch.

To each other.

And with threat of the Council, of her sister, hugging onto her shoulders. Weighing her down. Threatening to pull her under those dark feelings, to bring back those sleeping memories....

Aisha couldn't help but feel that blowing hot air as she'd run across the African plains. Feet bare and sore, but growing hard with each step. Calluses forming. The joy that had filled her senses.

So completely. So fulfilled.

She finally, *finally*, began to understand what was missing. In her Waystation, with her Familiars. But what was more, she needed to understand.

About the sickness. About Lanhi.

But she knew, her magic burning hot and true in her gut, that this sickness was created.

They—witches and wizards—had created it. And had somehow had hidden it. Kept the truth buried so deep, none could see.

The Council.

Nate had told her they'd buried the truth about Familiar Sensitives; who's to say they hadn't buried the truth about this? They might not be *behind* the sickness but that didn't mean they didn't know about it.

After all, they'd sent her sister to Paradise Grove to investigate.

Right after they'd sent someone else, and then changed his assignment.

Aisha shook her head. Pushed aside her braid.

She needed to focus.

Focus on why Timiculous thought her Waystation was safe.

Aisha weaved her fingers through her long, dark hair. Braided one strand, then another. Thinking, and fingers moving, as she paced.

But Lanhi hadn't contracted it first.

But she *had* been the one to change. The one to turn feral.

Aisha's now half-braided hair slipped from her fingers.

Lanhi was the key.

Aisha had no choice. Not if she wanted to stop the sickness. Not if she wanted answers.

She was going back into Lanhi's enclosure. And she was doing it, today. Before Darkwood got here.

Before he could stop her.

CHAPTER 35

*A*isha stood just out of striking reach from Lanhi's cage. In fact, behind that line she'd drawn in the dirt for Darkwood—how many days ago was that? Yesterday? A lifetime?

It all felt the same.

But the cage didn't.

It now vibrated and glowed with such a strong magic. One of the strongest spells she'd ever felt—something her budget couldn't have afforded even if she'd saved up a year's income.

The magic in her own gut swirled. Danced. Recognized Darkwood's magic, and perhaps, something more.

Finally, it settled down.

Lanhi lay on that now-dusty dirt ground. Her tattered tutu clutched in her large paws. Face pressed into the once-sparkling magic that flowed off the pink dancing dress.

Completely secure in that cage.

Completely unaware of the magic now pulsing around with the metal links. Keeping Lanhi—and everyone else—safe.

Darkwood's power.

Even now, Aisha felt him beside her. Body pressed against hers. Lips claiming hers—or hers claiming his.

She couldn't remember.

Didn't much care, either.

Instead, cared only about how her chest suddenly swelled. Suddenly hurt.

He'd done this.

For her.

Yesterday, after running into the aviary, she hadn't the heart to see Lanhi. Couldn't make her feet take her to care for the tiger…but Darkwood had. Had even left a note for her when she'd finally pulled herself together.

But she had no idea he'd done…this.

That he even knew the right spells to reinforce the caging.

As if he'd planned for it.

Was it the memory Timiculous had mentioned? Pushing Darkwood to learn these spells, just like he'd learned the spell that had taken out a fully grown, completely feral tiger?

Or was it done more consciously?

Aisha stepped over that line. Reached into the cage and gripped the metal fencing.

Lanhi still lay in the center. Unmoving. Orange-gold eyes closed.

Aisha moved to the locked and sealed cage door.

Steps slow. Quiet.

Still, Lanhi didn't move.

Didn't even twitch her ears, following Aisha's movement.

Aisha had no idea how she even knew this was something Lanhi *should* do. Only that she did. Knew it.

Knew it in her gut.

Just like she knew, this, right here, held all the answers she needed.

Aisha studied the cage—not with the eye of someone who was the owner and director of the Waystation, but as that other person…the person she might have been before her world had changed.

If her memories weren't blocked.

If she was who Timiculous claimed she was.

The Africa lady.

Her gaze took in the tutu. The sparkling sequins and limp ruffles.

The posters and elephant stands. Every little item and detail the witch Ghazille had demanded be placed in Lanhi's enclosure....

After she'd gotten backing from the Council. *After* Ghazille had wrestled controlled of Lanhi's enclosure from Aisha—and from what Aisha's gut was telling her the right thing to do.

Aisha took out her wand. Froze, just a breath from the lock.

"That's the answer."

Her voice, a bare whisper, slipped from her.

And it made sense.

All of it.

Her Waystation *had* been safe. Fine.

Except all the changes, the sickness, had started after Lanhi had arrived.

Aisha closed her eyes. Squeezed them shut until even the sun's bare lighting was dark beneath her closed lids. She thought back to that time. To when Lanhi had first been transferred to the Waystation —from Paradise Grove—to Aisha. Lanhi had felt...off.

There was nothing more Aisha's magic could identify. Even their volunteer Familiar veterinarian, Locksweep, had checked her out. Declared Lanhi to be physically fit and healthy.

But Aisha hadn't trusted the vet or what Asher had said. Again, she couldn't put her finger on why—except her magic had told her not to. And even that had been a vague warning. Just a sense, a feeling.

Still, she'd listened to her magic.

Had taken control over Lanhi's enclosure, supervising it as she saw fit. It was never easy accepting an unwanted Familiar from one of the Sanctuaries, especially when their owner was still heavily involved in their care. Aisha's Waystation was a different sort of place than the Sanctuaries. And everything she'd told Darkwood about it—and their differences—had been true. And Ghazille hadn't liked Aisha's changes.

Because Aisha had kept the enclosure simple. Down to the bare necessities, the bones of what Lanhi needed. She'd planned to slowly add in trinkets, to see what would help and what wouldn't...but then the kangaroo-hopping mouse had gotten into the cage.

And Lanhi had *played* with him.

Lanhi *had* gotten better.

Had healed.

Until Ghazille got the Council involved and won that battle of wills with Aisha. Oh, Aisha could have refused service to Ghazille, to Lanhi, but that wasn't what her Waystation was about. She didn't refuse care or a home—ever. That wasn't why she'd founded the Waystation.

Everyone needed a sanctuary, even those who weren't wanted.

But Ghazille had tossed every memento and reminder from Lanhi's circus-dancing days into her enclosure. And Lanhi had gotten sick.

Almost immediately.

Aisha opened her eyes. Now, for the first time in days, seeing clearly. She reached out. Touched her wand to the lock.

A spark flew out its tip. Unlocking the door.

Right then, she didn't care about protocols. About safety.

All that mattered was finding the truth.

The cage door creaked open.

Still, Lanhi didn't move. Didn't stir.

Just the barest rise and fall of her chest.

The sickness *had* started with Lanhi.

She was the one who'd brought the sickness, that dark, oozing net. She'd come directly from Paradise Grove when Asher claimed she wasn't working well with their environment. Asher, and the Council, who more than anything wanted to close her Waystation down.

Aisha closed the door behind her. Locked it. With her spell. One only she could undo.

In the distance, she heard a car door slam. Someone yell.

Feet padding hard, fast, down the steep-sloped dirt road into her Waystation.

She ignored the running feet. Ignored everything but the tiger in front of her. The tiger who'd come to her, looking for help, looking for a home.

She wouldn't let them close her Waystation. Wouldn't let them take away her home.

Even if she risked everything to stop them.
She would.
Starting with herself.
Starting, with right now.

CHAPTER 36

*N*ate ran.

Boots pounding down that slick, dust-dirt road. Slid as much as he ran. Stumbled once. Twice. Didn't notice. Didn't care.

Just felt that tightening in his chest.

Timiculous's words, fear, pushing him on. Faster. Harder.

"With Lanhi. Inside."

"What the hell is she doing in there?"

Nate darted past Lion's Row. Flew by the chimps—heard them calling out for him. Whistling.

Nate just kept his arms pumping. Breath heaving from his lungs.

He had to get to her.

Couldn't let it—no. It couldn't happen again.

Couldn't!

"Door locked, now. Darkness. Stronger. Hungry. Don't like. Must hurry."

Nate swore. Sort of. Didn't have much air to speak; barely enough to breathe.

He heard the fluttering of wings. Felt the connection between him and Timiculous grow. Stronger. Timiculous, nearly there. Must have left the aviary to come to Nate.

To help save Aisha.

Aisha who was now alone in that cage with Lanhi.

Just like his mother.

The image from that night crept into his vision. Fuzzy. Distorted. But the smoke was there. Like it always was. Clogging the air. Made him cough. Gasp for breath as he'd crouched lower to the ground. Hoped to stay underneath that black, smoky cloud.

Felt the squish of liquid between his bare toes. Red liquid.

Didn't care. Couldn't.

If Nate allowed himself to think, he'd freeze. He couldn't afford to freeze.

Not when Aisha needed him.

Not when his mother needed him. She was there. In the smoke.

Nate kept his new wand out. It shook. Didn't matter that he didn't actually know how to use it—but he had a wand. A weapon.

He could save his mother.

Help her.

Except as the smoke finally parted—enough to let his stinging, blurry, tearing eyes see...he saw them. Mother lying facing down. Dark hair sweeping over her bare shoulders—pieces of skin ripped open.

The image blanked there.

Became fuzzy.

Nate's stomach heaved. Churned up Chaz's foul-tasting beer from last night. Forced himself to swallow it back down.

He didn't have time to stop.

To puke.

Last time, he'd been too late.

Even though his mother must have killed Apollo, even as she lay there under that great cat's paws, her blood, the last bit of her life draining way, soaking onto the carpet he'd crept on with bare feet... but he'd been too late.

So had his father.

Nate's steps slowed. As if of their own accord.

Shock sliding through him. Holding him. Until he stopped.

A shard of a memory, settled, slowly, into place. One he'd thought lost. Forever.

Timiculous whistled at him, from somewhere, Nate wasn't sure— couldn't see other than through that smoke as his father crashed open the doors to his study. Hair splayed about him. Not perfect. Not spelled to show the great councilor he was.

The fear. The anger.

Both had blazed off him. A man who'd done his utmost to show nothing of the sort to the world, or even to his family.

Timiculous settled on Nate's shoulders. The beat of his wings against his ears. Blowing back his hair.

But still, all Nate could see was his father and that look on his face. Guilt.

A knowing.

Nate shook. All over.

Legs suddenly going week. Nate grabbed something—a bare, spindly tree—and held himself upright. Timiculous rubbed against Nate's cheek. Felt the warm, glowing comfort flow between them. That offer of strength, of support, of love.

"He knew," Nate whispered. "My father knew. Before he even saw her. Lying there, lying there in all that blood. He knew."

Nate closed his eyes, tried to force out the memory—but Timiculous rubbed at his cheek again.

"No force. Just...let go. Let come to you."

For the first time in his life, the first time since that awful night he saw his mother lying there in every clear and crisp detail. Everything. Because of this, because of what had happened, he'd given his whole purpose, his whole life into understanding, finding the answers....

Revealing the truth about his father.

But now, now Nate fully understood. Saw that the truth was right in front of him.

Always had been.

The truth was, his father had known. And had then covered it up.

Including removing all of Nate's memories of that night.

His father's voice rang out through the smoke. As if he didn't need to breathe the same suffocating, choking air has Nate had. His father had stood there, regal as always with long, dark and shining hair fallen free from its tie. As he'd called up the Council on his mirror.

"Send for a team. No. To my home. It's Apollo."

Nate stayed crouched in the smoke. Huddled there in that carpet and the soaking, sticking blood. Knew to move even an inch, to let out the swelling, burning cough would mean…would mean something.

He didn't know what.

Just knew he couldn't.

Not yet.

"Apollo has turned. Yes. You heard that correctly. Turned. And he took Trishia with him."

His father's voice had broken at that.

Strained.

Enough that only someone who'd grown up with the man, had lived every day in his shadow, in his unhappy gaze, would notice.

"I said she's dead, you fools! Send over a clean team before I have to inform my son!"

His father yanked away from the sight. His wife and the tiger. Lying there, peaceful and calm. Except for the blood. Except they were both dead.

His father's last words came to Nate. Seemed to bob and float in that smoke. Even as Nate's throat burned. Tears not stopping. From his stinging, red eyes.

Maybe.

"This mustn't get out. Not ever. No one beyond the Council must know we've had our first Familiar fully turn."

Which was when his father turned, and saw Nate. Crouched there. Hiding in the smoke and shadow. His own father, whose cold, gray eyes narrowed. Unfeeling. Uncaring. But determined.

He held out his hand towards Nate. Reached for him.

Then, cast the spell.

There was a scream.

Tore right through the air.

Timiculous pumped his wings. Smacked Nate in the side of the head.

Took him a moment to realize it wasn't his memory. Not where the scream came from.

But here.

The now.

In the Waystation.

"Aisha!"

He shoved off from the tree. Felt that same desperation. That same echo.

His mother screaming. Him, being too late.

Not this time.

CHAPTER 37

$\mathcal{A}$isha stood in front of a fully awake Lanhi.

Those claws as they extracted from her paws. Those gleaming orange-gold eyes. They'd snapped open. Gone black for a moment. Any intelligence, any understanding or remembrance of who Aisha was, faded.

As if it'd never been.

Aisha kept her feet apart. Balanced.

Ready to move.

To act.

A single bead of sweat trickled down Aisha's cheek. Dripped off her chin. Tickled, where it passed.

She didn't dare move.

Wand, still out, but it wasn't the wand Aisha thought of. Wasn't the wand she thought of as her first tool, as her first line of defense.

It was the spark of a memory.

A memory her body, her muscles, had kept, without her being the wiser. Even after all these years. Even when she couldn't remember anything except the African heat, burning heat, and equally burning sand against her feet.

Lanhi slowly curled up. Rose upwards on all fours.

Her massive body of stripes and orange. Stretching. Pulling. One long, giant muscle. One long giant body with one intent in mind.

Predator.

That was what Lanhi was. What every tiger like her, even if dressed in tutus or pink outfits.

Each was a predator.

If Aisha dared close her eyes—which she didn't—she could almost see, almost imagine the dripping black oozing down from above. Felt, right here, right around Lanhi, the netting grow closer.

Hungrier.

Knew in her gut that even if she'd moved Lanhi to another enclosure, it wouldn't have made a difference.

The netting, the spell, whatever it was would just follow Lanhi. Just as it had followed her into the Waystation. Just as it had then infected her other Familiars—starting with the ones nearest her.

Lanhi didn't take her gaze off Aisha. All her intention, focus, desire, speared at Aisha.

It took all of Aisha's willpower not to back up.

Not to run or flee.

Instead, Aisha forced her body to relax. To un-tense. To prepare.

In the distant background, that part of her mind that still registered things outside this cage, outside that feral gaze, heard running. Pounding of feet against the dusty dirt. Desperately rushing towards her.

Knew, in her heart, it was Darkwood.

Coming for her.

Again.

She didn't know him at all. But she trusted him then, just as before.

He wouldn't let Lanhi escape. And whatever happened here, happened now, he would see this finished. All the way to the Council, if need be.

And what was more important was, she trusted herself too. Trusted in herself. In her magic, even if it wasn't whole, even if she knew a piece of herself was missing. Still, she trusted in that piece of herself she hadn't remembered, hadn't believed in since that day with Blakeley.

When she'd stood up to him. To her parents. Blakeley, who was everything that their world represented. That little box her parents had wanted to stuff her into, the same one they'd shoved Racine into.

Aisha lowered her wand. Tucked it back into her pants.

Turned her attention, away from the past, from Darkwood, and focused only on Lanhi.

Lanhi, who now crouched. Lower.

Head nearly pressed against the ground

A tiger ready to spring. To attack.

That was when Aisha realized it.

When the pieces finally began clicking into place. As if her lost memories were slowly appearing—even if it was only the shadowy outlines of a few.

But it was enough.

Enough to see what—and who—was standing before her.

Aisha *was* staring at a Familiar.

But a tiger too.

Lanhi had never, ever stopped being a tiger.

Aisha felt her body, her self, fade away to something more primitive, something that hummed with her soul.

The place where her people had come from. The place she'd gone to reconnect, to understand, even at her parents' direct disapproval and orders. She'd done it anyway.

And Blakeley had come to reclaim her.

As was his right. As he believed.

Her magic swirled within her gut. Felt, a little more solid. It arched up. Reaching for her heart. Wanting to become one with her, fully, completely.

She didn't ignore it. Simply moved. Simply followed.

Aisha slowly breathed.

In. Out.

And so, came the memory.

As it did, a scream tore out her throat.

CHAPTER 38

isha stood just outside the females' camp. Couldn't quite leave the comforting, spindly shade of acacia tree, even though its sharp, spiked branches had sliced through her skin just this morning.

Still, she couldn't make herself move. Couldn't take herself away from the guttural clicks and murmuring chants slipping from the camp.

Sounds of home.

They surrounded her. Made her heart beat, hard.

Then harder.

Could barely breathe as she watched Daniel Blakeley, the dashing, slick, graceful High Lord's son of Tanzania slide off his pegasus. The flying horse's snow-white fur and long, arching wings had already turned a pinkish red from that unforgiving, harsh sun.

The same went for Blakeley.

Aisha had learned that, out here in the bush, it as if like no spell was strong enough, good enough, to protect against another kind of magic here.

A wild magic.

A deeper magic.

Ancient, even.

As if the very sun, the land, was alive with it. As if it revolted against the kind of magic Blakeley and the whole of magical society brought with them. Wielded like it was a mere trinket and right they claimed simply by existing.

Sweat clung, stained, and ruined Blakeley's silk robes. And the second his boot touched the harsh, crackling dry grass—the nearby thorn bushes pulled at him.

Scratched right through that beautiful silk.

He cursed.

Then wiped that sweat from his forehead and just glared at her.

Glared, as if he hated everything about her.

"Enough of this game, Aisha! It's time to go home."

"This isn't a game."

How could it be? How could discovering who she was, where she and her family came from, be a game? How could they hope to provide a haven for Familiars if they didn't first understand where such animals came from?

Not that her parents actually cared. Especially her mother, of all people. Her mother, who'd been raised a Hadzabe and who, instead, turned her back on her people.

"Playing primitive? I'd call that a childish, immature game." He spat onto the parched ground. Precious water he shouldn't have dared waste. "Especially for someone of your status. Do you have any idea the embarrassment your disappearance has caused? The speculation? Enough of this. Before you cause any more damage to your family and to mine."

Blakeley made a fast, jerking, shooing motion with his hand. As if she should just hurry along so he wouldn't miss afternoon tea.

The truth rammed into Aisha.

Of Blakeley.

Of his so-called "love."

Of why, exactly, he was here.

Come to fetch her, the heir of one of the most prestigious families in Africa, to save her from the embarrassment of running off with a tribe of people barely classified as "human."

At least in the great and powerful minds of those who ruled above them.

That truth, undeniable, unrelenting. It speared her bare feet into that hot, smoky-red dirt.

Daniel Blakeley didn't wait for her answer.

Her blessing.

Not even her consent.

Just grabbed her hand. Clenched it.

As if he owned it.

Owned her.

Around her, the chants kept coming. Beat into her self. Her heart.

That ring on her finger, sparkling and beautiful, bit hard and deep.

She yanked herself free.

Stumbled. Toes stubbing on the hard, sharp grass.

Dead grass. Moisture sucked clean out. Left behind only husks.

These torched plains, which, until now, had felt like home.

"You will return with me," he snarled.

Aisha's chest hurt. As if she couldn't breathe.

Maybe because she couldn't.

Or, just maybe, because she finally could.

Breathe. Again.

She didn't have to go. With him.

Could make a choice. For herself.

On her own.

Aisha lifted her head. Felt that blazing, unrelenting sun.

Welcomed it.

"Take your ring. Take your promise."

He stepped forward. To reclaim her.

No more. Never again.

"I'm taking my life back."

The life she wanted.

Not his. Not her parents'.

Hers.

Which was when she saw him. Not Blakeley, but the shadow man. A man who shimmered into being from the shadows of the acacia tree. Not there one moment, a solid being the next.

His wand held out to her and not a single regret or feeling in his eyes. Just determination.

Which was when the spell hit. Slammed right into her chest.

A scream again swelled within Aisha's chest. Burst out her throat.

Even as Lanhi moved.

Sprang at her.

Aisha pivoted. Called on the her magic.

Not the magic from her wand.

Not the kind she'd been instructed in since birth from the greatest instructors high society could provide—even in the middle of nowhere Tanzania.

This magic came from her heritage.

From the long walks with the Hadzabe, as her grandfather taught her. Spoke of the land. The plants. The animals.

The land of Tanzania.

Even as Darkwood slammed into Lanhi's enclosure. Desperate. Calling her name. Wand out and ready….

The magic sparked from her fingers.

Came at Lanhi. Even as the tiger came at her.

Lanhi's claws never touched Aisha. Didn't pierce through Aisha's skin or clothes.

But Aisha's magic pierced her.

Stripped away that feral light. Stripped away that darkness, the darkness straight from Lanhi's soul and that pooling, oozing blackness dripping down from above. Ripped it right out of Lanhi, until Aisha saw only that poor trapped Familiar within—trapped between the magical world and the one she'd been born for.

The wild world.

The same world Aisha had been born for.

Meant for.

$\mathcal{S}$ylvester shoved open the doors to his study.

Light blinked in from the curtained balcony windows, slipping passed cracks that hadn't been properly concealed. Bathed his whole sanctuary in light.

He growled. Came forward and yanked the curtains fully closed. Jerked those inferior pieces of cloth until he could finally, *finally* think straight.

Sylvester sank into his armchair. Hand pressed to his head.

The headache pulsed.

Warning. Deafening.

She was doing it. The girl was actually breaking through.

Sylvester squeezed his eyes closed. Forced himself to think. Move beyond that first, traitorous sign of panic, to re-find and regain the control he was so known for.

That he'd practiced and studied. The cold, shadowed life he'd lived long before he became a politician.

His sleep robes were disarrayed and wrinkled. Hair no longer neatly brushed, combed, and slicked as when he went to sleep mere hours ago. He took a moment to straighten himself, the very act soothing, slowing replacing his mask and his persona.

No, he realized.

Reached within himself and examined the connection between him and the girl. The powerful spell he'd laid over her to make her forget that very dangerous knowledge she'd inherited.

He tested the red-gold strands within his own mind. Carefully poked and examined. The spell held strong. It was weakening in some areas, yes. Fading. Allowing just enough, bits and pieces—perhaps glimpses of her time in that horrid desert with those savages.

But the core of the spell, and the failsafe, hadn't been removed.

Aisha hadn't broken through.

Hadn't reclaimed those memories that would ruin him, ruin the Council. But she was getting close.

There was still time to right this, but he needed to act.

Now.

His fingers tightened on his robes. Left behind bunched, ruffled wrinkles.

It'd need to be thrown out. Replaced by a newer, finer quality of robe. One that didn't disappoint when he needed it the most. Just like Aisha and her Waystation. They'd set up another facility, this one in complete control of the Council, that took in those…broken Familiars. And if any did show signs of the wasting sickness, they'd be disposed of before it passed to the others.

Dealt with.

Quickly. Efficiently.

Just as he needed to do now.

Sylvester reached for the calling mirror. Used his mind to dial that fool, Asher. Fool though Asher might be, he was also a part of this. Had been, from the very beginning.

Sylvester would not be the only one to face this. To face what happened next. The possible disaster he needed to circumvent.

There was still hope, though.

There was still the contract with the Proper to consider, and, even just as important, the one holding the land itself there hostage. But first things first.

The mirror's surface shimmered. A rippling water that finally solidified on that fool's twisting mustache. Uncombed and unstyled. And Asher himself, with those robes actually revealing portions of his chest, hair and all, looked little better. As if the man hadn't taken half a moment to make himself presentable to the High Chancellor, rather than display the rabble and discord he really was underneath all that money.

"What took so long?" Sylvester snapped.

Asher blinked. "Ah, my Lord Darkwood, I was not anticipating your call—"

"Of course not! That does not mean you shouldn't be ready and prepared to accept my call within a moment. Do you think I have anything better to do than contact you as the sun rises?"

"No. No. Of course, I just—"

"You will remain silent or your sanctuary, the whole *empire* you've built, utilizing those Familiars as glorified pets and servants, will come crashing down around you. Do I make myself clear?"

Asher went pale. Nodded. The only color left came from his twisted mustache and his too-red lips.

But at least he remained silent.

Sylvester took the time to smooth his sleep robes once again. To calm himself just as he'd scolded Asher to do. He needed to think. And more than that, to act and act decisively.

"The plan," Sylvester murmured, "the one you came to me with all those years ago, after your personal and rigorous study on the matter of Familiars living side by side with their masters in complete co-existence..."

"Y-yes?"

"It is about to fall apart around both our heads. Do you understand what I'm saying?"

"I-I don't see how that's possible. We were very careful. The Familiars we've allowed to live, the few Sensitives that are even allowed—all of which are in control of the Council in some way—I really don't understand how it's—"

"Aisha."

Asher's mouth clicked closed. There was a slight tremble to that no-longer curling, now-wilted mustache. "I thought the matter was dealt with. Before she arrived in the States."

It had been. Or, so Sylvester had thought.

But she'd surprised him now, just as she had back then. She'd rejected her parents' fortune and prestige, her place in society, even her advantageous marriage to Lord Blakeley's eldest son.

She'd chosen instead to live amongst the dirt and poor of those bush tribes. To find her magic.

Her *heritage* magic.

"The matter was dealt with, but it seems your decision to send her a sick tiger has created…holes in her memory block." Sylvester leaned forward. Pressed his hands into his knees. Glared at the now floating speaking-mirror before him.

"I thought it was the perfect excuse you'd need, my lord, to close the Waystation down. For good. I thought—"

"You are not employed to think. You gave her the perfect opportunity, the perfect storm to reconnect with what she lost. She *is* remembering. Do you understand what will happen when she remembers?"

Asher opened his mouth. Slowly closed it. His mustache drooped until it fell beneath his chin. He nodded.

Sylvester leaned back in his chair. "You see how serious this situation is."

"But the memory block…"

"Is breaking. Right at this moment."

Asher and his wrinkles went a pasty white. "We must act."

"Yes. We must. I've already sent an emergency missive to the Council." Which he had. The moment he'd been pulled from his much-needed rest. He'd planned on sending a team to close the Waystation down today, but it must happen sooner.

Now. With him leading.

"We will meet at the Waystation within the hour."

"An hour isn't nearly enough time to mount the proper defense and the media exposure necessary to blame this all on her—"

"Make it necessary. Make it work."

Lord Asher, fool that he might be, at least had the contacts, the name, and the prestige that came with running his empire of Sanctuaries. None of the reporters would question his word—certainly not over Aisha Faye.

"One hour," Sylvester ordered.

The mirror rippled to a blank, clear surface. Not even Sylvester's reflection mirrored back at him.

Sylvester stood. His robes fell around him in a wave of wrinkled, unclean cloth. Yes, he would surely have to rid himself of it. Just like Asher. Just like Aisha.

Just like the truth of his dear wife.

He'd do what was needed, what was *necessary* for the Council, for their wizarding empire, to remain untouched and unmolested.

And most especially, for his own place in that world.

But soon enough, he'd be done with this business. With these Familiars and their constant problems. They'd be what they were meant to be and nothing more: servants.

He'd see it through himself.

To the very end.

CHAPTER 40

Nate didn't give a shit that Aisha was safe. That the tiger hadn't ripped her apart.

Couldn't.

Not when a greater need filled him.

Aisha panted over Lanhi's unmoving form. Stood there. Hands braced on her knees. Long dark hair a straight and tangled mess. Swept down her back. The tail of it curling just above her rear.

But no blood. Not a scratch.

The great tiger's chest still rose. Still fell.

Aisha was fine. Unharmed.

But she'd done it. Damn it to all the heavens above, she'd gone in there again and without him!

He reached for the lock.

Timiculous screeched. Flew off Nate's shoulder in a quick beat of wings. Nate called on every magic he knew and tore the whole thing right off. Burnt the metal clean off until that smoking mess clanked onto the cement ground. Then, he nearly tore the door from its hinges as he rushed in.

Took two long steps.

Gripped Aisha by the arms.

Hauled her to him.

"What the hell were you thinking?"

He shook her.

So light. So easily taken from him. "You could have died!"

"Yes."

Aisha said that so, so calmly. So unworried.

All he wanted was to shake her until some sense started cracking through that thick, stubborn skull of her. That stubbornness that he couldn't stop thinking of. Caring about.

"Damn it, Aisha."

He was shaking. His entire damn body was shaking.

From the memory. From her being in there, in that cage…could still see his mother's body. The body of Apollo. Both almost unreal, both appearing ghostly in that haze and clogging smoke.

"I'm fine, Nate." Her hands lowered. Touched just above his. "I found it, Nate. I found the answer. Not all of it, not yet. But it *is* there. Inside of me. Timiculous was right. I *do* have the answers."

Tears slipped from her eyes.

Excitement. Happiness. Joy.

"I can stop it," she whispered. "I can stop the wasting sickness."

And her touch on him, on his hands. So gentle. Soothing.

And it didn't do a damn thing to soothe the fear in his soul. The memory of what had nearly happened, once again, in front of him.

"No," he growled. "It's not fine." Never would be again. Couldn't be.

"Nate, I—"

"Why did you go in there? You saw what happened. Hell, you were *there* and you went in again."

"I had to."

"Bullshit."

Aisha shook her head. Her joy and happiness vanished. "Lanhi. All this time. Lanhi was the cause of the sickness. Don't you see? I *had* to go in there. It all started with her. I didn't see it at first. Didn't know what to look for, but then—"

Nate didn't let her finish. He pushed her against that glow metal fence.

A fence that sparked with his magic. Sparks he felt right to his soul. His need. Desire to protect and more. So much more. They reached right through him and out of his fingers.

Into her.

Arms on either side of her. Trapping her. Even as he watched her own eyes flash. Anger, first. And he couldn't help but smile at that. Only his Aisha would get pissed at being pushed against a fence. Held there. But there was heat too. Her calm from earlier, dissolving.

About damn time too. He wasn't going to jump off this bridge alone.

"I. Don't. Care," he growled. "I'm not losing you again."

"You never had me to begin with!"

"No. But I want you. Everything about you."

Nate kissed her. Long and hard. Kissed her with every desperate beating of his heart.

He'd almost lost her.

Couldn't save her. He'd been too far away and she'd nearly died. No. She *could* have died. This time, he knew she'd been prepared. Had been ready. But he didn't care.

Just, just couldn't.

This was exactly the type of woman she was. And exactly the reason he couldn't stay away. Couldn't keep his mouth off hers. Couldn't keep from wanting her—every damn inch of her.

His fingers dug into that metal. Felt the chain-link press into the palms of his skin. He pushed her further into the fence. Buried his body into hers. And it wasn't enough.

Not nearly enough.

He showed her, with every inch of his body, with his mouth, his heat, just what her going in there without him behind her did to him.

He couldn't stand back. Stay away. Not any longer.

Aisha's arms slipped up to his neck. Pushed him even closer. Fingers digging in his shirt. Yanking. Pulling.

Just as hot and needing and desperate as himself.

Nate didn't know how long he lost himself so completely in her. Her hair. Still that tangled mess, which he wrapped his fingers around. Tangled, but soft and perfect. Just like her work-hardened body. The curves, the muscles. They pressed against his and all he could think about was her.

For the first time in years, Nate let all that fear, all his frustration loose for anyone, other than Timiculous, to see.

Needed her to see. To know.

Finally, he slowly pulled way—but not far. His lips only an inch from hers. Their heaving chests, still touching. Their breaths, mingling until they became one.

"Don't you get it," he whispered, breath sliding past her ear. "I can't lose you."

He didn't see the smile. Couldn't. Not when his cheek was pressed against hers. But he felt it.

"I thought great and powerful lords' sons like their women prettied up and dumb as a rock."

He chuckled. Held her even closer to him. "Maybe I was waiting for an powerful lady's daughter to shove me into a pond."

"And then force you up a steep hill in that soggy mess of very inappropriate robes?" Aisha pulled back. Smiled again.

At him.

A smile that reached her eyes. Made them sparkle.

This, he knew, was the woman. The one he'd been waiting for.

The one who didn't care who he was or how powerful his magic was.

Except, she didn't know. Not the full truth.

And it was time to tell her. He *needed* to tell her.

Standing in this enclosure, with a feral Familiar who could so easily have taken this amazing woman a second time, Nate knew. Not the truth he'd been searching for all these years, the truth his father and the Council had kept from him, from the world.

But the real truth.

The one that actually mattered.

He loved her.

Nate took her hand. Could still feel that heat sparking off them. As if it lived inside them and needed to get out. He wanted nothing more than to pull her into that steel shed and show her just how much he needed her.

Instead, he wrapped those callused fingers around his. Brushed his lips against hers.

The heat continued to build. But this, first.

"Aisha. There's something I need to tell you—"

Timiculous's voice broke through their hazy world. The sudden quiet of the Waystation, both out loud and in Nate's head.

"Company coming!"

Which was right about the time a very pissed-off, screeching, pink-haired witch came barreling down the Waystation road with a flapping, equally pissed-off raven on her shoulder, and a sputtering, flame-throwing flying broom spewing out black smoke and soot behind her.

"Get your lying filthy hands off her!"

arcelle?" Aisha blinked.

That one word, and that one action, was about all her fogged-up, sex-filled mind could handle. Even the scents and the sounds of the Waystation, the constant muskiness, the need for cage cleaning, slices of chicken and beef-fat breakfast sitting out untouched with the thousands of buzzing black flies hard at work on their part...all of that had dimmed.

Completely.

Faded because all she could focus on was Nate.

Nate, with his arms still pressing her into the fence.

Her own, grabbing him. Pulling him closer. Their bodies touching. Every inch. In every way. Almost every way. Still not the way that she needed. That mattered. And then there was him—that hint of leather and cool, breezy air.

But the shock factor of seeing Marcelle with her pink, spiked hair standing up on end. Her broom spilling out nitro flames as she kicked it into first gear and zoomed down the dirt road. Dust devils and choking clouds shooting out behind her.

Well, the shock factor was certainly working hard on getting Aisha's head to clear.

Even though Nate's arms were still wrapped on either side of her. Still pressing her into the fence while her chest, chest still rose and fell with every breath as his. So close. So perfect...until Nate backed up.

Let her go.

His arms fell to his side. Shoulders drooping.

In resignation?

Timiculous squawked again. High and piercing—even over the rumbling noises from Marcelle's souped-up broomstick. He settled on Nate's shoulder. Large black claws digging in, holding on.

Nate gazed at her with those gray eyes.

Full of sorrow.

Apology.

"What?" Aisha strangled out. Somehow. Somehow spoke around her pounding heart. Heat filled her cheeks. Right along with the confusion. "What is it? What's going on?"

Darkwood shook his head once. Lowered his eyes, breaking the contact, the moment they'd shared.

"I'm sorry, Aisha. Truly."

Which only made her head spin more.

Her heart, though, slowed.

Thumped once. Twice.

Her awareness magic, her gut, telling her—warning her—what was coming.

Even if she didn't know what that was. Her magic knew.

"I was going to tell you," he said, "but...."

Marcelle flung herself off her broom the moment she reached Lanhi's enclosure—Lanhi, who still slept quiet and peacefully on the dirty, dusty ground.

Marcelle's gaze fixed on Lanhi, eyes widening just slightly, before she yanked out her twisted alder wand. Her eyes glowing pink—as pink and shimmering as her hair. Even the spiked collar around her neck was glowing as well. As if Marcelle had a few spells up her sleeve, ready to fire and attack.

Aisha stumbled away from the fence. From Darkwood.

He let her.

Her face still burning, and even with her dark skin, she knew her blush blazed from her. A telltale sign that Marcelle seemed to immediately notice as her pink, glowing eyes narrowed further.

Or maybe she was using her own magic and saw the clear, heated trail that had once connected Aisha and Darkwood. The heat and tension Aisha had never believed she could feel again.

Could want to feel again.

Except she did.

Aisha swallowed. Straightened her back. Raised her head.

Managed, somehow, to speak. "What is going on here?"

Which was about all she managed to get out because Marcelle's wand suddenly gleamed with red sparks and the jaws of a snapping dragon from its tip. A tip still very much pointed at Darkwood.

"I'm here to take out this Council-trash," Marcelle snapped.

Aisha stepped back. Or stumbled. Couldn't quite tell.

"Council?" The word strangled out of her.

She gazed at Darkwood. Blinked. Tried to see straight. To think straight.

Failed at both.

"Aisha," he said. Opened his mouth to say more. Nothing came out.

"Council?" she said again.

Marcelle didn't lower her wand. "That's right. Remember? I told you the Council had sent an investigator before your sister. But he didn't stay long. Had been *reassigned*. And guess who that investigator was? Guess where he was sent?"

Again, there was only sorrow and apology as Darkwood stood there, with Timiculous perched on his shoulder.

Darkwood. Tall and imposing.

His lips that had locked with hers in such fear, such determination…now, he lowered his head. A simple, slow shake.

As if not denying anything, anything at all that Marcelle had just said.

Neither did Timiculous.

Both of whom she'd trusted.

Had come to love.

Her whole body shook. Legs barely keeping her upright. But she managed. Managed to stand. To hold her head high. Even managed to feel the first stirrings of anger beneath the hurt, the soul-wrenching pain that tore her in half.

She loved him.

God, in such short amount of time, she'd fallen in love. Even after she'd sworn never to do so again. Because he'd been there for her. Stayed by her side. Had her back. Had *understood* her and hadn't once, not once, asked her to change.

And all of it, all of it, had been a lie.

"It's true," Aisha whispered. "You're from the Council."

"Oh, it gets even better." Marcelle inched closer to Aisha. "Are you going to tell her, Mr. Tall, Dark, and Handsome, who your father is?"

Marcelle slid in front of her. Probably felt the intense confusion, the hurt, coming from Aisha. Or worse, the real truth that she had only just realized.

"Father?" Aisha parroted. As if that was all she could do. As if she'd lost the ability to think on her own. To be independent.

But she hadn't.

She closed her eyes for a moment. Did her best to shove aside the pain and the hurt. Enough to listen to her gut, to the magic there.

And remembered the first time she'd seen Darkwood...in the aviary. Yes, that's where, right? When she'd pushed him in the pond.

He'd felt familiar to her; she hadn't known why. Which wasn't surprising. She'd locked herself away from magical society, from the politics of the witches and wizards on top, had ventured into Enchantment Avenue only on rare and required occasions. But hadn't Lord Asher made sure she knew the politics when she'd first arrived, when she'd taken her first step off that dragon transport and into the Los Angeles Magical Sector?

And she remembered.

"Sylvester Darkwood."

The image slowly appeared to Aisha. Also, familiar. The same as Darkwood had been. As if they had met before. Sylvester. Who was a silver-haired, aging man. Unkind gray eyes. An unkind face. He'd been the first person Asher had introduced her to, and he'd cared only about Tanzania and what she remembered from "the incident" with Blakeley, which had been next to nothing.

At the time, anyway. Now, though, it was coming back.

And so, also, was the nagging, tickling memory that that hadn't been the first time she'd met Sylvester Darkwood.

Aisha shivered. One shock at a time. One memory at a time.

She'd deal with the rest, if she could, later.

Aisha opened her eyes. Looked straight at Darkwood—who had the same color eyes as Sylvester. "Of course. Lord Sylvester Darkwood. The Chancellor."

Her breath breezed out, but enough where she could still say the words, the words her gut knew without a doubt, was true.

"You're his son."

"I am."

Her hands bunched into fists. "He sent you here. To spy on my Waystation. To close me down."

"He did."

Darkwood didn't move. Didn't offer an apology or an explanation. Just met her gaze.

"That's it?" She snapped. "You're not even going to try and explain?"

"I know you. Your past. Would you really listen to anything I said? Would you really believe I was telling you the truth?"

It didn't matter that the answer was no. She wanted it anyway. Some part of her, the part that broke and bled, needed to hear it.

But he just stood there. Unwavering and intense. Just like that first day she'd met him.

Which made her hate him all the more.

Made her *hurt* because this whole time, from the very beginning, this had been nothing but another set-up.

It was all she needed.

To take those few steps separating him. To raise her right arm. Punch him. Right in the cheek and damn the consequences. That soft tissue area between jaw and skull.

Pain split through her hand. Just like it continued to split through her middle. Her heart. Soul.

Damn Nate Darkwood. His father. The Council.

Everyone.

"I'm not letting you, your father, or that damn Council take away my Waystation."

Not even someone she'd fallen in love with.

Especially when she'd finally learned how to fight back the wasting sickness.

She raised her hand to hit him again, but Marcelle flung herself forward. Grabbed Aisha. Hauled her back.

"Aisha. Jeez, girl. Calm down. I'm all for you beating up on the High Chancellor's lying, cheating son—"

"Then let me go!"

"Except the Chancellor's going to be seriously pissed when he gets here."

ate's heart about stopped. Not because Aisha had a seriously wicked punch—the kind that'd give even Hilda a run for her money—but because of what Marcelle had said.

His father.

Coming here.

Timiculous was flapping on his shoulder. Sending squawks and dust up into the air. Hitting Nate in the back of the head with his wings. Making such a racket he thought for sure Lanhi would jump right to her feet and attack them were they stood.

But Lanhi kept sleeping. Those black stripes just rising and falling with each breath. Peacefully. Completely unaware of the drama in her cage.

"Quiet," he whispered to Timiculous. "Please."

"Can't. Must leave. All must leave. Noooow!"

Nate cupped his cheek. Hurting and swollen and puffy. And suddenly, completely, forgot about it. His attention snapped to Timiculous. A cold, cold dread filling him.

Understanding crept in.

The real truth. The real game his father had set in motion.

And he'd been so caught up with Aisha, caught up in his own memories, to notice. To realize.

Aisha didn't stop struggling with the pink-haired, firecracker witch. She speared Nate with such a glare, he slid back a step.

And nearly tripped over Lanhi's overturned breakfast dish with the untouched chicken carcasses and red-purple meat—and sent about a thousand, hungry buzzing flies into the air.

Which made Timiculous flap and squawk all the more.

"Darkness gone from tiger. Netting falling. But must go. Angry. Coming quickly!"

Marcelle finally just let go of Aisha, who stumbled and nearly fell. Marcelle thrust her hands on her hips, right at the elastic of her short, narrow little gothic-black skirt. "Enough! All of you."

Nate stopped swatting flies.

Aisha stopped trying to reach him—to claw his eyes out.

Timiculous just whistled.

Fantastic.

"Your bird's right," Marcelle snapped at Nate. "And I'm right. Your dearest father is on his way here. Right now. With the full force of the Council behind him to shut this place down. We're lucky those foppy lords take so long getting dressed or we wouldn't have time to even pee before taking off."

Marcelle stepped forward.

Smacked Nate right in the chest with her wand.

At least the snapping dragon's mouth with the red sparks wasn't there anymore.

"He's coming here," Marcelle said, "because *someone* tipped him off that Lanhi went nuts!"

Nate threw his hands up. "I haven't spoken with him since I got the assignment."

Aisha, he noticed, had wrapped her hand, the one she'd slugged him with, and pressed it against her middle.

"He did send you."

"Yes, he did. I won't lie. I was just going to tell you—" He cut himself off. Shook his head. "It's too late for apologies. Even for an explanation. For either of you."

He said this to both Marcelle and, more importantly, to Aisha.

The warming sun heated the enclosure. Seemed to lift off that dry sand. Sending the waves back at him, or maybe just reflecting the heat and anger that was already here.

"My father," Nate said, "trusts no one and leaves nothing to chance. I should have realized sooner. He would *know* about Lanhi."

But Nate hadn't.

He'd been so caught up in Aisha—in the return of yet another lost memory—to think of the consequences.

"But you're right," Nate said. "This is still my fault. I should have realized he wouldn't stop until he had what he wanted. And for whatever reason, that's closing down your Waystation."

Aisha lowered her hand.

The one, even now, that he could see was swollen.

Knuckles bruised. Purple and red. Puffing.

Even a trickle of blood.

And all he had to do, this whole time, to prevent that hurt, prevent the hurt he knew was splitting her in half, was to tell the truth.

To be honest with her.

"I'm sorry," he finally said. "I want to explain. To tell you everything. But I can't. Not now. You need to leave."

"I'm not leaving my Waystation." Aisha stood there, hands on her hips—even the swollen one. And not once did she flinch. Show any sign that she was hurting.

That *he'd* hurt her.

Instead, she dug her hiking boots into that ground and he doubted even a mountain slide could move her.

"You need to." Nate kept his voice low, quiet. "Because you found the answer, didn't you? You can stop it. You *know* how to stop it."

"Stop what?" Marcelle asked.

"The wasting sickness." Nate stepped towards Aisha, hand half-raised, but when she immediately backed away, he froze. Lowered his hand. "That's what you said. Earlier. That you had the answer. Inside of you."

She wouldn't meet his eyes. Wouldn't even look at him.

Probably because of where they'd been earlier.

What would have happened if Marcelle hadn't shown up? If the Council wasn't nearly here?

The Council.

"You need to leave," he said again.

Hurting, knowing she'd leave and he'd let her. Go. Without him.

"My father will stop at nothing. He won't let this get out."

Aisha finally glanced once at him, and then knelt beside Lanhi. Her fingers just a hairsbreadth above the tiger's massive forehead. "He will, won't he? He'll destroy her. Destroy all my Familiars. Even though she's healed."

Aisha wasn't wrong.

That was exactly what his father would do.

Marcelle moved to her friend. Gripped Aisha's shoulders in a tight embrace—without ever once taking her untrusting eyes off Nate.

He'd always known this quest, this search for answers, would come at a high price. He'd always expected it to be his father's disinheritance, his disapproval and anger. Nate had never expected to hurt the woman he suddenly couldn't live without.

Because Hilda had been right, all those years ago. He hadn't be willing to fight for their love, their future...but now, he'd give anything to make this right.

Even though he knew he couldn't.

Not now.

Not anymore.

Except, maybe, for one thing.

Nate wanted to reach for Aisha. To touch her face one last time, to let her know in that small way, that small gesture, he loved her. Hadn't wanted, hadn't meant to hurt her.

But he didn't move.

"There is a way," he said. "But you'll need to trust me."

Marcelle's eyes snapped back to their glowing, angry pink. "Trust you? The son of the very man—"

Aisha reached up. Her hand touched Marcelle's.

The other witch quieted.

"You can save them?" Aisha asked.

"No."

Nate did move then. Knelt across from Aisha, with only that tiger separating them. And for once, didn't feel any twinge or sharp fear in his gut. This tiger wasn't Apollo. Wasn't the tiger who'd killed his mother.

But his father didn't care about that.

Neither did the Council.

All they cared about was complete control over the knowledge, the real truth about Familiars.

A truth which, now, Aisha had.

Aisha, who looked him in the eyes. Who didn't move away.

"I can buy you time," he said, "but you, only you, can save them. Whatever answers you need to stop this—stop this sickness completely—you better find them. Fast."

There was a high-pitched whistling in the air. Then a trumpet. Loud. Screeching. Quaking.

A herald. Announcing the Council had come.

CHAPTER 43

$\mathcal{N}$ate stepped back from Lanhi's cage, surveying his work. An obvious blue-tinted glow surrounded the entire enclosure. Heard the sizzling. The warning that this cage was fully reinforced. Fully charged. Fully armed.

Lanhi still lay on the ground. Breathing growing more shallow. Ears flicking once. Then twice. Her tail twitched. A long curl of her black-and-orange stripes.

Twitched again.

She was finally waking up from whatever Aisha had done to her. Whatever the healing, the ridding of that darkness, had done to her.

Well, having her awake would only make what happened next easier.

He hoped.

Nate had placed a double-spell on her enclosure. Added on to the one he'd done just yesterday. But this time, spelled not to prevent Lanhi from getting out, but to prevent their visitors from getting to her.

Killing her.

Nate rubbed the sweat dotting his forehead. Running down his nose. Glanced behind him and up that narrow, steep dirt road he'd only run down himself…just an hour or so ago.

That was all. An hour. An hour in which everything had changed.

At least the one good thing about the Council, and his father, was just how predictable they were. And how long they, and their entourage, usually took to get somewhere.

Anywhere.

This wasn't a raid that happened within a heartbeat, but a full-on march complete with all the usual pomp, press, and media frenzy—after all, the magical world simply *loved* the drama of witches and wizards making headlines—especially the bad kind. Which made Nate just smile as he heard the swearing. Wished Aisha was here to enjoy it too. All their slipping and sliding and carrying on, mostly cursing, as those from Enchantment Avenue, who'd probably never set foot outside their protectively spelled beach community unless it was on a Dragon-Back private charter transport complete with cocktail and tea service, came face-to-face with Aisha's world.

Aisha.

His stomach twisted.

She'd had enough time to leave. To go wherever it was she'd thought she could find the rest of the answers. She hadn't said more than that. All he knew was there'd been a look in her eyes. A sudden understanding. A puzzle piece finally, after years, sliding into place.

He didn't ask where and she wouldn't have said.

Didn't matter.

All that mattered was she'd had time to leave.

He watched as the Council and their entourage created such a dust storm down that dirt road the chimps were already screeching and making catcalls. The whole small valley, that little slit of a ravine Aisha had managed to stuff an entire Waystation compound in, shook from the noise.

The pounding feet. The fiery tension.

Whatever reason his father and the Council had something against the Waystation, whether it was just some blight on their perfect little world or something more, Nate didn't know. Only knew that they were pissed and hell-bent on seeing this place gone forever.

Which he wouldn't let happen.

Not with a damn good fight.

"All right, Mr. Council-Toady Henchman. That's the last of it." Marcelle, all five feet of her, hauled the last of Lanhi's trinkets and memories out of the enclosure. Her arms were filled with the last of the clown noses and shredded confetti balls made to look like pink elephants. Including a bright red nose slapped onto her face.

He moved forward to help, but she danced out of her way.

Nate shook his head. "I could have handled it."

"And trust you to not do something sneaky? Leave some clue that gives your dear daddy all the reason he needs to destroy Lanhi? I don't think so, buddy."

At least she'd let Nate haul out the full-length, elephant-decorated, copper-carved mirror from Lanhi's sleeping shed.

Sleeping shed, of all places.

Marcelle dumped the last load right in the pile—nearly three times her size—and even snatched off her own clown nose. Then, she dusted her hands off, turned, and sent Nate her customary glare.

Which she'd started doing the second Aisha had left, and hadn't let up since.

It had taken a few minutes—precious minutes—to convince Aisha to go. Even more when Aisha realized Marcelle wasn't leaving with her. That Marcelle was staying. That Marcelle wouldn't dare leave the Waystation in the hands of Nate.

He hadn't argued with either woman.

That had been one lesson he'd learned from Hilda.

Especially when women dug their heels in and had *that* look.

The same look Marcelle was shooting at him.

So he kept his mouth shut. As did Timiculous—who was huddled in a nearby, spindly desert tree with its bare-leaf branches. Conveniently giving them a play-by-play of his father's arrival until Marcelle had told him to shut the hell up as she could sense those bastards just fine.

"You sure about this?" he asked. "Staying?"

"There goes that trust issue again. You hard of hearing?"

Marcelle's raven, just as foul-tempered as her, cawed from the same tree in which Timiculous perched. Glared at Nate, then went back to glaring at Timiculous.

"Your choice." Nate just shrugged, turned to Lanhi's enclosure, and pulled out his wand.

The slender wood slick from all his years of practicing. From never letting it far from his reach.

From the promise he'd made all those years ago.

He locked Lanhi's enclosure door—what appeared to be a simple spark and snapping of lights. But wasn't. It was his spell. His signature lock.

Marcelle snorted. "Fancy."

"Not even my father can force it open."

She lifted a perfectly plucked brow at him.

"Not, at least, without half a day trying to break it." Nate tucked his wand into the pocket of his mud-stained pants.

He surveyed all of Marcelle's fast—and good—work. The pile was huge. The pink tutu with its sequins no longer shimmering, no longer shining with the magic of its Familiar. The posters. So much. So much had been stuffed in that enclosure.

No wonder Lanhi had lost it.

Her owner had thrust every reminder of her former life in there— except it was only *half* of who Lanhi actually was. Her owner had completely ignored the tiger part of her. Had, instead, thrust only what she'd deemed necessary and appropriate right in Lanhi's face until that poor tiger had no choice but to turn feral. To lose what little hold she'd had over her magical self.

To allow Lanhi to contract the wasting sickness, which had slowly broken down the barrier separating her and her magic. To think, all this time, the answer had been right in front of them. The answer to all this had been so simple, so right in front of his face.

He still didn't fully understand. Didn't know what the wasting sickness was. Why it had formed such a dark, complete, and infectious netting over the Waystation. Why it stole and ate the magic of Familiars. His father, the Council—they probably knew and wouldn't dare say.

Nate could only hope whatever Aisha was searching for, the answers, would tell him the rest of the story. Prevent *this* from ever happening again.

Still, this whole time Nate had *known* it felt wrong.

Every time he'd stepped into a sanctuary. Every time he'd glimpsed those magically spelled pipes, and Jesus, a lavatory!

It'd turned his stomach.

A red-tailed hawk screamed overhead.

Timiculous screamed right back at him. As did the raven.

Nate couldn't help but look up, watched as the hawk circled above them. Again and again, riding the heated wind, and he knew how his father had known about Lanhi.

His father had never trusted Nate to inform him about the Waystation. About what was truly happening. He must have had Artemis watching the place, probably watching him, watching Aisha, the whole time.

Which only pissed Nate off even more.

"You ready for this?" he snapped to Marcelle.

"You ready to stand up to dear ol' daddy?"

He was.

And it was about damn time.

Nate leaned into the cage. Crossed his arms.

The dust cloud was finally drawing nearer. This fight with his father, the one that had been brewing for nearly two decades, since he'd lost his mother, was finally here.

No matter what happened next, Nate wouldn't give in. Wouldn't back down. Not like he'd done with Hilda.

This time, he had something worth fighting for.

CHAPTER 44

*A*isha slapped her tattered duffel bag onto the back of her dirt bike. Her movements jerky and stiff. Angry and hurt. Hated how hard she was working to keep herself from shaking.

To keep herself from crying.

She glanced back, down that narrowed, small road. Twisting and turning back into her main compound. Back to the Waystation. To Nate.

To the Council members descending on and threatening everything she loved.

Aisha kicked the wheel of her bike. "Damn it!"

Mud chunks rained down. Plopped onto the parched ground and onto her boots. A few chunks had tumbled off when she'd rolled out the bike from the barely holding-together shed near one of the small game trails, but there was still plenty there. Heck, even the padding poking out from the seams had its own pocket of stained and dried mud.

She'd forgotten to clean it—forgotten because of so many chores she always had to get to and never had enough time for.

At least the bike had a full tank.

That was one chore she never, ever skimped on.

One she'd learned the hard way back...back then. In Tanzania, before she'd run away from that life her parents and everyone there wanted her to have. Insisted that she wanted the same as well.

And now she was running again.

But this time, she was running right back to where she'd started from.

Aisha slapped her hand on the seat. Forced herself to get on that bike. Straddled the seat. Yanked on the ignition key. Kickstarted the gear with her foot.

Hard.

The bike revived and hummed beneath her. Shook so hard it made her teeth chatter and clatter. The rumbling growls would have filled her small valley if the Council wasn't, even now, entering her Waystation with all the pomp and frenzy and mass they were known for, complete with what sounded like goddamned blaring trumpets.

Her home.

While Marcelle and Nate worked fast to dump all the crap from Lanhi's cage—to make sure the sickness didn't retake hold of her.

Aisha should be there.

With them.

Not running away.

Not again.

She swung off the bike. Shut the whole thing off. Yanked off her helmet. Felt her braid grab at a strap and pull.

"I am not running! This is my home."

Aisha turned, hiking boots sliding in that always-dry dirt, ready to storm right on back and fight for what was hers—and came to face-to-face with the most beautiful witch she'd ever seen.

Even if that witch lounged against a biker-broom, had brilliant pink riding gloves currently braced on her hips, and wore black, spider-silk lace as if it were a skirt.

"So," Miss Blond and Sexy Witch murmured, though it came off as more of a rumbling purr (Aisha was betting there was Siren blood somewhere in her genes). "You're the witch that's got Nate finally standing up to his father."

"Who the hell are you? Council?"

Hilda snorted. Wrapped a long-ass lock of that hair around her fingers. Twirled. Like she was trying to reel Aisha in like a damn fish.

"I am not having a good day." Aisha stepped forward. Gripped her helmet as if she was going to chuck it at the witch. "You want to test me? Play with me like a little mouse? Be my guest. But you are on *my* property. And I am not going to ask you again."

She also tried damn hard not to think about the part where this gorgeous witch—biker or not—said Nate's name.

Nate.

Aisha clamped down hard on anything, anything daring to resemble emotion from leaking to the surface. Not in front of an enemy.

"Peace, Aisha Faye." The witch released her hair like a playful bit of string. "I'm here because I haven't had a very good lifetime, and you can thank your dear boyfriend—and his bastard dad—for that."

"He's not my boyfriend."

"Right. Because Nate's not back at your precious little Waystation, standing up to the one person he's afraid of, the one person he wouldn't stand up to even for his fiancé…"

The word hit Aisha in the gut.

She actually, *actually* stumbled back a step.

Then caught herself.

The witch's red-lipped smile grew. "Oh, my bad. He's my *ex*-fiancé and you, my dear, are the one who matters."

The witch pushed away from her broom, which Aisha noticed, was rumbling softly. Quietly. There must be some damn good compression spells on that thing to have kept quiet—and to have not triggered her protective alarms about her Waystation. Not that she'd renewed the spells in some time, but they were *supposed* to be good for a couple of…years after the expiration date.

Shit.

Just another chore she'd forgotten.

"Enough." Aisha balled her hand into a fist. "Nate's old girlfriend or not, I don't have time for you or your games. Now. Get out of my Waystation."

The witch didn't stop moving. Just sashayed her way over as if she hadn't a care in the world—as if she owned the very ground she slinked on.

"But I'm here to help. You do want to get away, right? To some place"—her gaze fixed on Aisha's bike—"fast, I assume?"

"That's none of your—"

"It sure as hell is, sweetheart. It is because I swear, that guy might be an ass breakin' it off with me because daddy said so, but he's sure as hell not being an ass to you. And—"

Here Miss Gorgeous took a deep breath.

Lines appeared along her mouth. Her eyes. Made her look not so gorgeous. Not so perfect and made up.

"And I deserved every bit of it," the witch finally said. "I'm not Council, but I'm not clean either. I've known about this sickness and I've been covering it up trying to cover my own ass."

Aisha nearly dropped her helmet. "What? Who—who are you?"

The witch held out her hand—nails practically dripping with the reddest nail polish Aisha had ever seen. "I'm Hilda Davenspear. Doctor, actually."

"The Familiar veterinarian." Aisha's mouth went dry. She'd known of Dr. Davenspear. Had even tried requesting her to see Aisha's Familiars when she'd first opened the Waystation—but had been promptly shown the door.

Every time.

"You knew?" Aisha whispered.

"I did. And I did nothing about it. Not like you. So, you, I'm going to help."

Aisha didn't move. Didn't dare.

"Why?"

"Because it's about damn time I did the right thing. Now." Hilda surveyed Aisha's bike. Shook her head. "You're never going to drive all the way to Africa on that thing, and any chartered dragon or pegasus flight is going to be monitored."

"What? How do you know I'm going to—"

Hilda tapped Aisha's nose. "I am a doctor, after all. I may have kept quiet, but that doesn't mean I haven't *studied* what was right in front of my face. But studying and actually fixing the problem are two very different things. And the only way you're getting out of this country is in a way that the Council would never suspect."

Aisha's stomach rolled. Plummeted, just for a moment. "You're not suggesting...."

"I hope you have a Normals passport up to date and forged?"

$\mathcal{N}$ate adjusted the brim of his floppy cowboy hat lower. It was the only shade in the whole area. A hat that Marcelle, of all people, had scrounged up from somewhere in that metal shed before she'd purged Lanhi's cage of anything magical and "human"—it also happened to be the same shed he'd been hoping he and Aisha would have slipped into hours early.

Which actually felt like an age ago.

Maybe two.

Aisha.

Nate's stomach knotted. Forced himself not to look down that narrow, barely trodden path behind that same metal shed—the path Aisha had disappeared down when they'd finally convinced her to leave.

Part of him wished she'd turn around. Come back to her Waystation. To him.

But no. This was something he needed to do. Now.

Trumpets lit through the small valley. Heralding. Announcing.

Colonizing.

Inched closer, just like that dust-billowing cloud of fog from the Council and its entourage.

"You sure you can handle this, Council-boy?"

Marcelle sided up beside him. Thrust her hands on her hips. The tips of her spiked-pink hair seeming to lean forward, as if they wanted to jab him in the chest. Probably the same way she wanted to do.

"You a mind reader?" Nate shoved his hands in his stained pants pockets.

"Psychic, actually."

"Great. Aisha didn't mention that."

"She didn't mention you either." This time, Marcelle did give him a hard poke with her black-tipped finger. "She also didn't mention how close she was to yanking you into that shed and forgetting about all those promises she'd sworn she'd never go back on."

Nate blinked. "Huh?"

"You really think I'm that dense?"

Actually, he didn't know what to think of her at all, but thought better of saying anything of the sort.

Not that it mattered.

With her being a psychic.

"You think I can't tell you're in love with her?"

Nate startled at that. Practically fell back against Lanhi's chain-link fence—which, come to think of it, probably wasn't the best place to be.

Especially how Lanhi was finally curling awake. Her whole body unfurling. Stretching. Long and lean and graceful. And those eyes... Nate glanced to Timiculous, still shivering the tree with Marcelle's unfriendly raven.

"Safe. Now. Tiger safe. Netting going away."

"Thank the heavens," Nate whispered.

"What?" Marcelle jabbed him again. "You're seriously trying to avoid the question. Seriously?"

He pushed her hand aside. "Not at all."

Never, actually.

Not when he knew damn well that he was in love with Aisha.

"It's just that we've got company, and considering our tiger is up, clean, and safe, maybe we should focus on the guys who really can ruin Aisha."

Marcelle scrunched her nose. Grabbed his chin. Studied him with seriously bright pink glowing eyes....

And she let go. Just, boom. Dropped his chin, stepped back, and clapped her hands together.

"You've got a point there. Now. If you're really going to do this—have it finally out with dear daddy, you better put your game face on and not the puppy-dog one."

"I don't have a—"

Nate didn't get a chance to finish.

Not when his father broke through that billowing, choking dust. Dust that seemed to snake around the man. Curled about his ankles. Up his legs. But never seemed to touched him.

And those gray eyes, the ones narrowed in silent but completely controlled fury at Nate.

Just like they always were.

But this time, it was different.

This time, Nate stepped forward. Lifted his own chin, just an inch, nothing more. And narrowed his own, identical eyes.

This time was very different indeed.

"Hello, Father."

"Nathanial."

Nate simply stood there. Ignored that tightening in his gut. How his father couldn't even call him "son."

With his hiking boots worn and muddied. Pants just as filthy. Just as dust-stained as his face. His dark hair. Nate never looked so different from his father—and yet, felt so confident.

So comfortable.

Aisha had done this. Aisha, just being Aisha, had allowed him to find himself—a self outside of his father's and the Council's shadow.

Nate stood there, with that short distance separating them, with the lions over at Lion's Row doing their calling and roaring, the chimps with their catcalling and quite a few sailor-swearing curses flying about as if even they knew what was happening was bad. That the witches and wizards who'd invaded the Waystation were a whole lot worse than putting up with Aisha and Marcelle.

Behind his father, the great lord and mighty Sylvester, came the rest of the Council.

All of them.

A dozen of the most powerful witches and wizards lined behind him. Their robes seeming to gleam and sparkle even in this desert valley. The dust didn't touch their fancy clothes, but their eyes were a bit red-rimmed and a few had smudge stains along their chins. Foreheads. Probably from rubbing off the sweat.

The unrelenting sun was doing its thing. Making the Waystation into one giant sauna and not a single Council member—or the fancy press or high society members crowding and shoving and jostling behind them—had actually thought to prepare their wardrobes with a bit more care.

Nate didn't fight the smile.

Especially when he saw a single bead of sweat slip down his father's forehead. Drip down his nose just like sweat on the rest of them.

Nate bowed, as was required by his office. As he was, still, indeed a member *employed* by the Council.

But not controlled.

Never again.

"Father. Council members. What a pleasant surprise." Nate straightened. Adjusted the brim of his hat in a more informal greeting.

Something he'd caught on those Normal Western films before his mother had died, before his father had closed off from Nate and turned serious—well, even more serious.

Nate heard Marcelle come up behind him. Also, the soft, almost silent padding of very large, very deadly feet come within inches of the cage. Lanhi's rumbling breath, which swished out from between her teeth.

Letting him know she was there as well.

They all were.

"Help all around. Not alone," came Timiculous's strong words.

Nate could practically feel Timiculous's comforting weight on his shoulders. The gentle rub against Nate's cheek.

He wasn't alone and never would be again.

Regardless of what his father wanted him to believe.

Even if Aisha and Marcelle didn't believe in him. Didn't trust him.

It didn't matter. Because he was going to do this. Right now, and forever finish this. No more, no more being controlled.

As Nate crossed his arms, met his father's unwavering, furious gaze across that short distance, he couldn't help but feel that Hilda would be proud. Of the man he was finally owning up to being.

No more being the Council's puppet.

CHAPTER 46

$\mathcal{N}$ate watched as the one man he'd learned, while growing up, to look away from, to never bother or pester, to never love, separated himself from the group.

Sylvester Darkwood.

Sure and confident and cold, just like always. Moved with a fluidity and grace he'd honed until it was as sharp and razor a skill as his commanding voice. The flies that hummed and buzzed, dark clouds that flittered about the cages looking for their next meal, steered clear of Sylvester Darkwood.

Sylvester, who didn't glance or scowl at the pocked dirt road he was now being forced to walk on, but also didn't summon any magic carpets or flying horses either.

A man too proud to spell something so mundane. Who wanted, instead, to appear real and in control by anyone who saw him. Which was one of the many reasons he'd remained High Chancellor for so long. One of the many reasons Nate had always found it simply easier to bow, to obey his father's wishes.

His commands.

"Nathanial. You've done well, I see." His father's voice cut through that suddenly still and quiet air. "Even better an outcome than I could have hoped for."

With every step his father had taken, the animals had slowly quieted. Only the rolling, hot breeze made noise as it picked up tumbleweeds and shoved them against cages and enclosures. The swirling dust devils. Even the chimps ceased their calls and lurid remarks.

Perhaps they could smell the danger. Could smell the predator standing not far from them.

The predator, and not themselves, who was uncaged.

In control.

Nate felt Marcelle tense beside him. He wanted to reassure her. Wanted her to say absolutely nothing. That this was just one of the many games his father played. One of the many moves and dodges he employed to retain that control of the entire playing field.

Nate slid away from Marcelle, from the panting Lanhi behind him. "I'm really not sure what you're referring to."

"I charged you with finding the evidence needed to finally close this monstrous place down. You succeeded."

There were murmurs behind his father. Nate finally glimpsed the spindly, curling mustache of Lord Asher somewhere in the back. Or perhaps it was just that beaming, smug smile. Of course he would be here. Of course Lord Asher would never miss this moment, this chance to see Aisha and whatever history between them fall.

Which Nate wasn't going to let happen.

"You mean those reports that I never sent?" Nate asked. "Or my failure to alert the Council of a Familiar turning feral?"

"The evidence was obtained, nonetheless."

"Nate," Marcelle hissed—warned—behind him.

Nate waved his fingers at her. She needed to trust him.

"Evidence. Interesting." Nate took another step forward. Somehow his feet moved. Somehow he didn't shake. Didn't quiver. Not even in his voice.

He knew the laws regulating Familiars.

Had studied them, had used them, even against the Council, as he'd done with Hilda—even though she'd gone and made her own side deal to keep her clinic.

All Nate had to do was trust.

In himself.

"The only problem," Nate said, "is I wasn't the one who obtained the evidence, was I? And if I recall, Ordinance number 4, section 58 B, in the Sanctuary subsidiary section, *Privacy* Act," Nate stressed on the privacy part, "that anything obtained outside direct Council observation is unlawful and quite—in your words, Father, as you wrote the section—illegal."

"The means does not change the truth."

"Really? So you are perfectly legal in your right to send *your* personal Familiar to spy on someone else's privately owned and operated sanctuary? And to use such evidence as you see fit?"

His father's face tinged. With red.

Just a tad, barely noticeable, but enough.

"That the tiger behind you turned feral." Sylvester used the same voice he had that night, while Nate had huddled and cried in the smoky shadows. "She has contracted the wasting sickness, and to protect all Familiars, she and this whole Waystation, must be destroyed."

His father whipped out his wand.

One fluid, easy stroke.

And very, very real.

His father never bluffed.

His father would do anything to protect his secrets. The Council's secret. His own place and power.

Even if it meant destroying his son in front of a legion of witnesses —witnesses it wouldn't take him long to convince of the justice and righteousness of his actions.

A curling red spell sparked from his father's wand. Destruction. Fire.

One aimed at Nate.

And the tiger behind him.

CHAPTER 47

Behind Nate, Marcelle sucked in a breath.

Heard the Council members do the same. The flashing of magic cameras. Recordings. The muffled reporters giving a live feed to the whole of Enchantment Avenue and beyond.

Recording. Watching. Witnessing as the High Chancellor prepared to attack, and to remove his defiant son.

The sun continued to beat down. Continued to soak through Nate's lightweight shirt. Sweat pooling under his armpits. Dripping down his neck.

Not once did he take his eyes off that wand. A wand now angry and hissing. Sparking with the spell that truly could destroy him—just as it had destroyed all proof of Apollo's turning.

Of the destruction and death the Familiar had caused.

"Only the truth," his father said, "matters."

Nate itched to reach for his own wand.

To defend. To fight back.

Instead, he managed a breath.

Then, a deeper one.

Thought of Aisha. All this place and the Familiars here meant to her. Nate couldn't attack. Couldn't draw his wand, as he knew his father was now hoping for.

That was one thing Nate had learned, growing up with a man he couldn't bother, couldn't love. Nate had learned how the great and powerful Council lord thought. Planned. Manipulated.

And for the first time in his life, Nate finally used what he'd learned. What Hilda had been pestering him to do for years.

As if he'd been waiting for this one moment.

"If that's the case"—Nate met his father gaze. Just as cold, just as unyielding—"then you'll see the tiger Familiar behind me, Lanhi, is perfectly healthy. That she does not, in fact, have the wasting sickness."

Nate stepped to the side.

Gestured, in invitation, toward Lanhi. So they all could see her. His father, the other Council members, those foolish members of the magical press who had no idea they were truly in pawns in his father's every scheming plots.

Lanhi sat right at the fence. Large paws facing out. No claws showing. Her long tail swishing. Once. Twice.

Calm, but alert. Watchful.

And not a hint of feral or wild in her eyes.

Nothing but pure intelligence—an intelligence that hid little about just how pissed she was.

She knew what they were saying.

Knew what his father's wand, being held right at her, wanted to do.

Sylvester snapped his attention away from the "evidence." Dismissing, as Nate knew he would.

In front of everyone.

"This tiger," his father growled, "is a danger to all of the magical world. To all our Familiars. She must not be allowed to live."

Lanhi gave a low, warning growl in return.

So too, did the rest of the Waystation follow. The lions. The monkeys with their high, yelping screeches.

"You mean, like Apollo?" Nate whispered.

Nate watched as his father flinched. Slightly.

Enough that only Nate, who was watching, would notice. That just for a moment, Nate saw the real man behind the spelled mask, the wrinkles, the years he'd lost after her death. Even now, Nate could still easily see his mother. Her unmoving body on that carpet—a carpet soaked in blood. And all that smoke. Clutching. Clogging. Suffocating smoke.

And all the while his father, standing there, giving the orders to bury it.

Bury the truth of his own beloved wife's death.

And not once had he shed a single tear or moaned in that gut-wrenching way as Nate had when he'd run from that smoke and back into his rooms. As his whole world fell apart around him.

Sylvester may have never loved or cared for Nate, but he had for his wife.

His wife who'd only just gotten in the way of what he, and the Council, needed to protect.

"The truth," Nate said, "well, that is an interesting way of looking at it."

His father's eyes narrowed. "Nathanial."

A warning.

"Because the way I see, as my Familiar Sensitive, Timiculous, sees it"—Nate nodded in the tree—"the truth is all the proof we need."

Timiculous spread his bright wings—the gold feathers underneath catching in the sun. Flapped and stirred up the dust devils even more—as well as murmurs from that entourage. From the Council.

Each of whose gazes became heated. Furious.

Knew exactly what Nate was about to do.

Reveal.

Timiculous took off from his perch in the tree. Landed easily and safe on Nate's shoulder.

What happened next was something they'd see through. Together.

Lord Asher laughed. The tips of his mustache curling up his nose. Holding his belly. "This is a preposterous claim. Everyone knows there is no such thing as a Familiar Sensitive—"

"Good place, now," Timiculous screeched. Loud. Clear. "Africa lady make better. Darkness gone. Tiger safe. Well now."

No one moved.

Spoke.

Couldn't.

Not when they all knew a Familiar couldn't lie. And Timiculous had just told everyone exactly who and what he was.

Timiculous gave another loud flap of his wings. Bobbed his head and whistled. "All you, go home. No welcome here."

Nate only lifted his eyebrow at his father.

As if to say, *Your move.*

But it wasn't his father who accepted the move.

It was another.

A witch came forward. Tall and graceful. Sliding past Lord Asher until she stood side by side with Nate's father. "The Familiar speaks truth. I sense no malice here, no sickness. Though there is a darkness but...it is dissipating."

A witch with familiar long, dark hair.

Hair, so similar, almost identical, to the hair Nate had ran his fingers through hours earlier.

But her eyes—her eyes were completely different. Where Aisha's held love and compassion, especially every time she looked at a Familiar, this witch held a deep, cold disdain.

His father nodded towards her. "Lady Racine. You have something to add?"

"The darkness here is what should concern the Council, and *how* precisely it came to be. Something that does, indeed, fall within the Council's ordinance and law."

Nate went cold. Didn't dare move.

Because Racine was right.

Racine slipped a hand through her hair, which gleamed in the sun's light, making it shine almost silvery. Nothing at all like the tangled mass of Aisha's hair. Always pulled back in a braid, out of her way so she could work.

"But she doesn't know, does she?" Racine asked. "Doesn't know exactly what this darkness is or how to fight it?"

Nate's father glanced back at Nate. The man he'd glimpsed before, who was still, deep down, grieving for his wife, was gone. Now, now there was just the High Council member Nate had grown up with.

"No," his father murmured, "she wouldn't. She is unable to...tap into the truth. I believe the Council requires a great deal of words with her. An explanation as to what happened here. And, account-ability."

His father stepped forward.

Nate dug his boots into the soft dirt.

"But the lady isn't here, is she?" his father asked. "Aisha Faye is gone."

Nate didn't dare answer.

But again, it was Lady Racine who answered.

"No." Her lips curled up. Like a snarl. Hungry. Predatory. "But the Familiar answered that as well. She's gone home. To Africa."

CHAPTER 48

*A*isha clutched the armrests of the tin can with wings and watched, from that pint-sized window, as something called flaps rose up and out, mechanically, creakily, from some hidden slot on those wings. She nearly ran for the closed hatch doors at that point, but instead settled for attempting to remove the armrests from the hard, no-leg-room chair those flight attendants had strapped her into.

So far, the chair was winning.

But it was a long, long flight to Tanzania.

No one else seemed concerned, though. But then, they were Normals and seemed perfectly at ease in flying thousands of miles above the earth where, if escape be needed—whether by flying carpet or dragon—you couldn't actually escape, the air being too thin and cold after all.

There was a reason most of the magical community thought Normals odd and beneath them.

Right now, Aisha was holding off on her prejudices too.

Not even the old lady with the oval-shaped glasses, compete with rhinestones, on a chain hanging from her neck, seemed bothered or concerned or scared shitless as the plane rumbled, bumped, *turned*. Nor the kid behind Aisha's seat who, she swore, started kicking it the *minute* she sat down.

Aisha tried for breathing.

Long, deep, rejuvenating breaths.

Except the air the was stale. Hollow, even. Lifeless.

And it really, really didn't help when that male attendant stood up in front of the ocean of flimsy seats in this sealed, very trapped-in plane, and began demonstrating the procedures in case something bad happened.

Like, the plane crashing into the ocean, and how to use the seat cushion as a flotation device.

Sweat rolled down Aisha's forehead.

She gripped the armrests harder.

The airplane slowly rumbled and moved on a huge strip of nothingness—okay, not nothingness. There was a whole lot of thick, black asphalt out there. Huge stretches of it, actually, with just as many scattered and crowded dots of airplanes, private jets, and giant, Normal-human-trafficking carriers. Each seeming perfectly at ease with their intent and destination: to take off from the Earth's surface at inhuman speeds, powdered by a mechanical device that may or may not spontaneously combust or just blow up, and land somewhere else.

Like on the other side of the globe.

Aisha nearly lost her breakfast right there.

Thank goodness the snack bar she'd had didn't quite count as breakfast.

"There, there, dear." A wrinkled hand descended from nowhere and patted Aisha's hand.

Came from nowhere, because, well, at some point Aisha had slammed her eyes closed.

Now, she peeked them open—slowly—and saw her seatmate, the old lady with rhinestone glasses, who smelled surprisingly like the midnight lavender lily cultivated by the gorgons she'd visited last year....

"Are you all right, dearie? You look a little pinky."

"Oh. Yes. I mean. No. I've never flown. On a plane." If Hilda had suggested Dragon-Air Service or Phoenix-Fire Lift Off, Aisha would have had no problem.

None.

Totally been fine.

But flying in a mechanical contraption she not only didn't understand, but which was being controlled by a bunch of Normals she'd never met, vetted, or analyzed (to make sure they were in peak condition for a flight across the world)... Well. Right. Liking Normals and their duct tape and their hoses was one thing.

Trusting her life in their flying machines was something entirely.

"I'm just wondering," Aisha said, somehow, through clenched teeth, "if the person who suggested the flight was just trying to get me out of the way so she could have another go at her ex-fiancé."

The old woman laughed.

Throaty.

Deep.

Cackling.

Aisha blinked. That was not what she thought of when she heard Normals going about their usual business. And, you know, laughing.

"Hilda wouldn't touch the Darkwood son with a ten-foot dragon feather. Not that she wouldn't want another shot at the lad."

"I'm sorry. But what... What did you—"

"Because of course the problem really comes down to the trust issue. And, of course, he's not exactly in love with her. Can't be. Not when he's got his eyes set on someone else."

The plane *jerked*.

Aisha bolted upright. Or would have, if she wasn't strapped down by that lap belt that the stewardess had *insisted* she tighten.

Not that it would actually save her from dying if they suddenly spontaneously turned into a plane-sized flamethrower.

The witch—because seriously, this old lady was definitely a witch—snapped her fingers in front of Aisha.

"Come on, girl. I heard you were made of sterner stuff." She snapped that bony, wrinkled hand again. "It's just a plane and believe it or not, those Normals are fairly competent at keeping these things in the air. Now, get ahold of yourself."

Listening to the witch seemed like a much better idea than panicking, so Aisha closed her eyes and just breathed.

"Would you mind, keep talking? Distraction helps," Aisha said.

"You can handle tigers turning feral and going for your throat, but you can't handle this metal bucket picking up speed—now, hold on. This is normal. Just getting ready to take off. Gonna be a bit bumpy. Gonna get fast and you'll flatten against the seat like a Normal pancake and then you won't even know we're in the air. Ah, see?"

Aisha had no intention of *seeing*.

She kept her eyes shut. Kept on breathing. Kept on listening to the witch just explaining the process of Normal flight abilities and what was, well, "normal."

As the witch kept on talking, Aisha learned her name was Mattie Dee, who not very surprising, was an associate of Hilda's.

In the witch biker-like gang, anyway. And Aisha did take some comfort that Hilda had the forethought to not only book her this flight—which, truthfully, the Council wasn't going to think *twice* about her taking—but Hilda had also thought ahead to send her a companion so Aisha actually arrived in Africa.

And not vacating the plane halfway above the Earth.

Or even before leaving Los Angeles.

"You ever been to Africa?" Mattie Dee asked.

At this, Aisha opened her eyes. Noticed the rolled up magazine in Mattie Dee's hand, and how she reached over the seats and smacked the little boy kicking Aisha's seat (while dear mom was away, probably the tiny bathrooms a league away from them) and warned the kid she'd turn him into a toad if he did this one more time.

When the kid blew a raspberry at Mattie Dee Aisha felt a small spark of heat and a pop behind her.

Mattie Dee straightened around, grinning from ear to ear.

"You didn't?" Aisha whispered.

"Turn the kid?" Mattie Dee waved her hand, then slipped her glasses off her nose. She no longer had the rolled-up magazine. "But he won't be bugging you no more, Miss Aisha. One of the best benefits of being what we are and flying on Normal transportation. Cheaper too."

Aisha couldn't help it. She risked a glance between hers and Mattie Dee's seat—sure enough, a blond boy no bigger than a wolf pup on enhancement foods was shaking in his seat. Eyes wider than plates. And had a mud-gray toad sitting on his bony knee.

"Perhaps I shouldn't be so keen on thanking Hilda for the company."

Mattie Dee only waved the comment away. "No, dearie. You were 'bout to tell me all about Africa. 'Cause you've been there, right? Grew up there, from what I've heard? Now, me, the only lions and tigers I've seen are Familiars wearing pink tutus and sweaters, and I don't think those count at all."

"Tigers aren't in Africa."

Mattie Dee shrugged. "Well, looks like I've got to book a trip to India next. Now, about those lions and bears...."

It was, truly, going to be a long flight.

But as Aisha talked, recalling up the bits and pieces of her childhood, bringing alive the memories she'd buried or blocked, or just simply chosen not to remember, she felt herself settle.

Prepare.

Not only was she returning to Tanzania—the place that had booted her out when she was no longer the darling daughter of their most darling wizarding couple and household—but she was well and truly, going home.

Going to visit her parents.

At their sanctuary. To piece together the missing puzzle pieces of her memory, her magic, and just where, exactly, she'd learned to understand the wild.

Mattie Dee, while she might be wrong about the tigers in Africa, wasn't wrong about the kid.

It was nice not having her seat kicked for a change.

Now, she was just going to have to do some seat-kicking of her own. The Council's seat. Because they weren't going to let this go.

Not now, and, she had a feeling, not ever.

As if this had actually happened before. If only she could remember.

CHAPTER 49

"Gee. That went well." Marcelle snorted. Turned her pink-spiked hair and that spiked neck band towards Nate and gave him a look that made even Timiculous shudder.

But Nate didn't shudder. Simply stood there on that now mostly empty dirt parking lot, except for his Mustang. And the burnt-dirt scorch marks. Tire tracks. Revved-up broomstick bristles that had frayed during liftoff.

All this was the only remnants of the Council. The only sign at all that they'd been here. Had nearly taken everything from Aisha.

The sun's noon glare didn't seem to mind. Just beat down on him until he felt like taking even that last thin, sweat-soaked shirt off. It was almost as if the weather itself was doing its part to drive the Council out as quick and painlessly as possible (well, mostly painless, because that heat sure was a killer today).

Nate wiped his brow.

It didn't matter that they'd finally, *finally* seen the last of the Council off. That he and Marcelle had waited patiently and with mouths as closed and tight-lipped as possible while the Council did their "inspection."

As Racine had predicted, and then all the present psychics confirmed, the darkness was dissipating.

Thankfully those other psychics seemed to be a bit...overwhelmed by Aisha's Waystation setup. The wildness of the place, that scorching, unrelenting heat, and the way it just sat on top of the gouged-out valley. Marcelle had explained, in a whisper early in the inspection, that the lack of familiar surroundings made it harder to get accurate readings.

Especially if you weren't properly attuned.

Which none of the Council's stooges were. Just as Nate hadn't been when he'd first arrived.

Which turned out to be a good thing because, according to Marcelle, while the "big, nasty, oozing net thing" was on its way out, it was still there, and quite a few Familiars still showed glimmers and signs of the sickness.

Which she needed Aisha to fully get rid of.

Aisha, who was currently on her way to Tanzania, wherever in Africa that was, with his father and Racine right on the tip of her broomstick.

If she was even flying by broomstick.

Nate swore. Shoved aside the dark, sticky hair that stuck to his forehead. His cheeks.

"Hey. You're not listening, genius." Marcelle snapped her black-tipped fingers at him.

She was right. He hadn't been.

"You got the Council out of the Waystation, and I'll give you props, that was some serious legal tap-dancing. A bit of a cheating hand thrown in there, but I guess it worked."

Nate managed not to smile at the half-compliment. "I am my father's son."

"Yeah, seriously, don't remind me. And speaking of dearest daddy, you know it's not over, right? That he's on his way to do Aisha serious harm? Probably lock her up. Burn her at the stake. Whatever needs doing to keep all his precious secrets, secret?"

"I do."

He knew just how far his father would go. Even covering up necessary deaths.

Like his mother's.

Possibly Aisha's, if it came down to it.

A shudder passed through Nate. Started in his chest. Ended in his chest.

Timiculous shifted on Nate's shoulder. Rubbed his head against Nate's check.

Still safe, now.

She was, at least for now. Even his father could pop in and out across the globe as he wished. He'd still need to get there using the normal means as any other witch or wizard (though fancier).

At least Timiculous was one secret that was finally in the open. A secret the Council couldn't refute or ignore—not when Timiculous's statement, truthful and unaltered, had been caught live by the newswitches and wizards.

It was one small victory.

But it wouldn't be enough.

He had no idea what that backlash would be—but had no doubt that there *would* be some. Somewhere. Somehow.

But he couldn't think about that now.

Because Marcelle was right.

Aisha was in trouble. If not now, she would be soon.

"I don't know much about her family history," he said to Marcelle. "Where she would go in Africa. Who she'd ask for help. Why her parents disinherited her. The reports were...sparse on the details."

Again, Marcelle snorted. "You can probably thank the different Councils for that. Or her stuffy parents. But the truth is, she's going into a pit of vipers and other not-nice reptiles who want to eat her."

Marcelle stepped forward. Shoved one very pointy, very sharp nail at Nate's chest. "You get what I'm saying?"

He had a feeling Marcelle and Hilda had the same nail lady sharpen those talons every week.

She jabbed at him again. "Me being the psychic that I am, I'm not going to rely on magic here and am just straight up going to ask: Are you gonna hang in there, finish this thing off, or do I need to find a different knight in shining armor?"

"I thought Aisha made her mind quite clear."

She didn't trust him.

Didn't want him near her.

Nate reached up, absently, and stroked Timiculous's beak as the macaw perched on his shoulder. Timiculous gave a whistle in return.

"Seriously? So, that's it?" Marcelle waved her finger at him as if he were a child. "She yells at you one time and you just what, throw in the towel? Decide maybe she's not worth fighting for and all that?"

"Because fighting off the Council, my father, didn't count?"

Nate's anger rose. Swirled up in his chest. His gut. Anger he'd locked up, holed away, and simply let simmer most of his life. Let his father decide the bet course, guidance, just as he'd done with Hilda.

Except walking away from Hilda, and their possible future together, wasn't the same.

Not now. Not with Aisha.

"Don't you think I want to go after her? That I don't want to see this through? That she's walking into whatever heaven-knows trap that my father has *clearly* been prepared for?"

"Really?" Marcelle piped up. "A trap, huh? Wonder how long he's been planning that for."

"Years, most likely." Nate half-turned, boots digging into the soft dirt. And froze. Years.

Dust kicked up. Stung his eyes. Clogged his throat, but he didn't care.

"You heard him," Nate whispered. "He said she couldn't tap into the truth."

Which meant Aisha did know the truth...but didn't, because that truth, whatever it was, had been blocked from her.

He closed his eyes. Balled his fists. Tighter and tighter.

"Son of a bitch," he growled.

He'd thought this was over. Thought what he'd done today, before the whole Council and all of Enchantment Avenue (all because, well, every reporter and society member of note had been present) would be enough. Enough to keep the Waystation, the Familiars, Aisha...safe.

He was wrong.

His father was going to finish what he started. What he would do to keep everyone in the dark about their Familiars, the stability of them, allowed them to keep them as less than pets and more like subservient slaves living a life their nature, their magic, could no longer tolerate.

Something had been the tipping point, clearly.

And that something, for whatever reason, was pointing right at Aisha.

"I need to get to Africa."

Marcelle nodded. Spikes bobbed up, then down. "Good. I happen to know of a quite fast, though a bit on the worn-out side, magic carpet that might just do the trick."

Nate lifted an eyebrow. "Fly. On a magic carpet. To Africa."

"No, actually. To Tanzania." Marcelle looped her arm through Nate's. Tugged him to follow. "And just think, this way you won't have to stop at any customs agents or crossover territory fly zones, because, well, no one keeps regulation tabs on magic carpets anymore. Seeing as how they're so old school."

She waved a hand at Nate's Mustang.

"Or, we could get you on a private, Normal charter jet or something."

"I'll take the carpet."

He didn't much care, really. He'd take whatever means, whatever transportation, just so long as he got to Tanzania in time.

So long as he got there, got to Aisha, before his father did.

CHAPTER 50

*S*ylvester clasped his hands behind his back. His robes, usually so smooth and silky, usually another piece of his many layers of armor, now felt constricting. Tightening.

To think he'd come so far, so close, and now one woman—barely more than a girl, even if she was his son's age—threatened everything.

He'd washed himself. Changed. Made sure every speck of that Waystation was off his person, and yet still he felt dirty. Sullied.

He resisted the urge to pull at the collar. To fidget.

Only simpletons fidgeted.

Still. He stood facing that ocean on his balcony, the endless sea of blue stretching out across the horizon—a view ruined by the rumbling of airplanes and screeching metal as they descended. Those bobbing white dots of boats on the waves. An eyesore destroying the perfect serenity of their world.

Just as Aisha was doing her best to his own world.

His hands tightened. Fingers digging into palms.

He should have destroyed her back then. Shouldn't have been lenient, shouldn't have allowed the dear memory of his wife to cloud his judgment.

But he had.

He'd allowed the girl to live, but with a memory spell blocking the most dangerous and threatening magic she had possessed.

And now it was all raging back. All of it, threatening to take him down and those fool Council members who had no idea—*none*—of the scrutiny that would be unleashed if the Familiars, and the truth of their nature, were uncovered. All the inquiries. Investigations. No decision the Council had made, probably even before their final relocation to Enchantment Avenue, would be safe.

Untouched.

Sylvester needed to stop it.

Would stop it.

By any means necessary.

The speaking-mirror floating beside him, catching his calm reflection and the magnificence, the beauty which anyone else would see of the ocean, was just another part of his armor. His unwavering control.

Sylvester clamped down on every hint of his worry, his doubts, and projected outwards the man, even his son, had grown to fear.

The shimmering image of Daniel Blakeley appeared in the mirror. Lean, almost to the point of gaunt, with a smooth face that was a complete mask of emotion. His blond hair slicked back and fair-white skin a complete contrast to the harsh, unrelenting world Daniel Blakeley and his family stepped into every day. Ruled. A place Sylvester had never intended to return to. Not after the day he'd stolen Aisha Faye's memories, her heritage.

Now, he would have to.

"My lord Sylvester?" Daniel said, his voice a bit echoed as if coming through a long, thin tunnel. Or perhaps the boy was merely surprised. "This is, ah, an unexpected call. Is all well with Enchantment Avenue? Should I call for my father?"

But Sylvester had no time for neither unsure boys or surprise.

"Unexpected? I'm not so sure of that." Sylvester glared at the image, spoke with his highest, commanding voice the Council had learned to shy away from. "I wouldn't be in need of calling if you'd handled the Faye girl with more delicacy and surety."

"Racine? But I haven't seen her since she signed the agreement with the Council. I thought all was going well with her transitioning there...?"

Sylvester barely kept from snapping at the boy. "Aisha, you fool. Aisha Faye."

The girl who'd been nothing but a headache, a constant sore on the back of his impeccable, unblemished record.

The one loose end he'd left dangling...

This time, Daniel swallowed. His arrogance, his inbred attitude that his parents—and Sylvester—had been sure to cultivate and nurture, finally faded. Enough to show discomfort.

"I'm not sure I understand, Lord Sylvester. I've heard no news of Aisha since she left the Proper, and her conditioning, of course. I was under the impression that your...help with the situation would be permanent and cause no lasting problems. For us. Or any of the Councils. Is the situation not progressing well?"

Sylvester wanted to reach through the mirror and smack the boy. Daniel, as inbred and trained as he was, was just like Asher and all those other fools underneath him.

Unimaginative fools.

"Aisha Faye's situation was never 'permanent'," Sylvester said, his voice as steely and cold as that monstrous metal plane screeching overhead. "As you should know from your studies. Memory spells can be, and often are, dangerous tools. There is no guarantee for a lifetime hold. Not even when the caster is a master in the art."

Which Sylvester was.

Sylvester felt the strands of his control fraying. Anger. Frustration. Everyone else's ineptitude. Each took its tool, stripped his power from him, bit by bit.

He took a deep, calming breath.

Listened to the call of gulls beneath his ocean view villa. The plane was gone, and for once, he only heard the gulls and that constant give and pull, the crash and recede of waves against the craggy rocks and *not* the engines of airplanes or sounds of distant cars backfiring and smoking up the crystal view.

"So, then," Daniel broke into Sylvester's calming breaths, "Aisha's memory is returning?"

"An unfortunate series of circumstances has allowed some of her memories to resurface," Sylvester explained. "The Council was not able to intervene in time, even with those of our employ in place beforehand."

Because Sylvester had trusted in Aisha's sister, Racine, to figure out the threads of how to stop it before Aisha did.

Because of his son.

Daniel licked his lips. Nodded. "She's coming here, then, isn't she?"

"To the place, I believe, that opened her heritage magic in the first place. Do you know of it?"

Daniel shook his head. "I wasn't with her then. She'd snuck out of the Proper. Even did so without her mother being aware, which was a real surprise when I learned of her escape the next day. And then, of course, you and I found her. But I can find out where she went," Daniel quickly said when Sylvester leaned in closer to the mirror.

His nose practically pressing down on the boy.

"See that you do so."

"Of course." Daniel glanced away. "Will you be returning then? Is there anything else I should plan for your arrival?"

He'd need to hurry. Rush. And Sylvester hated rushing.

Too much would be left to chance. But there was no choice. He'd set up blocks and passport declines all throughout the western states, any mode a witch would try to leave the States from, but she hadn't been spotted.

Or stopped.

He'd need to rely on the assumption that Aisha was already on her way to Tanzania, to the Proper and that backwater tribe her mother was birthed from.

Her mother.

Sylvester's lips twisted. Smiled, for the first time in what felt like in a lifetime.

"Yes. There is one thing you can do."

"Anything, my lord."

"Send a call request to the Faye family, specifically Rosaline." Daniel Blakeley might not know where Aisha had gone, but the mother would. Mother always did. "I will be staying with them for the duration of this event."

An event that would end in the destruction of their daughter. An event that neither of her parents could protest because of the contract they'd signed all those years ago.

With him.

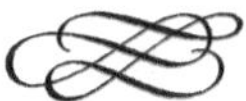

CHAPTER 51

Aisha gripped the strap of her duffel bag slung over her shoulder. The strap digging into the bare skin next to her tank top.

Couldn't move.

Couldn't seem to take that next step.

To cross that short distance that would bring her home.

So instead, she stared across the narrowed expanse of Lake Eyasi—and honestly didn't know what was worse. To cross that illusion tucked away beside the lake (along with the very expensive, very good counter-spell, repellent-charm to keep Normals and undesirables from stumbling into the Proper), bringing her right to her parents doorstep, or stand there, staring out into a world where her heart truly belonged—the same world she'd walked away from.

Even now, she could practically feel the lake's slow, lapping, shallow waters. Sliding against her ankles, sucking and pulling, not from any wind or breeze, but just from the nature's balance of all things as she walked barefoot across as the lake. The parched, dried-up lake, which had slowly vanished during the dry season.

Aisha slammed her eyes closed. Squeezed them.

Breathed.

That wasn't happening now.

But when had it happened?

She couldn't remember. Not the day. Not the time.

Just that it had been when she'd decided to visit her grandfather's people, to understand herself and her heritage. But still, try as she might, couldn't remember anything except that briny salt against her dried lips as she'd licked them. The feel of the warmed water around, disappearing even as she walked.

Even now, there was that salt against her lips. A slight spray.

It was the same as now, just as she had tasted then.

But right now she had on her boots. Right now the lake was brimming with water. Overflowing, even. Possibly even hippos were scattered about, having been lured down by the abundance of water from the Serengeti to the north.

But there no mistaking, none at all, the migrating flock of brilliant and pale pink. Flamingos with their long, spindly, stilted legs. Dark, curved bills scooping up the shrimp that gave their feathers such a beautiful color.

Just a sea of pink, really.

Aisha wiped a tear from her eye. Couldn't help the ease and comfort slowly sliding through her. Even if, just beyond the sight of what most Normals saw, was the hidden and famous sanctuary her parents ran.

The place she was raised.

And while she could stand here, stare all day (or to be honest, two days, because yesterday when she'd arrived hadn't actually gotten the courage to take those final steps either), none of that would change the fact that the Council was after her. That if Hilda and her buddy Mattie Dee were right, it wouldn't take Sylvester Darkwood long to get here. She'd even gotten a text from Marcelle warning her that Racine had told the Council exactly where she'd gone.

Marcelle, at least, hadn't mentioned anything about Nate.

As much as it hurt. As much she had wanted Marcelle to say something.

Anything.

Aisha shoved Nate from her mind. Heart. Had to.

She'd already lost a full two days to her hesitation, her fears. That was truthfully all the time she could afford. So, she made herself focus on Nate's father, Sylvester Darkwood. Thought again, and again, just as she'd done on the flight, why his very name brought such a tightening in her stomach. A cold, numbing sensation to her fingers.

As far as she knew, she'd never met the man before Asher had introduced them.

And yet, clearly, some part of her, perhaps the animal part, the natural part, was afraid of him.

Aisha swept a hand across her forehead. Wiped away the sticky, constant sweat pooling on her face. At least she knew Sylvester Darkwood was arriving by dragon flight. And while dragon flight was sure as hell a lot more sturdy and safer (though dragons tended to be temperamental, moody, and often hungry) than the Normal way with airplanes—a floating, flying tin can at elevations humans were simply not meant to go—the Normal way *was* faster.

Aisha turned from the lake, the ache in her heart, even as part of her looked—one last time—to see if she could spot any dark, spindly frames not belonging to flamingos but to her true heritage.

A man, or woman, from the Hadzabe tribe.

She saw no one.

And perhaps, she thought, that was for the best.

She shifted her duffel bag up higher. Felt the sucking heat already breaking through what energy and sleep she'd snatched on the plane. Turned to follow the shore and the palm trees bordering the lake, as if they'd been plucked straight from here, transported, and shoved straight down all along on the coast of southern California. As if they were the same palm trees lining the fancy cobblestone streets of Enchantment Avenue itself.

Aisha kept her focus in mind. Kept the reason why she was here— protecting Lanhi, her Familiars, her Waystation—as she passed through the shimmering barrier of her parents' sanctuary—a barrier that looked more like a distant mirage of some far-off water overlapping the grass plains beyond the lake.

And for the first time in years, stepped into the shining, glinting world of open cages.

Unlocked, unspelled doors.

She could see in the distance the tiny, dark forms of trackers and handlers as they rode horseback between enclosures. Enclosures simply meant to separate predator from prey and nothing more. The handlers also moved and dodged and corralled Familiars to and from pockets of that Familiar's wizard-like life, reminders and tokens like Lanhi's tutu and posters, and the natural home these Familiars were always a part of.

For a moment, her breath caught. Heart swelled at what was before her.

Not her home anymore. But it had been.

She'd found love and life and hope on the free-range plains of the Serengeti Magical Proper Sanctuary.

She'd also found betrayal. Rejection.

Hurt that ran deep, straight to her heart's core.

Still did. A hurt that, just by being here, she felt tearing open. Threatening to spill out. Overwhelm.

She couldn't let that happen. Couldn't, not when her Familiars, her Waystation, depended on her.

Aisha adjusted her duffel back and continued walking—right towards the heart of the Proper—the glorious, palm-crested buildings, thatched roofs. The wide-open windows that provided the perfect viewing experience, so perfect it was as if a Familiar's owner was right there on the plains with their believed pets.

She walked. One step. Then another. Focused on each one. Took strength that she was taking this, literally, one step at a time. All the while knowing she wouldn't reach the buildings, the Proper's headquarters, before he'd come for her.

Come to send her away. Again.

Her father.

CHAPTER 52

*A*isha's boots dipped into and bent the soft, spongy, moist grass. Grass that was only this green, this long and unchewed by the herders—the wildebeests and giraffes and spindly, lean gazelle —during the one time of the year when the rains came and poured life back into this parched, dried-up valley. When the overflowing rivers plunged back into the lake.

Everything was exactly like she remembered.

As if she'd never left.

Including the rider who veered off from the main group. Hair, she noticed, even from this distance and closing, that was now graying, especially where wisps stuck to the sides of his face. Wisps that had slipped free from underneath his cowboy hat.

Aisha couldn't help but reach up. Adjust her own hat.

She'd gotten the habit from him.

Had wanted to impress him. To be like him.

Just like the comfort and ease he had on horseback. The way which his body moved with the horse's, as if they were one, intimate, communicating—unlike the graying hair, which was new, how he and the horse rode together hadn't changed at all.

They were completely attuned. Were in complete communication.

Just like Nate and Timiculous were.

Aisha swept her hat from her head. Wiped away sweat with her forearm. Told herself, again, it was just the heat and nothing more. Then she, completely and fully, shoved Nate from her mind.

Just like she swept aside her heartache. The same ache she felt, swelling. Pooling. Wanting to escape.

To leave this place before he got here.

Smokey, the dabbled black-and-gray horse, had acquired some extra gray as well. Around the muzzle. Creeping up long, lean face. Smokey was more than a horse: a Familiar. Like many of the horses that the handlers used while on range duty. Made things easier to control; safer, too, especially when dealing with the larger predators.

And just, well, larger animals.

Elephants and hippos might not want to eat you, but that didn't mean they weren't dangerous. Aisha, along with everyone else who'd grown up in the Proper, who'd trained in the Proper, had learned that lesson.

Fast.

Still, as the rider rode closer, each hoof beat like a pounding of her own heart, she saw his narrowed brown eyes. And the hurt—definitely hurt—as her father, for the first time in years, saw his eldest daughter.

The daughter who had been disinherited and let go.

Her father, Albert Faye, known throughout Africa and beyond for his radical notions on caring for and raising wild-bred Familiars, for bridging the gap between the wild and luxury and prestige, slowed Smokey. He didn't even pull back on the reins. Smokey just seemed to know, probably because he did. Probably because her father simply told him to.

"You were told never to return."

Aisha dug her fingers into duffel bag. Pinched and squeezed the fabric until it felt as if it cut through her skin. She didn't let up.

"I had reason to."

"So you think. Your sister called. Told me to expect you."

Aisha flushed, thinking that perhaps she should have thought about that first over the fast travels of dragon flight. But there was no turning back. Not now.

"Daddy."

The word...hurt. Cut through her lips like it had been cut straight from her heart.

Her father didn't flinch. Didn't even move, as if the word meant nothing to him.

Probably because it didn't.

Aisha swallowed. Lifted her chin. Didn't back down. Even if the last thing in the world was for her to return here, groveling. Begging.

But her Familiars depended on her. Her Waystation depended on her.

"I need help."

"Again, so your sister said. But you won't find help here."

"So that's it, then? You're going to toss me out. Abandon helpless, *innocent* Familiars to their fate—which we both know what that will be—simply because you're still pissed that I didn't fall in line with the Family's way of doing things, and *only* the Family's way?"

Her father's face hardened. "You were told never to come back."

"Well, we both know how good I was at listening, so let's just get back to the point." Aisha dropped her duffel bag to the ground. It thumped down.

Right at Smokey's dancing hooves. The horse barely kept from squishing her undies, he was so agitated.

Which was fine. Just fine with her.

Aisha slapped her hands on her hips. "Let's get one thing straight here. You can be pissed all you want, but don't forget there is more than one Family in this bloodline, and if you're so ticked about a young woman being curious where she came from, maybe you should have thought twice before marrying Mom!"

Her father's dark brown eyes darkened to almost black. The roadmap of wrinkles and laugh lines, continuously touched by the sun's unbearable heat, stood out. Pinched together as he withdrew from her, physically, mentally, and, like always, emotionally.

Just like always.

Aisha felt her shoulders lower. Sag. "You know, for as insightful and 'before-your-time' that the different Councils and critics proclaim you to be, you really are just as prejudiced and bigoted as the rest of them. You may act like the bigger man, giving these Familiars as close to their natural home as possible, letting them choose to leave and return as they fit, but so long as it suits you."

Aisha took the short, but distant—wide—steps separating them.

Snatched up her bag. Yanked it right back on her shoulder.

"I guess the same holds true for daughters. Regardless how long they've been gone. Regardless that they've been raised exactly as you wanted them to be. Until they do something that doesn't suit what *you* want."

She turned on her boots.

Dug her heels into the moist, springy grass. Grass she used to ride across, day, night, and every time in between. The same grass she'd close her eyes and walk barefoot through, just exploring, just being.

Just living.

She'd find the answer on her own. Didn't need their help. Didn't need their disapproval or resentment.

"Aisha."

Her father. Calling her.

She didn't want to stop. Didn't want to turn. Didn't want to acknowledge that even now, even after all these years, he could still hurt her.

But she did stop.

She didn't, however, turn.

"The wasting sickness." His words were short. Clipped. As if they carried across a great distance.

Probably because they did.

"We have had no cases here."

That was all he said.

All she heard next was the turning and pounding of hooves. Clicking up dirt and mud and grass. Away from her, just like always.

Aisha squeezed her eyes closed.

Couldn't help the single tear that slipped free.

CHAPTER 53

*A*isha wiped the tear away. Nodded, but only to herself. Her father's words were more help than she'd expected. And they'd have to be enough.

Had to be.

She adjusted her duffel bag. Slipped it higher up on her shoulder so the heavy weight didn't gouge a chunk of her out, or just leave a nasty bruise, and kept heading for the exit.

Not that she had any idea where she'd go next.

Where she could go.

Just that the answers were here. In Africa.

Somewhere.

But damn, Africa—even Tanzania—weren't exactly small little islands with answers right in front of her face. And she wasn't exactly on a lingering vacation where she could just pick up her feet and have a nice martini with those little purple umbrellas…unlike the clients her family currently hosted back at the Proper's headquarters.

"There's nothing for it," she said to herself. "I've got to head into the bush."

And hope she found Grandfather or another tribesman more willing to help her than her own parents had been.

Aisha again left the Proper without anyone to see her off, to wish her well and say they'd miss her when she was gone. Well, Aisha's tears were now gone, though her heart was still heavy—her heart that froze when she saw the small, compact woman gazing at Aisha.

The woman wore fine, close-fitting pants and a short tunic. Tailor-made and seeming to shimmer from the nearby illusion. Her long, black hair braided neatly together as if servants had spent hours making each plait and twist perfect.

And yet, despite the finery, despite the luxury that seemed to glow off her, the woman lounged, silent and at ease, just inside the illusion. Back pressed against the spiky bark of an acacia tree as if its harsh, unwelcome touch didn't bother her at all. Her head tilted up as if soaking in every ray of sun and light. Her skin, though, was just as dark as the evening's cloudy rains. She seemed so content, so at peace with this sweltering, unforgiving, and yet beautiful valley.

So calm as she stood up, just as silent as she'd arrived, without Aisha even noticing, and came forward.

Feet that weren't bare, but wore sturdy, comfortable hiking boots. But feet that, at one point, had walked these hills and valleys and over that same salty lake with only the calluses and hard lessons to protect them. In fact, she had spent most of her life living and breathing this bare, natural world.

Even if she'd never spoken much of it.

Aisha sucked in a breath. Couldn't speak.

Not as the woman came forward. Slow and careful, as if each step she chose with deliberate ease and care. Feet that should have been holed up inside headquarters, greeting and welcoming guests, seeing to comforts, and oftentimes, out riding the same plains as Albert Faye did.

But the woman wasn't there. She was here.

Greeting her eldest daughter.

"What?" Aisha licked her suddenly dry, parched lips. "What are you doing here?"

Her mother, Rosaline Faye (a name she'd changed when she'd shed the life of her tribe, adopting one more suitable for high magical society), merely tilted her head to the side. Her long braid falling over her shoulder.

"I am where I should have been, this whole time." Rosaline spoke with a slight deepening of her voice. As if the words, at least when speaking to family, weren't natural, but close enough to familiar. "Waiting."

"For what?"

"For you to come home."

Her mother's words hit Aisha in the gut. Made her stumble back.

Her duffel bag slid down her shoulder, nearly falling to the ground. She grabbed the strap with numb, cold fingers—despite the sweltering, unforgiving heat.

"Daddy's made his wishes pretty clear." Just like he always did. Always.

"He has. As I have allowed, and which has been required of us. But you did not come to return home. You did not return to the Great Valley for heart's yearning. You came for answers."

Aisha bit back her first reply. The one that wanted to spill out. Toss up all over the floor: what she wanted to know, more than anything else, was why her mother hadn't fought for her the first time.

Fought against her father, fought against society and what the great House of Blakeley had wanted her to become. Had instead stood up for the wild child of her heart. The child Rosaline had walked away from when she'd accepted Albert Faye's marriage proposal.

But Aisha didn't ask. Just like her mother hadn't stood up for her. Fought for her.

"You know about the sickness." This was the question, the information Aisha needed to know.

More than the truth of the past. More than why her mother had felt it better to watch her flesh and blood leave forever than to fight for her.

"I do. Just as your father does, but more, importantly..." Her mother came forward then. Reached out, touched Aisha right above her stomach.

A warm touch. Aching, too. Hurting.

Touched Aisha right where her magic was. Where it, even now, swirled and danced and did nervous little twists. As if it was slowly coming together again. Returning to what it was before…before it was taken from her.

And yet it hurt to even think that, even in magic, she was so like her mother.

And so very different.

"More importantly," her mother said, "*you* already know of the sickness."

Which was about as helpful as Timiculous and his cryptic comments. And, of course, thinking about Timiculous meant thinking about Nate. How he'd lied to her. Hurt her. As her father did, her mother.

Nate, who'd made her feel, for the first time in years, *loved*.

Aisha shoved herself back. From Nate. From her mother.

From her own, aching heart.

She let her mother's hand linger in the air.

"Look," Aisha said. "I'm glad you came out here. To meet me. Better late than never, but considering the Council wants to tie me to a stake without trial or a hearing, and simply burn me alive to keep *their* secret a damn secret, I'm not looking for cryptic word games. My Familiars, my life, my *freedom* is on the line. Again. And if you're not going to help—fine. Then leave me alone."

Aisha shoved past her mother. Made sure she didn't brush the smaller woman. Made sure her mother didn't see how her throat tightened. How the tears seemed to swell and clog within her eyes.

How badly, desperately, she just needed to run.

Far, far away from this place she'd loved—this place of hurt.

Except her mother's hand reached out. Touched Aisha's shoulder.

She froze.

Not from any magic. Not exactly. This went deeper. Further even than a mother's loving touch to a child.

It was a touch, tribe to tribe. Heart to heart.

"Grandfather awaits you. The bent acacia tree. Onwas awaits you there, to lead you to the tribe."

"How does he know I'm here?"

There was a soft tightening on Aisha's shoulder. As if her mother was holding on, digging in a little bit, so as to never let go. "Because I told him. But you must know, Grandfather is not the only one who knows you've come home."

Aisha slowly turned. But didn't pull away. Instead, let her mother's hand rest where it was, and she secretly, quietly, soaked up every inch of warmth and love as if it were her last.

"I thought you said I didn't come home."

"You did not. But others believe so. So long as they do, you will not be allowed to return. Not to the woman you were awakening to be."

Again, there was the cryptic answer talk.

Aisha *would* have stormed off—she really wasn't kidding when she'd said she had enough of that with Timiculous—but if there were answers to save Familiars, then damn it, someone should be responsible and just give them to her already.

But she didn't stomp off.

Because, because there was a slight pull along her mother's lip. Not a smile, but something else. A knowing.

A knowing that resonated within Aisha. Struck to her very core, even if she couldn't reach out and touch this feeling herself.

But it was there. Buried, and deep.

As much as her mother had shed her old life, Aisha knew there was much she'd kept. Hidden. Held close.

The memory of this, of this knowing and understanding, tingled. Nudged against Aisha's mind. Her memory. The one that had, she realized, been taken from her.

By someone.

The realization nearly caused her legs to give out. To sink right down into that grassy, springy plains. Amidst the herds roaming far across the Proper, content and one with life.

The sharp smell of nature and dung and life drifted to her.

Home.

Pulled again at the memory. Drew it closer.

Finally, her mother let go. "What was taken from you will return, but you must hurry to the bent tree. As I spoke, and even now, others are aware you've returned and fear what you do not remember."

Her mother waved at Aisha's stomach again—at the magic there.

"Who?"

"The one who'd claimed love and devotion, but only wanted one thing."

This time Aisha's knees did shake. Her bag did slid to the ground. Resting there on that grass and overturned, fresh, moist dirt. Watched as her mother turned, silent, without even bending the grass, and left her. Once again.

But there was nothing more that she needed to say. Not when Aisha already knew.

Blakeley.

It was Blakeley who knew she'd returned.

Blakeley, who, like the Council, like Sylvester Darkwood, would destroy her at all costs.

She raised a hand to her head. Touched the sweat-slicked skin, the buried and taken memories, and wondered if Blakeley already had.

$\mathcal{S}$ylvester wrapped a silk scarf around his neck. Raised it to his lips. Pressed it against his nose. Did his best to not directly breathe that hot humid air, the clogging, clutching dust and dirt that was intent on seeping through his very skin.

He hated Africa.

Almost as much as hated the man sitting on that wretched, aging horse. Barely more than a four-legged-bag-of-bones, and a Familiar too. One Albert Faye trusted his life to every time he sat on the thing.

Should have been destroyed long ago. Gotten a replacement. Younger. More docile.

Behind Sylvester was his entourage. Several of the Council members, and Daniel Blakeley as well, who'd met them at the dragon landing facility with all the proper transportation and convenience that Sylvester's station required.

Demanded.

Except they'd had to disembark from the air-conditioned vehicles when they'd reached the Proper's entrance gate.

Some time in the past few years, Albert had altered the requirements to enter. Only a driver of vehicles could remain inside, and while they might be *Normal* creations, they did provide a great deal of comfort. Like, constant cool blowing air. Filtered air. Chilled water and other such items.

Which was why Sylvester was standing there in this heat and dust and glaring up at the man who, Sylvester was positive, had made such a change to infuriate him. As if, as much as he denied Aisha's existence, he'd expected this moment.

Expected both hers, and Sylvester's, return.

That monstrous horse stamped its hooves. Called up more of that dust and dirt to billow out between the two men, and those behind Sylvester who hadn't the forethought to have some item to protect their mouths and nose.

They coughed.

Sylvester didn't. Just pressed the scarf closer. Was sorely tempted to end that horse's existence right at this moment.

With Albert Faye on top of him.

The hooves ground and clomped again before Albert got the beast under control.

Hooves that had come far too close to Sylvester and his carefully polished and spelled shoes. Not that the spells he'd placed on his person were doing anything to keep back that wretched, scratching brown and red dirt Africa insisted on having.

As if his magic barely had a foothold on this wretched, dirty land. In this country.

"You got here mighty quick," Albert said, in his most Western-like drawl, purposefully drawing out the accent just to irate Sylvester.

It had always been the way between them.

"I have great need," Sylvester said.

"Where's my daughter?"

"That was the question I had posed to you, remember?"

Albert tipped back the brim of his flopping, sweat-stained hat. "I've only got one daughter. Racine's the one you had get through to me, you and that Blakeley tricking me into taking your call. Before you so kindly *informed* me of the situation. So. Where is she?"

"Regretfully, this is not the task to which she's been assigned. She's needed back in the States, overseeing the unfortunate circumstances surrounding your *other* daughter's Waystation. The one I'd nearly succeeded in closing down."

Albert leaned over the side of his horse, somehow not falling off the thing, and spit.

A great glob of it. Sylvester didn't even spare it a glance.

"Don't know where she's got to."

"But she was here," Sylvester pressed.

Sweat trickled down the back of his neck. He felt some flying creature land there. Felt its tiny little legs exploring, nuzzling.

He slapped a hand. Squashing it.

This conversation shouldn't be happening here. Not in the middle of the Proper with all those beasts and Familiars eying them. Roaming free across that almost dead grass plains. That salty lake which looked barely bigger than a fishbowl. It took all of Sylvester's control not to squirm. To glance about. Study the possible threats. Prepare the spells that would destroy them all.

Instead, he glared at Albert.

He would not ask to take this conversation inside, away from the gossip ears behind him. That, after all, was what Albert wanted. A good move, truly, one Sylvester used on many occasions himself.

He just hated Africa.

Everything about it and this cursed land.

Which was why Albert had ridden ahead, meeting them at the illusionary gate. Kept the power, what little of it he had, in his control.

"I made my intentions quite clear," Sylvester said. "You are to provide accommodations for me, the other Council members and those who accompanied us, until the matter of your eldest daughter, Aisha Faye, has been settled. Per our agreement years ago. The one established before either of your daughters was even born. At your insistence, and creation of this...this *place*."

Albert didn't move. Just sat atop that beast, hands gripping the horn of the saddle, clutching those dirty reins, and sat there—as if he waited long enough he'd win this test of wills.

But Sylvester was beyond these games. Had lost his willingness to participate the moment he was forced to ride that dragon to get here.

Sylvester reached within himself. To the magic always at his command. Drew it closer to the surface, to his eyes, which he knew flashed and warned. A brightened red glow. No one, not even Albert Faye with his great sanctuary intentions that sought to change the whole of the magical world—and failed—could fail to notice just how dangerous his situation was.

This was a magic, a particular magic, Sylvester could call up because he owned them. Owned the land around them, and this forsaken place with its ancient bush-people magic couldn't do anything to stop him.

Not while the contract between him and Rosaline Faye held.

Albert Faye only twitched his lips.

As if smiling.

Enough.

Sylvester grabbed hold of his magic—didn't need a wand—not for a spell he knew with his whole being—ready to sent straight at the old, graying man—

"We give you greetings, Lord Chancellor."

A slender, dark, and slight woman *appeared* from the land itself. As if she faded in. Where before Sylvester knew there was only more of that parched grass, that damned tree littered with thorns and whatever it called leaves—then there was Rosaline.

She, like Albert, hadn't change much over the years. Her skin appeared darker, as if she were a true creature of the night, but there were more wrinkles. They lined her eyes, the corners of her mouth, as if she'd given up with those all-important protection spells any woman of breeding would take care to uphold. Maintain. Instead Rosaline seemed to have slowly faded from what was accepted and appropriate for a woman of her station.

More of those beads, gaudy things her "people" had taken a liking to. And more strips of leather instead of actual shirts or dresses.

At least, so it appeared to Sylvester.

But she was not *his* wife and if Albert enjoyed the company and companionship of a woman was barely above feral, such an uncivilized creature, then that was no problem of his.

Their daughter, as much as they pretended she no longer existed, was his problem.

Sylvester withdrew his magic.

There was a collective sigh behind him, which he didn't even bother with a glance. The fools had known what they'd signed on for when they'd accompanied him. They'd followed for the gossip and the prestige. They'd also deal with any unpleasantries that might—that *would*—arise.

"Rosaline."

She bowed. It was courtly and appropriate. At least some of her teachings hadn't faded through the years.

"Where is your daughter?"

Albert twitched on that beast of his. Sylvester spared him a narrow, pointed glare. "Unless you know where she is, Lord Albert?"

"I told you."

Sylvester waved his hand. "Yes, you did. Which we will deal with. Presently. But first, I believe the Lady Rosaline has some...information for me, do you not?"

She did.

He could feel it.

Feel it in the way his spell, the one that was still alive, active, and pulsing within Aisha, warned. Both parents had seen the daughter, but it was the mother who knew.

Because Aisha wasn't here.

That much Sylvester knew, not that he'd expected differently.

But it was that damn heritage of Rosaline that had started this mess. Even though it was her magic that had allowed the Proper to flourish, that gave the Council insights on how to best control the growing...stability issue with their Familiars.

Everything came at a cost.

"I am growing tired of waiting." Sylvester slapped at his neck again. Another crawling bug, he was sure.

Or just more sweat.

Either way, he was through with these games.

Rosaline nodded once. "Aisha was here, but it is no longer."

"Yes, I gathered that. Do you know where she is? Right this moment?"

Rosaline tilted her head to the side. There were a few beads braided into her thick, string-like dark hair. "She has gone into the bush. To remember. To relearn."

Sylvester breathed in. Barely kept his fists from clenching. "Where, exactly?"

Rosaline didn't flinch. Not even when his magic flared.

"Where?" he growled.

"The place," Rosaline said, voice sounding like the quiet threat of rain, thunder rumbling in the distance, "where you stole what was hers."

CHAPTER 55

Aisha kept her shoes on as she made her way through the bush. It was early, so early the sun was barely glinting over the top of the horizon. Her duffel bag was still slung over her shoulder, still heavy and still growing heavier with each step, with each new wave of heat slapping down at her.

Right along with thoughts of Blakeley.

She reached up. Touched her forehead. The slick sweat coating and dotting her skin.

It might be early but the sun didn't seem to care, and that made it feel a little more comfortable. As if she was back at the Waystation and not hunting through the bush for her elusive heritage and memories.

Her memories—which brought thoughts of Blakeley up again.

Had he been the one to steal them? She knew he was there that day. Knew, because he was the only sliver of a memory she could even grasp.

But did he have the magical powers? The cunning and skill required to cast so clearly a difficult spell?

Aisha lowered her hand. Adjusted her bag so it didn't quite dig as much into the raw flesh of her shoulder.

Last night, after returning from her confusing, and quite failed, trip to the Proper, she'd asked the small hostel owner about Blakely. Really, the hostel was barely more than a cot with an outhouse within trotting distance—but the owner had remembered her from before. Fondly, even.

Even if she couldn't remember him.

And while she'd asked about Blakeley, there wasn't much of relevance he could tell her. He was a Normal, after all, and only marginally aware of the political pull from the great house that was Blakeley. He'd told her only that the eldest son was around often, in his fancy clothes that suited a Paris ball than her, and what the blazes a boy like that was doing out here in the bush of the Great Rift, the hostel owner hadn't a fly's sense for a wildebeest's mud-pie.

Aisha had hoped to learn more, but only Normals came through and stayed in the hostel. Any magical folk would be clients or employees of the Proper—who mostly likely would have heard her father's stance on the matter of, well, of her.

The plain's grass bent and cracked underneath her feet. Thorns plucked and tore at her pants—she'd tucked the ends into her boots but swore it didn't make a difference. By the end of the day she'd be scratched and red from the ankles on up. She was absolutely not going to think about just how far *up*.

The further she moved from the lake, the further the land became dry and parched. As if the land itself had decided to avoid the tribes' restricted lands altogether. That small allotment of land the Normals of Tanzania had allowed the Hadzabe to live on.

A reservation.

All because the government was embarrassed by a people who continually rejected civilization, modernization.

She knew a huge push of that movement came from the magical community. Those who wanted to control the area around the different Sanctuaries, especially the Proper. Keep the secrets here, secret. Keep the Normals and their recorders and digital cameras and nosing, curious minds away from anything that might appear...magical.

Blakeley and his family were the biggest ruling bunch when it came to politics. They always had been. Riding between the Normal and Magical World, bending the one to suit the other.

Regardless of who—or what—was herded over in the process.

It was how she'd met him, initially. Not that there wasn't ever someone of the great house of Blakeley at the Proper, but until she'd turned of "proper" age, the Blakeley family hadn't paid her much mind.

Or Racine, at least, so Aisha remembered.

Perhaps the land saw this cracked ground as yet another form of retribution, as if the land blamed the Hadzabe itself for how much it'd changed, been developed over the years, as if it believed the Hadzabe had abandoned them and not the witches and wizards who actually oversaw its care, use, development.

She'd seen much during the flight—as much as her queasy stomach had allowed—and the sight itself had nearly sent her to use those little bags Mattie Dee had waved in front of Aisha's face like a white flag.

The farming and the livestock lands that now stretched even further through the Great Rift Valley. Cut like Normal, little cross-cut waffles with a stream or river of syrup running through. Like every section, every piece had its place.

Had lost its wildness.

Much like the Familiars had. Like Lanhi.

What would her grandfather have to say about this? Did he believe the land held them, its people and its caretakers, responsible?

Aisha shook her head. A silly question. Especially when she couldn't even remember the man, not really. Just a fuzzy blur.

A blur that became clearer in her mind, more solid with each step, but still not enough to see. To know and remember.

She also wondered, not for the first or even the fifth time, why and how she knew where she was going.

Why she knew, even with her eyes closed, which way to the bent acacia tree her mother had spoken of.

Aisha finally reached the acacia tree, bent from age and a lightning strike that had nearly snapped the trunk in two—yet still held on, still clutched onto life. Signs of baboons that had perched there, scraping up and down that thorny, uninviting trunk. The ground around it packed and trodden as if many animals had passed through here; had, at one time, called this place home.

Or perhaps just a place to rest.

Aisha unslung her bag. Collapsed onto the ground—a safe dirt spot with no ants or spiny bushes out to eat her—and took a long chug from her water. It spill down the sides of her mouth. Slid down her neck and into her shirt.

She leaned back. Closed her eyes and sighed.

Sighed from exhaustion.

Sighed from the energy thrumming through her. Her magic sparking and shaking. Dancing. It hadn't stopped dancing since she'd set foot out of the Proper, since she'd begun to follow a path she couldn't remember but her body did.

Her magic did.

Felt finally the worry and the tension releasing. Finally allowed herself, just for a moment, to wonder about Nate. She'd lost herself too long in the memories here. Had delayed too long before stepping foot in the Proper and now that she was finally giving herself this moment to breathe, to think...she couldn't help but think of him. Of the way her chest twisted and twisted until it felt like it'd come undone.

Had he followed through with his promise? Had he somehow managed to protect her Waystation? Her Familiars?

The anger in her, the hurt, betrayal, wanted to deny it. To squash aside any feelings and just live and thrive on that anger...

But she knew better. Knew one didn't thrive on anger. Only spiraled down, down, until hitting a bottom you couldn't see, couldn't fathom—only to then claw back up from.

And despite all that anger—she believed him.

Even now, even thousands of miles away, across a vast ocean and two continents, she believed in him.

He wouldn't let her down. Even if he'd lied about the truth—about who he was and who he worked for—it still didn't change the truth.

He would fight for her Familiars.

For her.

Aisha smiled and being here, in a place where her mind finally felt rested, peaceful, joyful, she allowed herself that smile. Didn't try to hide it or change what it was.

Because she cared for him.

Loved him, even still.

The magic in her gut bucked. Tried, it felt like, to ram itself up her throat.

Aisha's eyes shot open. "What the—"

But the words died because she found herself no longer alone.

An aging man stood before her. Thin and fit. Tattered shorts held on by sheer will as if he'd only had the one pair and it had worked well enough for the past twenty or thirty or fifty years. A hunting knife was strapped to his hip, but safe in a sheath of hide. Not drawn at her, either.

A face lined, not with wrinkles—although there were some—but more a roadmap of tattoos, like his chest. His dark chest bared to the sun—but they weren't tattoos, not exactly.

Scars.

Scars that ran from his face to his chest. A lifetime of living in the bush. In the wild. Leopard slashes. Snake bites. A long gouge that trailed down his rib cage from falling out of a acacia tree.

She could almost remember each one. Each scar that came with a story, a story of living and bravery, and most of all, wisdom, which followed alongside the proudly displayed marks. Could almost hear the throaty, deep words as if it were a breeze just touching the back of her neck.

But no closer.

And that knife—she could almost remember holding it. The weight of it. The feel of that worn leather binding beneath her grip. In her own hand. From a very young age.

Aisha's mouth lowered.

This wasn't just Onwas, sent to met her at the bent acacia as her mother had said.

This, this was her grandfather.

CHAPTER 56

*A*isha sat on the warm, dry dirt. The reddish-brown granules sliding over her boots. Couldn't help but stare up at the small man, thin and scarred, but who seemed, suddenly, so much taller.

As if her memory was trying its best to say that yes, yes he was taller. Older. Wiser. Much more than his small size allowed for.

And she knew that it was true.

Another puzzle clicked into place and she realized, she *remembered*, that she did know him. Had grown up knowing him. Always in the background, the outskirts, but often near. Checking up on Aisha, on his own daughter who now lived a life so different than his own.

Her grandfather's lips, thin and dry and cracked, pulled back into a grin. Not a toothy grin—he was missing at least half—but it was a grin, and the joy would have knocked her to her butt if she wasn't already sitting.

"Grand...grandfather?"

He spoke. But it was in the Hadzabe language. Tilting and gentle for a moment, and then jarring with clicks and pop-pops.

Her heart, her magic, soared.

Aisha shook her head. "I'm sorry—I can't, I can't understand."

His joy faded, but only a moment. Just a single nod. As if under-standing.

Completely.

"I can't remember," Aisha clarified. As if she needed to. As if she single-handedly needed to bring that joy back—to think that someone would look at her like that, as if she were the cause.

But Nate had looked at her that way, too.

Often. The more they'd spent time together.

Aisha swallowed. Pushed passed the lump in her throat.

"I'm sorry," she said. "I know we spent time together. In my child-hood and later, but I can't remember."

She tapped her forehead. "Something's wrong with my memories."

"Is okay, daughter of my daughter. Onwas is only joyful to see you home. To see you smile. And that you love, again. Maybe? Yes?"

There was a twinkle in his eyes, a knowingness that made Aisha shift on that patch of red-brown dirt. Squirm. Like she was a little kid looking at something, or someone, she shouldn't have seen.

Her face heated. How with, only seeing her for a few minutes, had he known? That she'd been thinking about Nate? Did her grandfather have some heritage magic of his own that both he and her mother never mentioned? She definitely wouldn't put it past her mother—especially if the order came down from father.

Aisha got to her feet. Wiped dust and dried grass from her butt.

"I'm not so sure about that. About love. I've come along way, but..."

But hadn't she just admitted it to herself? But admitting it to herself and saying it aloud were two very different things.

And she had a job to do.

The Council was still after her. Her Familiars were still in danger.

Aisha shook her head. "That's not why I'm here. I'm in trouble. My Familiars are in trouble and I think you can help me."

He peered at her with those darkened eyes she remembered so well. "Help, we can, I think. Maybe in both. But...."

Onwas came forward, steps sure and confident. No limp. No sign of aging that she could see even with the harsh life he'd led.

Onwas tapped her forehead with a bent forefinger—as if it had been broken or fractured at some point and not healed properly. "Memory problem, though. Need memory to touch your magic, yes?"

"It's coming back." Slowly. "Can you help?"

He sucked on his lower lip, then shrugged. "We see, yes? First, you come home, Great-joy-to-my-heart. We see then, where your mind and heart take us, yes?"

"Sounds like a plan."

A much, much better plan than the one she'd started with.

Aisha slung her bag on her shoulder (and then quickly promised her shoulders a nice break from hiking by the time they were done), and followed her grandfather deeper into the bush.

His home, and hers.

THE MOMENT they stepped into camp, Aisha froze.

Sweat clung to every inch of her. Dripped down her nose. Her neck. Soaked through her light-colored tank top until the whole thing just became a second skin. The heat and the trek all morning had taken everything she'd had, except the hope, the thrill of being with her grandfather. Listening to him. Watching and feeling as bit by bit, her memories had returned.

But all that had been nothing, nothing at all, compared to the camp.

Two dozen tribesmen and women flowed about the place. In and out. Traveling from the women's to the men's camp, except right now, during daylight, they were one and the same.

Hunters out into the bush. Women to collect berries and such. But all together; all connected.

The huts made of dried bushes and grass. Thatched together like it was one giant grass mess, except she knew differently. Remembered the care and skill required to build one.

Because she'd had one of her own. Built it under the steady, helpful guidance of her grandfather. Of others.

The Hadzabe stared at her. Openly. Many with curious expressions. Others with…with smiles?

Each wore scraps of shorts and leather shirts. Some barely covering even a small portion of their chest, or in the women's case, their breasts. Bright beaded headdresses slipping down over foreheads or tufts of fur crowning their heads—black and white, which could have come from nearly a hundred different animals.

The clicks and pops of their words, their language, freezing as well. When they saw her.

Except for the children.

They rushed forward. Dancing around and around. Arms up. Cheering. Speaking or whistling, she wasn't quite sure. As if they knew her, which they couldn't; they were too young. But they didn't care. They welcome her. Cheered for her.

At least she thought. Mostly, because her head couldn't stop spinning or thinking or just remembering.

The feeling of rightness settled over her.

Claimed her.

Onwas clasped a hand to her shoulder. Strong but gentle. Squeezed.

"Home, yes? As remembered?"

Aisha could only smile. A smile she felt from her heart, to the magic swirling and dancing in her gut, right along with those children.

"I remember."

"Good! Then we celebrate. You celebrate. And you find memory and love, yes?"

"What?" She blinked at that. "I came here to help the Familiars. About the wasting sickness, not—not love." Couldn't, because she'd left love behind. Back in the States. At her Waystation.

Onwas gave that grin again—the half-toothless grin splitting across his face. "You do both here, yes? Home can handle both."

Onwas lifted a scarred hand. Forefinger clearly broken at some point and healed at a slight off angle. He pointed through the crowd.

And it was a crowd as if the entire tribe, as small as it was, had suddenly showed up for the hunting and berry gathering.

And there was Nate.

Standing right in the center of the crowd. Of her tribe.

Bare-chested and burnt from the sun and didn't seem to care. Not that she could tell. Not from the intensity of his eyes. His gaze. His focus solely and completely on her.

A gaze that seared straight to heart.

Aisha didn't dare speak. Or move. Or breathe.

Nate, had come. For her.

CHAPTER 57

He came. All way here." Onwas released her shoulder. His comforting presence, the warmth, was about the only thing that'd kept her from backing away. Running.

A hot breeze picked up. Pulled at her sweaty strands of hair. Stuck them to her face. Got in her eyes. Made them sting, water.

Somehow, Aisha managed to keep her balance. To not sway from shock or, or something else.

Joy?

Relief?

All the while the tribe kept welcoming, dancing, joying over her return, and yet to her it felt like the world had slowed. Became a still being.

"What is he doing here?" she whispered. As if she didn't dare believe what was in front of her. What her eyes and heart said was true.

That was dangerous. Too dangerous.

Except Nate still hadn't moved. Hadn't disappeared or turned into a cunning, well-planned and executed illusion, one she wouldn't put it past his father to employ and succeed in. Except Nate wasn't an illu-

309

sion, because he didn't offer her any rings or veiled promises that were in truth shiny and perfectly fitting chains meant to bind. Meant to cage and trap. Just as the wizards and witches had done with the Familiars.

The connection was fleeting, tentative, and yet there all the same.

How they'd changed that special bond into something little better than slavery simply because one was better than the other. Just as Blakeley had seen of her. A wild beast of beauty meant to be caught, tamed. Broken.

But still, Nate just stood there, just outside the dancing children around her with their leather shirts and shorts and loincloths—if there were even any. He was a white speck amongst the dark—well, more like a crispy-red speck—and yet he belonged.

Because she did.

Because he cared for her.

This time, this time she did sway.

Onwas had said nothing during this, as the world slowed until it stopped, but his words came to her. Slowly. "You ask what the man called Nate has come for. Best answer comes from one who came, yes? You ask. We wait. Always wait, Joy-of-my-heart."

Onwas left then. She didn't turn or follow. Instead, just heard the subtle shift and crunch of his sandals on the hot-red sand, the cracked and yellowed grass here—so different than the fertile lakeside the Proper was perched in. The tribesman slowly peeled away to leave her and Nate still standing there, a village apart.

Except for the children, of course.

They stayed. They clapped their hands to their mouths. Giggled and squealed.

Part of her wanted to run right to him. Throw her arms around him. His shoulders. All of him, and just hold on. Forever. But the other part, the larger part, still hurt. Still felt the sting as the truth came between them. Startling and sharp and he'd never told her.

Hadn't told her.

Only one word mattered, and it was the only one she could actually speak.

"Why?"

Why had he come. Why was he here. Why did he care. For her.

So many why's and only one that mattered.

"Why?" she asked again.

Her voice, cracked. Broke.

She swallowed. Held back the hurt, the tears, the "more."

Nate came forward. One step. Then another. Boots even on the parched, cracking ground. Bending and crackling the yellowed grass. Kicking up the red dust until it seemed to swirl in that hot, sticky wind.

"Because I'll always come."

She shook her head. "That's not an answer."

He stopped just a breath from her. Lifted a hand as if to touch her cheek. Stroke or apologize or just whatever, she didn't know.

But he didn't touch her. As if he knew he was no longer allowed.

Instead, he lowered it.

"It's the only answer I have," Nate said. "I'll always come. Always follow you. Always fight the Council. My father."

"You didn't tell me. Why? Why when you knew how much it'd…"

It would hurt her. Tear her apart.

"Because I didn't know. Not then. At least, not how important you were to me. I've devoted my life to finding one answer: the truth about my mother. My father did everything he could to cover it up, but I was always searching, and that was true the moment I was assigned to your Waystation."

Aisha breathed in the hot air. "Because of your mother. To find out what happened to her."

He nodded. "And then I met you. Timiculous said you had the answers."

The children no longer danced, no longer closed in around them. They huddled in groups, whispering in their chitters and pops. She even saw a few hands exchanging brightly colored beds of red and blue. Some exchanging tufts of fur or tails.

Betting?

She ignored them. "So you lied to me. Gained my trust and all the while, you were planning on betraying me. My Waystation."

A smile cracked his lips. Lips, she noticed, that were parched. He looked chapped and windblown, like he'd ridden the hurricane winds itself to reach here. To reach her.

"I was always torn about that part," he said. "I might never have met you, but I knew of you and your Waystation. Compared to the Sanctuaries, including"—Nate shook his head—"Paradise Grove, I always respected what you'd done. Apollo was the name of my father's Familiar. A white-striped tiger who lived in the house, in my father's study. Never set foot outside. Even to my ten-year-old self, it felt...wrong."

Dark hair falling across his forehead. Sticking there to the sweat and heat, just like hers.

"And then, for some reason I still don't understand, Apollo killed her. My mother. And my father just stood there, didn't know I was there, not at first, standing in all that smoke. Her blood soaked through the carpet. He covered it up. The only person he actually ever loved, and he lied. To protect what he believed mattered most."

Nate swept that intense gaze of his. Gray eyes hard and hurting, and didn't hide from her. From the truth within him.

"What I did to you was wrong. Know that I would never have followed through with my orders. I couldn't."

He'd hurt her. Lied to her. So much, so similar to Blakeley—to her parents. All for his own ends. His own wants.

But he'd come after her.

"The Council?" Her heart thumped hard in her chest. "Did they destroy it? My Waystation?"

Pounded like the pounding beat of those children who'd resumed dancing—some barefoot, some in sandals, as they played over and over in the dirt and the water-starved grass.

"They left. In the end, the Council had no cause or jurisdiction to shut down your Waystation. Not after Timiculous, and then their psychics, confirmed the wasting sickness wasn't there."

She heard what he hadn't said.

"But?"

Marcelle had already told her, but she needed to hear it from him. The truth.

Nate's lips twisted, but he didn't look away from her. Didn't shy away or dodge. She could feel that; her magic felt it. And she was never more grateful. She braced for the truth, even though she knew the answer.

"But," Nate said, "my father is holding you responsible. You accountable."

"Of course he is." Because for whatever reason, Sylvester Darkwood had something against her. Her, and her alone.

She remembered what Hilda had said. How Nate had done for Aisha what he hadn't risked, hadn't wanted to do for Hilda—he'd stood up to his father.

For her.

"Thank you, for doing what you did. You didn't have to."

"Yes. I did."

Aisha closed her eyes. Breathed. She understood why he'd lied. As much as it hurt. She understood the drive, the need.

Nate looked nothing at all like the great wizard lord she'd first met in her aviary. In those dark, fancy robes ill-suited and completely wrong for her Waystation.

Not like now, though. Now, it looked like he fit. He belonged.

"Your father is coming. Here. After me. He's probably already here." She didn't even realize she'd stepped even closer.

That her nose nearly touched his.

They didn't, but their breaths did.

Mingled.

This time Nate did reach up. Did brush her hair back. Let his fingers trail down her cheek.

And she let him. Enjoyed the moment. The chill slipping down her cheek from where his fingers grazed. Echoing through her body. The thrill. Excitement. Joy.

"Because," he said, "it's not finished yet. With him. With you. I'm not leaving until it is."

"And when it's done?" She didn't dare ask. But did anyway. Somehow.

"I'm still not leaving you." He lowered his head. Forehead, with all the sweat and dirt, touched hers. "I can't. Because I love you."

CHAPTER 58

Sylvester stood in Albert's cool, carefully spelled private study. Gazed out those windows—walls really, the way he could see out over those plains in almost every direction. Made him want to close his eyes. To block out that sight.

All those Familiars.

Roaming free as they pleased.

Coming in to speak with their masters or those "wranglers" who cared for them whenever they damn well pleased.

Sylvester shook himself. The sight itself might be disconcerting—vile, even—but it was *Albert's* study, which was why he was here. Which was why Sylvester would push all those thoughts and feelings from his mind. To focus on the task at hand.

Which was yet another full day and no Aisha to be found.

Anywhere.

"I am growing rather impatient," Sylvester said to the young man behind him.

Daniel Blakeley, who huddled near the only door—unless, of course, Sylvester counted the door that led *outside* those windows to a *balcony*. As if anyone in their right mind wanted to stand out there in that sweltering heat. Those black buzzing clouds of twittering, biting bugs.

Daniel tugged on the collar of his shirt. The more he shadowed Sylvester, the more he looked less and less like the son of a great and powerful Lord.

Pity.

It was something he'd have to correct once this Aisha problem was attended to. Perhaps she had even been the one to break him when she'd failed to submit.

Sylvester turned around. Raised an eyebrow.

His silk robes flowed about his person as if a fluid, living thing. The reminder that everything about him was unexpected. Dangerous, even.

Blakeley flinched. Face drawn in tight and red around the collar. "I'm sorry, my lord. We have scouts, teams of wizards, truly, scouring the plains, but it's like she's vanished." Blakely shook his head. "They're deploying every tracking skill and spell they know of. They've even used those personal items Racine had sent along with you, but we haven't found a trace. Not once she left the Proper, anyway."

Sylvester's hands tightened. "She should never have been allowed to leave the Proper."

But that was only one problem; one irritant of many.

He'd deal with Albert soon enough for that transgressions. Or more to the point, the Proper would deal with the fallout soon enough.

Sylvester might not be the governing wizard in this country, or in this region, but he was one of the founding members of the Council here. He'd helped place the Blakeley family in such a position of power, both within the wizarding and Normal world. Not to mention the contract itself, the one that Albert had willingly signed when he'd first proposed this idea, this *sanctuary* that allowed Familiars to run wild and uncontrolled. A radical idea at the time, and it still was. Very few Sanctuaries had followed in the Proper's footsteps, and those that had had been under the careful supervision of Sylvester—or those, more or less, employed by him.

Because it didn't matter how popular the Proper had become. How the Fayes were viewed as wonderful, upstanding citizens of the highest order for what they'd done here.

What mattered was that Sylvester Darkwood owned them. They could never have received the sanctions to allow these Familiars any amount of freedom if it hadn't been for Sylvester.

They received the sanctions and Sylvester had a facility that successfully—or mostly successful—treated Familiars close to turning feral, with all the proper silencing spells in place as well.

He owned the Fayes.

Them, and their daughters.

But he needed to find Aisha first.

Sylvester massaged his chin. Rubbing his fingers back and forth over the clean, smooth skin. Not once taking his eyes off the Proper's vast plains. All those roaming Familiars.

"Rosaline said that she had now gone to the place where I'd stolen what was Aisha's. You do not remember, do you?" Sylvester asked. "The day where she told you no. Threw off your proposal and your ring?"

"Where it was? No. I…all of Tanzania, even around the Proper where I've spent much time training, it's all the same to me."

"Yes," Sylvester murmured. "For me as well."

To him, he could have placed that spell on Aisha right here on the Proper's grounds—but he couldn't pinpoint *where*. To him, all the plains were a parched, unholy, and desolate place with that dead grass. Red dirt that stained his nails. Turned his silks and robes into that horrid shade as well.

Which was the problem, for it was clearly *not* all the same to Aisha. Or her mother.

But her mother wouldn't say, that much was clear. He could force her. Could force another spell, just as he'd done with the daughter— but Sylvester had a feeling that tactic wouldn't work.

Just as the location spells weren't working on Aisha, even though they had all matter of items—hairs, snipped pieces from fingernails—which should have cast a direct beacon right to her. Instead, the spells simply faded, as if they couldn't take hold in this place.

This land.

Even with the hold he had over Rosaline, and over this filthy land, somehow they had both found a way to thwart him.

But only momentarily.

It'd mean more drastic measures would be needed; even if that meant using Rosaline and her life to make it happen.

"There is magic here." Sylvester turned from the window. Robes slapping about legs. "Ancient magic, and it doesn't seem to care much for ours."

"I don't understand."

"Of course you don't. Your family has lived here for two generations and you still haven't begun to understand."

Daniel's mouth moved. Face turned a slight shade of red, but the boy kept his temper. Pity, really. He wouldn't amount to much if he didn't learn to stand for himself. His family. Family, after all, was what mattered.

Here, too, in Tanzania.

To the land itself, it seemed. It was well past time that Sylvester used everything at his disposal. And he would, when the time came, if it was needed.

Indeed, even now, he felt Aisha pulling and tugging against the spell on her mind, the one blocking her from reclaiming her heritage. There was also the matter of his own son, who, Sylvester had learned in a message from Racine just this morning, that the boy had left for Tanzania as well.

Sylvester gazed up at Albert's display of primitive wooden masks and tufts of fur and sticks stuck to them. Some wore an angry grimace. Others laughed at him.

No one would be laughing soon.

Either Aisha would be found or she would break through his spell. And when she did…there would be no coming back. No revealing of whatever she'd learned of the wasting sickness.

Couldn't, because she'd be dead.

His son would try and save her, of course, and that would take care of Sylvester's other, smaller problem. Pity, because he did have need of an heir.

Some day, anyway.

Sylvester reached for and took down the mask. Held the rough carving in his hand. A splinter dug into his forefinger.

Blood swelled at the tip.

A fighting omen, and one, he hoped, the land here would answer in reply. A reply, in vengeance, when one of its own was threatened.

Threatened, and killed.

His failsafe spell would make sure of it.

CHAPTER 59

*A*isha wore a only simple black tank top and khaki pants as she followed after her grandfather, the other ten hunters, and... Nate as they crept through the darkened land. Her skin, like the others of the Hadzabe, blended perfectly with the deep night.

Her heart thundered. Seemed to out-beat and out-pound even the calls of lions across the dark plains. The hyenas yipping and thrilling in a hunt.

Or a kill.

Sweat lined her upper lip.

Not from the heat. But from the moment.

From what her grandfather was attempting to do.

Aisha focused in front of her. Saw the dim, slightly whitened form of Nate as he crept in front of her. He stood out in the night, even with a long shirt covering his chest and his arms. His pale skin wasn't suited for night hunting, but still she watched as he crouched along with Onwas and the other hunters. Watched, and couldn't help but admire as he did the best he could, felt his way across the angry land.

She smiled.

A small one, but it was there and she didn't fight it. Nor did she fight the way her heart paused in its anxious beating, the anticipation of breaking through whatever was blocking her memories, to feel another kind of anxious beat.

For Nate.

For what she felt.

She hadn't given him an answer earlier. Not in front of the dancing—and betting—children. Didn't throw her arms around his neck. Kiss him. Finish what they'd barely started before the Council, Marcelle, and the truth had ripped them apart.

She had something else to do first.

The Familiars needed her to do this.

But still, she smiled. Even as she watched Nate step right into another thorn brush. As he swallowed a curse before it broke out across their silent, stealthy trek.

Onwas had invited him to come, but she suspected the invitation was a mere formality. Onwas had a look about him that almost insisted Nate be there on this journey. That he was needed if Aisha were to…remember.

Still, despite the way thorn bushes and nettles grabbed him and bit him because he didn't have the night vision or understanding of the land the Hadzabe did, that they had gained generation after generation, Nate still kept going. Didn't slow in his speed or make the line wait for him as he stumbled. Jerked. Twisted his body as he stepped into yet another thorny and spiky bush.

Her grandfather and the hunters had the same kind of familiarity and understanding of this land, just as she did with every inch of her Waystation. Except their familiarity spanned a thousand miles. Not that she had this either, not when she'd been raised in the Proper. In fact, more than a few thorns had cut right through her pants. Bit into her shin and thighs.

She'd need help later, digging them out.

With knives, most likely.

And just like Nate, Aisha had grit her teeth. Swallowed, and kept following that slow-moving, single-file line.

But not as many thorns and spikes found Aisha because she had her magic.

Right now, it was flaring within her gut. Guiding her in a way that spanned those generations as if she was as much apart of this land as her grandfather. What was more, the longer she moved, the longer she allowed the land, the night, the sounds of stinging, warning insects to fill her senses, her memory opened.

Bit by bit. Returned to her.

Fell away.

As if all it had been waiting for was her to return home.

Return to the wild.

Just as the Familiars, those affected by the wasting sickness, had needed.

The whoops and calls of baboons filled the night. Split across the land with such a sudden, defining silence. Shock.

Aisha froze. Couldn't help it. It was as if her muscles stopped moving. Her mind skittered to a pause. All she heard were the calls. Deep and calling. Echoed off her soul. Down deep. Deeper.

Her shirt clung to her chest. Her armpits. But she didn't feel it. Didn't feel the sweat rolling down her chin. Dripping down her neck.

"Aisha?"

A voice whispered beside her. But it was distant.

Instead, she closed her eyes. Listened to the calls. Felt them.

"I've heard this before," she whispered.

As if speaking the words called up some time, some place and moment through the thick fog. A small light, a distant beacon flashing, working so hard to get through.

To be seen.

"Tell me about it," the voice said.

A familiar voice. One she trusted. Loved.

Loved.

Aisha sucked in a breath. All this had started because of love, right? Blakeley. He'd done this to her. Except, that didn't make sense. She remembered bits of that moment, the confrontation where she told him and his promises no and forever no—but it was her time with the *Hadzabe* that was blocked.

Stolen from her.

And Blakeley would have no reason to do so. Not if she'd still followed her mind; remained true to herself. She'd told him no and walked away, and he hadn't stopped her.

"It wasn't Blakeley," she said. "I thought it might be…"

"Forget about him," the voice said—though the voice sounded a bit strained. "Tell me about the baboons. Did you hunt them? Before, with your grandfather?"

"Yes."

The answer came to her. Sweeping. Truthful. Right.

Her magic felt like it swirled around her. Embraced her. Aisha didn't shy away from it. Didn't open her eyes. Just focused on that light. As if she'd push away that fog with her bare hands. Clawed it away with her fingers.

"I've been here. Before."

Her body could almost feel the distant gouges as thorns had struck and bit into her skin. A ghost memory, but there nonetheless. What her mind blocked, her body once again remembered.

Aisha stepped forward.

The others moved beside her.

Let her take the lead.

She opened her eyes. Trusted in her magic and followed the calls of the baboons. Followed them right through that fog. Right through some flash of magic. Bright and blinding all at the same time. Distorted and tearing.

A spell, she realized.

The one that had been used on her. But not by Blakeley. It was too clean. Too advanced, with a surgical and precise purpose that even now she couldn't see. Couldn't understand.

Not that it mattered. The spell, regardless of its intent or why it was placed on her, didn't care. Only that its purpose, even now, was to rip her apart. Bring her to her knees. Prevent her from breaking through. From seeing through the fog.

Prevent her from reconnecting with who she was. With the Hadzabe. With the wild.

Aisha took another step. Plunged deeper into the fog of her mind, the stolen memories.

And immediately swallowed a cry.

The spell tore through her. The ends of it had thorns of its own. Spikes just like the acacia trees. Ripped into her mind, shredded it. Tore relentlessly and without bias.

She didn't realize she'd been crying. That tears streaked her face. Barely realized that, even now, she was still somehow moving forward through the bush. Trying to reach those baboons.

The spell reared up again.

Talons arched into her. Clamped down. Pulled.

Aisha stumbled.

Someone grabbed her. Held her up.

"I…I have to keep going."

"Then I'll help."

Strong hands, familiar hands, gripped her arms. Supported her and she knew, without even seeing who, that he'd never let her down. Never let her walk through that fog alone.

Another hand, different, but still just as comforting and familiar, touched her forehead. This touch was leathery and strong, but gentle even as it was tempered by the same wild that called to her heart.

Her magic fluttered. Weak for a moment, then stronger.

Like calling to like.

"Spell break mind," the wild voice said. "Try to finish what began that night."

"What happened?" Aisha asked. Somehow finding the words, or thought she did. "That night. Why the baboons? Why this?"

Why this moment.

Why this memory.

Why her.

The wild voice answered her. "Is moment you connect. With heart. Mind. With wild. Baboons showed you self. True self, as do for every hunter who makes first kill of baboon for tribe."

The leathery hand left her forehead.

She felt its loss straight to her soul.

"I don't understand," she whispered.

"Is why you came home, to tribe, to grandfather."

Aisha thought through the fog. Forced herself to remember. To understand. "I...I was missing something, wasn't I? From my life. Something in me that wasn't fitting with my parents. In the Proper."

She could, distantly, see the darkened outline of a man. Dark and bare-chested, silhouetted against the night's thousand stars. Her grandfather.

He nodded. She felt the movement with her magic, more than saw.

"This night. Night of memory. Is moment you found magic. Your soul."

And Aisha knew, without a doubt, with her magic sparking and glowing and pushing through that fog, that he was telling her the truth.

That her grandfather was right.

This was the moment that whoever had done this, no matter why, had feared.

Which meant she needed to push through. All the way. Regardless of how much damage the spell did to her. Destroyed of her.

She had to keep going.

She reached up. Touched the hands still holding her shoulder. Warm and loving. She squeezed them.

"Then the only thing left to do, is to remember."

CHAPTER 60

*A*isha followed the sounds and the calls of the baboons. Shifting and moving, high and safe in their tree. Tonight, her grandfather and the hunters were not here to hunt, but instead to help her.

She understood that as she moved through the bush. Felt the scraping of thorns catching at her ankles. Tugging and gouging as she moved through the blackest night with only the stars above and the slim sliver of light from a faded moon to guide her.

But she wasn't relying on her eyes.

She was relying on her magic.

Her memory.

Aisha crested a small rise, an incline that made her muscles groan—already weakened and sore from the trek out to the tribe's camp, her sleepless plane trip—but she moved through the burning. Behind her came the others.

Her grandfather.

Nate.

She reached the top of the hill. Knelt down. Knees digging into the soft dirt here. Below, in that little dip of a valley, was a silhouetted acacia tree with its thin branches and trunk. The sparse leaves and the many bodies, some moving, some sleeping, of baboons.

The fog lifted. A tiny bit. Enough to see, to remember that night.

"The other hunters," Aisha whispered, pointed with her hand. "They fanned out around this hill. Silent. Climbing up from all sides. To startle them. To make them run."

"And they run, yes?" Onwas asked.

"They did."

She could see it. *Hear* it.

The crazed screeching sound. Startling and fierce through the night. Tore through all the roars and hyena yips and insect chittering. A warning, a single warning, to go away.

"The baboons sensed danger. But still the hunters carried on. They came closer." Aisha squeezed her eyes shut. "They came down. Branches snapping. Cracking. Dozens of bodies."

"And you, Joy-of-my-heart, you remember, what do?"

With her eyes still closed, Aisha reached behind her. Pulled an arrow, the tip poisoned, and nocked it to her bow. She drew back the string, just as she had done that night.

Felt the tautness of it. The strength, stealth, and ease.

It had been hard to see through that darkened night. But she *could* see. Was guided by the spark she felt, glowing, stronger and stronger in her stomach. Spreading outwards. Reaching for, and into, her hands.

She felt it. Felt it with every beat of her heart. Her breath.

It was a part of her, and for the first time in her life, she had allowed it *to be.*

She watched as most of the baboons fell towards the hunters. Ran right into them. But one went a different way. Towards her. Crested the boulders right before her, right before the hill dipped down towards that tree.

He'd landed on the boulder. Feet silent, but there. Saw her and screeched.

Aisha let out a breath. Its warmth tickled her lips.

She couldn't see much, not through the darkness, through the dim light of moon and stars. But her magic had curled up, reached further than her hands. Touched her eyes and she saw, as if she were seeing as clear as day.

"I saw him. With my magic."

Onwas knelt beside her. Sandals crackling a thorn bush. "You saw with heart. Is magic of tribe. Of people."

True magic.

Wild magic.

Aisha still held the bow, the arrow taut, and pulled back in the string—both from her memory and the reality she was reliving. She felt as the moment flared.

Even as it did so, the spell grabbed hold of her. Pulled. Tore. Pain, fierce and sharp and unyielding, ripped through her mind.

She cried out. Nearly dropped her arrow, but a hand was there, steadying her, holding her up.

"Keep going," the voice whispered, and she felt surrounded by love. Strength.

Somehow, Aisha managed to pull back the arrow again.

Somehow, with her hands shaking, shoulders quivering, she held it there. Sighted the baboon. Sighted the memory through all that fog and for a brief moment, even as tears slid down her face, became one with her shakes and quivering body, her magic flashing through that fog.

A beacon in the form of that baboon.

Blazing and bright.

Staring down at her with its twisted and yet beautiful face.

Beautiful.

Aisha loosed the arrow. It flew through the air. Cut through the fog, the darkness of her memory, just as it had done that day. Struck true. Fast and straight and unwavering.

She saw, only briefly, as the baboon arched its curved, furry back. Its screech that filled the night, her senses, everything—and then the spell, its last-ditch effort to prevent her, block her from reclaiming her heritage, her heart, struck. Just as fast and straight as that arrow.

Just as true. A pain so crippling, blinding, penetrating, cascaded over her.

All she saw, felt, was darkness.

Her mind torn into two until that was all there was.

Just blackness. Just darkness.

And she felt no more.

CHAPTER 61

*N*ate felt her go down.

Aisha fell, limp, into his arms. Would have crashed into the ground, into those damn thorny bushes, if he hadn't been there.

He caught her. Easily. Quickly.

She was too light in his arms. The strength he'd grown to admire, love, had vanished. Now just a woman, withering, moaning, face drawn taut as whimpers escaped her lips.

Nate called her name.

Knew his voice cracked through the night, right across the plains, and any predator or wizard would hear from miles off.

And he didn't care.

He had to reach her. Get to her. Before it was too late.

He didn't have Timiculous beside him. Didn't have Timiculous and his understanding, his sensitivity to others, including witches, to break through that spell and that haze he knew was descending on her. Breaking into her mind with sharp piercing talons. Tearing every last shred of her apart.

The spell was making one last effort to destroy what it had tried so hard to hide.

A failsafe trigger.

A spell, so damaging, so crippling, and almost impossible to destroy. Should have known. Should have realized what was right in front of him—what had happened to him. There was only one wizard who'd dare cast such a forbidden spell and fear no worry, no repercussions of getting caught.

His father.

"Aisha!"

He bent lower. His lips near hers. Felt her desperate pull and exhale of breath against his. Growing ragged. Weaker.

Onwas was beside him. Nate didn't know when or how and didn't much care. Just wanted the old medicine man to stay out of his way. But Onwas gripped her shoulder. Squeezed.

"You help? You reach?"

"I don't know."

He didn't know how. Not without Timiculous to guide him. Or a psychic like Marcelle. That was who Aisha needed right now. She didn't need him, the man who broke her heart. Betrayed her. The son of the one who'd done this to her.

"*You* reach." Onwas slapped Nate's chest. "Here. Here. Heart. Find true self. Forgotten self."

Aisha's hand reached up. Grabbed the collar of his shirt. Squeezed. Desperate, almost. Before going slack. Falling away.

He immediately grabbed her hand. Squeezed back.

"I'm here," he told her. "And I'm not going anywhere."

Nate was no psychic. Was not able to see or experience the colors or aura of others, and he didn't care.

Instead, he let instinct guide him, right to where he needed to go.

To his heart. Soul. Whatever he wanted to call it. The name didn't matter. Only the trust mattered. The knowing that he *could* reach her.

Just like Onwas had said he could. And Nate would.

He closed his eyes and fell within himself. Deep and then deeper. Reached down to his core, the place where he'd always believed his magic sparked and sizzled, nestled in his chest, protected by ribs and his heart. Hidden there, but always ready.

Always there.

Nate felt himself slide beside Aisha. Felt the dimming, but still strong pull of her own magic. His breath sucked in. Held there. Couldn't help but marvel at the beauty of her magic. Bright and sparking. The taste of Africa on his lips. The wildness of the dry wind and the wet season as it revitalized a dying, drying landscape season after season. Constant and flowing, as much a part of the rhythm as his own heartbeat.

Felt his father's spell turn towards him. Felt as it turned that hateful, angry, controlling gaze onto him. The spell ripped into him as if he and Aisha were one. Right into his mind. His soul.

He didn't care.

Only cared that it lost its focus, its attention on Aisha.

Nate grit his teeth. Ground them together.

The spell didn't care that he was the creator's son. Only that it had a job to do and it would succeed.

To leave nothing, no person, behind to speak the truth.

Nate felt his mouth open. His voice tearing out his throat, but he only gripped Aisha harder. Drew the spell and its attention, as much as he could, into him. To leave her alone.

He'd already betrayed her once. Already kept the truth from her about who he was, what he was; now, he would leave nothing unsaid. Even through the agony. Even through the red haze that became his whole center, his focus, he never once let go of her.

Always held her to him.

Nate felt his heart slow. Felt his mind fade. Grow sluggish and weak. Dry and just as parched as the land he now lay on.

Until water trickled into him. Into his soul, into his heart.

Not water, but magic. Revitalizing and pure. It flowed into him, first as the smallest of streams, but growing, growing. And as the water came, so spurted the green grass. The flamingos and their brilliant, pink-tinged feathers. The hippos and the wildebeests and elephants, all racing for that first taste of thirst.

Of life.

"It's my turn to not let you go."

Aisha.

He felt her hands on the sides of his face. Felt her lips, moist and alive, touch his. And the fiery warmth that was always between them blossomed. Grew just like the streams and rivers flowing into him did. As it shoved the parched and destroyed spell further and further back, until it had nowhere else to go but simply disappear.

There was no more room left in Nate to kindle its hatred. Its need to destroy. Nothing left for it to hold on to.

Nate reached up, pulled Aisha even closer, and kissed her. Kissed her like he had that day by Lanhi's cage, and swore he'd never, ever let her go again.

Aisha pulled back. Slightly. Enough where all he had to do was lift his—very much aching head—and reclaim those lips.

"You see," she said, "this time, I have no intention of letting *you* go."

"You? You heard me?"

In his voice. His mind.

She leaned back down. A smile on her lips as she kissed him again.

Heard a single word, that he felt through his whole being.

Always.

CHAPTER 62

Sylvester closed the heavy, framed wood doors to Albert's office. His muscles groaned and shook. Ached from the physical weakness he felt all over—from his magic straight to his soul. Of handling that amount, that strength of magic. The backlash as Aisha had finally broken through the memory spell.

The door's heavy thud resonated behind him. Made all those darkened windows shake and shiver. But Rosaline didn't turn.

Instead, she waited in that dark, silent, and unwelcoming study. Back rigid. Head held tall. Not the least bit nervous or afraid.

Just as she always appeared before him. Even that first day he'd finally met the recently conquered bush woman.

At least during the day, Albert's study had the familiar trappings of civilization to remind him who ruled here. The appropriate desk and reading books, and the special, rare ones lovingly encased in glass. Each item contributing to the whole that this was a place where those of a civilized nature ran supreme.

But, of course, during the day Sylvester would have to stare out at those plains that seemed to come up around him. As if to swallow him.

Except night was, somehow, worse.

With Rosaline's back towards him, facing outwards to those dark plains and prowling Familiars. A low-hanging fog seemed to skim the land. As if it'd risen from that nearby salt-drenched lake and sought to overtake the Proper during the night.

As if the land here wanted to overtake him.

Just as Rosaline had first warned, all those years ago, when he'd offered her the contract. That the land would rise up against him, take back what did not belong to him. Sylvester, of course, had laughed at her. Then, dangled the only hope she and her people had of surviving this intervention of the Magical High Council.

Sylvester had been requested by the High Council to oversee the negotiations and the...ramifications if such a place like the Proper existed. His reputation for...getting things done, as quietly as possible, was precisely what the High Council had wanted.

Needed.

Sylvester had had no difficulties setting up the perfect net.

The perfect trap.

One for Albert and his strange ideal, this *need* of his to advance the life and happiness of Familiars...and his recently engaged fiancée, Rosaline.

It was Rosaline who'd been the most difficult, at least until Sylvester offered her a deal she couldn't walk away from. She could either help Albert set up the Proper, this little "rehabilitation" center, and use her special little bush woman gift to heal the most broken Familiars, or she could see the last remnants of her people lose their land.

Their home.

Because, as the whole of the magical world knew and understood, those without true governments (which inconveniently protected all those fleas and mice called *Normals*) and those without magic had no standing. No say. No voice or claim.

Which the Hadzabe, thanks to Sylvester's carefully networked plan, did not.

The Hadzabe had no recognizable government, not even a ruling tribal elder, and they certainly had no *magic*.

Except for the matter of the land itself and their ties to it, which Sylvester had very carefully omitted.

And yet, even as Sylvester stood there in Albert's dark study, he could almost feel the land rolling beneath his feet. Creeping beneath the carefully laid and polished floorboards. How he felt, to his very bones, that the land wanted him gone.

His whole existence, swallowed whole.

But the land was nothing. Could do *nothing* against him.

Just like Rosaline couldn't.

The earth rumbled. Buckled. Quaked.

Caused some glass trinket on Albert's desk to fall, topple, clink and clank on the floorboards until it finally rested near his silk slipper.

Sylvester hid a shiver.

He was too worldly to believe in silly folklore or superstition and would instead focus on what mattered most: Rosaline.

She'd arrived even before Sylvester had sent for her. As if she'd known.

As if she'd also felt the magic backlashing.

Into him.

Sylvester's whole body shivered again, the memory alone of what had recently happened—even now, it was enough to have his muscles contract. Loosen. Tighten. As if still fighting to shake off the remnants of the broken spell.

Of Aisha breaking through the memory block.

He'd known it was coming, had braced and prepared himself, had Daniel standing nearby for just this moment. Except even now, even having used Daniel as a funnel for the worst of the backlash, Sylvester couldn't seem to fit the final brass button into place on his tunic. As if his hands couldn't hold steady enough to slip the button into its proper place.

Because of Aisha.

He glared at his hands. The wrinkles he could suddenly see with such clarity. The veins and bones standing stark as day even in the near-dark room. His hands still shook, a tremble that refused to go away—no matter how much he willed it to.

A tremble that swept through his whole body as if it were a living thing.

No matter. There was little he could do about this now.

Too much was at stake. Both for his own desires, and for the High Council once they learned of Aisha's reawakening. Of her heritage magic.

Which was precisely why Rosaline had come.

"Did the land warn you? Tell you what she'd done?" he asked.

Rosaline didn't turn. Didn't acknowledge with a bow as his rank required. Instead, she spoke.

"Anyone with a sense of this place felt it."

Including Albert, Sylvester was sure. But it wasn't Albert who'd come—because both Albert and Rosaline knew what would happen next.

What Sylvester would demand of them.

What the contract demanded.

The black sky shone like darkness through the room's three wall-like windows. Those windows making him feel like he was actually standing on those plains. Surrounded by those Familiars.

Familiars, it seemed that slowly, as if compelled, each turned their attention to him.

Which was absurd.

He was too far to even see such details, what with the nearly moonless night. Those thousands of stars that, while having some amount of beauty, cast hardly any light about the land.

Those Familiars certainly couldn't see *him*.

Unless, of course, it was Rosaline with her strange bush magic that was compelling them to do so.

That thought was enough of a reminder.

Of what had happened.

Of what the daughter had done.

How everything he cared for, worked for, was now in jeopardy.

Rosaline still stood in front of those windows. Hadn't turned when he'd opened the door—or when he'd slammed it shut.

The bare hint of moon silhouetted her person. Her dark clothing, dark skin making her blend into that dark landscape. Would have, if not for the moon.

"I'm surprised you haven't disappeared. Like your daughter." Sylvester strode into the room. Steps hard, but assured. Confident. No matter what he felt on the inside. How his magic quivered or wavered, she must not know.

"You hold the chains to our sanctuary. I could not without betraying my husband. You hold the chains to my people. I could not without breaking what little they have left. I will not run. This is my home."

"I thought your home was in the bush."

"I did not say one or the other was not my home." She turned at this, those dangling, gaudy beads in her string-dark hair clanking. He couldn't even see the whites of her eyes. It was like every inch of her being was wrapped in shadows.

"Yet, you stayed. Waited for my summons."

Rosaline inclined her head. Only the tiniest nod of acknowledgement.

"Even though I plan to destroy your daughter."

She shook her head. Once. The beads tingled like chimes. Or perhaps a warning bell. "You have already tried to do so, and failed."

"The memory spell," Sylvester growled out the world. "I'd enacted it to spare your family the loss of a child. It seems I should have retained a more harsh treatment for her actions."

Rosaline jerked her head up. "You promised—"

"No. *You* promised. When you were married. When you signed the contract to fund and sanction your little *Proper*."

"I never agreed to allow you to kill my children—"

"Then perhaps you should have taken greater care to dissuade your eldest's interest in your tribe, for I will not and never will allow your tribal magic or whatever it is to destroy what we have worked so long to build, to maintain." Sylvester moved forward. Slammed his closed fist onto the desk.

Another trinket toppled fell.

Something shattered.

"You and your husband were specifically warned about the ramifications of what would happen if your children did not comply. The same as any employees you accepted into the Proper. What happens next is on your heads."

He came forward. Grabbed Rosaline's arm. Muscular. Hard. Nothing at all like his dear late wife's softness. Gentleness.

Made him all the angrier that his own son would choose a woman like this over the loyalty to his family. His father.

Sylvester's hands tightened. Dug into Rosaline's arm.

She said nothing. Not even a whimper or a flick of her unnatural, dark-sighted eyes.

"Enough games, Rosaline. You know very well what is at stake. Your Proper. Your family. Your people. So. Let's stop pretending that you have any choice or say in this little matter, one that *you* did not solve all those years ago."

He released her. Took care then to straighten out any wrinkles he may have caused on her shoulders and her evening wear or whatever it was she even had on. He didn't care.

"Tomorrow, we will go to this place where Aisha's memory was taken. The place also where she acknowledged her magic. We will go to Aisha and tomorrow, we will see this little matter finally settled."

CHAPTER 63

*A*isha blinked away the few tears that managed to sneak past her eyes, but didn't wipe them. Just as she didn't wipe away those fragments of memories that slipped into her mind, which now, instead of dissolving like that fog, pieced together.

She sat with Nate, her back against his on a woven cot of weeds and grass and some kind of hide. The night stars continued to shine and twinkle, a great carpet of tiny white dots across the night sky.

A sky she'd missed so deeply.

The stars had witnessed everything that night. Just as they had that day when all of this was taken from her. Even if she hadn't been able to see them, they'd seen her.

Watched, solemn and silent, as the day and sun had reigned supreme.

But she had a feeling, this nagging sense, that they remembered her.

Aisha's hand slipped up and along the rim of the cot. The hide, familiar, comforting.

Wildebeest, her mind supplied.

Her hand ran across it, back and forth. Each touch adding to the memory. Fitting it further into place. A little uncomfortable at first, like putting on boots for the second or third time. They fit, but not quite right.

But the hide was both coarse and yet, somehow, smooth.

She'd helped hunt the wildebeest down herself.

It hadn't been the traditional role women of the tribe played, but one her grandfather believed was necessary. He'd said she walked both worlds.

He'd been right.

More right than Aisha could have ever realized.

Her night vision was still poor, at least compared to her grandfather and the tribesmen, but right now she didn't need her sight to remember that particular day, or how she'd gone about the tanning or the weaving of reeds for the day's chores. For now, though, she let those comforting memories slide past her. Bury themselves into her psyche, just as they were meant to be.

Those were easy memories. Ones that didn't hurt, even as she wove them back together.

Her grandfather had saved the cot. Kept it with the tribe even as they moved from place to place, every season, every moment as needed.

Saved it for when she returned.

The night was alive again with calls and yips, as if her moment by the acacia tree and the baboons, the spell turning back on her, had never happened. The deep hollering of baboons, the same ones that had helped her reclaim what was taken—what Sylvester Darkwood had stolen from her—carried long, deep, and far. So did the solitary, throaty calls of male lions marking their territory. Warning off predators. Intruders.

Aisha shivered.

Remembering. Everything.

Aisha gasped. Sucked in that hot, sticky air. Tried to breathe through it. Breathe the memory and what came next.

Remembered, even the day, that moment, when she'd given Blakeley back his ring and his promise, but even more importantly, what had come after. How she'd turned away from Blakeley and her family, to head back to where her grandfather and the tribe waited, to learn more of her heritage, of how she could help heal and guide those broken Familiars—because that had been what compelled her to learn. To understand. This need, buried within her chest.

A living part of her.

Her bare feet had slid in that hot, reddened sand, almost burning, but nothing like the burning in her heart. She moved away from Blakeley, forever, and then, suddenly, she and Blakeley were no longer alone. Sylvester Darkwood—she didn't know him at the time, but now, there was no mistaking him, that man with his robes whipping about him like he was some phantasm from a folklore, a nightmare the Hadzabe spoke of in hushed tones over a lit and quite large bonfire meant to drive away evil spirits—appeared from nowhere. He shimmered into existence, a watery mirage that she wasn't quite sure was actually real.

Not at first.

But then he'd narrowed his gray eyes at her, cold and unforgiving, and asked her once to change her mind.

She'd said no.

He'd simply nodded. Raised his hands.

There were no apologies, no sorrow lining his face or shining in his eyes. He hadn't felt sorry for what he was doing, as he cast the spell that had stolen her true heart from her. Took away all but the least bit of fragments of the Hadzabe, even most of her joyful time in the Proper.

She'd been cast out with barely more than the clothes on her back.

And she'd done the only thing she could.

She ran.

Aisha swept a tangled, sweat-stained strand of hair from her face. Even in the dead of morning, with the land mostly still steeped in night and sleep, it was hot. Sweltering. Or maybe she felt that way from the memories crashing back into place. Sometimes taking chunks of her soul with it.

She tucked the hair behind her ear. Her hand, she noticed, shook.

She forced herself to breathe, to let the memories come to her.

She felt Nate beside her.

His breath, even with hers. Deep and filling, then slowly exhaling.

"You're doing good."

"It doesn't didn't feel like it." Actually, it felt like every time another memory, another puzzle slid into place, she'd break apart into a million pieces.

His warm hand touched her shoulder. Back, still pressed against hers, felt a tad bit warmer. Heated.

Aisha leaned back. Her head pressing against the back of his.

"Keep breathing," Nate whispered. "It'll help."

She did. "Your father taught you this?"

There was a pause, and she didn't dare turn, didn't want to see something she'd regret on Nate's face....

"No," Nate finally said. "He didn't."

She reached up. Clasped his hand and squeezed. "Just breathe, right?"

"Yeah."

Breathe, and focus on the world she was surrounded by. Living in. Her home.

The all-consuming darkness of the plains, which would frighten most people, instead warmed her. Chased away those fragments of pain and hurt Sylvester's memory spell had placed in her, shards of discontent and her parents' disapproval.

But she understood all that now. Understood why they'd turned away from the Hadzabe, away from her, and finally, turned her out.

That made those shards hurt a little less.

Not much, but a little.

The sounds of the Hadzabe camp came in only soft snores, shuffles in the dirt, and soft cracking of grass as scouts kept their nightly watch. Her grandfather had set Aisha's cot and hut apart from the others, still with the group, but separate. Giving her the space, the chance to heal—as if he'd known that was what she'd need.

Maybe he was right. And not just from her stolen memories, but from the other parts of her self, her life, she hadn't been able to live.

Couldn't live, until now.

But maybe, there was more healing she could do.

"Everything I've done," she said, "was for the Familiars. I don't know why, they've just…always called to me. I felt them. Even as a little girl. In the Proper. When my father would bring in the broken ones. The ones that needed healing."

"You remember?"

"Pieces. But yes, they're coming together."

"It's just like your Waystation." Nate's voice was quiet, but deep. Comforting. Even though the tribe was around them, with him there, his warmth seeping into her, she didn't feel alone at all.

Nate laughed. Soft and quiet. "Father hoped to destroy that, when he took away your memories. But he couldn't, could he? Not when it was actually a part of you."

"No. He couldn't." Aisha again squeezed Nate's hand. "But I think when he cast that spell, he stole more than just my memories."

She turned slightly so her back was no longer resting against his. Brought his hand to her lips.

Nate straightened, but didn't move. Just sat there. Waiting.

For her.

And maybe, she'd been waiting for him.

CHAPTER 64

I think," Aisha whispered, leaning in closer, her chest closing that small distance on the thin cot. Her breath tickling and sliding against Nate's ear. "That I'd like to reclaim that too. The other part he stole from me."

Nate didn't move towards her, didn't even seem to breathe for a moment. Until finally, he said her name, like a sigh.

"Aisha...."

She could only see the shape of his features in that vast darkness. His dark shirt hiding what it could of his paler skin. The gouges the thorns and bushes had taken out of him. But it was the way his shoulders slumped that reminded her she wasn't the only one to survive his father's spell. That it had also taken a bite out of Nate as well.

Perhaps, even, long before he'd ever met her.

Still, she concentrated on the outline of his hard lines. His face. Reached up as if to trace his cheek, down to his jaw, but stopped.

She didn't need to see. Not when she could feel.

"He's taken more than enough from me, and for long enough. But this part, this one right here, I let him take from me. I let your father and Blakeley take it from me. I didn't fight hard enough to reclaim it."

To steal back her heart. To allow herself to feel. To hurt. To love.

"I know what my father took from you," he said.

There was longing in Nate's voice, but also hesitation. As if he really did understand what the spell his father had cast had done. How long it would take to heal, to put herself back together. That there was no rush and he didn't want her to look back on this moment, with him, and feel any kind of regret…that maybe, his father had somehow stolen the same from him as well.

Or maybe none of this was even assumption.

Maybe she wasn't even guessing what Nate's hesitation meant. Maybe, as she had guessed earlier, when her magic had returned and she'd touched him, all of him, that this was *exactly* what Nate was feeling. Thinking. That perhaps her magic put her on a different kind of level from others, unlike psychics, but perhaps more like Familiars.

Sensitive to the natural world. To the wildness in the land. In people.

Aisha didn't care.

Only wanted to move forward. To heal. To be herself, and herself fully. No more spells blocking the way.

She felt his hand on her bare arm. Fingers sliding down once. Over her biceps. Her elbow. Down to her forearm. Lingered on her fingers as if wanting more.

Aisha closed her eyes. Shivered.

Felt every moment, every breath of that simple touch.

Right now, with the sounds and calls of the wild plains around them, the stars still shining, still gazing down at her from overhead, the baboons, even, hollering and calling, as if still upset by the disturbance Aisha and the tribe's nightly visit had caused and now wanted to make sure every creature and beast in the gorge knew they were upset, it was all happening around her, except right now, none of that mattered.

Only Nate.

And remembering what it felt like to be touched.

To be loved.

"I can't show you what it feels like to be loved," he said, as if either hearing her thoughts, or knowing what was in her heart. "I can't. Any more than you can show me."

"Then let's learn together."

She still felt his hesitation, felt his fear, or maybe it was just hers. Maybe it was just her own heart pounding like that. Causing her chest to rise and fall, harder, faster. But there was more there than just fear. An ache, too. Longing. Need, even.

Aisha turned fully towards him. No longer back to back, but staring at him fully. Slid herself across until she was nearly on his lap. Made him stare at her, to not look away or hesitate as she could feel him wanting to do, as if he needed to. She stared into those gray eyes she could barely see in the night's dim, starlit light. Reached out. Touched his chest. Hardened muscles underneath her palms, hidden by that flimsy shirt. She felt the rise and fall of his breath. Felt her own, slowly, match the pace of his.

Aisha leaned in until their lips nearly touched, but didn't.

But their breath did.

Mingled. Intertwined. Became one.

Nate didn't pull away. Instead, his hands reached up, cupped her hips. Pulled her closer until she was sitting on his lap. And from there, she felt him. All of him, and couldn't help the smile spreading across her face. The same one, she knew, spreading across her heart.

"I'm tired of being afraid," she said.

"You never, once, seemed afraid to me."

"I was. Every minute, it felt like. That was what my anger was covering up."

She brushed her lips against his. A heat and a sizzle flared through her body. Started at that light, delicate touch and sparked all the way down, down. Heated something within her belly and she needed more of it.

Much more.

This time, it was Nate's turn. But his kiss wasn't light and sweet as she'd done, nor was it the heated one from the Waystation that had nearly sent the two of them into her storage shed.

This, this was different.

Tingled every sense in her. Swept right to her core. Her heart. Promising, even.

She moved with him, her lips against his, pressing her body even closer, closer, as close as she could and it still wasn't enough. Not to relieve the ache. Certainly not enough to reach that part of her that had been broken.

Oh, but the promise was still there and it was a long, long way yet until sunrise.

Nate finally pulled away, reluctant. Kept kissing her lips. Her cheeks. The side of her mouth. A little bit longer each time. A little bit deeper.

"So. You were afraid. Even when you pushed me into the pond?" he asked between kisses.

It took Aisha a moment to even realize he was speaking and these were words that she was capable of responding to.

She arched her back. Lengthening her neck, allowing him access… to which he gave himself. Fully. The same long, lingering kisses down to her shoulders. The spot, right there.

"Hmm?" he asked.

"Right. That. *That* part, you deserved." But she'd deserved him too. His relentless pursuit of what he wanted, allowing Timiculous into the Waystation, and finally, of her. "But I deserved it too."

And this moment, most of all.

Especially when she raised her arms, when his fingers slid under her tank top and slowly, carefully, pulled it up. Over her chest, her shoulders, her head. Especially as she did the same to his shirt and as her hands explored his chest, his hardened muscles that no regular wizarding lord would even care to have, to work on. Especially when they finally lay together on the cot she'd made of tanned hide and long grass all those years ago, when they finally lost themselves in each other, in their breaths, Aisha knew they both deserved this moment.

Most of all.

CHAPTER 65

*A*isha stretched out her bare arms, hips sore from sleeping on the cot, and other parts of her sore for entirely different—and much more pleasant—reasons. The threat of heat already laced the dry air, even with the sun barely brushing the plains, but it was still cool yet. Still comfortable. Even with the slender warmth of the fur blanket wrapped around her hips. And the warm and very wonderfully naked form of Nate sprawled out beside her.

Nate, who slept soundly, even a half-nasal snore, not all bothered by the sun peeking over the horizon, the sounds of the camp already in full movement…or the quiet giggling of nearby children.

Aisha strained to see over Nate's shoulder, most of it bare and uncovered, the blanket having been claimed by her—and her hips—at some point in the early morning hours when they'd finally fallen asleep in a heap of tangled limbs from exhaustion. She lifted her eyebrows at the children.

And yes, as expected, they were the same group from yesterday. All of them, in fact. It was still hard to make out their faces, the sun still working its way on lighting the day, but by their constant chitters and clicks, Hadza words that were just starting to piece together in her memory…truthfully, though, she didn't need her memories to under-stand what the exchange of beads and tufts of fur meant.

It wasn't at all difficult to know exactly what was going on.

She gave them a stern look, thrusting out her bottom lip like she'd seen Grandfather do many times before her memory had been blocked.

This caused yet another round of giggles—apparently they'd been on the receiving end of Grandfather's displeasure before. Most tossed up hands, hid faces, and the other half, well, they just didn't bother hiding their grins.

So, Aisha grinned right back.

It felt good.

Really good.

To be whole. Healing. Loved.

Nate grunted, then turned, half-crushing her with his body, half, well, simply scooping her up and pulling her close. He buried his lips into her neck. Nuzzled her there, oh, just so right.

"You people get up too early," he mumbled.

"Maybe you people don't get up early enough."

"I was a bit busy most of the night." He nuzzled her again, eyes still relaxed and closed, then planted a slow kiss on the nape of her neck. It sent another sizzle through her…as if she hadn't possibly had enough sizzling last night.

Which, come to think of it, she hadn't. Not nearly enough. All the time to make up for, what she'd missed out on, what she'd just discovered.

Of course, there was the matter of their audience.

Aisha pulled up the fur blanket a little closer even as she stretched against him, the full, full length of him.

Nate gave a wonderful, deep, low moan.

Damn. She really hadn't had enough sizzle last night. She was almost tempted to ignore their audience. Of course, there was no telling if one of the tribesman would shoo the kids away or not. There were pieces of their culture still missing from her memory. It was, unfortunately, best to play it safe.

"You do realize," she whispered. "We have an audience."

He trailed another long, lingering kiss on her neck. One on her collarbone. One a little bit lower….

Aisha sucked in a breath.

"You people don't seem to mind much about things like that."

"We don't. Which includes the children."

Nate immediately stopped the kissing, which allowed Aisha's breathing—and her brain—to catch up, to reorganize itself, and to take back some small manner of control.

A small amount.

"Seriously?" he asked.

"You can't hear the betting exchanges from here? The giggling would be enough to alert an entire tree of baboons."

Nate swore quietly, flipped the blanket long enough to get an eyeful of the kids, whose laughter only doubled, especially when Nate ducked back under the blanket—completely flushed and red. "I guess they start their days early here."

Aisha could only smile. It was so like him, she realized. Curious about one world but still quite firmly rooted in the other. And yet, he was here. He'd come after her, in more ways than one.

She kissed his forehead. Slow. Promising. Heartfelt. "But their nights end early."

Nate gave another quiet groan. "You mean I've got to wait till night?"

"You've waited this long."

He smirked. "I guess I have." Then, he pulled her to him, lifted her until she was spread out fully over him. He kissed her. Slow and just as promising. This time, it was Nate who made *her* groan. Made her want to kick those kids right out because she certainly didn't want to wait until nightfall.

Finally, Nate slipped his lips free of hers. Gave another slow touch, a rub against his lips. "And the wait was worth it. Every minute."

They somehow managed to get dressed, even with their watching audience. Well, Aisha had a much easier time of it. She wasn't quite as shy about her nudity as Nate, at least, now that she'd returned home and this way of life felt like home too. Although she did turn her back when it was time to put on her bra and shirt. Nate, on the other hand, had to do the fully shimmy under the blanket, which wasn't a very big blanket to begin with.

Aisha had a feeling he was half the reason the kids had stayed so long. They probably weren't used to such entertainment as a white man embarrassed by his own nudity.

She couldn't help but smile too.

A smile that she felt from her fingertips to her heart.

"Here, let me help." Aisha yanked a clean shirt from his bag, this one lacking the holes and gouges by thorn bushes, at least for the moment it, and pulled it over his head.

His dark hair was tangled in every way possible and reminded her of the day they'd met, not when she'd pushed him into the pond, but after. How he'd followed her, dripping wet in pond water and bird droppings, boots sloshing with every dirt-and-mud step he'd taken up to her home. Just like now. Now, where he looked nothing like that high lord, a member of the same elite class that had ousted her.

Aisha smiled, stood, and held out her hand. "Come on. If you want to eat your share of breakfast, you'll need to do your share of the work."

Nate grimaced. "What I could really go for is some coffee."

But he reached up, took her hand, and Aisha found herself in the middle of a shattering memory.

One, of a younger Nate, holding out his hand to her while she ran, ran, ran…from his father.

CHAPTER 66

She felt Nate's fingers, warm, slick, intertwined with hers. But they weren't what she saw.

Instead, Aisha stood in her father's study. Fog seemed to roll around her ankles. Clinging to the bookcases and book stacks. Slowly crawled up the rickety chair she used to sit in, the hand-carvings of the armrests and the slightly deep gouges her father had caused when he'd made it. The chair was right in front of the darkened windows overlooking the Proper. No light lit the plains except what the moon's deemed to touch. All was still. Silent. Quiet.

Except, it wasn't. Not completely.

Aisha took a step forward. A chill sweeping up from her bare toes, all the way from where her nightgown brushed her shins, to the back of her neck and the braid her mother always tied up right before bedtime.

The study was exactly how she remembered it, all those evenings she'd snuck in when her father's candles finally dimmed…but everything was larger now. Towered over her. The top of the desk brushing against her chin, just the perfect height where if she stood on her bare tiptoes she could see the massive stacks of books and ledgers—mostly handwritten with her father's scratchy scrawl.

"Aisha?"

Nate's voice called to her, distant and through fog. But whatever he said, it wasn't clear.

And besides, what was before her was more pressing. Made her heart race. The beating picked up. She felt another piece of her life slid back into place.

This *was* her father's study, but the rumbling of thunder in the distance, so loud it shook the windows, made her flinch and duck her head…the way it had sprung on her as if it came not from the land but from someone's fury.

A wizard's fury.

She'd felt it. Felt it, the minute that dark carriage with those dark horses—except for their eyes—had raced up in a dusty cloud at the Proper's entrance. Even from Aisha's bedroom, as high as it was and as dark as it was, with all those clouds suddenly colliding with each other, she'd seen the pinpricks of fire. The snap and crack of red and flame-lit eyes.

Demon horses was what Grandfather would have called them, before quickly disappearing into the safety of the bush.

Aisha had wanted to disappear too. But she didn't. Couldn't say why. Maybe it was because her father had been the one to stride out into the sudden, howling winds. Winds so strong it seemed they wanted to rip him from where he stood, wrestling with the carriage doors to for their visitors.

He hadn't used magic. He rarely did.

Always said he trusted what his hands could do over magic.

But Aisha had stood there, slender in her thin, pale blue night-gown. Face pressed against her bedroom window, trying to see, trying to make out the dark-robed figure who emerged from the demon carriage, wanting to hide, to flee as Grandfather would have done….

Except then she'd seen a pale, thin, and hollow-looking boy stumble from the carriage.

Face gaunt. Eyes so dim they looked dead.

The wind *should* have ripped him from the ground and flung him across the plains to the gods' mercy. But it didn't. He moved, not quite steady, but with a hidden purpose. A determination.

Aisha pressed her nose closer to the glass. Her breath puffing out. Making him and the carriage and her father disappear from view.

Lightning cracked. Streaked across the plains. A brilliant, deadly flash.

Aisha found herself in the same nightgown, but back in her father's study. Her memory, still piecing itself together. Still not quite right. Still out of order, but finally making sense.

She'd seen the boy and something had compelled her to not run, to not hide. Instead, she'd come to her father's study.

Again there was a loud crack. Thunder knocking right overhead. So hard, so loud, it brought Aisha to her knees.

Then, all went to stillness.

Except for the sound of footsteps padding on the hardwood floor.

Coming closer.

Aisha darted to the desk. Curled up underneath and shoved the chair behind her, closing off the view of the Proper—but not completely. It was as if she could still see the twin fires from those demon horses, the only persistent light daring to break through that storm.

The door to her father's study crashed open. Shook the study so hard it felt like another peal of thunder.

"*You* assured me that tiger was fixed."

A man's voice. Angry. Sparking. Just like the storm.

"I did nothing of the sort. I warned you, Sylvester. I told you it was too soon." Her father. Calm, just like always, but there was a catch in his voice Aisha hadn't heard before.

Didn't ever want to hear again.

"Rosaline also told you. We both did. Apollo was exhibiting strange signs. Erratic. Unpredictable."

Aisha knew about this. Knew what her father spoke of.

In fact, she spent as much time as she could with the other wranglers. Trying to understand why the Familiars even came to them; it was so very different than what her parents often told their clients.

How they were a sanctuary...but here her father was talking about healing?

A thought nagged at her. One she'd had before. A question she remembered asking her father, even her mother, a hundred times, that never got answered.

Why had the Familiars needed healing? What was wrong with them?

"He needed more time with us," her father was saying. "More monitoring. There was something not right, and both Rosaline and I tried to convince you to wait before returning him to the States, but you insisted. Apollo hadn't fully healed—"

"How dare you say this to me now. No, he didn't fully heal! That monster killed my wife!"

Another crash.

This time the sound shook Aisha's teeth along with everything else. She buried her head in her knees. Pulled them closer to her chest. Tears slipped out from the corners of her eyes.

"And do you know who witnessed it?" the man roared. "My son!"

Aisha shivered. Dug her fingers into the thin nightgown. Suddenly, understood that boy.

That dead look in his eyes. The dimming all around him from his magic, his aura.

"I...I had no idea," her father said. "I'm sorry. Truly. For what happened to your wife. The loss to your son. But I can't be responsible for what happened when you took Apollo against my advice—"

"I would be very careful what you said next, Albert."

She heard her father take a deep breath in the sparking, electricity-charged air. Her own hair felt like it tingled. The hairs on her arm standing on end.

Aisha dug her fingers tighter into her arms. Pressed her knees even closer to her chest. Barely dared to breathe.

"The hold you have over my Proper," her father said, "and my wife's allegiance is quite clear."

"The *contract* you signed is quite clear." The man's voice lowered.

The threat hung, just as sharp and biting and dangerous as that lightning outside.

Lightning, Aisha thought, that might actually be coming from the inside.

"You fix what's wrong with them, with these Familiars," the man warned. "And you do it quickly. Quietly. Without anyone in your employment, or your family, being the wiser. That was what you agreed to. Instead, I must now deal with the fallout of my wife's murder and you, Albert Faye, and your Proper are responsible for what happened."

Footsteps creaked on the floorboard.

Coming closer.

"I hear your eldest has been asking some intriguing questions. About this place. About the Familiars. Perhaps if you cannot find the answer I seek, maybe someone else with, perhaps, Rosaline's talents could."

"Aisha knows nothing."

There was a thud on the desk. A loud thunk as something was thrown down on top.

Aisha flinched. She cupped her mouth to keep from making any noise.

"I hope for your sake it remains that way. Fix the problem. Fix it now. Our deal was quite clear. You do *not* want me to return."

Both sets of footsteps faded. Padded away on the creaking floorboards, still sharp and loud, even over the rolling thunder. But even though the wizard and her father left, the storm continued.

Aisha didn't know how long she hid there, just that at some point she discovered she could actually move. Could crawl out from under the desk, and through the flash of lightning saw a leather-bound book on her father's desk, one that hadn't been there before.

The Rehabilitative Program for Magical Familiars was the title.

Aisha stood on her tiptoes. Reached out for it, when there was another creak in the floorboards.

Right behind her.

She spun, ready to scream, to throw something, anything—but it was the boy.

He sat huddled in the corner, against the only non-windowed wall in her father's study. Shivering controllably.

"I wouldn't touch that."

She barely heard his words over the thunder. "Are you…okay?"

The boy bit his bottom lip. Shook his head once. Then, finally, held out his hand to her. "We should go. My father…we don't want him to find us here. Find us, at all."

There was something about him. Not because he looked so scared, but there it was again… that little spark. That determination she'd seen as he'd stumbled out of the carriage.

"Okay."

Aisha stepped forward, bare feet on the hard and cold floors, and took the boy's hand. Squeezed it to reassure herself he was real and so was she, and that for now, they were both safe.

CHAPTER 67

*N*ate watched as Aisha blinked away whatever memory had slipped into her mind, as she looked down at their intertwined hands, a dawning realization growing on her face. She didn't look up from their hands, but instead, slowly, squeezed.

He exhaled a breath he hadn't realized he'd been holding.

She was coming back to him. Thank the heavens.

She wasn't lost.

Nate wanted to pull her into his lap. To hold her close until whatever memory had grabbed her finally let go. But he didn't. Instead, he curled his fingers tighter around hers. The sweat of their skin making the contact slick and slippery, as if she could so easily slip away from him. Gone, forever.

He knew, instinctively, to give her this time, this chance to realign herself. She needed to return on her own. If she didn't, there was no telling just what parts of "her" could be left behind. Left behind in those fragments, that fog….

One Nate knew too well.

Personally.

The Hadzabe children, he noticed, had finally taken their leave, as if they'd sensed something more was going on now. Not the funny taunting and play-pranks on two adults who'd just found each other, but something more. They'd fled the moment Aisha's eyes had gone glassy, the moment she slipped from the here and now, in the warming sun and heat of the bush, to...well, wherever it was she'd gone.

Soft footsteps padded closer. Brittle, stunted grass cracked underneath. Beads clinking together.

Nate looked up and saw Onwas, with his thick necklaces of beads wrapped around his neck. He leaned on some gnarled piece of wood, like a walking staff, and just stood there. Watching. Waiting. He closed his dark-black eyes and began humming softly in clicks and grunts and words Nate couldn't even begin to recognize.

But Onwas, and whatever he was doing, the steady beat of his chanting, thrummed in tune with Nate's own heart.

Helped him relax. To steady his own breath and believe that Aisha would fully pull out of the fog.

It helped him remember, too, his own struggle. His own fight to regain memories his father had stolen, and the aftermath, of when someone he loved and trusted had tried to pull him back when those memories were retaking their place, just as what was happening with Aisha.

Nate sucked in a breath of the hot air. Felt his whole body tense.

It had happened to him, after all. When Hilda had thought she was helping, that night when he finally broke through his own memory spell, the night she asked him to confront his father, to stand up for their engagement and their love.

She hadn't really understood why he'd walked away after that night, why he couldn't give himself fully to her, just as she hadn't understood what was happening to him—or when Timiculous told her to leave him be, to let the memory find its place.

But she hadn't listened, as was her normal behavior, and if it hadn't been for Timiculous...

Nate shivered. Tightened his hold on Aisha's fingers, just slightly.

And his memory spell had been nothing compared to Aisha's. His had been a small one, one his father had placed on him to help Nate "heal" from his mother's death. His hadn't been anything like Aisha's, where a death trigger had awaited at the end.

He'd nearly lost her.

"Nate?" Aisha whispered.

"I'm here."

Onwas, Nate noticed, had stopped chanting. Aisha glanced at her grandfather, but only briefly. Hair tangled in front of her face. Down her shoulders. Sliding between them. He wanted to reach out, to touch her hair, to touch her.

Make sure she had returned, fully, but he didn't dare.

"This happened to you," she said.

Nate sat back. Hard. Fast. Nearly rocked himself right onto his back. But he didn't let go of her hand.

"What?"

"The memory block," she said. "Your father put one on you, didn't he?"

"How…I didn't tell you." He'd told her parts of his life, but not all. Couldn't, because parts of him were missing and he'd never get them back. "How did you know?"

"Because we've met before. Here. At the Proper. I remember."

Nate watched, his heart pounding hard and fierce, hurt, even as she closed her eyes and pulled up whatever memory she thought she might have…one that had been a part of him that he couldn't remember.

"You came here, in the middle of the night with your father. He was furious. It was right after your mother died."

Nate didn't know when his head began spinning. The world seeming to tilt as Onwas went from an upright position to an almost horizontal one. Nor did he know when his head finally stopped the spinning. Probably because at some point he'd put his head between his legs.

All he knew was that the world, his whole world, went blank for a moment and all he heard, all he saw, were the words Aisha had spoken.

After his mother had died.

"You can't know that," he said.

Or tried to. Wasn't sure he succeeded.

In the back of his mind, he heard Onwas chanting again, but that was all. Even the heat seemed to slip away. The sweat pooling along his forehead, little droplets that slid down, and then he didn't register them at all.

He lifted his head and just stared at Aisha, with her eyes still closed, still holding his hand, as she told him her memory.

Of the first time they'd met.

Nate didn't know, truly, what it meant to feel true betrayal until this moment. Not because of what his father had done, but because of how far, of how deep his plot actually went. Nate's whole life had been based on lies and untruths, and some truths hidden in plain sight. And through it all, there had been Aisha.

Somewhere, always hidden from him, but there.

Helping him just as he'd helped her. Even if he couldn't remember it—those memories were lost to him, lost in the fog of his father's spell—but he felt it. Felt the rightness of Aisha's words. Felt the way her fingers slid beside his. Held him. Just as he knew they'd held each other that night so long ago when his world truly had collapsed, and his father, apparently, had taken away every memory associated with his mother's death—except for the ones Nate managed to find, on his own, through that thick fog.

But there was one thing Nate *did* know.

"Aisha."

This time, he did pull her into his lap. Pulled her close until their chests pressed against each other, heartbeats humming in tune, just as they did with Onwas's chanting.

"What is it? What's wrong?"

"He won't stop." Nate buried his face in her tangled hair. Took a deep breath of wild and earth and of everything he believed was this place called Africa. Tanzania. Niggled a little, at a memory he'd lost, but could still almost sense. Smell.

He wouldn't let his father take her away again.

Not again.

Nate pulled away, enough so he could look into her eyes. "My father won't stop. If this went back that far, back to my mother's death—"

"Before that, even. It was your father who allowed the Proper to exist, who...who held my mother's people hostage for her cooperation." Aisha growled at that last.

"Which means he's going to fight, hard, to keep this under control. Do you understand? Do you know what this means?"

Aisha didn't look away. Didn't flinch like Nate had seen so many others do when faced with his father's fury. Instead, she looked Nate right in the eyes and in a calm, steady voice, with the same steel he'd fallen in love with, said, "It means that bastard's coming here. To me. To end this."

Suddenly, he tasted wild on the air. Felt it sizzle and spark and stir.

Waking up. For the first time in a long time.

Onwas continued chanting. Behind him, many of the other tribesman arrived, chanting as well. Their heads, bowed.

In honor, and respect.

Aisha, he saw, noticed none of this. Instead, she got up. Slid right off him and thrust her hands on her hips. Glared in the direction of the Proper—or at least, where Nate *thought* the Proper was.

"He's coming to end this." A small cyclone of dirt, dried grass, and red sand swirled at Aisha's feet. Tugged at those tangled, dark strands of hair. "And it's about damn time."

CHAPTER 68

Sylvester glared at Rosaline. Glared at the calmness in her eyes. The graceful, fluid way that she moved over rocks and weeds and thorn bushes that should have immediately been eradicated for daring to bar his passage. And she simply stood there, at the precipice to the last remnants of civilization, and expected *him* to enter the *bush*.

On foot.

"You want to find my daughter? To find my people?"

"You know I do," Sylvester growled, but didn't take a single step. "But if you expect me to tramp through that bush without some form of transportation—"

Beside him, Daniel slumped forward. Feet stumbling in that dreadful, too-red, unnatural dirt. Shoulders slightly bent. His tall frame now hunched from the strain of taking the full impact of the memory spell's backlash. He looked nothing like the handsome man he'd been just a few days past.

"With all due respect, sir," Daniel somehow managed to croak, "we've been searching for Aisha nonstop for three days."

Sylvester glared at Daniel, who still couldn't muster the energy to even stand straight and proud, as his rank demanded. Weak. That was what he was.

Should have left the boy behind.

He'd do nothing but slow Sylvester's progress—except, Sylvester needed the Blakeley's presence here. Their name. All that power he'd built and helped create in the family: he'd need that support if he expected the High Council to accept his actions without doubt or inquiry. For as much as he'd boasted to Rosaline, the murdering of other wizards, even disinherited ones, was not looked highly on. Unless, of course, Sylvester provided the appropriate means and reason for the High Council to discreetly look the other way.

"You wish to find my daughter? Then this is where we most go. And how." Rosaline pointed at his feet. "That is all the transportation you need. Anything more and the truth will remain hidden from you."

The tiniest ghost of a smile tugged at Rosaline's lips. As if she didn't even realize or care about the knife he held to her throat.

He wanted to throttle her. Blast her with a spell that would wipe her and this horrid land off the map.

But he couldn't.

And since he couldn't, he *would* control it. Control this family. Rosaline. Even the land.

Except Rosaline, damn her, just stood there as if she was ready to meld into the land. Disappear right in front of his eyes.

He wouldn't put it past her. Leave them alone and stranded in the middle of this forsaken desert.

Another reason he'd brought Daniel.

Two ruling members of society disappearing was not something even Rosaline or Albert could simply make *go away*.

Not without threat to their contract.

The sun already beat down on him. Soaked through his robes even though he'd shed his more formal ones with their many layers and signals of his office and his rank, and still, he couldn't seem to stop sweating. Even while it was still morning.

He wiped a sticky hand across his forehead.

His discomfort didn't matter. He hadn't always been so high in society. Hadn't always ruled a Council. He would return to that man he once was, show Rosaline, her family, and this land exactly who—and what—Sylvester Darkwood was.

Exactly why he was so feared.

Sylvester ignored the sweat dripping down passed his eyes. Ignored the way the heat seemed to cling to him, even the way the land seemed to *breathe* under his feet.

None of that mattered any longer.

He had a mission, a job. He'd see it through to the end, just as he'd seen through the covering up, and truth, of his wife's death, and everything he'd done and been before then. Sylvester felt the layers slide over him. The layers that made him so cold and cunning. Calculating. Already drawing on his deepest powers, the well of power within him, the parts he'd kept carefully hidden away.

A part that not even the High Council was aware of.

The part that, at one point, had made him one of the deadliest, most accurate, silent assassins, along with the mind and deep understanding that made him into the High Chancellor without anyone being the wiser.

Sylvester bowed once. Slow, deliberate, to Rosaline.

She froze. Her dark eyes going wide for a brief moment.

Yes, she remembered who he was. Who he would be again.

"I think it's time we finished this game, Rosaline. You promised me your daughter. Now, take me to her."

CHAPTER 69

*A*isha felt the shift in the land. The hard-packed earth suddenly quaking underneath her worn hiking boots. Bucking. Warning.

She closed her eyes and let the land roll around her. Breathed long and deep. Felt, within herself, the spark of magic in her belly warm in response. A magic she recognized now. It was more than just her "gut magic." It was the magic of Tanzania. The one her grandfather, and all the Hadzabe seemed to have within them. That deeper understanding of this place, as if they were connected by blood to the drying plains, the gazelle leaping across the lands, the herds of wildebeest and their long, long migrations.

She acknowledged the land. Not so much in words, but in feelings. Allowed herself to feel the growing fear in the plains, as if it knew the change that was coming—or could come.

But there was anger there too.

Unforgotten anger from all those years ago, and it was rising.

Aisha opened her eyes. Stared at the bent and broken acacia tree in front of her. The same one at which she'd met Onwas at without every realizing the significance. How important this tree, this exact place was, for both the land, and for herself. Cracked and split in two, right down the middle of the trunk, a deep gouge of burnt wood cut nearly clean through. Anyone looking at the tree would have assumed it was a lightning strike.

They would be right.

And wrong.

She stepped forward, boots crunching the browning grass, and touched the trunk, careful to keep her hands away from the thorny spikes. And yet, she still felt them bite into her—not the spikes exactly, but the power there.

Within the tree. The anger.

The tree, like the land, remembered what had happened here.

Knew, exactly, what was coming.

Again. For her.

"Is this where it happened?" Nate asked behind her. "Where my father cast his spell?"

"It is."

Nate's voice had been quiet, as if in reverence, but it still seemed to echo. To roll across the land. She felt the land shifting underneath her in response, not quite sure, truthfully, what to make of him. As if could sense the connection between Nate and the man who'd done this to the tree, and to her.

The rough bark was cracked and aged under her touch, but warm, too. Welcoming, even though it still held so much anger, still hadn't forgotten what had been done.

Aisha continued to stroke, to soothe. "This is where Daniel came to fetch me. I don't...I don't know how he found me. I think my mother may have shown him the way."

"The way?"

Aisha glanced over her shoulder, a smirk pulling at her lips. "Just because you found me so easily doesn't mean just anyone can."

He frowned. "Your mother told me. I went where she directed."

"Yes, you did."

Just as Daniel had done. But unlike with Daniel, whom her mother would have had no choice but to tell, she'd shown Nate because... because she really did care about Aisha.

Aisha closed her eyes again. Sighed. Felt another piece of herself slipping into place. This one was still jagged, still hurt and worn in a few places, maybe even torn in others, but it was there.

Behind Nate, Onwas stood, still leaning on his staff, his own eyes closed as he swayed slightly. None of the other tribesman had come with them, though some had clearly wanted to.

She was glad they hadn't.

There were so few of their people left, so little of their way of life, and she understood now that Sylvester and the ruling Council of Tanzania controlled much of what life they did have left. If needed, the tribe could disappear into the bush. The land would protect them, so long as the land remained as it was.

Wild.

Free.

Aisha slid her hands down the trunk, then stepped away, her fingers black from the sooty and burnt trunk. The residue of magic clung to her skin, to her fingertips. Carried with it, still, the price to use this civilization' magic in a place that had its own magic.

Just as her father had taught her, once.

And it felt good, at least, to put some sense to her life. To the memories that had been blocked from her. At least she knew, now, why her father feared and distrusted magic so much. It hadn't been magic itself, per se, but the use of magic *here*, and why he'd worked so hard and long for her to understand this.

It was one small step closer to putting herself back together. Maybe one day, if she survived this, it'd be enough.

"Aisha?"

She hadn't noticed that Nate had come closer, was actually directly behind her. It would be so easy to take that final step backwards. To lean into his tall frame. To let his strength and confidence enfold her. The promises that, his very presence told her, he'd be there, he'd protect her.

But she couldn't.

Not yet.

First, she had to protect herself, and more importantly, protect what had always been her birthright.

"I'm fine," she answered. "Just...ready."

And she was. Felt it, right to her bones. Felt her magic in her gut growing, maturing. Which was good, truthfully, because it was at that moment that Aisha saw them appear. Out of the corner of her eye, from the same direction Onwas must have seen Aisha appear, came her mother, Daniel, and lastly, Sylvester.

Her breath hitched. Not at seeing Daniel, as the land hadn't been kind to him. The way his once-bright eyes appeared dim, his face and skin sunken, and the almost ghostly sheen that hung off him.

No, her breath caught because she finally saw Sylvester as she had that day. In his dark and billowing robes, tall frame and stature, so high and so noble that not even the harshness of Africa could touch him.

It was then, too, that Aisha realized how Sylvester had found her.

Her mother.

She'd told Sylvester, just as she'd told Daniel and Nate. It was the only way he could have found her, could have destroyed that ancient and powerful magic that flowed across the land, so strong and potent, just the same way the heat now beat down on them.

Aisha's gaze flicked to her mother, whose dark eyes immediately shifted to the ground. She bowed her head, low, as if in sorrow, but she said nothing. Offered no apology. And somehow, even knowing the truth of why her mother had done this didn't change the hurt Aisha felt as it struck right through her. Hard and fast, just as it had that day.

"Well," Sylvester said, stroking his chin, "I see that we have once again come to this place. But if this is where you feel it must end..." He shrugged. "Truly, it makes no difference to me. So long as I never have to return to this horrid land again. You will see to it this time, won't you, Rosaline, dear?"

But Sylvester didn't wait for an answer. Just gave a tiny uplift of his lips when he saw Aisha's mother flinch. He raised his arms, long billowy robes slipping down revealing two pale hands. Raised, towards Aisha.

A hazy purple-black color sparked from his fingertips.

She heard Nate shout behind her. A rush of air as if he wanted to push her down.

That was all the warning she had before the day turned into night.

CHAPTER 70

ate watched, helpless, as the force of Sylvester's magic smacked into Aisha. A hard thud that struck her first in the chest, causing her to gasp. The second, right in her gut.

Nate yelled. Reached for her.

Watched as she bent forward. Heard as her knees cracked into the hard, dry ground. She gasped again.

But his father's magic, that purple-black, unrelenting haze, kept at her. Seemed to flow straight and true for her chest. To keep her there.

Nate felt his own magic answering.

He was nearly there. Nearly beside her when Aisha, his father, and the others disappeared.

One moment she was there before him, gasping and fighting, and the next, she was gone.

"No. No. No." Nate fell to the ground, right where she would have been. Clawed at the air. The ground. But she was gone.

Gone.

He wasn't going to let his father win. Couldn't.

The magic within him continued to swell, pour from him, as he searched for any sign of his father's spell, any slight deviation or tear that his father might have left behind. But there was nothing.

His father was just too good a spell caster. Too good, Nate knew, to be taught just anywhere. Even for a high-ranking Council member.

Nate's mouth went dry. Didn't notice the heat. The bite of the thorny bush beside him as he again shoved his hands right where Aisha had been, feeling for any hint or sign of that spell.

Still nothing.

She was gone. Gone. His father had taken her. Taken her, right from Nate, and he hadn't been able to stop him. Again.

Nate pounded him fists into the sand. A small, jagged rock bit into him. Drew blood.

He didn't care.

"Dark magic strong here. Too strong." Onwas stood beside Nate. Gripped that gnarled cane. Black eyes narrowed into thin slits. "Strengthened by blood."

"Not mine," Nate growled.

Onwas nodded. "Land knows this. Knows too, who made him strong when should be." Onwas reached out. Gripped Nate's shoulder. Squeezed with a grip harder than Nate would have believed possible for someone of Onwas's age. "But can be broken."

"How?"

Onwas pointed at Nate's chest. "Daughter's-daughter already show you. Your magic not right here, not right for this place. But Africa magic, older. Stronger. You find?"

Yes, he could.

Panic rose within him. Every breath, every beat of that sun against him a reminder that Aisha was running out of time.

He forced himself to take a deep breath. To remember that night when she'd reached within him, healed him. Remembered too, their shared moment under the stars, before all the land, as if she'd somehow known the land needed to understand....

He was of his father's blood, but not his father.

Nate's magic came to him, an answering swell that filled his chest. Lungs. Heart. But it was more than just his magic. Tasted the difference. The hot, stifling heat. Rigid and unyielding as if each second was a test for worthiness to life, or of sacrifice.

A distant rumbling echoed....

Nate reached out again, right where Aisha had been, closed his fingers on the air, and rent it back—shoved himself through that rip and crashed into a world of pure darkness.

CHAPTER 71

The more Aisha fought, the more her world went dim. Darkness blinked across her vision. She struggled to breathe. Failed.

She was so easily suffocating.

So easy.

Too easy.

She *wouldn't* be so easy to kill.

Aisha stopped clutching at her throat. Grabbed a handful of soft, reddened dirt, focused on where she was. Who she was. A person whom Sylvester was afraid of, had always been afraid of. She felt each soft granule, the simplicity of the dirt, slide through her fingers. Felt within those tiny bits of sand, leaves, and bone, her magic.

Bit by bit, she felt the throttle of magic at her chest loosen. Ease, slowly. She managed one small breath. Sucked in a mouthful, then, another.

All took place within a single heartbeat.

Sylvester continued to shoot out his magic at her, but also at the land itself. Everywhere. Surrounded them. As if he wanted to destroy her and every inch of her tribe's land until there was nothing but ash left. Ash and death.

His magic was so dark and black, it blocked out the sun. Left only Aisha, her mother, Daniel, and Sylvester there in this world of never-ending darkness. And of course, that lone acacia tree, split down the middle, which had already witnessed this once before.

"Aisha!"

Nate's voice cut through that darkness. Cut straight through the thundering and pounding of magic. She blinked, then saw him shove aside that darkness, push right through it until he stood in that dark, inky-black world, right beside her.

He'd come for her.

"Nathanial," his father warned, low and cruel. "This is none of your affair."

"It's always been my affair. Ever since you covered up Mother's death. Ever since you stole my memories." And Nate thrust his own hands into that steady stream of magic. Face straining, sweat dripping down his forehead, off his nose, even as Aisha sought to catch another breath before her vision and all those dark spots overwhelmed her—

Nate grabbed hold of his father's magic and thrust it right back at him. Smacked it right into the center of Sylvester's chest.

Sylvester stumbled.

Didn't fall, though.

Not like Aisha, who fell forward on her hands, sucking in as much air as she could. Air that sparked and sizzled.

Sparkled as she felt—no, the *land* felt—Sylvester readying yet another spell.

"Nate," she tried to warn, but it was only a croak.

Sylvester straightened himself to his full height. Shifted his dark robes, so black they made him appear a shadow among all that darkness. "So this is how it will be, my son. Your choice. I wish I could say I was surprised, but I had hoped you'd turn away from this path."

Nate, who she could sense calling on his own magic, paused. Hesitated.

She wanted to tell him to keep going. To not listen. But her throat was locked tight. Refused to let even a single "no" out.

"Do you think I didn't know?" Sylvester asked. "All those years with you and your *Familiar* searching for answers? Your so-called great Familiar question?"

Nate slid in front of Aisha. Blocked her from Sylvester's view, his direct line of fire. Protecting her.

Sylvester lowered his arms as if unwilling to fight, but Aisha knew better. The land knew better. Because even as he stood there, Aisha felt the air continue to spark.

Swell.

A powerful, powerful spell building, growing...

"Yes, yes, I knew," Sylvester said. "Your silent little crusade against me. All those depositions you'd collected from former sanctuary employees...you will discover most have changed their mind about testifying before the High Council."

Aisha watched as Nate flinched. She tried to reach for him, but her fingers grasped only air, as if he were too far and distant.

"It was well played," Sylvester continued. "Careful, so I wouldn't notice. The way you choose your battles, especially when you convinced the Council to leave that Familiar veterinarian and her practice alone, but how you weren't willing to risk my displeasure for her love. Just like I knew your interest in that Waystation. It was my mistake to send you, but I'd hoped seeing the alternative would deter you. Teach you that my will would never be shoved aside."

"It doesn't matter anymore," Nate said. "You failed. We know the truth about the wasting sickness, where it came from, how to stop it. Soon, everyone will know."

Sylvester's lips quirked up. Just a tiny bit.

The air continued to spark. Sizzle. Heat that practically singed the air she breathed.

"Nate," she tried again. But it still wasn't enough. Couldn't speak. Sylvester's magic had done something more than try to suffocate her. She couldn't reach Nate, couldn't warn him, because all he knew was civilized magic. Didn't sense the danger...and then she remembered last night. When the memory spell had first tried to kill her, and then Nate...

Nate!

Nate's back went rigid.

Right as Sylvester thrust his hands out. A different spell sparking from them.

A red so dark it nearly appeared black.

Except Nate dove to the side. Rolled in that red dirt. Out of the way and safe. But no longer shielding Aisha. No longer protecting her.

Which caused that smirk of a smile on Sylvester's face to grow. Widen. As he turned his attention to her.

"You want to know how I'm suddenly so strong? Why your precious land magic can't fight against me?"

Sylvester waved a hand to Daniel. And then, to Aisha's mother.

Her mother was splayed against the acacia tree. Body bent backwards. Taunt and rigid. Face strained and eyes becoming more and more bloodshot. Daniel looked no better; in fact, he looked worse. He'd gone so pale and dim, as if only the tiny amount of life spark remained.

But it was Rosaline and Rosaline only who had Aisha's gaze. Her beautiful dark hair fell across her chest. Hung there, lifeless, growing fainter just as Aisha could sense that life within her was. Just like those beads woven among the strands, their color fading. Disappearing.

Rosaline somehow lowered her head until she looked right at Aisha. "Contract."

Then her back arched again. She screamed.

Aisha surged to her feet. "Mother!"

And then froze.

As if the land had grabbed hold of her. Was holding her back.

Except the grip on her shoulders, the way they tightened, felt familiar. So did that smell of wild wind and old, worn leather.

Her grandfather.

Holding her back. Keeping her from rushing to her mother and making a terrible mistake.

"That's right." Sylvester continued to grin. Held out his hands. Light streaked from her mother, from Daniel, right to him. "The contract binds them. The contract they both willingly signed. Not *legal* magic, of course. But then, I didn't get to where I am by following the natural order of things. Or perhaps I did. It's what your Africa would call 'survival of the fittest'."

Nate surged to his feet. Raced right at his father.

But Nate didn't have Onwas and the land to hold him back. Didn't know the trap he was willing running to.

Aisha tried to scream a warning. But it was too late.

When Sylvester opened his eyes, now completely black, and thrust a hand at Nate. A dark, thick, and snapping rope snaked around him. Bit into him. Right at his throat. At the all-important blood that would be pumping there, just as a lion would always target the jugular.

Nate fell.

Didn't move.

Again, she screamed. Torn from her throat until she felt nothing but despair. Tried to get to him, but the land held her fast. Held her, as she slowly watched him die. And within her, felt her own heart dying.

It was hopeless. Everything she'd done, everything she'd fought for and won, piece by piece—her Waystation, her memories, none of that mattered.

Sylvester was too strong. Too powerful. And her magic, her simple magic of helping Familiars heal and find their way back to their true selves, none of that meant anything.

Not here. Not now.

"You finally understand." Sylvester, finally, turned his attention to Aisha. "As I said earlier, I do believe it's time we ended this little game, Aisha Faye, and all the troubles you've caused me."

His magic struck again at her.

This time, striking for her heart.

CHAPTER 72

No sun broke through Sylvester's magic. The hazy darkness whipped around her. Tore at her clothes, her hair. Stung her face and eyes. Aisha tried shoving it aside. Tried using the new magic she'd found, but it was like grabbing a fistful of sand.

No matter how hard she fought, no matter how deeply she reached, it kept slipping through her fingers.

As if she didn't have the right net to contain it. Use it.

Not even a glimmer of light penetrated the magic as Sylvester stole precious amounts of life from her mother, Daniel, and Nate. Nor was there any hot breeze flowing from the nearby salted lake.

No help coming.

Not from her mother, who'd signed over more than just the safety of her tribe, but her heart's blood as well. Not from Nate, who was struggling to live against that viper rope. Stealing his breath, his life force. Feeding it right back into his father and the spell she felt thickening in the air. Making it hard for even her to breathe or move.

Sylvester was going to destroy her.

All of them.

The land.

Everything.

Sylvester raised his fingers to his lips. Sent her a farewell kiss.

And a swirling dagger of black-and-purple magic sliced towards her. Sliced through that already dark world. Striking right at her chest. Right where her heart beat.

Time seemed to slow.

The land no longer held her down, but she found she couldn't move. Not when despair held her there.

Hopelessness.

Everything she'd fought for, fought to save and protect, was dying. It had all been for nothing.

Right before that dagger sliced into her chest, tearing out her heart, it was shoved aside.

Deflected by another kind of magic. Familiar and yet different.

It sent that dagger spinning until it thunked right into the torn, burnt trunk of the acacia tree.

The dagger's killing magic exploded. Sent sparks of white and purple showering upwards. Sent the branches and thorns in a smoking-black fire.

Aisha shoved her attention towards Nate. He held out one shaking hand even while the other still clutched at that rope viper, gorging on his neck, his life. Still protecting, even as she saw the last of his strength, fade.

"Still so defiant," Sylvester murmured. He simply shook his head at the dagger, which was now smoldering, burning ash on the tree. "Both you and my son. But none of this would have happened if not for your family. For their inabilities and incompetency. If they'd merely held their side of the bargain...."

Sylvester shrugged. "It's no matter. I suppose it's only fitting for my defiant son to watch you perish first. Or perhaps, Nathanial, I should allow this woman you love, everything she's worked for, cared for, watch *you* perish first. Perhaps that will take that final spark from her, hmm?"

Sylvester tightened his grip on the air.

Nate jerked back. His body arching up. Then down. Mouth open in a silent scream.

Aisha screamed his name. Wanted to go to him, but couldn't. Held there still by her grandfather, the land…she didn't know and didn't care.

She needed to help. To stop this, to—

Nate's face went pale. Deathly pale.

He didn't look away from her. Even as she felt that thinning connection they had left, vanish. His eyes, clouded. Mouth, going slack.

A final word, drifting in her mind.

Contract.

Then, the connection was severed.

Except, she still felt a lingering trace of him…and something more. What he'd done with the dagger, and just now, that hadn't been *his* magic.

It had been the land's.

Hers.

The magic within her, which she'd somehow shared with him last night, under those stars with the baboons and calls of lions as witnesses. A magic he had access to, because of her.

Because of her tie to the land.

Aisha held her ground. Didn't slid back a step like every fiber of her being was screaming to do; to run, to survive. But she didn't. Couldn't. Because this was exactly where she needed to be.

Suddenly, began to understand.

"You used the contract my mother signed, didn't you?" Aisha got to her feet. Legs shaking, barely holding her up. But they did. "That's why the land can't stop you. That's why you can use this magic, how you were able to cast that spell on me."

"It has been to my…benefit, that your mother never truly understood *what* she was signing away. But yes. The tie between her and the land, and then therefore with me, has been most beneficial. If, of course, I'm able to settle this matter between you, me, and all those Familiars."

"Except by settle, you mean death."

"There is that, yes. Unfortunate, but I gave you ample opportunity to turn aside, my dear. You, and my son."

She felt the growing anger within the acacia tree. The magic within it swelling, pulsing. And even though she couldn't see the ground, the reddened dirt, or the thorny branches, she still felt them—even through all that darkness.

She no longer felt her grandfather there, holding her, but she felt him all the same. Because he was still there. He was all around her.

He was the land.

And so was she.

She wasn't afraid anymore. Not of the shadow she'd only glimpsed from her dreams, nightmares, memories. Wasn't afraid of the true assassin hiding within a Council member's robes.

Because she understood.

Aisha lifted her head. That was the real truth Sylvester had stolen from her. The magic had always been within her. She felt it now. Felt the way the earth moved and breathed underneath her boots. Felt the distant spines of mountains, that slow rise and pull as more mountains were created—and even farther off into the distance, destroyed. Felt the trickling of water as the land finally flooded with new life. Green spouts of grass spurting up from the ground. The flapping of pink-and-white flamingos. Faced the nightmare she'd been living for years. The man of shadows she'd seen in her dreams since that day he'd stole not only her memories, but her magic.

Her heritage magic.

Her magic, which wanted to act. To free itself from the chains Sylvester and the High Council held over it.

But it couldn't. Not as long as it was tied to her mother. And the contract she'd signed.

Aisha sucked in a breath of hot, dark air.

There was another contract. One that had been in place long before Sylvester came along and forced her mother to sign his. It was an older contract. Ancient. One that reached back for so long, so far into the past, since the first Hadzabe came to this piece of land.

It was so hard to not look at Nate. To close her heart to him when all she wanted was to go to him. Save him.

But she couldn't.

The only way to save him, herself, and the others was by freeing the land.

All it needed was her.

Her, and her blood.

"This tree remembers, did you know that?" Aisha carefully, slowly made her way to the acacia tree. The dagger was gone, but that wasn't the weapon she needed. "It remembers what happened. What you did here. To me. How you killed my Familiar."

"It is a tree. Should have been uprooted and tamed the moment we settled here."

"Yes, you'd think so." Aisha reached out to the trunk. Again, let her fingers slid down that rough bark. The magic there sparking from Sylvester's old spell. But within it, she felt that anger do more than stir.

It came alive under her touch.

Her coaxing.

She reached within herself. Deep. Deeper than she'd ever gone before; ever trusted herself before.

"What are you doing, young lady?"

Her hand touched the tip of those long, sharp thorns. "You said you'd made the contract with my mother. But the thing is, she was only one piece of another contract. Another promise."

"Aisha?" Sylvester warned. His eyes darkening.

She felt his magic arching, spiking to higher, more dangerous levels. Just as she felt those precious seconds slipping away from her mother, Nate, Daniel…who'd all finally stopped moving.

No.

She couldn't think of them.

Not now.

She had to finish this.

Aisha opened her eyes. Looked right at Sylvester. "I am Hadzabe. The Hadzabe are the land. My mother no longer speaks for the land."

She shoved her hand onto the pointed, sharp thorn. Blood spilled from her. Coated the acacia tree's thorns, its trunk. Dribbled down and finally seeped into the earth.

An earth that rumbled.

Quaked.

Came alive.

Sylvester thrust his magic at Aisha. Sent every sharpened, killing spell he'd learned from his years working in the shadows. Sent everything he had, every reserve of his energy right at her.

Should have known.

Should have seen the treachery.

Just like her mother's.

But no magic came from him. No magic poured from his fingers. The connection between him and the three vessels was gone.

Severed.

Sunlight pierced through his dark haze. So bright and hot, it seared his eyes.

He yelled. Raised his hands, covered his eyes, but the light was so bright it penetrated that feeble protection.

And the ground beneath him...

It came alive. Fierce and angry. It shoved Sylvester to the ground. His knees smacking hard into a jutted-up rock. Another tore into his side as he fell. Cut right through his robes, skin, as if they were nothing.

As if he was nothing.

Sylvester thrust his hands into the ground. Forced himself to stand. He wouldn't let it end like this. He wouldn't let some primitive child and this backwater country defeat him!

He stepped forward. Hands reached out for Aisha. Used the very last spell he had, taken right form the center of his soul. Aimed it right at her heart.

A true death spell.

The spell leapt from him. It tumbled through the air. Right at Aisha, who stood there in her torn and dirty pants and shirt. The blood that flowed down her hand and onto the earth. Her wild, oily black hair whipping about her face as if she were some African pagan goddess.

The spell didn't touch her.

Couldn't.

Not when the ground literally heaved itself upwards. Blocking her. Saving her.

His spell smacked hard and true into a mound of dirt.

Sylvester roared. Went to send another spell, another piece of himself, when his feet no longer found purchase.

When he felt himself falling. Falling…

A darkness, greater than any he'd ever created, engulfed him as he was finally swallowed by that terrible, wild land.

CHAPTER 74

*A*isha stumbled over the rocking, shaking earth. Slipped once, then again, as she tried to get to Nate. His body bucked and swerved with the earthquake. Still tangled and caught by his father's spell.

Sylvester Darkwood. Whose screams had been quickly cut off the moment the ravine had opened beneath him. Deep and black and so far down—he'd been silenced the moment the earth closed above him.

But even though his screams no longer cut through the mid-morning heat, the echoes of it vibrated still, as if the moment of his death was trapped within that shaking ground.

Aisha shoved off the acacia tree. Felt her other hand tear as another thorn cut deep. She didn't care. Not about the thorn. Not about the still rolling, angry earth that seemed to want more blood, want more vengeance....

She had to get to Nate.

She collapsed beside him. Her knees smacking into the hot dirt. Rocks gouged and ripped through her pants.

She barely noticed.

Aisha yanked and pulled the magical, binding rope off Nate. Away from his throat. The rope no longer glowed. No longer shown with magical powers. But he was still so pale.

Too pale. Still didn't move.

"Nate. Nate. Talk to me. Please." Her hands shook. Faltered when the loops wouldn't uncurl. Shoved harder. The magic within her gut sparking. Rolling in tune with the earthquake. Rising within her.

She tightened her hold on that gold-red strand. Poured her own anger into it. Her desperation.

The rope quivered in her hands. Shaking once. Then, fell away.

But he still wasn't moving. Breathing.

Her vision blurred.

Tears, she realized a moment later. She wiped them aside. Needed to see. Needed to help him.

Form the corner of her eye, she watched Onwas rush to her mother—who was also pale. Also not moving. But that was all the attention she could spare them.

Aisha ran her hands down Nate's face. Dirt smudged down his cheeks. Streaked across his forehead. He'd fought hard. With every-thing he had. But at some point, his eyes had shuttered closed.

She could no longer see that bright gray.

Aisha leaned closer. Lips right next to his. Hoping, praying for any slight breath. Any stirring.

Anything at all.

Nothing.

"There is…nothing left to save." It was Onwas's voice. Distant. Sorrowful. As if he spoke to her from across all of Africa.

From somewhere distant, somewhere even further than her grandfather and all the hope she'd bottled within her, that they could win this, they could see another sunrise, together…came the throaty call of a male lion. Deep. Calling. Stirring.

Another answered.

Tears slid down her face. Mingled with her own dirt and blood as she wiped again at her face.

Aisha slumped back onto her heels. Hard. As if someone had punched her in the gut.

"No," she whispered.

Didn't let go of Nate's face. She cradled his head in her lap. Trailed her fingers down his cheekbones, jawline. Every inch of him that she'd only just realized she loved and had, only so briefly.

"The binding between shadow man and daughter." Onwas's voice broke. "Too strong. Even for Africa. Even for binding with Hadza."

"No."

The word ripped from Aisha's throat. Animal and wild. Terrified.

She hadn't done all this, fought so hard, only to have Sylvester take away the one person who mattered. The one person who'd seen her for who she was, even when she hadn't known herself.

Onwas bent his head over Aisha's mother. Long hair and beads hiding his face. Aisha heard a mournful keen come from him. Sounded so much like those baboons. That touch and sound of wild she'd only just found again.

A sound she felt, vibrating through *her*.

Singing in her blood.

Still tinged with power.

The earthquake still rolled. Still rocked. But softer now.

Losing its strength. Losing, bit by bit, its desperate need for vengeance as the land's anger was finally appeased.

An anger that had awoke the ancient, powerful *magic* here.

"Oh my God. It's not done. It's not over." Aisha sat up straighter. Tugged Nate closer, as much as she could he was so much bigger, taller than her. Even with her strength.

There was a way. To save them.

Both of them.

"I can do it."

Onwas stopped chanting, but she didn't pay him any mind. Just bent her head closer to Nate. Her breath spilling over his face. She squeezed her eyes closed. So tight until even the light from the sun was blocked from her lids.

She focused. Concentrated. Everything she had on that magic burning with her gut. The magic she felt still tied—always tied—to the land. To the wild here.

Help me. Please.

Save them.

The land rolled again. She held Nate tighter so he wouldn't fall away. Almost as if that were a test. A test to see if she meant what she asked. If she would hold on, even if another ravine opened beneath Nate as it had his father.

She didn't let go.

The earthquake eased, but the power around her did not. It flowed into her from the dirt. From the shifting amongst granules of sand as hot ants made their way to large, cavern-like homes nearby. The tiny scrip-scrape as their food moved in a continuous line. Then there were the lions lounging in the sun. Long, tan-furred tails whipping back and forth to ward off flies while cubs tumbled and played unheeded and uncaring about the heat or sleepiness.

All of this flowed into her.

Through her.

The strength was incredible. So vast, so powerful it spread across all the land and plains, north and south. Touched every piece of land that was called Africa.

Aisha sucked in a breath of hot air. Gasped.

But this strength was not meant for her. This power, that of life and wild, wasn't meant for anyone to hold. Not even her.

The magic flowed right out of her again.

Right into Nate.

Her mother. Even into Daniel.

The gift of life. And wild.

Aisha kept focusing on her own magic. Her own soul as it bridged that gap between the land and those she cared for. The bridge she'd created by honoring the ties between her and the land. She kept holding on until her head spun. Dizziness? Exhaustion? Lack of air?

She didn't know and didn't care. Didn't let up until she felt Nate's hand reach up. Trail down the side of her face. Weak, but moving.

"I knew you'd come for me."

Aisha's eyes snapped open. "Oh. Nate."

She flung herself practically on top of him. Didn't fight the tears as they fell. Again and again. As he held her, rocked her, and she held him right back, and her soul touched his.

A touch of Africa still flowing between them, even though the earthquake had finally ceased and its magic returned back to its quiet, ancient slumber.

Still, Aisha felt him and knew, without a doubt, she'd never let him go again.

"I'll never let you go either," he whispered into her sweaty and tangled hair.

Aisha only tightened her hold and buried her head deeper into his neck.

They'd never let the other go again.

CHAPTER 75

*A*isha waited for Nate outside the Proper's main headquarters. She glanced up at the windows that had been hers as a child. Her room. She couldn't see much from here, just the glinting of sunlight off glass panes, and she was glad for it.

She'd been invited inside upon their party's return—all stumbling, bleeding, and a little bit broken—but even though she was bleeding herself, it didn't feel right to step inside those walls. To stare outside through those vast, far-seeing windows. Across all the plains and herds of healing, mending Familiars with their wranglers on horses, helping to guide them along in the process.

Aisha stomach twisted.

It was hard enough just standing there now, waiting, staring at the outside of the building, looking out from the plains, watching the Familiars of all kinds, from parrots to toucans, to African native animals to exotic bears from the northern continents with their heavy, dark fur as they panted under shade. It wasn't their home, but it was a wild place and for many Familiars, the only chance they had to heal.

This had been a place Aisha once called home. But it wasn't anymore. Not after her parents, the choices they made, their decision to let her go on first without knowledge of her heritage, and then later, allowing that knowledge to be stolen from her.

So, she'd declined their offer.

Her father, when he'd met them at the enchanted entrance, hadn't protested. He'd just taken a long, slow look at her, nodded once with those eyes she'd wanted for so long to love her, accept her, but even now, though she felt a warming in his cold, hard eyes, it wasn't enough. Too much had come between them, and this place just wasn't hers anymore.

Maybe it never had been.

And besides, she had a place back in the States, a home, waiting for her.

Her father had rushed her mother, Nate, and even Daniel inside. To be cleaned and changed. Healed further. And Aisha just waited outside. Alone.

Which was fine too.

She couldn't help but feel the deep, aching loss in heart, and in her gut. Knowing she was leaving this place that sang with her blood's magic, the same place that had stolen so much: her memories, her parents' love, even her own Familiar.

A few wranglers waved as they rode by, but none came to say hello, which was fine by her. She wanted nothing more than to get Nate and go back home—go back to her Familiars.

To *her* Waystation.

The back door to the Proper creaked open. The hinges still needing oiling, which she remembered now—a memory she hadn't had before yesterday. As a child, Aisha had oiled it routinely. Secretly, of course. It was a useful exit when she didn't want her parents or any of the Proper employees to know she'd gone off again.

The screen door banged shut.

Her father strode out, turned towards her, and adjusted the floppy brim of his hat. His boots clanked and thumped on the wooden patio until he climbed down the stairs. Stood beside her. Not close, but beside her still. That was something. For both of them, maybe.

"Your mother will be all right."

She nodded.

"That fool, Daniel, too. And your boy."

Aisha nodded again.

Her father swept off his hat. Rubbed his forehead. "Hell, Aisha. You know what happened wasn't easy on me. Or your mom."

"I know."

"'Course, that don't make any of what we did right. Thought it was right at the time."

She could understand that.

She'd thought that, too, about many things. Even how she had viewed and thought of Nate.

"All we can do is keep learning," she said.

Her father's cold eyes softened for a moment. Just like earlier when he'd offered her sanctuary and she'd said no. He hadn't pressed. Hadn't pushed. He'd let her be.

Let her be wild.

And free.

Just like he'd always done. Even when he'd known the risks. Her sneaking out. Finding her way to Grandfather and the Hadzabe.

Aisha sucked in a deep breath. Her chest, tightening. "You knew this would happen. All along. Didn't you?"

"Figured it might. Soon as I saw the girl you were shaping up to be. You were gonna be who you were gonna be. Even if that meant hard times for us all. For you." He nodded at her. Slapped his hat back on his head. "But that, too, seemed like the right thing at the time. Maybe that one I didn't do half bad. Or right. But you're on your way now. Always had been; even with half your memories missin', you still found your way to those hurt and broken Familiars."

Aisha's throat closed. As if something were lodged there and couldn't seem to slip free. Not after all this time.

"Father…"

He shook his head. "Lied to you about a couple of things. About Daniel being a good man for you. About you not fittin' in proper-like with the high life who pays us." He grinned at her then. Silvered hair seeming to shine just a bit lighter and brighter in the smacking heat of the sun. "'Course, me and your mother never did so well with that. Except when the Council was looking."

This was the longest, she realized, that her father had ever spoken to her.

Knew, for a fact, because her memories were back.

"Also," he said, "before you head on out: I talked with your sister. She knows everything."

Aisha's back tensed. Her breath, catching. "Racine? What does she have to do with anything?"

Other than telling Sylvester exactly where she'd gone.

But her father was shaking his head. "I know how it looks. That's how we planned it."

"What?" Aisha's head spun. She knew so little of her sister; they were so different, so at odds, and her parents had never encouraged love between them. "I don't, I don't understand. Racine hates me. And she hated it here."

"You don't think I was about to lose two daughters to that monster and his infernal contracts? Nah. Your sister knew better, learned to hide that curiosity you had nipping in your blood—I blame it on your mother's side. But she knew better, 'cause we learned from our mistakes with you. She'll be meeting you when you arrive. See if she can't help sort out that Council mess you've got chomping at your Waystation."

Aisha was honestly having a hard time standing. She held out a hand. Leaned against the wooden stairway rail. Just focused on breathing and keeping her knees from turning into jam.

Just then, the screen door opened a second time, and all her confusion slowly ebbed away.

Because Nate was there.

Looking, with those gray eyes sparking and alive, at her.

One of his hands held open the door; the other supported by her mother. Or, perhaps, they were supporting each other. They both looked better than a few hours when they'd limped into the Proper. Pale. Eyes to dimming to almost nothing. But they looked better now.

As if they'd gotten a full serving, or two, of the finest meat and potatoes found on the plains.

They still looked wane and gaunt, but they were *alive*.

Nate smiled at Aisha then, a smile she felt all the way to the tips of her toes and straight into her heart. "You ready to go home?"

Home.

She had a home now, and always would. No matter what happened next. With the pissed-off Council waiting for her, the wasting sickness, and the news that would spread when she did—and she *would*—not only leak that news but scream it from the highest mountain peak. Not to mention a sister that apparently didn't hate her.

Aisha's head was about to spin yet again, but she shoved aside all her worries.

Right now, none of that mattered.

"I am," she whispered, both out loud and in her heart. "Let's go home."

Nate just nodded.

Hearing her.

All of her, and loving her in a way that her parents hadn't been capable of.

"I just wanted you to know," her father said, "that we did wrong, but I lied about you not being our daughter. 'Bout you not being welcome here."

"The Proper isn't my home."

"Nope. But if you ever need a sanctuary, it's here for you. Always." He tilted the brim of his hat at her.

Aisha's gaze strayed to Nate, and felt, for the first time, that last piece of her sliding into place. The part of her that had wanted to go back into the Proper, into her old room, and pick up the old pieces of her life, but couldn't.

Couldn't, because she wasn't that girl anymore. She was changed, now.

Aisha smiled.

The truth was, she had a sanctuary of her own.

Had finally found it.

She just hadn't realized it had been in front of her the entire time.

Her Waystation.

Her own heart.

She made her way to Nate. Offered out a hand, which he took. A warmth flooded through her the second their fingers touched. Held on to each other. Supported each other, and always would.

"Thank you, Father," Aisha said, without taking her gaze from Nate, from the future she finally saw before her. The future she finally, *finally* welcomed. No longer ran from or feared. Accepted. Embraced with every fiber of who she was.

Her, and her wildness. Her magic. All of it.

Aisha's grip on Nate's hand tightened. "But I've found a sanctuary of my own."

SNEAK PEAK: DRAGONS IN PRESCHOOL

AN ENCHANTMENT AVENUE SHORT NOVEL

New school. New partner. New beginnings.

Dragons in Preschool: An Enchantment Avenue Short Novel, on sale now from your favorite retailer. Turn the page for a sample chapter from that book.

When the magical world and the Normal one collide, bad things happen. World-ending kinda bad. Mina, a Magical Boundaries Investigator, keeps those bad things from happening.

She now faces her biggest challenge yet: finding the right preschool for her four-year-old daughter.

Just... not this one.

Set in the dazzling world of Enchantment Avenue, "Dragons in Preschool," weaves together motherhood and magic, and the sizzling first sparks of attraction... and, a possible future.

"Wonderful book, chockfull of unexpected surprises. If you like sports novels, you'll like this—even if you don't like romance. If you like romance, you'll like this—even if you don't like sports novels."
—Kristine Kathryn Rusch, *USA Today* Bestselling Author.

CHAPTER 1

*M*ina's back pressed against the white-plastic gate that guarded the exit and kept the tiny, toddling children inside (really, from escaping). Her buttoned-up black suit pulled tight across her chest. Instincts kicked in, warning her...to run.

A single drop of sweat slipped down from her forehead. Already, the morning's heat warned just how hot today would be.

Especially for running.

Even if that meant running in her classy, heeled boots.

And if that weren't bad enough, a sun-sized, yellow smiley face glared at her from behind the front desk. Not to mention the desk itself was anything but inviting. Not with its perfectly arranged, perfectly placed vase of fake red and purple blooms and a box of (mostly-gone) Kleenex. There was even a sign in bright bubble letters saying, Welcome to: Days Are Sunny Preschool!!

Again with the smiley face.

In fact, the smiley faces covered every inch of white space on the banner and, where they didn't, the glitter made up for it. And the glitter was *everywhere*. Great globs of it that looked like a child her daughter's age had gotten the container open and dumped the whole thing on a mountain of glue.

And the whole thing was meant to entice her, to drawn her in.

The brightly lit fish tank with its glowing purple- and yellow-tailed swimmers who were making a run for it in and around the double-masted, sunken pirate ship. Never mind the giant sign above the tank, which declared, quite boldly (and with necessary smiley faces): DO NOT TOUCH.

In fact, most parents would nod their head in approval, understanding, and agreement. Would automatically relax at what they saw here—the gate, the sign, the plastic coverings over electrical sockets—and would be convinced and reassured that these fears and silly mommy-and daddy-worries were unnecessary, that leaving their small, precious daughter or son in their loving and absolute care was the right choice. That he or she would be welcome, and safe.

Not Mina, though.

Her skin tingled, the tiny hairs on her arm prickling as they stood straight up.

Something…off.

Leila, her beautiful little daughter, just stood there; waiting, yes, but clutching Mina's hand as if she were going to drown if she set a single toe here. It didn't matter that she was wrapped in her favorite Disney sweater—all pink and complete with each princess ever created—her usual shield of comfort.

Leila barely reached Mina's stomach, short as she was for her four years, but her springy curls and dark hair made up for it. An unruly gift from her father, but one that was better than the alternative.

Still, neither Mina nor Leila moved from their spots by the baby gate.

Not even when they heard a sudden burst of giggles and laughter and high-pitched squeals from the outside. As if seeped *through* the walls and rebounded off the tiny, escape-proof entrance. Mina strained to see—to confirm—that those sounds came from actual living children, not recordings, not even some spelled illusion-charm concealing a bunch of crusty, chain-smoking ladies in their late sixties who styled themselves as "caregivers" but whose actual expressions were more along the lines of angry and alone.

Which was silly thinking, as her husband…ex-husband…would have declared, and quite angrily.

Silly.

Foolish.

It was how she'd gotten into this mess in the first place. Sent away from family and friends. Sent *here*, of all places. Enchantment Avenue. Here, where they were a mere stone's throw from the busy, bustling Los Angeles. Surrounded by concrete and metal and the ever-constant, flow of cars. It was the Normals' world, and it was powerful. And yet, Enchantment Avenue was right here, clinging to this southern strip of coast. Here, because of the pulsing power of the Pacific Ocean, the thundering and quaking power living beneath their feet.

A place of true and deep magic.

It just also happened to be right smack in the heart of the Normals' world. And it was the one place where people like her, liaisons between the magical and the Normal, the Magical Boundaries Investigation, were seen with a barely-above-snarling tolerance.

The MBI wasn't wanted.

But…it *was* needed—regardless of what the Detectors and those governing the Board of Enchantment Avenue thought.

At least, that's what she told herself when she tried to calm and quiet her mind enough to actually fall asleep at night. Yes, she'd made a mistake. Yes, she'd "jumped the gun" (as per the Normals' speech) on her last investigation…but that did not mean she'd been wrong or that her intent had been wrong.

Except, she had been wrong. And if there was one place fitting for punishment of an MBI screw-up, it was here.

And, truth be told, she was lucky to still be here at all. Still working with the MBI and not being given her outright notice.

They'd wanted to. Desperately.

But she'd fought them off. So they sent her here.

Here, where there were no illusions or charms or talking dragons. Just like there were none in this preschool that was perfectly normal for Normals, and as soon as she got it through her thick skull, she could report to work and get transferred to a place that actually wanted her help. Some place else, *any* place, where she could make a difference.

Except right now, her traitorous, unruly Time magic prickled at the *something off*.

It certainly didn't help her unease that she couldn't see much through the black-tinted, three-inch-thick (and probably bulletproof) windows blocking her view of the playground outside. Actually, they looked almost like the same windows as the Magical Borders Investigation vehicle.

Minus the curse-and-tamper-proof charms, of course.

Still, she thought she spotted one child running barefoot, a glimpse of red hair, and a whole herd of them following after as they raced up what looked like a plastic tower before pounding across a drawbridge. They slid, one, then two, then in great clumps, down a bright, hunter-orange slide before streaking across the ground in a very important, elaborate game of chase....

But the ground looked like it was rubber-foam. Not sand. Not even dirt or grass created by the great and powerful Oberon himself.

Rubber.

The white gate pressed harder into Mina's back. She felt herself tensing, wanting to run.

The tingling continued. It crept up her arms, buzzed at her shoulders like persistent fireflies with a light-up problem. She shifted her vision, and the world went slightly out of focus, but just a bit. Just enough to cast a shimmering overlay, making each color and shape brighter and bolder...but no...no gold.

No golden strands connected magic to Time, and back again.

At least, none that she could see.

And her Sight, well, it wasn't exactly bulletproof these days. Not anymore.

And seriously, everything *looked* fine. Even the children were laughing. Enjoying themselves. That, at least, was clear. That counted for something...right?

But try as she might, she couldn't take another step onto the preschool's cold tile floor that shone with a sparkle and smelled as if someone had doused the whole thing in lizard's fire and gave it a Mr. Cleaner-Upper spit shine to cover the stench up—and the ash —afterwards.

Mina's severe suit pulled tight again about her chest as her breathing came faster, harder, fuller.

Her unruly, opinionated Time magic or not, this couldn't be the right place. She couldn't leave Leila.

Not here.

Her wand, tucked in the secret, inside pocket of her jacket, dug hard into her side.

Pinching. Poking.

As if it, too, had an opinion—and it agreed with her.

Leila certainly had one.

Leila's whole body, her whole being, usually had the same springy steps, like spring just waking up from a long nap and barely able to contain itself. Certainly not to sit still long enough for a bath or a meal or a hug.

Not now, though.

Right now Leila was squeezing as if her grip alone could convince Mina to *Not Leave Her Here.*

She knew she couldn't…but what choice did she have?

The call had come this morning, bright and early. And when she hadn't responded, it had come again.

As it did now.

The phone in her jacket pocket buzzed as if by magic, which it most certainly was. The phone's sudden vibrations and wind chimes kept going, kept ringing, and sent her own magic reeling and…confused.

Confused, because…

Hadn't she turned it off earlier?

She had. Right before entering the preschool. Just in case.

But it was back on, and Mina didn't need to look at the screen to see who was calling. Or that she knew, without a doubt, that *he* had turned it back on.

To continue reading *Dragons in Preschool*, visit ChrissyWissler.com or your favorite bookseller.

Any Normal person thinks magic a myth. Anyone worth knowing, knows differently. Magic wanted and it took. Free pizza delivery, free Wi-Fi, freewill.

All of it, fair game.

Blessa of the Blessings Bridge made sure all her landing platforms, from the golden arches to the inter-dimensional voids, remained clear of seaweed and seagull shit. An important job, really. Essential, even.

Too bad she hated it.

"The Blessings Bridge" will transport you to living, breathing world where magic resides alongside freeways, fishing piers, and funnel cakes. A world you never knew about, but always knew existed... right outside your backdoor.

By joining my list you'll receive wonderful benefits such as being notified of upcoming book releases as well as the free story, *The Blessings Bridge*.

To enjoy your free copy of *The Blessings Bridge* and keep up with the latest news and releases, go to chrissywissler.com/free-book/ and chrissywissler.com.

ABOUT THE AUTHOR

Chrissy Wissler's writing has garnered praise both from readers and professional writers. Readers love her characters and the emotional grip she engenders.

About her novel *Home Run, New York Times* bestselling author Kristine Kathryn Rusch said: "Wonderful book, chockfull of unexpected surprises. If you like sports novels, you'll like this—even if you don't like romance. If you like romance, you'll like this—even if you don't like sports novels."

Chrissy's short fiction has appeared in the anthologies: *Fiction River: Risk-Takers, Fiction River Presents: Legacies, Fiction River Presents: Readers' Choice, Deep Magic,* and *When Dreams Come True.* She writes fantasy and science fiction, as well as a softball, contemporary series for both romance and young adult.

Before turning to fiction, Chrissy also wrote nonfiction for publications such as *Montana Outdoors, Women in the Outdoors,* and *Jakes Magazine.* In 2009, *Inside Kung Fu* magazine awarded her with their 'Writer of the Year' award.

Follow her blog on being a parent-writer at Parents and Prose.

To enjoy another story by Chrissy Wissler and to keep up with the latest news, releases and more, go to: chrissywissler.com/free-book/

For more information:
www.chrissywissler.com
chrissy@chrissywissler.com

Prom Dates & Softball Bats

Throw Like a Girl, Catch a Date

Fly Away

No Crying in Softball

More to Life than Softball

A Pitcher's Unexpected Date

A Catcher's Christmas Wish

Stolen Bases, Stolen Kisses

Softball Baby

Off-Balance

Batter-Up Pucker-Up: Collection

Everlasting: Collection

All or Nothing: Collection

Home Run Series

Home Run

Romance Video Game Series

Second Chance: Novel

Anything Possible

Changing Perspective

www.ingramcontent.com/pod-product-compliance
Lightning Source LLC
Chambersburg PA
CBHW050606170726

48283CB00001B/128